DUKE CRAIG,
TEN YEARS A GRIDIRON STAR,

is thirty-one and still loves to win. He likes to ram his shoulder into a man and knock him down, thrives on the fans' screaming approval. Duke is a clean-living, clean-thinking hero of the football world.

But when Duke meets the woman who becomes his mistress this world is shattered. For the first time Duke sees that his ex-campus-belle wife is viciously immature—that football is a sport full of schoolboy cruelty, physical agony, and cold-sweat fear—that the game to which he and his teammates had given their lives and their manhood is

ONLY A GAME.

Other SIGNET Titles of Special Interest

ONLY
A GAME

by Robert Daley

A SIGNET BOOK from
NEW AMERICAN LIBRARY
TIMES MIRROR

Library of Congress Catalog Card Number: 67-29730

This is a reprint of a hardcover edition published by
The New American Library, Inc. The hardcover edition
was published simultaneously in Canada by General
Publishing Company, Ltd.

SIXTH PRINTING

SIGNET TRADEMARK REG. U.S. PAT. OFF. AND FOREIGN COUNTRIES
REGISTERED TRADEMARK—MARCA REGISTRADA
HECHO EN CHICAGO, U.S.A.

SIGNET, SIGNET CLASSICS, SIGNETTE, MENTOR AND PLUME BOOKS
are published by The New American Library, Inc.,
1301 Avenue of the Americas, New York, New York 10019

FIRST PRINTING, SEPTEMBER, 1968

PRINTED IN THE UNITED STATES OF AMERICA

For
Kevin

CHAPTER | 1

The morning sun slants over the roof of the stadium. It is already very hot. Craig jogs toward the group waiting for him on the shady side of the field. After so many seasons he is keenly aware of stadiums, and he can feel this one rising up all around him. He can feel a slight breeze, too. That is because the stadium is empty. Tonight, full, it will be a hotbox.

This is Nashville, where tonight the Big Red will play the Lions in an exhibition game. Craig jogs toward the photographers, and some girl or other, who wait in the shade on the bench. He does not have to jog, but for him jogging is a conditioned reflex. The first commandment of football is hustle, and from the eighth grade, when he played on his first organized team, he has obeyed it without question. He jogs with his fist around the face guard of his helmet. He jogs mindlessly toward a function he has performed in towns like this for ten years.

Malverde, the team publicity man, jumps up and brings the girl forward.

"Wallace Craig meet Margie Berger, Miss Pepsi-Cola."

Her hand is cool. She looks questioningly at the publicity man.

"I thought it was going to be Duke somebody," she says.

It is clear that Craig's name means little to her.

"And I thought Miss Pepsi-Cola was going to be sixteen years old," Craig says, smiling.

"You mean they call you Duke?"

"Sometimes."

"But you don't enjoy it when they do?"

"Do you enjoy being called Miss Pepsi-Cola?"

He is still smiling, but when she seems to bristle, he decides that she has no sense of humor. Probably she takes herself seriously. He has found that most of the good-looking ones do.

7

They gaze at each other. He knows from the magazine covers what she is looking at now: curly hair, some freckles, a rather long nose and fairly heavy chin; a man whose crinkly eyes contain, hopefully, a strong glint of intelligence. He is six feet one and weighs 195 pounds. He has narrow ankles, thick thighs, and flat hips, and his wide shoulders look even wider now under the freshly laundered red jersey that is stretched taut over his shoulder pads. It is the jersey he will wear tonight, with the silver No. 6 front and back.

The grass has just been cut, a stronger odor than her perfume and one he has always loved. Nonetheless, her perfume is what he is aware of. She is a tanned young woman who is twenty-five at least, and probably older. She has smooth cheeks. She wears makeup around the eyes, and false eyelashes, and too much lipstick. She wears a sleeveless rose-colored dress that is very tight, and above it there is no smile. She is stunning looking and he supposes she is a movie starlet; who else could they get to play Miss Pepsi-Cola?

He shakes hands with two public relations men from the company, while the photographers set up their gear. Under his low-cut cleats the field is a little damp, and the odor of fresh-mown grass comes on again strong. One photographer says to Craig: "We want to get Miss Pepsi-Cola holding the ball for you on kickoffs."

Craig is not a kicker. Normally he is not even on the field for kickoffs.

But it is no sillier a photo than dozens he has posed for in the past, and he knows it might appear in a hundred newspapers tomorrow, or in several, or in none at all.

Miss Pepsi-Cola takes the ball, arranging her skirt so as to kneel on the grass on her bare knee, her bare arm outstretched to hold the ball. Craig is conscious of a flash of thigh, of the tightness of her dress, of a girl here in the middle of a football field where he had never expected one; he is also aware that her looks excite him and that he has been celibate since training camp opened two months ago.

Coming forward, he kicks the ball gently up over the photographers' heads. He is afraid she might jerk her finger away, but she does not, having eyes and smile only for the cameras. As he makes the kick again and again, he is careful not to scare her or kick into her hand, though she seems scarcely aware he is in the picture too. So on the last take he suddenly comes through the ball with a rush and a thunk, booming it all the way to the goal line, wanting to impress her with his power or maleness of something. At least wake her up.

She watches the ball sail off, then gives him a puzzled look, and begins trying to wash the grass stain off her knee with a Kleenex and spit.

Walking in toward the clubhouse, one of the PR men from Pepsi-Cola says: "Tonight Margie will hold the ball for you on the opening kickoff."

This sounds preposterous.

"Suppose we receive instead?" asks Craig.

"Then she will hold for the other team."

"It's nice to feel needed," jokes Craig.

"We've had to arrange for the contingencies," the PR man says.

"Has Miss Berger practiced sprinting off the field after the kick?"

"What do you mean?" she asks. But she knows what he means, and is obviously irked that the idea amuses him.

"Well, suppose you get caught in a runback?" He is imagining seven or eight 250-pound football players galloping right over her.

"No runback," the PR man says.

Craig almost laughs.

When he comes out of the clubhouse after changing, the photographers are gone, but the PR men, Malverde, and Miss Pepsi-Cola are waiting for him with a car. They drive back to the hotel where they enter the coffee shop.

"How about a drink?"

"I thought this was a dry town," says Craig.

"Brown-bagging is legal." The PR man says, producing a pint bottle of whiskey in a paper bag. "The waitress will bring ice and setups."

It is nearly lunchtime, and the coffee shop begins to fill up.

"Usually I'm drunk by this time of day," says Craig. "But we have a game tonight."

"Sorry, I forgot. Have some coffee then."

Miss Pepsi-Cola orders tea. Craig sips coffee. The two PR men and Malverde have whiskey on the rocks.

The restaurant is cold from the air conditioning. The background hums with piped-in music.

"You're allowed to drink, aren't you, if it's not a game?"

"Well," says Craig, "it's a two hundred and fifty dollar fine if you get caught in a bar."

Presently the men go off to see about sideline badges for the game. Craig, to his surprise, finds himself alone with the girl.

He is not particularly pleased.

"Where are you from?"

"California, originally."

9

"Have I seen any of your movies?"

"I don't know. Have you?" She gives him an oversweet smile.

He thinks: A simple question, but it managed to offend her.

"Well," he says defensively, "you didn't know who I was either."

"I'm sorry. I haven't paid much attention to pro football in recent years."

She is twisting a paper match in her fingers.

"But I do remember you now from your college games. You went to Texas, didn't you?"

People entering the restaurant stare at them, recognizing Craig at least. He doesn't like the idea of what they might be thinking.

Several of his teammates enter, wave at him, and go out again.

He can imagine the dialogue later.

"Who was that stuff we saw you with, Duke?"

"Mighty tasty."

"You getting any of that, Duke?"

Craig looks at the fine line of her profile. He thinks: She probably supposes that since I'm a football player I'm an idiot. This is an attitude he is used to recognizing in people. Persons either fawn over star players, or resent them on contact, and Craig has come to see the resentment anytime he does not get the adulation. That's my complex, he thinks. But I bet she has more complexes than I do. Because I am famous, and she only wants to be, because I never heard of her. Otherwise we are more alike than she thinks. Because for both of us any success depends on physical qualities that will be gone in a very few years.

Craig drains his coffee and sets the empty cup down.

"You don't care for football, I guess."

"Football is all right."

He sees she is beginning to perk up at the stir they are causing in the restaurant. Craig, who does not like to be seen alone with strange women, is uncomfortable.

"We're sponsoring the games this year. I'll be doing some of the commercials on TV."

"That's fine."

"Are you going to have lunch?"

"No. We have dinner at four o'clock, today."

"Oh."

After a moment she says: "I'm in this hotel, too."

"Is that so?"

"Yes."

10

What is that supposed to mean, he thinks. An invitation?

He says, "Well, I better get to our meeting." There is no meeting.

"Do you have to go?"

"There's this meeting." He is an expert at escaping from unattached women.

"I enjoyed the coffee with you," he says, giving her his big smile.

He goes out of the coffee shop wondering if anyone really means to let her hold the ball for the kickoff.

The answer is no.

Francis Xavier Boyle, owner of the team, reads about the plan in the Nashville *Banner* while having supper with his friend, Father O'Malley, whom he has brought down for the game.

"Who's Margie Berger?"

The special edition of the paper has the rosters of the two teams on the front page, and in the middle the picture of Craig with the girl.

"There's a Mrs. Berger on the cardinal's committee," the priest offers.

"Not this dollie," says Boyle showing the photo.

"Isn't that the woman involved in that divorce action in Hollywood?"

"Well," demands Boyle, "is she?"

"Sounds like the same one." The priest names a famous male film star.

"That pervert!" snorts Boyle.

"He's divorcing her, if it's the same woman."

"She looks like the type." Boyle folds the paper and stands up. "We'll see about this."

Outside the hotel, the players are filing on board the two buses for the ride to the stadium. It is six P.M. Boyle says to Malverde: "Get Duke Craig off the bus."

When Craig joins them, Boyle shows the paper and says: "Whose idea is this Miss Pepsi-Cola?"

Craig answers with a grin: "Not mine."

"I don't see anything funny in my team giving publicity to this—this actress."

Boyle believes in "his" team. Its image is precious to him.

"Sorry," says Craig.

Malverde scuffs the sidewalk with his toe, then says: "The promoter thought it was a good gimmick."

"And you did too, I suppose."

Players' faces stare out the bus windows at them.

11

"Well, since Pepsi-Cola is sponsoring our games this year I thought—"

"That's what I get for hiring thinkers."

Malverde is discomfited, and Craig is a little amused.

Boyle says to Craig: "I know it wasn't your fault, but you should know better than to get mixed up with such a notorious woman. There are people just longing for such a situation to drag your spotless reputation down in the dirt with them."

Boyle says to Malverde: "If you get any more brilliant ideas you check them with me, understand?"

"Yes."

"I don't want that actress on the field."

"Well, the promoter gave sideline badges to all the Pepsi-Cola people."

"Get them back."

"Well, I mean I can't take them away by force."

Boyle stares at the publicity man until Malverde drops his eyes.

"I'll see about this when we get to the stadium," the owner snaps.

An assistant coach emerges from each bus.

"I got twenty-four here."

"I count twenty."

The head coach, George Dreuder, says: "That's all of them then. Let's roll 'em."

Only the players are counted. The other assistant coaches, the team doctor, Boyle and Father O'Malley, and the reporters traveling with the team quickly board the buses. The equipment manager and the two trainers are already at the stadium.

In the bus, Craig sits next to Malverde, who is staring sullenly out the window.

"Is she really a notorious woman?"

"How the hell do I know?"

"She seemed ordinary enough to me."

"Whose great idea is Miss Pepsi-Cola?" asks Boyle of the promoter. Unlike Malverde the promoter does not work for Boyle; therefore Boyle is smiling, and his voice, he thinks, is carefully noncommittal. Boyle's only thought is to keep Miss Pepsi-Cola off the field, but he cannot order this without damaging his relationship with the promoter of this profitable annual game.

Boyle has an attractive smile, but a manner that is so stiff that the promoter is immediately discomforted.

The promoter says: "We can drop it if you like."

"Well, that's what I'd prefer."

"Okay. It was only a ceremonial kickoff. Nothing to get excited about."

They stand at midfield. The dusk is deepening, and the floodlights have just come on. There are lights under the eaves too, and they can see that the stands are already about a third full.

"I would really prefer not to use my team to give publicity to a woman like that. Especially a player like Craig."

"He's certainly been a great player," says the promoter uncomfortably.

"On and off the field. Maybe the best we ever had."

"Yes, I've heard that."

"I'm fond of that boy, and he thinks a lot of me too, I don't mind telling you."

"Well, he's not a boy anymore. He must be over thirty now."

"He's still a boy to me. I won't have women like that taking advantage of him."

"The thing is, I can't imagine Pepsi-Cola hiring any notorious woman or anything. Are you sure you've got the right name?"

"I've got my information," says Boyle stiffly.

"Yes, well. They've got sideline badges, you know. I can't very well take their badges away at this point."

"I hope they can be kept away from our bench, though. We've got priests on there and everything. How would *that* look in a photo?"

"I'll try to keep them away."

"Some of these photographers have no notion of good taste."

So Miss Pepsi-Cola does not hold the ball for the kickoff. Ken Jones, the Big Red's left-footed kicker, boots the ball off the tee in the normal manner, and on the first play from scrimmage the Lions fumble. A few seconds later Craig bursts through the middle, tacklers, converging on him, pawing him, but bouncing off him and off each other. He concentrates on running as compactly as possible, hunched over on pistoning legs, so that he caroms from tackler to tackler in a clatter of shoulder pads and helmets. He hears the grunts of contact close by and the crowd roaring a long way off. Although Craig, running, is trying only to maintain balance, to keep his legs under him as long as possible, there are too many tacklers, they get in their own way, and Craig suddenly realizes almost with a laugh that they are not going to manage to knock him down until after he has crossed the goal line.

As Craig at last goes down under everybody, the referee's

13

arms go up signaling the touchdown. Craig comes to the bench delighted with himself. Hands reach to shake his.

"Great run, Duke," cries Lincoln Hamilton, the big Negro center.

"Your block sprung me, Link."

"I only got a piece of him, Duke."

This is true, but the small piece made all the difference.

"You made me look good, Duke," says Lincoln Hamilton.

The crowd applauds, but the best applause is that which he is getting from his teammates—and also the ovation he is silently giving himself. He is hardly winded. It will be fun looking at that run in the movies on Tuesday.

Toward the end of the first half, needing seven yards for a first down, Craig goes eight yards down and out to the sidelines for a pass. He catches the ball despite the cornerback lunging for it, then ducks under the cornerback who should never have tried to intercept that particular pass. The cornerback is a rookie trying to make his reputation intercepting one off the great Duke Craig, but Craig has the ball and is sprinting for the far corner of the goal line sixty-two yards away.

A quick glance has told Craig where every player on the field is standing, and which ones are starting to run, and which are already running hard, and he can see also with an almost geometric precision a twisting, zigzag line to the goal which seems to be open all the way; although he can never simply outsprint everyone to the end zone, he can reach every point on this line before anyone else can.

He sees this line in advance, and then adheres to it, running hard, stopping, starting, changing direction, running a course ten yards longer than his pursuers, making the closest ones overrun him so they have to double back—by which time he has veered off on still another angle. Crossing the goal line he is laughing inside, his principal emotion pure delight that he was able to work out this complicated, difficult run in advance, and then to do it. He listens, pleased, to the cheering.

Both benches are on the same side of the field. As he jogs up along the sideline, the faces on the Lions' bench are hard, and no one meets his eyes. He is trying not to smirk. The crowd is still cheering and stamping.

He passes Miss Pepsi-Cola. Her eyes are alight and she says to him: "You *are* exciting, aren't you."

He feels so pleased at this that when a photographer brings her over a moment later, though he is still breathing hard, he poses with her, grinning.

Nearby, the band is forming for the half-time march. Groups of players, standing, edge toward the locker room.

Her arm is around his waist. His jersey is wet with sweat and stuck to him, and her hand feels like it is on his skin.

The photographer says: "Give him a kiss, honey."

She gazes doubtfully at Craig.

"Go on," says the photographer.

He feels her lipstick on his sweaty face. In the background is the impact of the two lines colliding; someone cries out.

"On the lips this time," says the photographer.

Craig feels her brief kiss and is blinded by the flash.

"Thanks, honey."

She smiles at Craig, then pats him on the rump, saying: "Why do football players always pat each other there?"

To conceal his surprise, Craig says: "Say, I like the way you do that. Do it again."

But instead her eyes drop, and she stirs the turf with her toe.

Still excited by his touchdown, by his own excellence, Craig asks the question that is on his mind.

"Are you some kind of" —unable to think of any other, he uses Boyle's word—"notorious woman, or something?"

She looks at him, then watches the Lions' huddle break. "I thought that expression went out with the Victorians."

Abashed, Craig says, "That was a thoughtless question to ask. I'm sorry." But he blunders on, "It's just that somebody told me you were getting divorced."

The Lions go into punt formation.

"Maybe I will, I don't know. Does that make a notorious woman?"

Craig says: "I guess I'm so excited I don't know what I'm saying."

She nods at him, then turns and walks away. The punter is barking signals, but Craig is noticing how narrow her waist is, how fine her legs.

In the second half of this exhibition game, Craig is replaced by a halfback named Mangrove, new to the team. For three seasons Mangrove was a reserve on the Bears, and he came to the Big Red two months ago on a trade.. The crowd lets out a roar to see him, for he is a local boy who once starred for the University of Tennessee. He does not disappoint. He sweeps left end for twelve yards. After two passes fail, he sweeps right end for twelve more. The Lions are cooked now. A few plays later Mangrove takes a swing pass and goes into the end zone with it.

The locker room afterward is jubilant. An easy win over a big team. All the rookies have got into the game. Nobody played more than two quarters, so nobody is exhausted. Nobody is too badly bruised.

They look forward to the buffet supper and two cans of beer each waiting back at the hotel.

A few of the rookies are solemn. Three, possibly four players will be cut from the team here. They will get fifty dollars (the week's wage) and a ticket home. Which ones will they be?

The shower room fills up, empties, fills up again. Eight burly naked bodies stand before a row of sinks, shaving. Craig, wearing only a jock, plus a coating of dried sweat and dirt, swills a Coke while talking to reporters. At last he gets into the shower. When he comes out, many of the players are dressed and the crowd in the locker room has thinned out. As he dresses, he watches the stack of game programs on one of the gear trunks diminish. The rookies take programs. So do some of the borderline veterans. This could be the final souvenir of a pro career: the last program in which one's name appears.

Lincoln Hamilton waves a playbook over his head, and calls to fullback Mel Slade going out the door: "Don't forget your brains, Mel."

Slade rushes back to claim his playbook. To lose one is an automatic $250 fine.

Pete DiGiacomo, one of the trainers, is distributing bridge-work and valuables out of a box; the box was locked in one of the gear trunks during the game.

At the end Pete stands in the center of the locker room holding a row of molars.

"Whose teeth?"

No one answers.

"I got a wallet here too."

Coach George Dreuder comes over. "Jesus Christ. Forgetting a wallet I can understand. But who do I have is so stupid he forgets his teeth?"

He reads the name in the wallet, then sends Pete out to the bus to hand over the teeth and wallet.

Another playbook is being waved by Mangrove. "Hey rookie, don't forget your brains." Mangrove is feeling cocky, and Craig smiles to himself. Mangrove has a right to feel cocky tonight.

Back at the hotel, the buffet is laid out on long tables with men in chef's hats serving it. There is a special waiter to put two cans (and two cans only) of beer on each tray. The veterans wear team blazers and ties. The rookies, not having been measured for blazers yet, wear sports coats and ties. Though

16

the room is cold from the air conditioning, some of the heavier players are still sweating.

Craig, sipping beer, stands with Lincoln Hamilton, who is offensive captain; with Jim Pennoyer, the quarterback; and with Mangrove.

"They were sure easy," Mangrove says.

"You played a heckuva game, Jimmy," says Craig.

"The luckiest day of my life was the day I got traded to this team."

A whisper runs through the room. "The Turk is out." Everyone glances around looking for coaches.

No coaches are present.

"The man with the ax," someone whispers.

The coaches must be upstairs deciding who to cut. The rookies begin to evaporate, as if, when the coaches appear, the first players spied will be the ones cut. Out of sight, out of mind, the players hope.

"Poor bastards," Mangrove says, watching rookies bolt a final scared bite and scurry from the room.

Suddenly Coach Dreuder stands in the doorway, searching the room. He makes his way toward Craig's group.

"When you finish that sandwich, Jimmy," he says to Mangrove, "can I see you a minute, please."

Mangrove, who has been chewing, stops chewing. He attempts to swallow, but it seems to lodge in his throat. The color goes out of his face. Without a word, he puts the sandwich down and follows Dreuder out of the room.

Craig, Pennoyer, and Hamilton have stopped chewing also. They watch Mangrove go. Other veterans hurry over.

"What happened?"

"He just cut Mangrove."

Several voices curse Coach Dreuder. But another says callously: "We got too many backs already."

"Why'd they trade for Mangrove then?"

"Insurance."

"Those bastards."

"He gonna cut you next, Pennoyer," says Hamilton to the star quarterback. But nobody laughs at the attempted joke.

"We'll all get cut sooner or later," mutters Pennoyer. He seems a stoical man. He rarely speaks. But he tries never to learn rookies' names. That way when they go it does not affect him one way or the other.

"Mangrove is from around here," somebody says bitterly. "Cheaper to cut him than a guy who lives in California."

They know they will not see Mangrove again. To avoid the humiliation of meeting anyone, he will slink away tonight, or tomorrow after they have gone. In the plane they will look around and try to work out who else has been cut.

After a while, the players resume eating and drinking as if nothing has happened.

A little later, Craig sees Miss Pepsi-Cola. She comes into the room with the two PR men and the manager of the hotel. Fearing a scene, Craig looks around for F. X. Boyle, but the owner is not there; he must be upstairs writing out fifty-dollar checks and airline vouchers for the cut players.

Most of the players have drifted out by now, but Craig is stuck with a reporter who is telling him what kind of pass patterns will work against the Giants next week in New York in the team's final exhibition game. Craig keeps nodding politely, for his parents drummed politeness into him at an early age, and he called every man "sir" until recently. Politeness, Craig feels, is important anytime, but especially if you are a celebrity. He does not want to be accused of having a star complex.

So he listens. When several others join the group, Craig is able to move away. From the corner of his eye he watches Margie Berger, whom he still thinks of not as Margie Berger at all, but as the mysterious, possibly notorious Miss Pepsi-Cola. Once he catches her staring at him. He keeps hoping she will come over and talk to him, but she does not, even though he lingers in the room until only a handful of players are left, lingers until she and the three men with her have gone out, and he sees her, a moment later, go past the door alone with a key in her hand, not looking to see if he is still there or not.

Then he gets his own key and goes upstairs to the room he shares with the stoical quarterback, Pennoyer.

Feeling guilty, he phones his wife.

"Everything all right there?"

"Do you realize what time it is?"

"It's not so late."

"You woke me up out of a sound sleep."

He holds the phone away from his ear. Carribel is always grouchy when she first wakes up. When Pennoyer glances over, Craig gives him a wink, as if getting shouted at is fun, which it is not.

He interrupts: "I just wanted to tell you about the game."

"Well tell me then."

"I ran for one and caught a pass for another. Jim threw me a beauty."

"Congratulations, but you could have told me tomorrow."

"The plane lands at eleven thirty in the morning."

"You better catch the limousine."

18

"Well, try to be there."

"Ah cain't. Ah've got a P.T.A. to go to."

He has not seen her in two months.

"The kids all right?"

"You might have sent them some postcards."

"We really have the horses, this year."

"Ah'm going back to sleep."

How much Pennoyer has overheard, Craig does not know, but when he hangs up he is embarrassed.

"I really do think we're going to have a great season, Jim." Pennoyer grunts.

"There's only us and Cleveland," Craig says. They began to discuss the league. The Eagles have no quarterback. The Cardinals have no defense. The Steelers and Redskins are weak. Craig does most of the talking as always. Pennoyer listens. He mumbles something from time to time. They search for weaknesses on their own team, but tonight there do not seem to be any.

"Barring injuries—" Pennoyer says. He raps on the bed-stead for luck. Superstition is rife on football teams.

"Yes," Craig concedes. But they both know that for the most part it is not injuries which cause teams to lose, but losing which causes injuries. Losing teams don't try hard enough, and so always get the worst of it.

"You ready?" Pennoyer says.

Craig swings his legs into his bed, and Pennoyer snaps off the light between them.

Craig lies in the dark. Talk of the season has dimmed thoughts of his marriage, but now that comes back to him.

He tells himself in the dark that he is probably no prize himself; he should try to see her side of it a little.

Nonetheless, when he tries to empty his mind for sleep, he finds himself thinking of Miss Pepsi-Cola, and in her he sees all the excitement that his life lacks, and he wonders what being married to her would be like. Or even going to bed with her. Then he imagines Miss Pepsi-Cola holding the ball for him on the kickoff, and the runback wedge thundering down upon them, and the fear on her face, and then the bodies caroming past them in such a way that, as they batter her about, a cleat catches in her skirt stripping it off her so that he, Craig, can see her thin panties over her bottom and her fine long naked legs.

With this image filling his mind he finds that he is aroused, and he tells himself that he could probably be up in her room right now, rolling around with her. But that isn't what he wants, is it? No, that isn't what he wants, he tells himself. That kind of thing is out for him.

Still aroused, he tells himself he will be home with his wife tomorrow night, which will take care of that problem for a while, and for now he better start thinking of something else.

So he begins to concentrate on the two touchdowns that night, but they are less fun to remember than he supposed at the time they would be. So he lets his mind run off remembering others over the years until he comes to the three in the Sugar Bowl game when he was still in college and life seemed more grandiose than it seems now.

Thinking about touchdowns still works, calms him, helps him avoid thinking of the tight-fitting dress she wore.

He remembers how her teeth gleamed.

You are exciting!

Does this mean she thinks she would find him exciting in other ways, too?

He wonders what she is doing right now, two floors above him.

He lies in the dark waiting to fall asleep.

CHAPTER | 2

Carribel is not there waving down from the promenade deck with the other wives. After collecting his suitcase, Craig accepts a ride with the Pennoyers into the city. From here he can catch a train out to the suburbs. The direct limousine would be a bit quicker, but would cost ten dollars, an amount Craig considers worth saving. Although his fans imagine that he has a fabulous contract, he has arranged to draw only sixteen thousand dollars per year now, with the rest to be paid at the rate of five thousand dollars per year for as many years as the accrued money lasts after he stops playing. At present, it will last less than three years. He can't afford to retire yet.

In addition he can count on earning about six thousand dollars this year in endorsements and appearances. Some of this will go into household spending, and some he will try to buy stocks with. However, Carribel resents buying stocks, wanting, he supposes, to spend everything now. But then Carribel is not worried about the future. She does not worry about some bigger, younger player coming along next season or even, possibly, next week.

At the station Craig thinks to buy *Playboy,* for there is a girl in a tight sweater on the cover and his mind is running all that way now. But he does not want to be seen reading *Playboy* by (perhaps) some impressionable kid, and anyway, the *Saturday Evening Post* is cheaper.

But he gets no reading done. On the train a fan recognizes him, and for the next thirty minutes is half in Craig's lap asking what is wrong with Cleveland's offense, then providing answers for Craig's approval.

Craig, absently fingering the unopened magazine, keeps nodding politely.

At home, when he sets his suitcase down and calls out, his voice rings through empty rooms. But he does not really expect Carribel to be there. He goes upstairs to their bedroom and unpacks on the unmade bed. Nearly everything from his suitcase goes into the laundry.

Then he peers into the kids' rooms, looking for something of them in there: new toys, a drawing on the wall. But there is nothing.

He stands indecisively at the top of the stairs, pleased to think he owns these walls, this house. He is—home. But he does not know quite what he wants to do, so he goes into his study. There are stacks of unopened letters on his desk. Most, he can see from the handwriting, are from kids. But he picks out several important letters, one a missing check. Carribel should have sent these on. Carribel assured him the check had never come.

Going downstairs to fix himself lunch, he feels more and more glad to be home, glad even to be alone in his empty house. Approaching the icebox, he decides he wants a beer and perhaps a leg of cold chicken—something to remind him he is home. No more training camp food until next summer. No more restaurant food until next weekend in New York for the Giants.

But there is no beer in the icebox, and no cold meat either. There are many plastic containers of leftovers. One has a crust of mold on it, so he throws it out and begins looking at the others. Several more are bad. He throws them out thinking, There goes the ten dollars I saved coming home on the train.

He fries and eats some eggs, mopping up with toast. He drinks a glass of milk.

The phone rings.

"You got home all right, Ah see."

"Where are you?"

"Sorry Ah couldn't meet you. Ah'm at a P.T.A. luncheon. Now Ah couldn't let them down, could Ah?"

The breakfast dishes are in the sink. He puts them in the dishwasher with his own dishes, and turns the machine on.

Up in his study, he decides to go through the mail. His study is a pine-paneled room with trophies in a case on one wall, and a big blowup of himself on another. He gets out a stack of photos of himself in the air catching a pass, and stacks of matching envelopes and cardboards and, although each photo is already signed by machine, he signs each again with the kid's name: For Jimmy, with best wishes from Duke Craig. Then he inserts the photo in the envelope, scrawls the kid's name on the outside, stamps and seals it, and goes on to the next letter.

Soon he has a shoebox full of stamped envelopes to be mailed. By midseason he will have sent out five hundred or more photos in this way, although if he gets too far behind he will have to hire a secretary to help. The expense is his own, but it seems worth it if you think of the joy he has given each kid. He imagines them calling each other up.

"I got the Duke's picture and he signed it himself."

The notion makes him smile. Sammy Baugh sent Craig a photo once, when Craig was a kid. He has never forgotten this.

Now on his desk are other letters, most asking him to speak before groups. He gets out his schedule book, which has many entries already, and works out which he can do. Some he might be able to get a fee for, and some that are for charities he will have to do free. People seem to think players should speak for nothing, or the club should pay, and often they are offended if money is mentioned at all. Craig never asks for a fee himself, but Malverde can usually squeeze fifty dollars out of groups for him. Sometimes a hundred dollars. He will pass some of these letters on to Malverde to try for a fee.

Still other letters on his desk offer endorsements. Craig has an agent who also handles many of the country's other name-athletes on endorsements. He will mail these letters to his agent for action.

This leaves many bills to be paid, some dating from early summer. Carribel should have paid them. Opening the checkbook, Craig finds that she has not kept any entries since he left for training camp. He has no idea how much money is in the account.

Hearing voices, he goes downstairs. His son Bobby, aged nine, is eating crackers with milk in the kitchen. The boy hugs him, then screams into the house, "Daddy's home!"

His daughter who is four and goes to nursery school, comes in and begins kissing him.

"Daddy, you know what? I get Mrs. Murphy's mail for her now. I can reach the mailbox all by myself. I'm a big girl."

"I passed the junior lifeguard test, Dad."

With his children in his arms, Craig beams and is content.

"How about a game of football, Dad?"

Craig stiffles a groan at the thought of handling a football today.

But he says: "Sure, why not?"

Bobby gets on the kitchen phone.

"My dad's home, come on over and play."

"My dad's home, get the gang."

23

"My dad's home. We're going to have a game."

The eager, small boy's voice makes Craig smile.

Before long, a dozen boys of the neighborhood congregate on Craig's lawn, which is forty yards long and bordered by big elms. He plays quarterback and passer for both teams, for although they catch well enough, their hands are not big enough yet to pass a football properly. Craig tries to throw the ball softly, not wanting to sting them.

An hour passes. Craig is lost in the game. He listens to the voices. he notes the glow of pride when he praises a player. He loves the smell of the grass, and the feel of the rough leather of the ball against his fingers. He watches each team strive desperately to beat the other. Competition, victory: that's what football is all about. Proving yourself better than the other guy. You can prove it when you're nine years old. It is heady stuff then, and it is still heady stuff when you're thirty.

It pleases Craig to note that his son appears to have the same instinct he himself has: don't go for the five-yard gain, go for the touchdown. Win.

He is so lost in the game he does not hear Carribel's car on the gravel.

"Get off that lawn!"

The boys look at Craig.

"Y'all're ruining it. Get off," Carribel shouts. "How many times do Ah have to throw you boys off this lawn?"

A boy guiltily tosses Craig the football. They all back nervously toward the street.

"The game's over, fellows. I have to go in now anyway," Craig says.

In a moment all are gone. Craig, football in hand, approaches his wife.

She offers her cheek to be kissed.

"You ought to have more sense," she chides Craig.

"Well—"

"Ah worked all summer to keep that lawn nice." Craig, expressionless, tosses the ball from one hand to another.

"Got a car full of groceries, have you?" he asks.

He helps her in with them, then watches her put cans on shelves.

"Ah don't know how Ah get done all the jobs around heah."

Craig's own accent, after ten years in the North, is neutral. But Carribel still drawls every word.

She wears a white blouse, a tan skirt, bobby socks and loafers. The same costume she wore in college. She still wears the same hair style, also.

"Well, where you fixing to take me tonight?"

Craig, after two months on the road, says: "I sort of hoped to stay home tonight."

"Ah know what you're thinking," says Carribel coyly. "Naughty boy."

"Well, I just meant that a home-cooked meal would sure taste good after all that training camp food."

"Think about it from my point of view, darling. Ah've hardly been out at all for two whole months."

"That's true."

"Anyway, Ah promised Flora Pennoyer we'd go out to dinner with them."

"Oh."

"You're supposed to call Jim and say where and what time, and then call and make reservations."

Craig goes out into his garden. The marigolds are in bloom. He hates the idea of dinner in the city: the long drive through traffic, the difficulty parking, the crowded restaurant, dinner interrupted by strangers, the need to be smiling and polite.

When he touches them, the marigold petals seem as smooth and cool as a woman's breast. This thought reminds him at once of Miss Pepsi-Cola, whose breast he has never touched, nor ever will touch.

Inside, he phones the Pennoyers, then the restaurant, then several babysitters before landing one.

By the time he drives to get the babysitter, it is raining. He has convinced himself that Carribel deserves the night out.

He hands Carribel's umbrella to the hatcheck girl.

"Hi, Duke, how we going to do Sunday?"

The maître d'hôtel shakes hands with him.

"How does it look for us against the Giants Sunday, Duke?"

The waiter, arriving to take their order, says: "Are we in good shape for Sunday, boys?"

He tries to seem pleased by each of these questions, and to make an appropriate answer.

During dinner, a stranger comes over from the bar. Drink in hand he stands talking down at them as they eat.

Craig, trying to be polite, notices that Carribel is boiling. She considers this an outrage, and is on the point of telling the man so. She has no fear of scenes in restaurants, and has created some beauties in the past. Just in time, the stranger departs.

"Of all the nerve," Carribel says.

"Not so loud," says Flora Pennoyer mildly.

"Ah was just about to explode."

With a grin, Craig says: "I pity the next poor fan who runs into Carribel."

"Ah say he was damn rude," snaps Carribel.

"You're right," concedes Craig seriously. "What he did was rude."

Presently an elderly lady approaches their table and says: "I know who you are, you're Duke Craig, aren't you?"

Craig, standing, says politely, "Yes, m'am."

"And you're—don't tell me—you're the quarterback, right? Pennoyer, right?"

Pennoyer, also standing, nods.

Craig, glancing at Carribel, sees the explosion coming and searches frantically for a way to avoid it.

"And you're Carribel Craig, right?" the lady says. "I remember your photo on the cover of *Life* with Duke when you were college sweethearts."

Carribel beams. The crisis is averted.

Craig says politely: "And you're Mrs.—?"

"Miss. Miss Turner. I'm one of your greatest fans. Why, you have no idea what a thrill it is to meet Duke Craig and Pennoyer. To actually meet them and their lovely wives."

She begins to describe games she has watched them play.

At last she is gone. Sitting down, Pennoyer says: "My roast beef is cold."

"She's waving at us," Craig says. "Give her a nice big wave, Jim."

"You wave. I'm eating."

"Imagine remembering that cover on *Life*," says Carribel.

After dinner, as they move out through the tables, menus are proffered for Craig and Pennoyer to sign.

"Let's beat those Giants," the maître d'hôtel says.

So Craig slips him a dollar.

"Let's smash those Giants," the hatcheck girl says, handing out Carribel's umbrella.

Craig lays a dollar, folded, on the counter.

Pennoyer too is distributing money. He is thirty-five years old, hair shot with gray. Like Craig, like most players, he was so tight those first years, he scarcely tipped at all. But his role, which he loves, now demands tipping, and he has become scarcely aware he is giving away real money at all. To Pennoyer, as to Craig, the attention seems worth it.

Outside, Carribel says: "That was a lovely dinner. What did you and Jim talk about?"

Craig thinks: Formations that might beat the Giants. What else?

26

"You mean between the drunk and Miss Turner?" Pennoyer mutters.

"She was a nice old lady."

"Jim liked her, didn't you, Jim?" says Craig.

"Y'all sounded terribly technical," says Carribel. "Ah don't see how you keep it all in your minds."

Carribel suggests a nightclub. Flora is willing.

Craig says: "Let's do the nightclub some other time. I'd rather go home."

"Ah know what Duke's thinking," says Carribel coyly. "The naughty boy."

But Craig, who tossed restlessly most of last night in the hotel in Nashville, is thinking principally of getting some sleep.

However, since Carribel has raised the subject, his mind is pleased to consider that prospect also, and does so during the long drive home.

Stepping from the shower, Craig is toweling himself off when Carribel, in pajamas, unexpectedly enters the bathroom.

Seeing the state Craig is in, she remarks: "Look at that ugly thing."

Craig frowns.

"Well it is ugly," she says.

"I wish you wouldn't keep saying that."

"And anyway," drawls Carribel grinning, "it's not going to do you a bit of good. Ah happen to be having my period."

Craig snaps: "Why didn't you tell me that earlier?"

"You really had your hopes up, didn't you?" giggles Carribel.

Craig keeps silent.

"You shouldn't have been thinking all those naughty thoughts," says Carribel.

She drinks a glass of water. "There isn't a thing Ah can do for you," she says, prancing out of the bathroom.

Her attitude should be enough to cool him off, but after two months it is not. He finds her sitting in bed reading a magazine. Her hair is in rollers.

Gazing at the state of his pajamas, she says: "You look pretty silly like that, you know."

Craig says nothing.

Carribel giggles. "All dressed up and no place to go."

Craig gets into bed on his side.

Carribel says: "After two months, you surely can wait another week."

"Sure."

Carribel laughs. "Because this week Ah'm on vacation."

He watches her reach to turn out the bedside lamp.

Lying in the dark, he concentrates on pass patterns to use

27

against the Giants, hoping this will calm him down. But it does not. He supposes there are things other wives do for their husbands at times like this. But he does not expect any of them to occur to Carribel.

Nonetheless, after a minute she snuggles up to him. He is lying on his side, facing away from her. Her hand slides over his hip.

"What's the matter with my honey?" she says.

But he is angry, and this would be like accepting charity.

"Never mind," he snaps. Without a word, she turns away.

He cannot get comfortable or relax. He shifts position constantly. Sleep feels hours distant.

"Will you please stop tossing," Carribel says. "You're keeping me awake."

"I'm sorry," says Duke Craig.

CHAPTER | 3

On Friday, excused from practice, Craig goes alone to New York to receive an award from the Football Writers Association there: he has been voted outstanding visiting player to appear in Yankee Stadium the year before.

There is a luncheon upstairs over an important New York restaurant. After coffee, rising to accept the plaque, Craig looks out over smiling attentive faces and says into the microphone: "I want you to know how appreciative I am for— I can't thank you men enough for"—he stares down at the plaque in his hands—"for getting me excused from practice today."

They laugh.

"I mean, I don't mind the games too much—"

They laugh again.

"Really, thanks. As you know, we beat the Giants here last year, and I had a good game." Craig's sense of timing is acute. It tells him to pause right here, and grin out at his audience. "In fact, it was about the only good game I had last year, and I think it's real perceptive of you to single it out this way."

Everyone laughs.

Craig as always is aware of the sense of power. He is good at addressing groups. He can hold them rapt, make them laugh, or provoke applause as he chooses.

Since he gives fifty or more talks a year, he has developed four set routines to choose from, all of them now polished to a shine. Three are funny, with most of the humor belittling himself. One, inspirational, is aimed at high-school boys. Even it is funny in spots. He knows how to project charm, and once the charm is there in his talks, it is not hard to make people laugh.

". . . People ask if we are aware of the crowds. Sometimes I make a good play, and I look over into a certain section of the stands and the people are going up and down, up and down, and I know immediately that"—the dramatic pause—"that there's probably a heckuva good fist fight going on in that section."

The men laugh.

"—Sixty thousand people in the stadium, and half of them are watching the fist fight."

More laughter.

"Really makes a player feel, well, you know, *loved*."

The public performer in Craig is intoxicated. His audience leans forward. Not only is there no coughing, there aren't even any spoons or coffee cups moving. Craig feels almost the same power he feels on the football field; the power to enthrall others; the knowledge he can do things other people can't.

"—Some players hear the applause, and some don't. Personally, I *hear* it."

More laughter.

"Sometimes you get a very average player—maybe even below average. But when he hears the applause he goes berserk. He plays way over his head. Now, basically, he's not a football player at all, he's an actor."

They laugh, and then applaud.

Craig thinks: basically I'm an actor myself. He decides to speak this line now, though it reveals more of himself than he cares to reveal, now or ever. But it will get a laugh, it is a good line to close on, and he imagines nobody will see that he has exposed a truth about himself.

He strikes a bashful pose, and says: "I guess I'm basically an actor myself."

They laugh, and when he thanks them for the award and sits down, the applause is tumultuous.

He listens to it, pleased with himself, but outwardly deadpan. To grin happily might appear smug. Smugness in an All-American, Craig has been taught and believes, is extremely unattractive. Humility is the quality to strive for.

Outside, watching men climb into cabs, Craig wonders what to do with the rest of the day.

A sports columnist moves up to him at the curb and says: "Why don't you and I have dinner together tonight?"

But this means an interview, and speaking guardedly all through dinner, so as not to say anything which, printed, might offend somebody. Football people are as touchy as politicians. Perhaps touchier. You have to watch what you say.

Smiling warmly, Craig answers: "I sure wish I could, but I've got to meet some people. Thanks so much for asking me though."

Walking out toward Broadway, he feels at loose ends. He goes over his talk in his mind, thinking where to polish it further, making sure he has not exposed himself too much. He is afraid to show people too much of what he thinks or feels. He does not trust what they might do with the information. He believes in dazzling people with charm, then slipping away. Serious questions he tries to turn aside with wit, dropping quickly into the correct and somewhat dimwitted role of All-American boy. This role after so many years is easy for him, and a guarantee against false steps.

The only trouble is it makes some people, usually the ones he would like to impress, think him shallow, or unfeeling, or dumb.

On the traffic island in Times Square he stops to stare around at the giant signs and flashing color: atop one building is the cascading waterfall for Bond Clothes; further on the Camel Cigarette sign belches smoke. New York always makes him feel like the country boy which, deep inside, he knows he still is.

When the traffic thins he darts across to the other shore, but the shops are the same here: windows filled with nudist magazines, stag records, erotic souvenirs. He disapproves. He is sure this kind of thing would not be permitted in Texas.

He enters a movie.

When he comes out it is late afternoon. He does not want to have dinner alone. He phones the Giants' defensive captain whom he played with in college at Texas, but the man has a TV show that night. It's just as well; they're not supposed to be seen together before a game anyway.

Craig then phones two other acquaintances, but neither is free.

Looking out through the glass booth, he watches the traffic going down Broadway. He has one dime left.

Go ahead and do it, he tells himself; you've been planning to all day. He dials the number.

The operator comes on, "Good afternoon. Pepsi-Cola Company."

"Will you give me Margie Berger, please?"

Craig, waiting, finds his heart thumping. It is like the moment before a crucial play, and not unpleasant.

He will offer her a drink. See what happens after that.

Another voice comes on. He gives Margie's name again.

"May I ask who's calling please?"

But Craig doesn't want to give his name.

"Well, do I have the correct number? Is this the place to get in touch with her?"

31

"I can see she gets your message. Can I have your name, please?"

"I was hoping to get in touch with her today."

"I'm afraid she won't be in this afternoon."

"Can you give me her home number?"

"I'm afraid we don't give out home numbers. May I ask who's calling, please."

"I'm a good friend in New York only for the day—" He floods the phone booth with charm, trying to wheedle the number out of her.

"I know Miss Berger will want to know that you called. Who shall I say called?"

Defeated, Craig hangs up.

Through the glass booth, he stares out at the Broadway traffic.

Searching the phone book, he finds two pages of Bergers, and another column and a half of Burgers. Also some Burghers and Berghers. There are two Margaret Burgers, and one Marjorie Berger. It seems hopeless.

He walks down Broadway past the Astor Hotel and the Paramount Theater. Coming out onto 42nd Street, he stares down rows of lurid movie marquees. The cinema nearest him is playing *Cover Girls Uncovered,* a film purported to be "Painted in Passion, Drawn in Desire."

To bump into Margie more or less casually is one thing. But to phone her at home having tracked her down—

Salacious films ought not to be allowed, Craig thinks.

Walking back up Broadway, he enters Toots Shor's restaurant, for this is the sports hangout in New York. Perhaps he will meet someone he knows. He orders beer.

"Any special brand, sir?"

Automatically loyal, Craig orders the brand of the team's radio sponsor.

The proprietor's arm falls around Craig's shoulder, and Craig is led to a table and introduced to America's favorite comedian that year, and to a famous retired baseball player.

Craig is pleased. It is good to be famous and seated beside your peers. From the bar, envious glances fall their way. It is even pleasant to know that there are too many celebrities at this table now; no stranger will dare approach them. Even their privacy is assured.

"How's the team, Duke?"

"How's your pulled hamstring muscle from last year, Duke?"

Craig is the focus of conversation, the way the star athlete whose sport is in season always is.

At length it is late, and Craig is hungry. No one mentions dinner. Unwilling to suggest it to men who might refuse, unwilling also to be seen in such a place dining alone, Craig excuses himself.

Outside he is hungry and lonely, and he walks along 52nd Street looking for a place he can eat without being noticed. There are many stores, closed, and a coffee shop still open. Entering, he finds a stool and orders scrambled eggs and toast and drinks two coffees.

When he comes out the city is dark. He does not know where to go next, but feels he can't go back to Toots Shor's.

Well, he can try to phone Margie Berger.

But he knows she is married. She might be in the book under her husband's name. Maybe Berger is her husband's name. Maybe they are still living together. If the husband answers the phone—

Maybe she does not live in New York at all.

So instead of phoning, he walks toward Rockefeller Center, where he looks down on the ice skaters whirling about in the warm night.

Some girls come up the steps past him. He forms the notion that if he waits here long enough, something exciting will occur. Some girl might ask him for, say, a match. This could lead to—anything.

An hour passes, and though he eyes every pretty girl coming up the steps, none asks him for a match or anything else.

After a time he laughs at himself. He thinks: You're willing to be picked up by a girl, but unwilling to try to pick one up yourself.

That's because I wouldn't know how to pick one up, he thinks, disgusted with himself.

Stopping a cab, he has himself driven up through Central Park, through Harlem and then across the bridge to the Concourse Plaza Hotel, which is opposite Yankee Stadium. This is where Craig's team, and most other teams, stay when in New York.

He goes to bed with a magazine instead.

The team comes in at two o'clock the next afternoon, Saturday. Buses take them directly from the station to the stadium, where a brief workout is held. The Yankees will not win the pennant this year, and they have no more home games, and so turf is already down on the skin part of the infield. But Craig and Pennoyer, walking the field before practice, find it has not adhered too well. They decide to eschew tricky stuff if they have to move the ball over that turf.

33

It is late afternoon when the players enter the hotel lobby in a mass, most wearing the team blazer and ties, a few with topcoats over their arms, a few (principally the Negroes) wearing hats. Lincoln Hamilton, the offensive captain who weighs 250 pounds, wears a bowler and carries a furled umbrella cane, like a British banker. A few players carry small suitcases, but most, since this is only an overnight trip, carry just shaving kits. Hamilton carries an attaché case with his initials on it in gold and diamond letters. In the case is his toilet gear. All of the players are freshly showered and combed after practice. The impression they give is of health and cleanliness and, in that hotel lobby, immense weight. They are all very large men. The lobby seems swollen with them.

The team's rooming list was sent down two days before. There are a few new pairings, because players have been cut since last week. Otherwise it is the same as always: guards room with guards, ends with ends, backs with backs, and so on; except that rookies room with rookies, and Negroes room with Negroes. However, since there are five Negroes at present, one, Hamilton, rooms with a white man, a veteran lineman from Maryland. Though he is a Southerner, the lineman and Hamilton have been roommates before. They respect each other as great football players. The supernumeraries traveling with the team also are paired off: the two trainers together, Malverde with Dr. Flaherty, the line coach with the end coach, the two defensive coaches together, and Head Coach Dreuder with his Number one assistant, Beady Stein, the backfield coach. Reporters are paired with other reporters. F. X. Boyle rooms alone in a suite.

As the players swarm into the lobby, the rooming list lies on the counter with room numbers penciled next to each pairing, and piles of keys to either side. There is much jostling and calling out. Keys are passed over heads, and within five minutes the lobby is empty of players.

The supernumeraries step forward to claim keys. Father O'Malley finds this time he is paired with the equipment manager. Boyle's two sons-in-law, who are general manager and business manager of the team, respectively, are together.

Boyle now corners the hotel manager.

"You received the menu we sent down?"

"Yes, sir."

"We don't want any substitutions on the menu. What kind of steaks do you have?"

"Same as last year." Although Boyle thinks he is speaking in a normal voice, his impatience, which is always just on the border of irritation, is a palpable thing. The hotel manager is so uncomfortable he feels he has to hurry his speech. "Small sirloins. The price, four dollars a head, as I quoted."

"Make them big sirloins. Don't you read the letters I send you?"

"Yes, sir. Canned or fresh orange juice?"

They are talking about the team's steak breakfast tomorrow (Sunday) morning.

"Fresh. The kickoff has been moved up to one thirty this season. So breakfast will be at nine thirty, understand? I don't mean nine forty. I mean nine thirty exactly. I want all the food on the table exactly at nine thirty—steaks, baked potatoes, peas, orange juice, toast, the works. Never mind that your cook wants to cook the steaks individually. I want them all there at nine thirty. Cook 'em all medium. If they're not ready when the players come in, the players won't wait for them."

The manager nods.

"Too nervous," Boyle explains. "Some will wait, but most will get disgusted and walk out. They'll all walk out anyway ten minutes after they're served. They're big eaters, but they're fast eaters. Ten minutes and it's all over. Any questions?"

"No sir."

"We'll have about sixty to breakfast, counting the writers and all."

Craig, relieved that what he will do and say and think—whom he might meet or telephone—has been decided for him for the duration of the team's stay in New York, dines with Pennoyer, with Fullback Mel Slade and End Wilson Cambridge, at Downey's. The team, broken down into its three basic components for the first time this season, is scattered all over the city. Offensive players dine with offensive players. Defensive players dine with defensive players. Negroes dine with Negroes in Harlem. Curfew is eleven P.M.

In the morning, going downstairs to buy a paper, Craig runs into Boyle at the newsstand.

"Father O'Malley is saying mass for the Catholic players in my suite in ten minutes," the owner remarks.

Craig nods.

He understands this for what it is, an invitation, and thinks: Why not, what else do I have to do?

They stand together in the nearly empty lobby.

Boyle waits for Craig's answer.

Craig has the Sunday New York Times under his arm, and would prefer to read it. But he knows having him at the Mass would mean a lot to Boyle. Boyle, who is forty-eight years old, hero-worships great players in general and Craig in particular.

Craig knows this, having long ago learned to recognize, and in some cases expect hero worship of himself. He also knows that the only thing he lacks in Boyle's view is that he isn't Catholic. Craig corrects himself: isn't *a* Catholic. That's how the Catholics say it, and if you say it wrong they know you're not one of them.

The trouble with Catholics, Craig thinks, is that for them there are only two kinds of people: Catholics and non-Catholics. What a presumptuous thing to think. Suppose football players thought there were only two kinds of people: players and non-players.

Of course, in a way they do.

Craig rather likes Boyle; it is hard to resist so much admiration. Boyle is an old style paternalistic employer. He takes care of his own people. As long as you keep your humility, you have a job with Boyle. The only ones Boyle ever fires are those who get too big for their britches. He keeps old players on the payroll for years afterward, sending them money for scouting and other small jobs. Some people say he is cold and mean, but he has always been generous to Craig.

Craig thinks: I might as well go to the Mass.

Entering the suite, they see Father O'Malley in his vestments waiting to begin the Mass, Boyle, grinning proudly, has his arm around Craig's shoulders.

"I brought you a Protestant, Father," the owner calls to the priest.

When the Mass begins, Craig stands among two dozen Catholic players. Stablinski and Gene Gardner (known as Mean Gene) are there; also Jonesy, the kicker, and Joe Morris, the defensive captain. Mel Slade, who is from Notre Dame, is there, as is Ox Polski, at 275 pounds the biggest man on the squad, although not by much. Craig sees Jimmy Finney, the club's Number one draft choice this year, a halfback from Georgia whom the veterans call Laughing Boy; the southern players are not usually Catholics and Craig is surprised. Dr. Flaherty is there of course, and the two trainers, and all the coaches except Beady Stein. The middle linebacker, Salvatore DiRico, is there in his thick glasses. A reporter once described him as "the house that moves like a man," so now he is known as House DiRico. He weighs 245 and wears contact lenses when he plays.

With downcast eyes Craig listens to the Mass. All over the league, Craig reflects, this scene is being repeated this Sunday morning, for this is a Catholic league and in many ways a Catholic game. The owners are Irish Catholics like the Rooneys, the Maras, Dan Reeves; or Italian Catholics like Spadia

36

and the Morabitos; or middle European Catholics like the Halas family. The commissioner is a Catholic, as are forty percent of the players, and there are priests on most of the benches. League rules forbid outsiders on benches, but a special clause was added to allow "chaplains."

Call it religion or its brother, superstition, but in this league games are played on Sundays, and on game days even many of the Protestant players go out to church.

When the Mass comes to an end, Father O'Malley asks for three Hail Marys for a good game, and that nobody gets hurt. The final prayer is repeated three times by the players and coaches present, but not by Craig.

"Our Lady of Victory, pray for us."

"Our Lady of Victory, pray for us."

"Our Lady of Victory, pray for us."

Father O'Malley comes over, still wearing his vestments.

"We'll be receiving you into the Church yet, Duke," he says, smiling.

Not *our* church, *the* church, Craig thinks.

"Well," he says, "I don't think so."

Boyle says, "That'll be a proud day for me, Duke, I don't mind telling you."

After the steak breakfast, Craig lies on his bed trying to read the paper. But he cannot concentrate on it. Presently he goes out and walks down the hill to Yankee Stadium. It is very early and only a few cars and fans have arrived. But there are masses of cops on the sidewalk, and the flags are already blowing on the rim of the stadium.

Craig goes inside the walls and down the tunnel and out onto the grass and looks around at the empty seats and wonders what, in two hours time, is going to happen to him in this place. He wonders if Margie Berger will be there in the crowd watching him. He hopes the wind will die down a little. He realizes that he thinks of Margie Berger often—too often.

It is a game in which both teams fight for four-yard gains, the two lines bashing each other, and nothing happening, and the backs struggling to advance the ball with tacklers all over them. Every first down is a triumph, for there aren't many. The Giants' defense is, as always, tremendous, but the Big Red's is as good.

Several times Craig wonders if Margie Berger is there, but he has no way of knowing, and does not wonder long, just keeps plunging into the line, sometimes wrestling forward for a few yards, sometimes being stopped cold. Late in the game, as his strength ebbs, he wonders how much longer he can go on doing this for a living. It is difficult to get his breath, and the backs of his hands tingle from what science would call oxygen starvation.

It is as hard a game as he can remember playing, though technically only an exhibition game. The rookies do not get in the game until late in the last quarter, and some, who do not get in at all, will get cut tomorrow without ever having had a last chance to show what they can do. In the final minutes the few veterans on both teams who have now been taken out of the game stand or sit, breathing hard, watching their replacements with grim faces. A hard game, hard to lose, but not satisfying to win either, for all the players will ache too much when it is over.

When the game ends, Craig finds they have lost it, 14–10, but for the moment he is too tired and beat up to care. In the dressing room he sits in his filthy uniform with his head in his hands. He realizes that he is exhausted, though the season doesn't even begin officially until next week.

At last he starts to strip off his uniform. Everything is muddy; dirt on a sweaty uniform becomes mud. His pads come off. He sits on his stool and works the scissors under the tape on his ankles and his right leg, and slowly cuts it off.

When he has finished he notes that his left thigh is tender and swollen. He has carried the ball twenty-six times and does not remember having taken a blow there. When he prods the flesh with his thumb it hurts, and he gets up to take his shower quickly and get an ice bag on this bruise, which in the trade is called a charley horse, which does not sound like much, but which can keep a man out of next week's game. Craig knows he won't be able to run on it for days.

In the trainer's room he shows the painful swelling to Doc Flaherty.

"Nothing to it, Duke, you'll be fine."

But he can tell from Doc's manner that this is serious. A little later he hears Doc tell Coach Dreuder that Craig is doubtful for next Sunday.

Dreuder comes over.

"How'd it happen?"

"I have no idea. An elbow maybe."

The coach nods. Both realize that most injuries come not from brutal head-on collisions, but from small pointed objects like elbows. Blows a player isn't even aware of at the time.

In the bus Craig sits with an ice bag on his thigh. He can feel the cold through his trousers. He can feel his thigh still swelling, too.

On the train the team has one car and a diner. Most of the players go directly into the diner. Craig sits with the ice bag on his leg, staring out the window. He hates defeat. Defeat ruins everything. The evening is ruined, the dinner is ruined. There is nothing to talk about with anyone. The future looks gloomy. He gazes out at the dark country, no longer believing in a good season. If the Giants can outplay them— After a victory a man feels his team can defeat any other. But after a loss he sees his team absorbing beatings one after another. Craig's leg throbs. He knows this is because of the loss too. If they had won he would be standing up waving a beer can.

He realizes again the major truth of his life: winning is everything.

A little later he goes into the diner and toys with his steak. It seems to have no taste, though he has usually enjoyed eating on trains, enjoyed watching the lighted stations blur past, and then the dark country beyond, and eating the dinner and gabbing with his teammates. But tonight, having lost today's game, nothing is fun.

Across from him, Ox Polski has no trouble wolfing down everything.

"Remember when we used to travel everywhere by train, Duke?" says Polski.

"Remember the time we went all the way to Los Angeles by train?" Wilson Cambridge says.

"Three days," says Craig with a wry smile.

"Jesus."

Every player who made the trip remembers this. They broke the trip in Chicago for a morning workout and a shower, then piled back onto another train for two days more. By the time they reached Los Angeles they were as bored and irritable as convicts. Of course they lost the game.

"Boyle was afraid to risk us all in an airplane at once."

"He wasn't worried about us. He was worried that a crash would put him out of business."

"I used to love to sleep on trains," Craig says.

"Not me," says Polski, who is six feet four inches tall. "Those short bunks. If you got beat up in a game, in those bunks you couldn't stretch out. Couldn't make your bruises stop hurting."

Craig remembers overnight trips after games in Pittsburgh, Chicago, Detroit. They used to open the partitions between each pair of compartments, so that they became compartments for four, instead of two. This gave walking-around room, and room for card games, and the porter could usually be bribed to bring them a bottle. With the doors locked they could play cards and gab and laugh and drink. It doesn't take much to get a player drunk after expending all that energy in a game, and half the car would be drunk by midnight. In the morning they would have to smuggle the empty bottles out past the coaches, but they would be ready to face another week, next Sunday's opponent coming up. Being a member of a winning team is, to Craig, the finest experience he has ever known. All that love for each other. All that oneness against the coaches. Against the owners, the fans, the world too, but first and foremost against the coaches.

After each other, the only men players love and understand are opponents. Opponents are themselves in different uniforms.

"Overnight train rides are finished now."

"I like rides like this well enough."

Craig does too. He realizes that every train ride will always be, for him, that first ride out of a small west Texas town to play in his first big high school game somewhere else.

At length the diner empties. Players straggle back into the other car. Craig sits by the window alone. He has asked the waiter to refill his ice bag. The man comes back, all grin and eyeballs.

"There you are, suh."

Craig gives him a dollar.

"Oh no, suh. Mr. Boyle has already taken care of that."

"Well, thanks. I really appreciate it."

"Hope it's not too bad, suh."

At last the train pulls into the city. Not wanting to wait for a suburban local, Craig takes a taxi home.

He is in considerable pain, and has already swallowed four aspirins. At home he takes two more and refills the ice bag. Dr. Flaherty has given him sleeping pills. They are in a bottle in his pocket.

He asks Carribel, who is watching television, to make him a cup of tea.

"As soon as this program is over," she says.

But the program seems endless. He limps down to make his own tea.

When he comes back upstairs, he says irritably: "You might have made me some tea at least."

"Ah hope you're not fixing to limp around heah all week wanting to be waited on."

"I hope not."

"Ah don't want to go through last year again."

Neither does Craig. He missed four games with minor injuries such as this one.

40

"What is it?"

"A charley horse."

"You're probably babying yourself again."

"Probably," Craig says sarcastically.

As they get ready for bed, Carribel says: "We had a call from some woman from Pepsi-Cola."

Craig feels his stomach contract.

"Did she leave a name?"

"Ah wrote it down somewhere. Molly Bergman. Something like that."

Craig carefully removes both his shoes before saying: "What did she want?"

"She wants the kids to appear on television. Pepsi-Cola is sponsoring the games this year."

Craig says: "I thought we decided we weren't going to subject the kids to any of that." But he is thinking about seeing Margie again.

"If all the other players' kids are on, we cain't let ours feel left out."

"What did you tell her?"

"That you'd call her."

"You call her," Craig says. He feels jeopardized. "Tell her no."

"Ah don't see where it's my job to call her. That's a man's job."

"Everything's a man's job around here," Craig mutters, but not loud enough for her to hear, for he doesn't want a fight. He is tired and in pain, and confused by Margie's call. He limps into the bathroom, where he sees the sleeping pills, but decides not to take any. He brushes his teeth. When he comes toward the bed, Carribel drawls: "Ah hope you don't think you are bringing that ice bag into my bed."

"I'm going to wrap a towel around it."

"You got no consideration at all, do you? Every time Ah touch against it all night long, it'll wake me up. And I have a lot of work to do tomorrow. There's a pile of ironing, and I have to clean the whole house."

Craig looks at her.

Changing moods, she says sweetly: "Now give your honey a big kiss, and go sleep with your ice bag in the spare room."

In the spare room there are no sheets on the bed. Craig takes his ice bag and gets under the blankets and tries to sleep. With nothing else to think of, the pain comes on strong. At last he gets up and swallows two sleeping pills and a little later is groggy enough to doze.

CHAPTER | 4

At the stadium in the trainers' room Craig sits sweating in the whirlpool bath. His arms rest outside on the rim of the deep aluminum tub. The swirling water is hot. He can feel it pounding gently against the hard mass of his thigh. The ache in his thigh is constant.

When the phone on the wall rings, Pete, the trainer, answers it. In the tub, Craig sweats. It is like sitting hip-deep in the current of a hot river.

"Call for you, Duke," says Pete.

Craig, who has been in the whirlpool almost thirty minutes, is glad of this excuse to climb over the rim of the tub and out. He wipes his face off with a towel, then wraps the towel around his middle and takes the phone.

"I called last week," Margie's voice says. "I don't know if your wife told you or not."

Craig makes some reply. Other players move past him, and he is conscious of the medicinal smells of the warm room.

"Well, we were wondering if you or your wife might bring the children down to the studio tomorrow or the next day."

"They've got school."

"Saturday, then?"

"Look," Craig says. "My wife and I decided we don't want to get the children involved in this kind of thing." He thinks, but does not add: And I have decided not to get involved with you.

"You don't even know what kind of thing it is, yet." Her voice, though pretending confidence, is a little too bright.

"We'd rather not have them on television."

"There'd be a fee, of course."

"I'm sorry."

"—And possibly a scholarship to the college of your choice."

"They're only four and nine years old."

42

Sam, the locker room boy who is a middle-aged man, has gone out to a delicatessen for sandwiches and beverages, which he is now distributing to players out of a box. He hands Craig two roast beef sandwiches in waxed paper, and a styrofoam container of coffee; Craig places them on a nearby rubbing table.

"Am I interrupting practice?" Margie asks.

But she must have got the locker room number from Carribel, who would have told her to phone at this time.

"We've come in off the field and are having lunch. In about ten minutes we start watching films."

"Could I possibly see you to talk to you about this?"

There is a pleading note to her voice. Craig, wanting to see her, but having decided not to, says: "I'm afraid we've already made up our minds."

"You haven't given me a chance."

But what chance does she deserve? A chance to break up his home?

He says: "Give me your number. I'll call you later." He is not sure if he says this to get rid of her, or if he really means to call.

The pleading note is still there. "If you don't call, could I possibly call you back tomorrow?"

"I'll call," Craig says after a moment.

Later he makes arrangements to meet her for a drink at five thirty. He is scheduled to give a talk that night, and is not expected home before midnight, but now he switches off with Joe Morris, the defensive captain. Morris will make the talk. Craig does not know what his drink with Margie will develop into, but he wants the evening free for whatever might happen.

However, when he waits for her at a cocktail lounge, his principal emotion is surprise that he has arranged this at all. He no longer wonders what the evening will develop into; he is convinced it will develop into nothing.

When at last she enters and comes toward him through the tables, he rises to greet her, and they shake hands. She wears an oilcloth raincoat, white with zebra stripes, and a matching, floppy hat. Oilcloth, to Craig, is something to cover dining room tables with in Texas. He is disappointed.

But she is smiling, and her face is stunning as always.

"What would you like to drink?" Having said this much, he cannot imagine what to say next.

Removing her hat and gloves, she shows off the coat. "It's the latest thing in fashion. Do you like it?"

"Oh yes, it's very nice."

43

As he helps her off with the coat, he finds that just to touch her excites him.

From the waiter she orders a negroni.

All around them is the low hum of conversation. Glasses clink.

"What's a negroni?" Craig asks.

She tells him, and for a moment they discuss drinks. She gives him a smile: "It was nice of you to see me."

He gives an embarrassed shrug.

He feels that being with her is basically illicit, and that no one who sees them here will believe this is strictly a business meeting. She is too good-looking for business meetings.

She wears less makeup today. She has a bigger bosom than he remembered, and a wider mouth. In Nashville she seemed to him a hardened career woman, but now she seems unsure of herself, almost innocent. He imagines she would be shocked to know that his plans for her tonight include the possibility of more than just one drink.

They make small talk, which from time to time dies out. He learns that she has lived in this city since her marriage.

"Then you weren't in New York last weekend?"

"Oh yes."

They sip their drinks.

After a pause, she says: "Why do you ask?"

"No reason."

"If you mean did I see the game, yes, I saw it. A man I know took me."

She says this with a confidence which makes him wonder which man. Did they go to bed together afterward?

To him she is a woman of mystery.

They get closer to talking about the television. She is now obviously nervous, and her nervousness pleases him.

She begins, nervously, to describe how she hopes to interview different players' children every Sunday as part of the half-time show. She would ask Craig's son, for instance, if his father was the best player in the league, did he watch any other player when his father was on the field, what was his father like at home after a victory, after a defeat.

"Kids being kids, we should get some very cute answers," she says brightly.

Since the program will be taped, embarrassing answers can be edited out. Each child will be paid a $250 savings bond.

The pleading look is in her eyes. He almost expects to feel her hand on his.

"So say you'll allow us to use your son."

He sips his beer, which he puts down on a moist napkin.

44

"Why is my son so important?"

"Because you and Pennoyer are the stars of the team, and Pennoyer doesn't have any children."

"Do you have children?"

She looks down at the table. "No."

They watch a couple being seated at the table next to theirs. Craig asks the question most on his mind.

"Are you divorced or separated or what?"

After a moment she answers: "Separated. My husband lives at his club."

He detects bitterness. But mostly he is aware that formerly married women now living alone are supposed to be easy to seduce.

"Do you think you will reconcile?"

She does not answer immediately. "I don't know if I really want to."

He imagines he can detect pain as well as bitterness, as if she worked hard to be a good wife, but failed.

She asks: "How did you know about this?"

Craig decides to evade the question. "I don't know. I heard about it somewhere. Isn't your husband a famous actor?"

"He's a stockbroker."

Craig thinks: F. X. Boyle got you confused with someone else.

"No one else knows about it yet, really," she says. "My parents think we're still living together, for instance. So does Pepsi-Cola. Even though it's three months since he moved out." The bitterness returns as she adds: "After five years of marriage."

By now Craig finds her so appetizing that he thinks: How can any one move out on you?

"Whose idea is interviewing the children on TV?"

"Mine," she says brightly. "The network seems very pleased. They're sick of those band shows at half time."

Craig considers. She will need at least fifteen kids, allowing for sicknesses and all, to get through the season. Are there that many old enough to be interviewed? The players, after all, are mostly very young. If Craig turns the idea down, it might sink the program before it gets launched.

"I've been reading up on you," Margie says. "You're very happily married, aren't you?"

"That's what the stories say," answers Craig. What else is he supposed to tell a woman he scarcely knows.

Her eyes drop to the table. "You're very lucky."

Craig nods.

45

He makes an abrupt decision. "Listen, if you'd like to have Bobby on your program, that would be fine."

"Thank you."

When he looks at her, her eyes seem deep blue in the gloom, and perhaps a little damp, too. Tears of gratitude?

She takes a deep breath. "Can I have another drink as well?"

Craig laughs. Smiling at him, she wipes her eyes. "I don't know what's the matter with me."

But he is moved. "Will you have dinner with me?" he asks.

"Why, yes. Of course I will."

Now they are both nodding at each other. But when the emotion of the moment passes, Craig realizes he doesn't know where to take her. He is a public figure and he does not want to be recognized.

Perhaps she reads this change of heart in his eyes. "Don't you have to get home to your wife and family?"

"I'm not expected until late."

He raises his arm to signal the waiter—not for the check but to stall for time—another round of drinks, perhaps. Where can he take her?

Coming to his rescue, she suggests a small French restaurant near her apartment. "It's quite dark and intimate and out of the way."

He is warmed and grateful for what he imagines is her delicacy and thoughtfulness.

Nonetheless, following her down three steps off the street and into the restaurant, he worries what his attitude should be if recognized. The place is small and dim. Almost all the tables are occupied. When no one stares at him, he is at first relieved, then a little disappointed too. His fame does not extend even this far. People who go to football games don't go to French restaurants, and vice versa.

"What would you like to eat?"

Their thighs brush together under the table.

"I don't know."

They study the menus. He is strongly aware of her perfume.

"Let's have some champagne."

"What made you think of champagne?"

"I just feel like ordering champagne," says Craig, who cannot remember ordering champagne ever before in his life.

"I think champagne would be very nice."

"What else would you like?"

"Do you feel very hungry?"

"I don't know. Do you?"

"I don't know."

A waiter with a French accent hovers above them.

"Perhaps just smoked salmon and some toast," Margie decides.

"Anything else?"

"No, I'm not really too hungry, actually."

"I'm not either," says Craig, ordering smoked salmon as well. He hands the menus back to the waiter.

"I had quite a big lunch," Margie says.

"I did too."

In the dim lamplight her eyes seem frightened. Her teeth gleam in a nervous smile.

"It's a nice little restaurant," she offers.

"Very."

"I've eaten here several times already."

"Have you?"

"Yes."

Their knees press together like teen-agers in a movie. Their eyes meet, and they grin nervously at each other.

When the champagne is poured, she proposes a toast.

"To a successful season for you."

"For you too," Craig says.

She is pleased by this.

Presently she says: "You're a very kind man."

This stops the conversation dead.

Both of them search for a topic. They exchange grins again.

"Football players are supposed to be just, well, dumb," she suggests.

It is something to talk about. "Not dumb. It's just that the football world is so narrow. At the end of the season you find that the only new people you've met are basically autograph hunters. People who are impressed with you as a football star. You might like to meet other people, but they're not interested in meeting you."

They smile at each other.

Craig adds: "Football keeps you in this state of arrested development. You keep asking yourself how to break out of the mold."

"You mean the game isn't everything to you?"

But he isn't willing to say this.

"It's very important to me."

"You could quit and do something else."

To keep silence from falling again, Craig sees that he is going to have to reveal some of his deepest feelings.

"There's nothing else—yet—that I can do to earn so much money and applause and"—he smiles—"good tables in restaurants, that sort of thing. That's hard to give up. But the game itself is even harder to give up. The joy it gives me—"

He is embarrassed to go on, but does so. He tries to tell her something of the animal excitement of making what the papers the next day will call a great play.

"Do other players talk this way?"

"I imagine if you mentioned the word joy in the locker room, everybody would think you were queer."

She laughs, sipping her champagne.

But he feels close to making someone, and himself too, see his life clearly. "It's a life lived on your nerves. You live from Sunday to Sunday. And that's not a bad way to live. And then to win—"

She watches him over the rim of her glass.

"When you cross the goal line the joy is intoxicating. Sixty thousand people screaming. You are drunk with it. I did it. Me. You come to the bench and your teammates have such love for you they practically want to embrace you. And you want to embrace them for having made the moment possible."

They fall silent. Margie is impressed, Craig embarrassed.

"I don't mean to bore you."

She says in a low voice: "You could never bore me."

Silence. Both pick at their smoked salmon. The old aura of sexual tension settles down again. Both push their plates away, the salmon scarcely touched. Craig wants to hold her hand, but someone might notice. He could squeeze her knee under the table, but that is not the same thing and she might not like it. He feels almost the same tension as in a game; the big play is coming up soon now. Her perfume reminds him of the excitement of dating girls before his marriage. His trousers are too tight. What will happen next?

Instinctively, he decides to keep her off balance by questioning her.

"How is it that you didn't have children?" he asks.

"They just didn't happen." She puts her glass down. "It's just as well—now."

"Were you trying not to have them?"

"No," she responds. "We just never—had them."

It reminds him that she is no teen-ager, and neither is he.

"How old are you?" he asks.

"Almost as old as you."

"I'm nearly thirty-one."

"I know."

"Yes, you read some things about me."

The waiter is at their table.

Craig finds he cannot call her by name yet. "Do you want some dessert?" He is half afraid that to call her Margie would seem too—well, forward.

"I don't know." She has not called him by name either. "Do you?"

"I don't think so," he says, meaning: Whatever is going to happen to us, let's get on with it.

"I don't either."

"Coffee, then?" he asks. If she says no, he thinks, will that mean that she too wants to get on with it?

"No coffee," she replies, "unless you do."

"Not unless you do."

"Let's not, then."

They go out through the tables.

In the street, Craig thinks: If the defense can read your emotion, perhaps they can stop your play. Now, though he is tense, his manner betrays nothing.

As they walk along a street lined with trees and parked cars, Craig thinks he can feel tension in her equal to his own. They are not teen-agers. They know what the tension means, and what is to happen next.

"Well, this is where I live." She peers into the hallway through glass doors.

"Oh, are we there already?"

She nods in a distracted way.

She says: "I really feel like a cup of coffee now."

"I do, too."

"I wish I had ordered some at the restaurant."

"Yes."

"If you'd like to come upstairs, I can make some."

"That would be very nice."

"Well, if you have time, come on up then, and I'll make you some."

As he follows her into the building, he thinks with some disappointment that this is no different from the way it usually happens in the movies. There are mirrors and potted plants in the hallway.

In the elevator she stands leaning back into the corner. When their eyes meet she offers a nervous smile, like a cornered animal. He knows that her invitation is to more than coffee, and she knows he knows. It must cost a woman, any woman, a great deal to issue such an invitation, Craig thinks. Suppose the man says no? This idea has never occurred to Craig before. He realizes how much a girl's pride is at stake, how much courage is required.

So he admires the courage of the girl in the zebra raincoat and the brave smile now huddled into the corner of the elevator. But he is prude enough to consider her conduct a little unseemingly, too.

The door to her apartment closes behind them. She takes Craig's coat, and he stands alone in her living room.

The carpet is deep blue. There are love seats facing each other in front of the fireplace. They are in a satiny material that is a paler blue than the carpet. There is a sofa against a wall; it is velvet, in still another blue. There are paintings on the walls: a medieval portrait over the fireplace, the paint cracked and old; some still lifes, also very old looking; an abstract painting over the sofa that is all black and green. On either side of the fireplace are inset bookshelves, the books interspaced with stone and bronze figurines and some vases which Craig supposes are Chinese. There are some antique, highly polished pieces of furniture: a desk, a cabinet which must be used either as a bar or a phonograph or both.

It is a tasteful, comfortable room which somebody has spent a lot of love and money furnishing. Craig hardly sees it.

When Margie comes back, Craig is gazing at the abstract painting over the sofa. She begins to tell him who did the painting, and how she and her husband happened to buy it. She stands apart from him, ten feet of blue carpet between them, a flesh and blood girl in a red dress—he is aware of the rounded surfaces of her body. He is not interested in the painting, and neither is she.

"I'll put the coffee on."

While she is gone, the worried Craig stares at the cover of an art book on the coffee table and tries to work out a plan. If she is anything like Carribel, everything must be done at just the right time in just the right way. Otherwise the whole seduction will fall to pieces.

Margie, in her red dress, comes back into the room. The room's subdued light glints off a gold brooch above her left breast. He is conscious of her nearness, and her presumed availability.

"There, the coffee's on," she says.

Craig nods.

"It's electric. I don't have to watch it."

"You have a nice apartment."

"Shall I put some music on?"

"All right."

"What would you like, a piano concerto or something?"

"That sounds nice."

He watches her body move as she bends over the cabinet.

"Who is it by?" Craig asks.

"Rubenstein."

Taking a chance, Craig says, "No, I mean the composer?"

"Beethoven."

50

"I don't mean to deceive you," Craig feels obliged to add. "I don't know much about music."

"I'd be happy to teach you the little I know." Her smile is a bit too bright.

On the velvet sofa they sit a yard apart waiting, presumably, for the coffee.

"One doesn't have much opportunity to learn about music around a football team."

"What will you do when you finish playing?"

"That's my big problem. I haven't found anything yet."

"Will you coach?"

"I've never wanted to coach. That's the same world as now, only smaller. There ought to be more to life than football."

There is thick blue carpeting under his smartly shined shoes. He is more conscious than ever of her perfume, but this time of her breath, too.

"You'll find something."

"The trouble is, I don't have too much longer to look."

There are curtains and drapes in the windows. He is aware of the mass of the apartment buildings with lighted windows across the street. Though he cannot see the buildings, he knows they are there. He wishes she would draw the drapes.

"I'd like to learn."

"What?"

"About music."

He cannot think how to start the seduction. At last he decides there is no graceful way. Or if there is, he cannot see what it might be. He decides to begin anyway. Instead of the slick attack he hoped to stumble upon, he grabs both her hands and says her name.

"Margie—"

Her face with its overly bright eyes gets larger and larger. Then he finds his mouth on hers, while still holding both her hands.

He feels great relief. The game is started at least.

Being new to seduction, he has no idea what she might be feeling, so he goes on kissing her, both arms around her now. He is trying so hard to think what to do that he feels no passion at all. He gets a hand between them, strokes the line of her jaw, and then begins to massage the front of her dress.

Her mouth opens under his, and to his surprise her tongue flicks across his underlip. His hand now drops into her lap, but she sits with her knees together, her red skirt taut around them, and she does not shift position, or spread her legs.

He is trying to decide if she is expert at this sort of thing, or a novice like himself. He is not even sure if she means to go

51

on with it much longer. If she wants him to continue, why has she not spread her legs?

Reaching behind her, he fumbles with the neck of her dress, getting nowhere until she breaks their embrace and, with her own hands, releases the catch, saying: "There's two of them, see?"

His fingers, returning to the attack, find she has even started the zipper halfway down, so he lowers it all the way, and then peels the dress off forward, so that it falls into her lap.

He peels her slip down, exposing a lacy half-bra. Getting this undone in the back, he slips it off, and then buries his face in her bosom, automatically comparing her in size and taste to Carribel. Her nipples are darker than Carribel's, and this puts him off a little. First love is best, he thinks vaguely, for you compare her with no one.

The music is playing, though he does not hear it, and the lights are dim, though bright enough to see what there is to see. The undrawn drapes he has forgotten. He supposes he can take her to bed anytime now, and tries to think of a smooth way to suggest it, but nothing comes to mind. She sits very straight, naked back rigid, her collapsed dress very red against the blue velvet sofa.

Raising his head, he says soulfully: "I want to make love to you." It is the slickest line he can think of.

Her eyes still look too bright to him. "I think that can be arranged," she says. There is a quality in her voice he can't name, but it does not seem like passion. "I don't see any reason why not."

They rise, fingers plaited, and she leads him out of the living room, holding her dress to her throat with her other hand. She leads him down a hall, around a corner, past several closed doors and into a bedroom.

There is a big bed with a silken coverlet in pale green, and a dressing table with a matching green skirt and mirrors above, and some paintings on the walls, and a single dim lamp, lit, on a bureau.

He stands kissing her naked shoulders and then removes her hands from her throat so that her dress falls again. He pushes it down over her hips, and she steps out of it. On his knees on the carpet, he undoes her stockings and slips them down, then carefully peels them off her feet because he knows how delicate stockings can be, how much they cost, and how many pairs Carribel throws away a week. He does not want to cause this unknown girl any unnecessary expense on his account.

Undoing her garter belt, he draws it out of her panties,

which also are lacy, matching her absent bra. When he starts to lower her panties, she holds them, saying with false coyness: "That's not fair, what about you?"

He lets her undo his shirt buttons. When she begins to tug on his tie, he pulls it off himself, afraid she might stretch it. He lets her stand there in the dim light, wearing only panties, while he shucks off his shoes, socks, trousers, T-shirt, and shorts, letting her see the body he is so proud of, that can do so many wondrous things on a football field, and that now in its proud state can arouse and delight a woman, assuming the woman is receptive to it, which in Craig's experience is almost never the case. He is afraid it isn't the case now either, for Margie looks more frightened than passionate. But he slides her panties down her legs and she steps out of them.

When he has torn the coverlet and covers off the bed and turns to her, she says: "I never go to bed with men I don't know," adding as she lies back across the sheet with her legs spread: "And very seldom with those I do."

Which makes him wonder whether ten men or a hundred have stood where he stands. Perhaps she is more passionate than she looks.

He feels to know how ready she is, but she takes his hand away. Her own hand brushed him a moment ago, but it was almost accidental. She has not touched him solidly yet. Is she timid, demure? Who is she?

"I'm afraid I don't know how to do this very well," her voice says.

He is eager and aroused, but most of all confused.

He has not made love to Carribel for years without a lubricant. Now, turning aside to hide what he is doing, he moistens himself with saliva from his dry mouth.

The mattress is firm under his knees, rubber like at home. Towering his body, he aims gently, but the target seems a fraction higher than on his wife and it is a moment before he locates it.

Fearing resistance, he pushes gently, but slides to the hilt. He is surprised. What does this tell him about her?

On his elbows and knees, he rocks gently, watching her. She holds both his hands beside her ears, their fingers plaited together. Soon her mouth is open, her eyes closed. She is breathing hard, alone in some other country.

He thinks he has never seen any woman look so beautiful.

Her eyes are fluttering as she says: "Oh you feel good to me. You feel—so—so good to me."

Her body begins to move, as if against her will.

It is all too much for Craig.

"Shall I get out," he cries, not knowing what other men do or say at such a time, but giving her the option. His body's swelling, throbbing, oncoming eruption is familiar to him, but all the rest is new, and he has no idea how to behave.

"No." She is breathing through her nose, her eyes closed, her body undulating. "You can stay. No. Stay, stay, stay."

Her mouth fastens on his as the violent spurts begin.

He lies on her; emptied, warm skin to warm skin the whole lengths of their bodies. But he thinks with disappointment that now it is all over, for it always has been in the past. Great fun, but only a minute of fun, he has always believed, and so why risk his All-American reputation, his family, risk everything for that? For pleasure that lasts only a minute?

It has been easy for Craig not only to remain continent, but not even to contemplate any other course, and now he wonders why he has given in at last to what, at this moment, seems to have been, for him, only the ordinary temptation. A temptation rejected many times before.

But he lies on her, skin to skin, though with most of his weight on elbows and knees, pressed into the foam rubber mattress, and he kisses her out of a kind of gratitude. He also begins to think about escape, for of course he has no experience in that technique either. But she is very beautiful in the dim light, flushed, with beads of sweat on her upper lip, the pillow under her head, and their limbs are still entangled if not their lives, and he is still in the moist hot place diminishing far less quickly than he is used to, in fact not really diminishing at all. She kisses him back, hugging him to her, seeming to want more as Carribel never does, his skin tingles all over. Now he can feel her fingers and hands sliding up his body to the muscles of his shoulders. He feels more proud of his body and his manhood than he can remember for a long time, and to his amazement he begins to swell, filling her, and then, proud and delighted, to move rhythmically, powerfully over her.

The phone rings.

"Why don't you—answer—it?" he asks.

"You—answer it."

"I'm too busy."

"I wonder—who it can—be?"

"Probably some man wishing—wishing he was up here doing—this to you."

"No," she says almost sorrowfully, "I'm afraid there's no such man."

Still later they lie quietly on their sides. Her fingers caress his face.

"Was that the kind of joy you were talking about before?"

"I don't want to sound like a queer."

She laughs. "I don't think you're too queer."

He moves.

"Actually, I don't feel at all queer—right now."

It makes her bite her lip. "You're very greedy."

Her eyes begin to flutter. A cry escapes her mouth.

"I don't even know if you are Mrs. Berger, or Miss Berger."

"Mrs."

"Then Berger is a fool."

"Do you know what—my maiden name—was?"

She tells him, though he does not want to know. There are too many Margie Bergers already, one wanton, one scared, and he does not want a third with even a different name.

He kisses her, his mouth on her mouth, his chest on her chest, the length of her legs outside his own.

"Oh Duke, my Duke."

"Do you think your husband would mind you doing things like this with people?"

"If he minds, let him stay home. Oh, oh, oh."

Craig's body goes rigid, then cold, then hot. Wave after wave of pleasure courses through him.

"Oh I love you," he hears himself say. "Oh Margie, I love you."

He looks at his watch. He does not want to leave her, but he has become aware of time.

"It must be late," she says.

"I wish I could stay all night."

"So do I."

"Go take a shower," she says. "I'll get you a towel."

Though her back is to him, he sees her thrust a Kleenex between her legs. The clinical end to love. Carribel has done this only since the babies. Margie has never been widened by babies. By an army of men, then?

He knows so little about her.

After handing him a towel, she strokes his face. They stand in the doorway to the bathroom. "You're a very good lover," she said. "*I* think you are, anyway."

No one has ever told him this before, and he feels proud. But also disappointed. How many lovers has she had?

In the shower, the water streams off him. Through a rift in the curtain, feeling almost like a Peeping Tom, he watches her bend naked over the sink to brush her teeth.

Finishing, she sees him, opens the curtain, and smiles. "Your legs are shaved," she observes.

"So are yours," he says.

But he feels faintly embarrassed under her gaze. He explains: "That's for the tape."

"I like to look at you, but if you mind, I won't."

"I don't mind." He has always wanted to have his body admired by his wife, by women in general, but it has never happened and he is not used to it.

When he steps from the shower, they face each other across the bathroom mat.

She stands in the smooth suit of her skin, smiling at him. He towels himself off.

"I like to look at you too," he says. "I had no idea you had such a big bosom."

Her skin is flawless, whereas Carribel's is laced now by stretch marks from the pregnancies. Marks he has put there, he realizes guiltily, and he frowns. His thoughts turn toward home and stay there.

"Well, I guess I better get dressed and get home," he says after a moment.

He can almost feel the confidence go out of her. In the bedroom she puts on a peignoir and watches him dress. He is amazed at how acutely she senses his moods, and he wants to reassure her. But at the same time he is very late, and he is afraid that when Carribel sees him, what he has just done will show in his face. He is preoccupied by home. He sits on the bed to put his shoes on.

At the dressing table she picks up a hairbrush, then sets it down again."

"I suppose the coffee's ready now," she says, "if you'd like some."

He sees that they have become strangers to each other again.

"I don't really have time."

She nods, and precedes him out of the bedroom, down the corridor to the entrance hall. From the living room he can hear the record still turning raspingly. When he opens the front door, he half expects her to shake hands. Not knowing what to do, he gives her a brief kiss to her unresponsive lips.

"I'll call you tomorrow," he promises.

"Well, you don't have to."

"I'll call about noon."

"About your son, if you felt—now—that you'd rather not have him on the program with—with me—well, I could probably get some other player's child."

He has forgotten the program.

"No, of course not."

The peignoir is pale yellow and filmy. There is a big bow at her throat. Below that the peignoir is loose and flowing, but it

56

seems to him that he can still see the form of her body beneath, still taste her skin.

They listen to the record turning in the living room. "I'll turn it off after you go," she says. They look at each other.

He wants to reassure her, but does not know how to, and it is very late.

"I'll call you tomorrow."

She nods and the apartment door closes behind him. He stands alone in the hall waiting for the elevator. Behind her door he imagines her moving to turn off the phonograph, to unplug the coffee. He does not know what she may be feeling, nor even exactly what he himself feels.

Outside he smells the air, then inhales it, filling his big chest. He finds it is fun to breathe. Locating his car, he drives toward home. But soon he begins to brood. Where does one go from here?

When he comes into his own house he is afraid the odor of Margie might still be on him, so he decides to shower again—his third shower that day. Carribel is watching TV, as always.

"Hi," he says, looking into the TV room.

"How'd the speech go?"

"So-so."

"How much money did you get?"

"How can you watch that silly program? I'm going to take a shower and go to bed."

When Carribel comes to bed later, he pretends to be asleep. He is afraid she might, this particular night, volunteer to make love. To Craig, the idea of two women in one night is repugnant. Still, how could he tell her no (since she volunteers so seldom) without making her suspicious?

He lies in the dark. His leg now hurts less than it has all week. He might be ready to play Sunday. Tomorrow he will try to run. He listens to Carribel breathing regularly, asleep. He feels relief to see *that* danger past. He thinks of Margie's hand sliding over his tender leg. He wants to play next Sunday. He dreads the idea of the team losing a game for want of him; but the idea of victory without him is unpleasant too. He doesn't want proof that he is not vital. Various parts of his body still feel contact with parts of hers. Most of all he still feels her fingertips on his injured thigh.

This evening has left him a little blinded, like after a flashbulb goes off. So love does not have to end in a single minute. It can last an hour or more. An hour of intense and pleasurable motion and emotion—as against the few cataclysmic seconds which were all he knew of love before.

To give up the seconds was always easy in the past, if what

57

you got in return, All-American respectability and admiration, was worth more.

But what is worth more than an hour such as he has had? How can he go on living as if such an hour does not exist in any real world, now that he knows it does?

He lies on his bed—a foam rubber mattress like hers.

He kneads his tender thigh. He wants to play Sunday. And he wants more of the same with and from Margie Berger, yet cannot afford to pay her price, whatever that price might be. He cannot afford any price at all. He knows he can't play Sunday, that his injury might drag on through several more games. Because of his age, and probably because he has been beat up so much, he does not heal as fast as he used to. He can't afford to worry about—about this other thing too. He feels guilty. Retribution can be expected.

But as he kneads his fingers into the sore muscle, it seems to him that he can still feel her fingers there.

In the morning at the stadium he goes under the heat lamp at nine A.M., as hot as he can stand it. There are other players on other rubbing tables under other lamps, but they will play Sunday and he won't. He thinks of phoning Margie. The skin of his thigh is broiling. The heat, or perhaps the pain, makes sweat pop out on his brow. The other players are joking with the trainers, with each other from table to table but Craig is silent. He is afraid to see her again. He wants more. But there is no point to more. He kneads his leg above the machine, trying to dull the pain of the heat. But he has promised her Bobby for the program.

Outside in the empty stadium, while the team runs through dummy plays in sweatsuits, Craig jogs up and down the sideline, putting as much pressure as he can stand on his injured thigh muscles. He jogs up the steps of the lower grandstand, past the rows of blue box seats, and the yellow reserved seats. He jogs back down, jogs up again. There are phone booths up there next to the empty concession booths. He has a dime in the pouch of his sweatsuit. From up there he watches the workout a moment. No one is looking at him. He ducks into the phone booth.

"So this is Bobby."

"Bobby, this is Mrs. Berger."

"How do you do, m'am?" The child shakes hands with her. Craig has taught his son politeness. Texas style, the only style Craig knows.

Margie says with a smile: "He's like his father, very polite."

"Politeness is important," Craig says soberly.

Her smile fades. "Oh yes, I agree."

She leads them into a studio. They step over thick cables into the lights.

Before the camera, Bobby is almost brash. Introduced by Margie, he nods at the camera and says, "How do you do."

The interview starts.

"Does your dad enjoy practice, Bobby?"

"Not my dad, boy. He hates it. He thinks they're trying to run him to death."

Craig, offstage, smiles.

The interview is charming. When it ends and Margie thanks him, the boy says: "Much obliged, m'am."

They come back to him out of the lights, across the cables.

In the hallway, Margie says to Craig: "He certainly doesn't have stage fright."

"Neither do you," says Craig.

He had not expected her to be relaxed and professional on camera and she, realizing this, is offended.

"I've been doing this kind of thing for years," she says.

"I'm sorry."

She decides to smile again. "I hope the other children are as good."

He realizes she is elated because she has made one good program and believes now the series will be a success.

"You were excellent," he says.

She beams.

But not wanting her to have any hopes about himself, he says: "Well, we better start home."

"I promised Bobby a Pepsi, first."

"Well, it's really quite late."

He sees that she has got his message.

In a subdued voice, she says: "When will I—" she stops.

Craig says nothing. She bites her lip.

"Well, anyway, thank you," she says. She ruffles Bobby's hair and says brightly: "Thank you for coming, Bobby."

"You're welcome, m'am."

Craig looks at her. *I never go to bed with men I don't know, and very seldom with those I do.*

This is accompanied by a vision of her breasts over the sink as she bent to brush her teeth.

But all Craig says is, "Well—good-bye."

He has his son by the hand, and he does not look back. She might be standing at the end of the long hall watching him go.

In the car Bobby says: "She's a very nice lady."

"Yes, she is."

"But she promised me a Pepsi."

"We'll stop and get one on the way home."

"I made a lot of money today, Dad."

"You can buy your own Pepsi, then."

"Aw, gee, Dad."

CHAPTER | 5

Every morning after Mass and communion, Francis Xavier Boyle reads the paper while breakfasting on coffee and toast at a drugstore across the street from St. Jude's church. Today, Monday, he immediately opens the paper to yesterday's games. He has known the scores since late yesterday afternoon, getting most of them off the stadium scoreboard, but there is much more he wants to know: how many spectators did each team draw, who made the big plays, who has been injured.

The biggest headlines say the Big Red beat the Eagles yesterday. It pleases Boyle to read the story of the game, every play of which he remembers by heart. They won without Craig too. Going down the page Boyle reads how the Giants were upset, and in the West the Bears were upset. He tries to work out what these defeats mean. The Steelers are not drawing. The Cardinals are not either, but they never have. The Rams had 82,312. The Forty-Niners have lost their quarterback; at any rate, he got carried off yesterday. President Kennedy watched the Redskin game.

Boyle, too, lives from Sunday to Sunday. Yesterday he bit down all that was left of his fingernails. He chewed two packs of gum. He has ulcers, and his stomach tortures him still. But his team won in the final seconds, and, lingering at the counter, he is happy. Later his pals will call him up to congratulate him, and to bum tickets off him for next week. This morning he believes his team is invincible, and this will make him an easy mark for tickets.

Leaving a quarter tip beside his coffee cup, Boyle carries his check to the cigarette counter to pay, then goes out into the street.

At his office a few minutes later, he finds the mailbag waiting outside the door. It is eight A.M. He drags the mailbag inside, then relocks the door. Pouring the mail out on his broad desk,

61

he makes a guess at how much money is in it, and writes this figure down. It is a game he plays with himself every Monday morning after a victory.

He begins opening the mail. All ticket orders go into a box on his desk. As soon as the first of the secretaries arrives, he will have her add up the checks, and if his guess is close, he will send her out for coffee and Danish pastry for everybody.

He sorts out mail for all the office personnel. His own personal mail, he notes, is mostly requests from charities. His name must be on the list of every charity in the state approved by the Cardinal. At least the Protestants and the Jews leave him alone, he thinks. He is a soft touch for Catholic affiliated charities, and will send a check to most of today's requests, although if in doubt, he will verify the organization first with Father O'Malley.

The films of yesterday's game come in shortly after nine o'clock. Boyle, who has been waiting for them restlessly, puts his coat on and takes them up to the stadium. There he watches the films with the coaches. The films are stopped, backed-up, and re-run often, and it is noon before the first showing is complete. The coaches have made many comments and many notes, and Boyle has taken all this down in his head. He has an excellent memory, and his whole life is football. He forgets nothing. By noon he knows who played well yesterday, and who dogged it, and which plays worked and which didn't and why. He is a tall heavy man whose florid-faced, bald head is stocked with old games. To remember one more is easy for him. It is necessary too, for he will use such information when making trades, or when beating down players' salary demands next spring. Even now he can hear himself telling Mel Slade next April:

"The Eagles got to Pennoyer three times over you on opening day, Slade. I got a million dollar property in Pennoyer, and the Eagles get to him three times over you, and you have the gall to hit me for a two thousand dollar raise? Don't be funny, Mel."

Of course Boyle likes Slade, and respects him. But Boyle is a hard businessman first. Slade, asking for a raise, will hear about every missed block all season long, every fumble. He'll feel lucky not to take a pay cut.

So will certain others.

Similarly, Boyle knows which players the coaches are sick of almost before they do from comments during the films. He knows which opposing players they like. He does all the trading, often without discussing it with Coach Dreuder first, though of course always giving Dreuder a chance to okay the finished deal.

Monday is the players' day off, so after the films have been shown once, Boyle sits down with the coaches over sandwiches and beer, and listens while a game plan for next Sunday is discussed.

"The way to beat the Redskins is to keep popping them over middle," Beady Stein says.

"But Pennoyer hates to throw it over the middle," says Dinsmore, the end coach.

"He hates to throw into traffic," admits Stein.

Boyle offers: "I'd like to see us go with screens and flares to their right. Their right end weighs only two ten, and their right linebacker the same."

Head coach George Dreuder, who is six feet six inches tall and prematurely white haired, chews his sandwich and says nothing. The other coaches discuss Boyle's suggestion.

"I want to look at their game with us last December before I decide," Dreuder says.

This is fair enough.

"Neither one of those guys will be able to cover Craig," Boyle says. "They'll have to bring the cornerback up, which will open them up to the deep stuff."

"If Craig plays."

"He'll play," Boyle asserts. "I talked to Doc an hour ago."

Dinsmore suggests: "If we put Slade out in front to clear the linebacker out—"

If Dreuder is annoyed at interference by the owner, he does not show it. Dreuder knew before he took the job what the setup was on this team. Some teams are owned by businessmen whom the coaches never see except on Sunday, but most are owned by football men. Some of the football men prefer their coaches to be drinking companions also, and some like to give advice that the coach is free to reject, and some like to be in on every detail.

Of the latter Boyle is the most astute.

After lunch, while the coaches go through the film again to grade the players and to begin to work out next Sunday's game plan, Boyle returns to his office. He checks the box office to see how long the lines are, and he goes over some publicity releases Malverde wants to send out; on this team, all front office decisions are made by Boyle.

Sam, the box office man, is at Boyle's door. "You want me to hold back Section Twelve?"

"How are they moving now?"

"Good. I think we'll go in with an advance of forty-seven."

This would leave only a little over 12,000 seats to be sold at the gate. With good weather, a sellout.

"Hold them."

A little later, moving through the office, Boyle stands behind the box office to watch Sam work.

A well-dressed middle-aged man peers through the bars. He asks politely for two good seats.

"Are you kidding?" says Sam rudely.

"Well, the best you have."

Sam thrusts across the poorest two tickets he has left. "You're lucky to get these, Mac. Ten dollars. Next."

The money goes into the drawer. The well-dressed man departs, humiliated. A laborer is next in line.

"End zone," says Sam rudely. But the laborer is immune to rudeness.

"You must have something better."

They bargain. Sam parts with two tickets on the ten-yard line.

Boyle enjoys watching Sam work. Sam is rude to everybody. That keeps each transaction short. He gets rid of the worst tickets whenever he can. If a customer hesitates, Sam stares off to the side, rapping his hands impatiently on the counter. If this doesn't work, he growls: "Make up your mind, buddy."

No one is encouraged to plead with Sam. Behind the grill, Sam's face and manner are cold, impersonal. He never looks anyone in the eye, never offers a choice. The tickets he selects go down on the counter, take it or leave it.

"I ain't got all day, lady," Sam's gravelly voice says. Sam's hands rap on the counter. The lady in fur, cowed, pays for lower deck tickets behind the goalposts.

A broker's runner comes in.

"Lower deck, end zone," Sam says loudly. "That's all I got." But from a drawer he takes out twelve upper deck tickets on the fifty and thrusts them into an envelope. The runner gives Sam money. Boyle is not sure, but thinks he has just seen a hundred dollars paid for sixty dollars worth of tickets. He knows Sam black-markets tickets on the side, but so would any other box office man. In return, Sam has connections with all the brokers and can get Boyle excellent tickets to other events and plays on a moment's notice.

Boyle does not consider Sam a thief, and petty larceny does not rank high in Boyle's litany of sins anyway. Boyle's father was Irish Jimmy Boyle, the politician, who never held high office in his life, who nonetheless could afford to buy the Big Red in the twenties and run it as a hobby for years, paying the players one hundred dollars a game but losing money anyway, and who died leaving an estate of half a million dollars. The great sin of the Irish, Boyle reflects, is the bottle, and the great sin of Irish politicians is robbing the city. These are small failings compared to, say, whoring. Thankfully, the Irish have never been whoremasters. Boyle considers himself Irish. Such weaknesses as the Irish character has shown, in Boyle's view, do not amount to much.

Sam's name is Leahy, he is an irreproachable family man, and he is an artist at moving bad tickets. Besides, he has been with Boyle a long time. The Irish take care of their own. This is called loyalty. It is one of their many strengths.

The club's ground floor offices face out onto Colonial Avenue. The ticket line, Boyle notes proudly, extends from the box office almost to the door. There is an armed guard out there hired by the day from the Burns Agency, but Boyle has no faith in such guards. They keep the crowd in line, that's about all. Every hour he has his bank send over for the money that's been taken in. The bank guard comes in a rear door, and slips out with a sack of money (no checks accepted). Two other armed guards wait to escort him to the bank. A stickup man wouldn't get much robbing the Big-Red box office between pickups.

Leaving the box office, Boyle looks into all the other offices along the corridor. Kevin Tierney, his son-in-law, is going over the books, and has a stack of bills to pay. Kevin, twenty-eight, is business manager of the club. In the next office is Pat Dolan, also Boyle's son-in-law. Dolan, thirty, is general manager. He is on the phone arranging for buses to meet the team in San Francisco in eight weeks' time.

Then comes the big room; one girl on the switchboard and three secretaries working on mail orders. There are many file cabinets containing names of season ticket holders, and information on college players.

Malverde has a small office without a window, and next to him is a conference room with projection facilities which is sometimes used by the coaches out of season.

Becoming conscious that his phone is ringing, he enters his own office. A friend congratulates him on yesterday's victory.

"Yes, thanks, Vinnie. Good of you to call. What's that? How many? Let me see what I have here."

In a locked drawer of Boyle's desk are stacks of tickets. He scrawls Vinnie's name on an envelope and inserts two tickets.

"They'll be in your name at the press gate Sunday, Vinnie. Don't mention it."

From week to week friends can tell where they stand with Boyle by the closeness of their tickets to the fifty-yard line.

There is pleasure in giving tickets to his pals today. Suddenly, not for the first time, Boyle wishes he had a son to leave all this to. A boy like, say, Duke Craig. Boyle's wife has been dead for many years, and he raised his two daughters without a mother. The girls turned out very well, married fine Catholic boys. But that isn't like having a son of his own, especially one he could really be proud of. Someone like Craig.

Malverde, obviously nervous, enters Boyle's office. Nervously, the young man says he needs a raise.

"As I've told you before, my boy, the system here is: when the team does well, we all do well."

It is Boyle's habit to keep the payroll small and tight. At Christmas, if there is money left over, Boyle likes to distribute it in the form of bonuses. He likes to keep his employees grateful and loyal.

The club, in recent years, has earned a good deal of money and now in the 60's seems to have entered on a decade of unprecedented popularity and prosperity. Nonetheless, Boyle has been through all the lean years when crowds were small, when old teams folded overnight and other teams sprang up in new towns—most of them folding in their turn. He has no real confidence that prosperity will last.

"When the team does well, we all do well," he says again.

Two years before, Malverde, whose salary is $125 per week, was handed a $1,000 Christmas bonus by Boyle. But the team won the championship and each player's share of that money was $4,000. Malverde now mentions that the bonus system doesn't seem quite fair, since he got only a quarter of what the players got.

"What about last year?" demands Boyle.

Though the team finished only third last year, Malverde was given another $1,000.

Malverde remains silent, no doubt hoping that Boyle will see that this still totals only $2,000 as against $4,000.

But Boyle sees only what he chooses to see.

"If you want to cut in on the players' share, speak to them about it, not me," says Boyle coldly.

Malverde, hastily changing his plea, insists he does a good job of great value to the team.

"When I win I don't need publicity," says Boyle with a smile, "and when I lose I can't get it. Your job is not that important to me."

Malverde stares at the floor.

"When you got a winner, you can go to dinner."

Malverde says nothing.

"Publicity has nothing to do with it. When you got a winner you can go to dinner."

Malverde dispiritedly asks if he might expect a raise or promotion sometime in the future.

"The job pays one twenty-five a week," Boyle says curtly. "As for advancement, this is a family business." He does not have to add: you're not family.

Having just denied money, promotion, and recognition to this employee, Boyle now asks expansively why Malverde needs more money. It seems that Malverde is moving, and will have to carry two houses until the old one is sold.

"What do you need?" asks Boyle expansively.

He writes out a check for $25,000, which he hands to Malverde. "No interest. You pay me back when you sell the old house."

Malverde stares at the check.

"Why didn't you say so in the first place," Boyle says. "Glad to have been able to help you out."

When Malverde leaves, Boyle feels good, for he loves to be generous. He especially loves to make generous gestures that will be talked about. Also he is pleased that he has insured Malverde's loyalty while still keeping the payroll tight.

He shoves some fresh gum in his mouth.

More pals call up, chiefly politicians and influential men about the city. Some are golfing pals from the country club. For six months during the off-season, Boyle plays golf nearly every afternoon; two hours work a day in the off-season are more than enough to keep a pro football team going, as long as the staff works full time.

At last Boyle asks the switchboard girl to turn off his phone. He begins to go over figures pertaining to his radio and television contracts.

Late in the afternoon he hears Craig's voice in the corridor.

"Come in, my boy, come in."

Craig wears a dark suit and knit tie. He holds tickets in his hand.

"How's the leg, Duke?"

Craig prods the thigh of his leg.

"I've been up at the stadium under the lamps all afternoon. Feels pretty good now."

"A little sunburned, though," suggests Boyle with a smile.

"Just a little," says Craig wryly.

"Well, we won without you yesterday, Duke. Couldn't win many without you, though."

"Didn't Jimmy Finney look great?" asks Craig.

It is the type of modest, correct remark Boyle has come to

expect from Craig. With twelve seconds to play, Finney, the Number one draft choice from Georgia, scored the winning touchdown in Craig's place.

"Finney's good, but he's no Duke Craig."

Craig, no more immune to praise than the next man, smiles.

Boyle is pleased to have the famous player in his office. Sickly as a boy, he always idolized great athletes, and he still has something of the small boy's awe in the presence of Craig. He feels football must be a great game to produce heroes such as this man.

"Did you get what you wanted, Duke?"

"Sam fixed me up in the box office."

"What did he give you?"

Craig shows his tickets.

"Didn't he have better than that?"

"He said not."

"He's probably sold all the good locations to the brokers under the table," Boyle says with a laugh.

Seeing the puzzled look come onto Craig's face, Boyle says: "Sam's been with me a long time. Many years. He's a good man."

Opening the drawer, Boyle removes a stack of tickets.

"Are these for people who are important to you, Duke?"

"I don't want to take your good tickets."

"Think nothing of it, my boy." Boyle feels pleased to be able to do something for Craig.

"Here you go, Duke. Smack on the fifty."

"I didn't mean to take your good tickets."

"It's nothing, my boy."

Boyle is enjoying Craig's presence in his office.

"I hope whoever you give those tickets to realizes you players have to pay for them," Boyle says.

"Well, they never do."

Boyle stuffs fresh gum in his mouth. "Why don't you and I have dinner together some night soon."

"Swell, any time."

Boyle is not used to asking favors, and does not know how to proceed. The owner gives a brief laugh. He chews his gum.

Boyle is suddenly anxious to shift the subject. "I saw a tape of your boy on the half-time show yesterday, Duke."

"How'd you like it?"

Boyle is on firmer ground here. He remembers that no one asked his permission for the show; he didn't even know it had been made, and seeing it was a nasty surprise.

"I didn't."

"It seemed harmless."

"You know how these actresses are. Morals of cats."

Craig, studying the floor, nods.

"I don't like women like that around my ball club."

After a moment, Craig remarks: "Well, I'm sure you're exaggerating."

"That's the same doll from Nashville. I put a stop to her there."

Boyle becomes angry. He was not consulted on the program, and he does not like pinup girls around his team. The Los Angeles Rams are always being photographed with starlets, which may be why the Rams don't win, and Boyle considers sex-oriented publicity a disgrace to the game anyway. Girls and sex have nothing to with football. Boyle wants to keep football pure, and he also does not want things happening around his team that he doesn't know about.

"I don't want some oversexed show girl getting publicity out of my team." He thinks of thirty-five healthy young men ogling her. Craig too, probably. "The reputation of my team is important to me."

"It's just a half-time show," says Craig.

"What's the matter with showing the band as always?"

"I guess the network thought this would have more appeal."

Boyle snorts. "We've been having marching bands at half time for fifty years. That's football. If it's good enough for fifty years, it's good enough for this year."

Craig says nothing.

"These TV people don't give a damn about tradition."

Craig tries a smile. "I guess you didn't like the show."

"I'd appreciate it if you'd advise the other boys not to get involved with this thing."

"Well, she seemed like a nice g—woman," says Craig. "I'm sure an outfit like Pepsi-Cola would have checked her out pretty carefully."

"She's probably sleeping around in the company."

"Oh, I don't think so," says Craig nervously.

But the owner nods his head several times.

"That's how all these girls get ahead."

Boyle shows Craig to the door. "Take care of the leg, Duke."

Boyle changes to fresh gum. Picking up the phone, he asks to be put through to the network. But no one there can tell him whose idea the program was, or who is in charge. They promise to call him back. Well, he will hound them every day until he gets some satisfaction. The TV executives don't seem to realize that the owners run pro football, not the networks.

He thinks of Craig with fondness. Craig is a winner.

At five o'clock they close the office, and behind closed doors

Sam begins to stuff tickets into envelopes the girls have prepared during the day. Tickets ordered by mail are sent special delivery in plain brown envelopes. When Sam finishes, he will drop the sack off at the post office on the way home.

Boyle himself begins to read the out-of-town papers which have come in that day. He subscribes to the Sunday papers in the home city of every major college team in the country. These arrive Monday and Tuesday wrapped in brown paper, and Boyle now strips the wrapping off a dozen of them. His office has a trophy case on one wall, and many blowups of famous players of the past on the other walls. He settles down in a leather sofa to read reports of last Saturday's college games. He loves to read reports of old football games. Beside him is a ledger with the rosters of the college teams, and after he has read game accounts, he checks off against the rosters the starting lineups as given in the papers. At the end of the season, the ledgers will tell him how many games each college player started. This gives a line on how highly each boy's coach thought of him.

Boyle could easily pay someone to do this job for him, but he prefers to do it himself because it helps him memorize the names, sizes, and to a certain extent the skills of every college senior in the nation each year. There are more than two thousand college players in his head at this time.

For two hours he works on the papers, then locks up the office and goes to the Athletic Club for a swim and a steam. Not meeting any of his pals there tonight, he eats dinner in the club dining room alone. After that he goes back to his office and starts in on the papers again. It is work that has to be done, and he has nothing else to do tonight anyway. Even when he was married he often used to work nights. He finds himself thinking of Rose, but she has been dead so long he can no longer remember what she looks like. He dines with one daughter Tuesday night, and with the other every Friday. Saturdays and Sundays he is often on the road with the team. That leaves only three nights a week to get through by himself.

Up at the stadium, he knows the coaches are working late too, endlessly studying yesterday's film of their own game, and also films of the Redskins' game last week with the Lions. He briefly considers going up there to share the work and the conversation, but realizes there is a line between his coaches and himself which he must not cross. To watch the films this morning and to discuss a game plan for next Sunday is okay; but to seem to be around their necks night and day would not be.

Much as he wants to, he can't go up to the stadium tonight.

As he studies the newspapers, he feels a little lonely, and does not know why. Perhaps he should have got married again. But to whom? Anyway, he has the team. He's married to that.

At last he takes a taxi home. His housekeeper, whom his father brought over from Ireland forty years ago, is asleep. His footsteps in the hall have an empty ring. After kneeling beside his bed to say his prayers, he lies in the dark worrying about the Redskins next Sunday. He worries about the weather, and the size of the crowd, and the Redskins' running attack, which will be very hard to stop, and whether or not his own team will be "up" for the game.

In his mind the Redskins roll up touchdown after touchdown. His stomach is burning and he gets up to take a Bromo. Then he gets his beads out and lies in the dark saying the rosary. You win football games with preparation and attention to detail, and you score points in heaven with prayer. Boyle means to be a winner on both counts. Saying the rosary always helps, and at last he falls asleep.

CHAPTER | 6

Another week and game have passed. It is Monday again.

Outside the hospital, Craig searches for a parking place. But there are none, except in the doctors' section, which is half full—Cadillacs and Thunderbirds mostly. Though Craig drives round and round, looking to park, he never considers usurping a spot with a doctor's name stenciled on it. He is used to obeying rules without question; besides he lives in a country taught to revere doctors. Though he has had a great deal to do with doctors and no longer quite trusts them, basically Craig still accepts the idea that their skill and devotion have earned them their Cadillacs and half-empty lots. Craig is a mid-century American with a mid-century American's ideas, and perhaps part of the reason he has known so much adulation is that he holds more of the country's ideas than his own.

Craig searches so long to park that he vaguely considers not stopping at all. But Wilson Cambridge, injured in yesterday's game, is up there, and somebody has to go visit him. Craig knows none of the other players will think to do so, and he has lain in enough hospitals himself to know how eager a man can be to see a teammate.

Upstairs Cambridge, who weighs 225 and stands six four, lies in a semiprivate room looking very healthy and much too long and heavy for the bed.

"When do I get out of here, Duke?" demands the patient.

"You gave us a heckuva scare," responds Craig carefully. "We thought you were dead."

Craig, thinking to prepare Cambridge for the bad news to come, describes how Cambridge lay unconscious, barely breathing on a rubbing table when the team trooped in at half time, and he still lay there when the game was over and the team trooped back in a second time. Doc Flaherty was afraid to move him, though the ambulance waited outside the stadium. Players, naked, stood over the table for a moment en route to and from the showers.

"When do I play again?" demands Cambridge.

Craig knows that Doc Flaherty has marked Cambridge out for the season. The concussion was so deep that another blow could kill him.

But Craig has come to cheer his teammate up. "They put you on the injured list today."

This means Cambridge is out four games at least. When tears come to his eyes, Craig looks away.

After a moment, Cambridge says: "What happened to me?"

Cambridge does not remember even the kickoff. With head injuries, Craig knows from experience, one usually cannot remember even breakfast that day. "You were running a square-in pattern. Looked like his shoulder caught you between your helmet and shoulder pads on the blind side."

"Who was it."

"Number 59."

"On purpose?"

"With that guy it's hard to be sure."

They are silent, considering; Number 59 is one of the players in the league who likes to hurt people. He is small for a linebacker, 215 pounds. He is hurt a lot himself, and perhaps that is what makes him so mean. He aims principally for knees and faces, hurling himself shoulder first, a 215-pound projectile. His target often is out of play and relaxed, or relaxed because the play is over—only to get clobbered from the blind side. If an opponent is down, Number 59 likes to come skidding knees first into the small of the man's back.

Through the open door they watch a nurse leading visitors to an adjacent room.

In pro football most injuries are accidents. But some are not, for most teams have at least one player who likes to hurt people, one who survives in the league partly because opponents fear him and spend so much time looking around for him that they concede him that extra step, that extra fractional second. This makes him appear to be a great football player. Football players, like most men of great size and strength, tend to be mild souls. So coaches are happy to have a hatchet man around too—they fire up the mass of mild players. Given two players of equal ability, and one of them a hatchet man, any coach would keep the hatchet man, for he would be more consistent. Ability some days isn't there, but the desire to maim opponents, if it exists at all in a man, is constant.

"If I turn my head sharp, it's a moment or two before I can refocus my eyes," says Cambridge.

Craig knows this feeling well. "You've got the double blinks."

Cambridge becomes conscious of the pale youth in the next bed who, since Craig's entrance, has been all eyes and ears. Knowing the boy wants to meet Duke Craig, Cambridge performs the ceremony.

"Duke, I'd like you to meet my roomie."

The boy says: "You sure played a great game yesterday, Duke."

"Thank you."

Craig politely inquires about the boy's operation, which the boy is pleased to describe at length.

Presently Craig turns back to Cambridge.

"This place still on the same schedule, Will?"

"How many times have you been in here?" Cambridge asks. His voice is mournful and Craig knows he is thinking about all the games he will miss.

"Three or four. Only once with the double blinks."

Cambridge says: "They wake you up for breakfast at six thirty, lunch is at eleven fifteen when you're not hungry, dinner is at four forty-five when you're not hungry—pretty lousy food, too."

This room costs the club thirty-five dollars per day or more, for which money, Craig knows, a patient gets treated like a kid in a boarding school. All the hospitals Craig has been in have seemed barbaric.

He tells Cambridge with a smile: "In hospitals the rules come first, the convenience of the staff comes second, the doctors come third, and the patients come last."

"The patient doesn't come at all."

"Dinner comes, though. At four forty-five."

Cambridge laughs. But in a moment he is morose again.

"What am I going to do if I can't play."

"There's other things besides playing."

"Like what?"

Cambridge is so forlorn Craig doesn't know what to say. He pats the knee under the blanket.

"I guess you'll be getting on home, Duke?" Cambridge says presently.

"No. I have a speech to make later. Then tomorrow I'm supposed to be on the morning show at seven A.M. It's hardly worth going home to bed."

"Why don't you stay in my apartment."

Craig thinks: Perhaps Will's apartment is what I've been thinking of all day. Immediately he imagines himself spending the night there with Margie.

"I'll lend you the key," offers Cambridge. "Hell, why let it go to waste? That way, at least you can get some sleep."

I never go to bed with men I don't know.

Craig gives a hollow laugh. "No, I'm better off going home."

"That's silly. You'd have to leave for the station before dawn tomorrow. Probably not even any trains at that hour."

I'm afraid I don't know how to do this very well.

"Well, it's nice of you and all—" says Craig.

"I don't know why you live so far out anyway."

"Still, I really should go home."

It's probably some man who would like to be up here doing this to you.

No. I'm afraid there's no such man.

"Go on," Cambridge insists. "The key is in my pocket in the closet."

"Well, maybe—"

"The apartment's only going to waste since I'm stuck here."

Craig allows himself to think that fate is making this decision, not himself. He is sure he must be meant by fate to spend tonight with Margie.

"Well," says Craig. He grins. "What the heck. It's too tempting to resist."

"The key is in my pants in the closet."

Craig at the closet says: "I've got it."

"Good."

"I'll sleep at your place tonight. That way at least I'll get enough sleep and not get chewed out at practice tomorrow for acting half asleep." He scarcely knows what he is saying. He grins. "So long, Will, and thanks."

As he turns to leave, he remembers to shake hands with the youth in the next bed. He pats his knee, small and skinny under the blanket. Then he pats Cambridge's knee under his blanket —it feels huge by comparison.

"You boys get out of here real soon, you hear?"

From the hospital lobby Craig phones Margie's studio. Miss Berger is gone for the day.

"Who should I say is calling, please?"

But Craig hangs up.

He looks up the number of her apartment, and lets the phone ring, but there is no answer.

Craig phones his wife to explain about Cambridge's apartment. He won't be home tonight.

"I have this dinner to speak at."

"—While Ah stare at the walls all evening."

"Watch television," Craig suggests.

75

"You have the life, don't you—"

To cut her off he says: "You sure looked beautiful, lying there asleep when I left this morning."

"Now you're trying to sweet-talk me."

"No, it's the truth—the way your hair lay on the pillow."

Through the wire he can feel her giving in to the compliment.

"You say the nicest things sometimes," she says at last.

"You looked lovely."

"Are you sure you're not just flattering me?"

Though he feels guilty as he hangs up, this passes and he hears Margie's voice again: *I never go to bed with men I don't know.* A shiver runs through his body and he rubs his eyes thinking: Am I sure I want to do this?

Later, in the hotel ballroom, waiting for the banquet to begin, he stands surrounded by eager men, most of them middle-aged. He sips beer, wishing it were bourbon, trying to listen. It is hard to concentrate on the questions the men are asking him.

"Will you excuse me, I have to make a call."

But there is still no answer.

He rejoins the same group, or perhaps it is another.

"How much money does Pennoyer get, Duke?"

"Who's the dirtiest player in the league, Duke?"

He parries these questions, not sure who he is talking to or what they might do with his answers. His smile is fixed to his face, and he uses charm like a shield.

When he looks at his watch another half hour has passed.

"Will you excuse me, I have to make a call."

I'm afraid I don't know how to do this very well.

Still no answer.

On the dais he toys with a chicken dinner cooked, apparently, yesterday. He wishes he might have had a strong drink before dinner. Where is Margie? Why is the food at these dinners so awful? Sipping his ice water, he looks out over a sea of tables.

Perhaps he should dine elsewhere, and arrive at these dinners just in time to speak. But that would be rude. They are always so eager to have him. He can't repay them with rudeness.

He glances at his watch again. Perhaps she is home now. Is there time to get to a phone booth—

But the toastmaster raps on a glass; in a moment Craig steps forward to the microphone. His own performance now crowds everything else from his mind. He makes his audience laugh once, then again, and after that they laugh at every line. When his speech ends, he stands parrying questions from the floor.

In public he must be even more careful than in private.

"Duke, on a flood left pattern, how many receivers do you send out?"

An easy question, but followed by a harder one: "What about dirty players?" They are not supposed to talk about this subject, even a joke is out here.

"Who's the best running back in the league?"

This is also difficult. Perhaps there is a reporter present. Whatever he answers could cause a storm somewhere. In Cleveland, the headline could read: Craig Rates X Better than Browns' Ball Carriers. The coaches paste such articles to the lockers, firing up individual players with them, or perhaps the whole team. The players (or team) get so mad they want to destroy you, and when they take the field against you, sometimes they do.

"Where do you rank Cleveland this year, Duke?"

"I'd rather not say until after we play them."

At last the sustained applause.

Craig makes his way through grinning, backslapping men, trying to get to a phone.

"That was a great game you played yesterday, Duke."

"Thank you."

"Great speech, Duke."

"Thank you."

"Good luck Sunday, Duke."

"Thank you." They crowd between tables waiting for him, and as he makes his way through he must shake a hundred hands.

At last he is dialing the number.

No one answers.

Hailing a cab, he gives Margie's address. Perhaps by the time he arrives she will have come in.

But there is little traffic, the driver gets there almost instantly, and when Craig peers up, Margie's windows are dark. Disconsolate, he gives the number of Cambridge's place.

He walks about the unfamiliar flat; in the kitchen he finds a can of Campbell's clam chowder, which he heats and eats, for he ate little at the banquet. But the soup tastes flat to him. He decides restlessly that all Campbell's soups taste the same.

But they are considered very good soups. The entire country seems to think so. So probably the country is right, and there is something wrong with him.

He phones again. Still no answer.

It is now nearly midnight. He finds a magazine and pages through it.

An hour later she answers. "Well, this *is* a surprise!"

His mind fills with the way her breasts looked over the sink when she bent to brush her teeth.

"I've been calling all evening," he confesses. His fingers curl and uncurl the cover of a magazine on the coffee table.

"I was having dinner with somebody."

A pang of jealousy. Who? Is he there with her now?

"I was hoping to see you tonight."

"I'm sorry I missed you," she concedes.

"Could we meet and have a drink, or something?" He forces himself to leave the magazine alone.

"Well, I don't think so. It's very late."

"Still—"

"I have to be up early tomorrow."

Craig admits the lateness, pleading for just a few minutes. When she laughs nervously, he sees a glimmer of hope. She seems tempted. Perhaps she is even pleased he has called.

"I just want to *see* you," he says, which is not the truth.

I never go to bed with men I don't know.

"Well, I can't invite you up here. The place is a mess."

His heart falls. She sounds wary. Perhaps there is a man with her.

You feel so good to me.

But it is all falling to pieces.

"Meet me in a bar then, or come over here."

"The trouble is, I don't know any bars."

"Come over here, then."

She hesitates.

"I just want to see you," he lies.

"You mean just to see me?"

"Yes," he lies.

"I want to see you, too."

He gives the address of Cambridge's flat.

"I could take a taxi."

"Yes."

"But just to *see* you for a few minutes. Really."

"All right."

"Promise?"

"I promise."

You're a very good lover; I think so, anyway.

"It will take a few minutes. I have to get dressed again."

He paces back and forth, waiting.

He keeps going to the front window. Parting the curtains, he peers out at the street. At last a yellow cab pulls up under the streetlight.

He stands at the open door listening to her shoes on the steps.

But seeing her face rise up out of the stairwell, then approach him, it seems that nothing has ever happened between them. She is a stranger. He doesn't know her well enough to kiss her.

With a smile, she says: "May I come in?"

His instinct is to say something charming, but the moment seems too delicate for that, and anyway, nothing comes to mind.

"Let me take your coat."

When he returns from the closet she is sitting on the sofa with her knees together. Her handbag and gloves lie on the coffee table. Craig knows nothing about fashion, but he knows when a girl's clothes look expensive. Though the word chic is not even part of his vocabulary, he recognizes it now as one of the qualities which haunts him about this girl. The players' wives, like Carribel, are still bobby-soxers at thirty. He has never known a chic woman before.

"Would you like a drink?"

"It's a little late for that."

"Oh."

It is as if they do not know each other (which they don't, Craig reflects) and this time there is none of the former sexual tension drawing them blindly toward each other.

And yet he wants her badly, partly for the sexual pleasure he knows will be there, though he feels none of that now; partly because he thinks that if he can just find out more about her, she will cease to haunt him. Then his life can return to normal.

But she is not sending out any signals, and he does not know how to begin.

So he decides to say something unexpected. "Who are you?"

"What kind of a question is that?" she asks. But he can tell the question pleased her.

At once they are friends again.

This is the first and probably last night he has ever spent apart from his wife when in the same city, and he has plans for what he and this girl will do together presently, though no idea how to get her to agree. What should he do or say next? All he is sure of is that personal questions will keep her off balance.

"Why did you and your husband separate?"

"I don't know, actually."

"Haven't you talked about it?"

79

"Not really, no." She stares at the coffee table.

"He just said he was leaving, and walked out?"

"More or less."

"Another woman?"

"I don't think so."

"Was it something you did?"

"Not that he ever told me."

"Were you faithful to him?"

She hesitates, then says: "Yes, I was really quite faithful to him."

Now what does that mean?

"But one day he just—left?"

She nods, and stares at the floor.

"Why did you say you weren't sure if you wanted him back or not?"

After a moment she replies: "Because we've never been able to communicate with each other. I mean really talk to each other about things that matter." She does not look up. "Some nights he would come home all tense and not say a word to me. Later we'd go to bed and I'd fall asleep beside him and he'd lie there still tense. All night he would lie awake, no doubt hating me for being able to sleep, and in the morning he'd get up exhausted and go to the office again, and never tell me what it was or anything."

Craig sits at her feet. His finger draws a pattern from her knee down her shin to where her toes disappear into her shoe. Her stocking, in this light, is nearly invisible, but the texture, as always, is surprisingly rough.

She says: "You don't know what it's like to live with someone for years, and suddenly realize that you don't know and never have known what that person is thinking or wants or even thinks of you."

Craig thinks: Yes I do. "And then one day your husband leaves you."

"Yes, one day he leaves me."

"And what does that do to you?"

"You can imagine. All of a sudden I have to ask myself who I am and how I appear to others, and in what way did I fail, and I wonder if I can ever be confident about anything—ever again."

She gives a hollow laugh. "You see, no man had ever rejected me before. That was what made it all so traumatic. I had seen girls around me rejected all my life, but never me."

"Because you were always prettiest?"

"I always understood how to make a man want to be with me, and want to make me happy and—or thought I did. This

80

summer, when your team was cutting players, I understood what it must be like for them. Because they had always been the best, before that, hadn't they? Every place they ever played they must have been the best, the way I was always the best and prettiest girl, or thought I was. And then they got cut. I saw some of them in the lobby in Nashville the next morning, after the team had left. I suppose they couldn't even comprehend it, the way I couldn't at first. How could such a thing happen to *me?*"

Craig, on the floor, embraces her legs, his face against her knees.

"Did I help you over that. Even a little?"

"I think so."

"I want to help you again," he says, and moves his hands up her thighs.

She runs her fingers through his hair. "I thought we said we wouldn't."

"We're going to have so little time together."

She strokes his head.

"So little time," he says, not explaining it to her or even to himself. But the future belongs to her husband and his wife. There is only tonight, and perhaps a day or two more.

Standing between the sofa and coffee table, he embraces and kisses her, then unbuttons her dress. A little later they stand together. The room feels cool on his skin, and her touch on him down in the dark between them, her delicate, long-finger-nailed, groping touch, feels cool, too.

He has scars three inches long on either side of his right knee. Sitting up beside him, she traces them with her nail.

"What are these?"

He gives a laugh, for it is hard to believe that in the real world, as opposed to the closed-in world he belongs to, such scars are so rare as to go unrecognized.

"That's where I used to have cartilages in my knee, just like everybody else."

"Was that *your* traumatic experience?"

"That was one of my traumatic experiences, yes."

"Tell me about it."

You sonuva bitch, you've cut both of them out.

But he still cannot bear to remember that. "Well, it wasn't anything interesting."

You promised not to cut both of them out.

There is a moment's brooding silence.

"All right," she says, "you don't have to talk about it."

81

He sees he has offended her. "I don't mind, some day. But not now."

"All right, tell me about your wife."

But he cannot do this, either. It seems too disloyal. What can he say except that it is hard to get used to two different perfumes, two different smells of skin.

"Do you talk to each other. I mean really talk."

"Yes, of course," he lies.

"Then it's a happy marriage."

He nods.

"You're very lucky. I think I said that to you before."

Craig, brooding, says: "I guess I'm as bad as your husband. I can't seem to talk to you either. I mean tell you what I really feel."

"I know. I guess it's just something wrong with me."

"Please don't think that. I've never been able to say what I truly feel. Least of all to my wife. Since I was about fourteen everyone has treated me like a hero, and depended on me, and so it never seemed fair to admit that I was as weak as they were; I mean, somebody had to act dependable. Right?"

"And how are you really?"

He laughs, as if to make her disbelieve the truth of what he is about to say. "Terrified, like everybody else."

She kisses his chest.

"I'm not a hero. I never was. I just was able to do a few easy things—hard or impossible for everyone else, easy for me." He thinks of all the off-season jobs he has, well *failed* at— failed because he was looking for something that promised the same excitement and glory he has already, and they were looking for a man much more amazing than Duke Craig turned out to be.

She is lying against him, and he holds one breast cupped in his hand. She makes him feel, almost for the only time in his adult life, that he is not alone.

"You don't know what it's like to be a hero. Every time something rare needs to be done, everyone looks at you. The strain builds up and up. Because nothing is as ridiculous as a hero who flops. If you fail, no one can look you in the eye."

After a moment, he adds: "Anyone who tries the impossible and fails looks and feels ridiculous."

"But you don't fail often."

"I fail more often every year. But for the moment it's habit for everyone in football and for me to disbelieve it. You see, I'm superman. I can make the big play. Only I can't. Not every time. And soon, probably, not at all." He adds: "And then what?"

She kisses him. He feels her lips surround his, and it helps.

"Off the field it's the same. I'm expected to be a model for America—young and old. I have to be on my guard all the time. I have to be eager to do what people expect me to do, always. The right thing."

With a smile, she asks: "How do you know what the right thing is?"

"Well, it's easy to know what the wrong things are."

"What, for instance?" she teases.

But he is serious. "Well, for instance, one doesn't go around having affairs with other people's wives."

She says in a low voice: "But one does. One does."

"I don't."

He still holds her breast in his hand.

"Well, you better let go of me, then."

Instead he tries to get on top of her and kiss her into submission. But she won't cooperate.

He subsides beside her.

"I think perhaps we better not see each other any more," she says.

"But I've got to see you. I can't let you go yet."

Perhaps he sees her illuminating for a moment the constricted life he leads. With her he might find a way out. Without her it will all go dark again, and what he has been on the verge of learning will be lost forever.

"I can't let you go yet," he insists.

At last she smiles. "Well, let me go for tonight at least. It's very late and I have a busy day tomorrow."

Watching her dress, he feels more haunted by her than ever.

"It helps to talk to you," he says.

She bends to hook on her bra. "And the other thing helps, too?"

"Yes."

"Yes, that always helps."

"You too?"

"Yes, me too."

But he has the feeling that that part of it has not helped either of them much tonight.

He wishes he knew more about her. Who is she, really? How many men has she been to bed with? What is being married to her like? What does she think of him? But he can't ask any of this now. The mystery is as deep as ever.

The dress goes on over her head, and the mystery is complete.

He, too, dresses. He draws his crew-necked sweater over his naked torso. "I'll walk out with you and put you in a cab."

Her hair is in some disarray. She takes both his hands and smiles at him.

"My hero."

He laughs and says, "You know, I've never been anybody's hero in any personal way."

"Not even your wife's?"

"No."

"But at least you're able to talk to each other about things that matter."

Craig shakes his head.

"You're a hero to your kids."

"But they'd accept anyone as their hero, if he was their father. Don't you see?"

"You're a hero on Sundays."

"The hero on Sundays is Number 6. The mob cheers me as a number, not as a man. They cheer the result of a run, they don't cheer the thought and experience and—and imagination I put into a run. They don't know who I really am, and they don't care. The touchdown is all that counts. The number is a hero to them, not me."

Together they walk down the stairs. Outside Craig flags down a cab.

"I'm sorry to have been so cheerful all night," he says, opening the door.

She puts a finger to his lips. "Don't apologize for that. I'm flattered and grateful that you wanted to talk to me that way. Thank you."

"I've never talked about those things to anyone. I wonder why I could talk to you."

She smiles. "Perhaps it was like being in a foreign country. You can afford to show what you feel, because you know you'll never be in that country again."

"But I will be in that country again," he says. "Won't I?"

She looks dubious. "Perhaps it would be better not to."

"But I can't let you go yet."

The cabdriver fidgets impatiently behind the wheel.

Craig feels her lips on his. "It must be nice being married to you," she says.

Standing alone, he watches her cab drive away down the street between the rows of parked cars, watches its brake lights come on as it slows for the corner, watches it turn and disappear.

CHAPTER | 7

The prospect of the game oppresses Craig, who sits in his underwear on his hotel bed trying to read a magazine. The other bed, Pennoyer's, is mussed, but empty. Pennoyer is now out prowling the streets, alone. Craig, brooding, goes to the window and looks down on Cleveland far below. The streetlights have come on and tiny car taillights wink red in the dusk.

He tells himself that the game is still a night's sleep and half a day away, and to ignore it. But there is a muscle or pulse twitching under his rib cage on the left side.

After five games, both teams are undefeated. To beat Cleveland tomorrow *solves* nothing, for it will have to be done again later in the season; but it will *prove* which is the stronger team. It puts all the pressure on them—or on us—all the rest of the way. Craig thinks: it's all a question of momentum; the people in the stands don't have a clue how important momentum is. If we beat Cleveland tomorrow we can lose to the last-place Cardinals next week and Cleveland will be tied with us again, but we will still know we have defeated them, and Cleveland will still know it too. Tomorrow it's not undisputed first place that's important, it's making them know we are better than they are. Football is emotion and psychology as much as it is bashing, and this is infantile if you like, but what we settle tomorrow is which team, this year, is the rougher team.

Craig's mind insists on going over the formations still again, and on contemplating the physical beating a team always takes against Cleveland. While he stares down on the city, his flesh seems to move, composing itself for the pads, judging the weight of them. They always seem heavier now than tomorrow when he laces them on in the locker room. The extra weight now is the weight of worry. Tomorrow the Big Red must destroy as much as possible that other big team. He himself must punish his own body and will for two and a half hours.

He must pay each Sunday for the place he occupies in society. Each Saturday night, too.

He watches the traffic moving far below. The muscle in his side goes on twitching.

A night, a morning, flags flying on top of the stadium.

Very soon.

It is ten minutes to six. Though not hungry, he decides to go downstairs and have dinner. Get it over with.

But the descending elevator seems to stop at every floor. People and football players step on. Most of the people are conventioneers with lapel tags. Craig reads the nearest tag.

MIDWEST DAHLIA GROWERS ASSOCIATION

Leonard Einseidel
Youngstown, Ohio

The players wear business suits, sports coats. A few wear the team blazer. They are very much younger and bigger than the conventioneers.

"Say, where you boys from?" a voice asks.

But no player wants to elect himself spokesman by answering. The question hangs there until Craig politely explains: "We play the Browns here tomorrow."

The man wishes them luck; his lapel tag gives the convention he attends: The Polish Roman Catholic Association of North America.

The rookie halfback Jimmy Finney, alias Laughing Boy, says: "We got a lot of players who would be right at home at your convention: Ox Polski, Stablinski, Chaplowski—"

Other players chime in with other names.

But Craig is visualizing himself trying to run a square-out pattern against the Browns' Number 40; he keeps seeing the ball intercepted.

"I'm a Pole, too," says Norm Youngelman, a linebacker.

"You're no Pole, Norman."

"My people come from Poland. That makes me a Pole."

"I'm the only Irishman here," says Finney.

"Where did your people come from, Duke?"

"From west Texas."

"Trust a Texan to say that," says Finney.

But Craig is tired of Americans claiming to be some other nationality. At least Texans claim only to be Texans.

The elevator, overloaded, lurches to a stop two feet below the sill of the lobby floor, and the door won't open.

"What's the matter?" cries Einseidel, the dahlia grower.

"Are we stuck here?" asks his wife.

"Ring the alarm," cries Jimmy Finney in mock terror.

Stablinski, a 250-pound guard, says to Ox Polski, the 275-pound defensive tackle: "Polski, you weigh too much. You have over-weighted the elevator and made us miss the floor."

To prove they're not nervous, several of the dahlia growers laugh nervously.

The plaque on the elevator wall reads: Capacity Twelve, Maximum Weight 1800 pounds. After counting, the dahlia grower says: "There's only twelve of us on here." But seven are football players, of whom only Craig weighs under 200 pounds. The average weight of the players is probably about 240.

To Craig it is no new thing to be stuck with teammates in a hotel elevator that has missed the floor; he pushes the up button and then, as the cabin laboriously starts to rise, the stop button. The two sills are even, and the doors part.

"Well, that's a relief."

"I don't see how the Browns have any chance against boys as big as you fellows."

The lobby is crowded. Lines of people wait at the desk. Many groups stand about: three airline stewardesses in blue and, not far away, four others in brown. There are groups of dahlia growers all first-naming each other off the name tags, and groups of North American Roman Catholic Poles doing the same. There are conventions in progress in every hotel all season, and Craig is no longer surprised at the esoteric groups that meet regularly and are unaware that a football team is in their midst.

Jimmy Finney, six feet three, 225 pounds, and twenty-two years old, dressed in a loose suit, has taken up station with his back to a pillar. He watches the crowds move through the lobby. Craig thinks: Even if you didn't know the team was here, you would recognize Finney as a player immediately. What else could he be, as big and young as that? It is years since Craig has stood gaping in hotel lobbies, and seeing Finney now makes him feel old.

"Come on, Jimmy, let's get something to eat."

There is a choice of restaurants downstairs. The Town Room has colonial murals, but there is a wait for tables. The dark, paneled Falstaff Room is full, too. It is six P.M. and midwestern America is at dinner.

Craig leads Finney past a tiny waterfall and an Oriental garden into the Kon Tiki Room. Craig sees some of the coaches already seated under a canopy of palm fronds, and this surprises him. Football people are not adventurous eaters; probably they couldn't get a table in the other restaurants.

Across from Craig, Finney is nervous, and Craig knows why. On the plane each player was handed six dollars to have dinner on, and Finney, like most players, has looked forward to dining on a sandwich and pocketing as much of the six dollars as possible. Now he fears the Kon Tiki Room will exceed even the six dollars.

"Relax, Jimmy. Spend some of your bonus money."

"I didn't get any bonus money."

Craig is sure Finney did, and bonuses are bigger now than when Craig started. Players often lie outrageously about their salaries, and the wives sometimes carry true tales back and forth.

On the whole, true figures are impossible to determine.

The cuisine being Polynesian and presumably unknown to them, the Oriental waiter suggests dishes. But Finney orders steak and Coca-Cola. Craig, glancing across the room, notes that the coaches eat steak also.

"Is that Number 40 as good as he looks in the films?" asks Finney.

Craig nods.

"Looks like he gobbles up square-outs."

"But if we can catch a few balls on him, he will start trying so hard to intercept everything that we can possibly get behind him for a bomb."

Craig sees that Finney does not comprehend this. "How can you be sure he'll start trying to intercept everything?"

"Well, he's been behaving that way for about six seasons."

Craig sees Finney file this away. He thinks Finney will probably become a great pro, for all he is interested in is football. To Finney, conversation is strictly a chance to perfect himself at football. The steak will give him strength to play football and he isn't interested in food anyway. He can eat steak twice a day and never notice, but he notices everything on a football field. Not that he tries to understand what he notices. He simply memorizes it. That way is quicker. The information about Number 40, for instance, Finney sees as fact, not as an expression of the man's personality. For as long as Finney plays, and Number 40 plays, Finney will never forget it. And for as long as Finney stays single-minded and doesn't get hurt, and continues to enjoy bashing people and being bashed in return, then he will be a good or great pro.

Craig is eating something he can't identify. Bean sprouts? Bamboo shoots?

Finney says distastefully: "Don't you wish you'd had steak, 'stead of that mess of worms?"

"It's really tasty."

"I don't believe you."

Craig laughs.

"Steak is my dish," says Jimmy Finney. "That's all you need to play this game."

With dessert they talk football again. Craig has found it easier to discuss football than to avoid thinking about it. The muscle in his side has stopped twitching.

Craig thinks: If you are not single-minded, then there is no place for you in pro football, and there has perhaps been none for Duke Craig for some years. But he has kept one nonetheless by keeping his mouth shut so no one can suspect how open his eyes are now, and that he is looking around at the world. He has kept a place because he has no other, and because parts of his role he still loves, such as winning games, such as being part of the big team, such as learning to get by no longer on sheer talent but on what he has learned about himself and the game and the people he plays with and against.

The only trouble is, he thinks, that you have to love it all or your attention will wander at some crucial point. You will get found out trying hard not to get found out. On the field you will get hurt trying hard not to get hurt. This game is meant to be played headlong, and once you no longer love it totally you can't play it that way, for you begin to notice all the bruises, all the brutality and cruelty and stupidity too. There is a lot of stupidity. Pro football is the new national game. Every Sunday teams collide, and the issue is settled in two and a half hours. The country is in love with this. Pro football is a square game played by square people, Craig thinks. But Craig doesn't want to be square anymore, but to grow and learn and expand his life.

He remembers the old joke: to be any good at football you gotta be smart enough to understand the game and dumb enough to think it important. This notion makes Craig smile. Of course it is important in many ways. It is spectacle, and mankind can't live without spectacle. Every Sunday it takes millions of people out of their own drab worlds. It enriches people's lives.

Craig thinks: But sometimes it seems to me we are like knights of old engaged in useless combat. Helmets, visors, everything.

The Oriental waiter pads up with the check.

And yet football has to be your whole life, if you are to be good at it.

"I wouldn't like to be in your shoes, Duke," says Jimmy Finney.

"How's that?"

"I wouldn't like to go to bed with all them worms crawling around inside me."

Craig laughs.

He tells himself that he likes Finney's brashness, and respects his dedication to the game, his determination to grasp for success and to trample (literally in pro football) anyone who gets in his way. But after an hour with Finney, Craig yearns to be alone.

Outside the night is fine. Two Negro shoeshine boys squat close to the wall, and Craig puts his foot up, his back against the wall of the hotel, feeling the boy's strong fingers through the leather, feeling the Terminal Tower, the world's tallest skyscraper outside of New York, rising fifty-two stories high straight above his head. He watches the people go by and the taillights blinking, feeling surrounded by Cleveland and by America, feeling himself a very poor kind of national hero of the national game.

"You got nice shoes," the boy says.

"Thank you."

"The Browns, they gonna eat you up tomorrow."

"We've got some secret plays."

"They gonna eat you up. They *hot* this year, man."

"Now you've got me worried."

"You got any tickets to the game?"

"I wish I did," says Craig, meaning it.

He gives the boy a dollar.

"Thanks, man. You not so bad after all. I wish you luck, but I hope you lose."

Pro football is a physical game, and after a time a player comes to feel that if there is no physical contact between himself and another, then there has been no contact at all. This is part of the reason it is so difficult to find a slot in the nonphysical world outside.

Craig now feels the need for physical contact with the shoeshine boy. He cuffs the boy on the shoulder. "Thanks for the shine."

White teeth shine in the dark.

Craig considers walking down to where the stadium looms up out of the dark lake. But this might demoralize him further, so he crosses Public Square, opting for the bright lights of Euclid Avenue. In the windows of the May Company stand wooden girls in fall attire. The manikins in Higbee's windows are dressed for rain. I hope it doesn't rain tomorrow. Craig thinks. The plays are designed for dry fields, and in the rain you must constantly improvise, all the while terrified that the wet ball will squirt out of your hands. You are on your nerves the whole time, and playing the Browns is hard enough without that.

Next come the three national ten-cent store chains in a row: S. S. Kresge, W. T. Grant, and Woolworth's, all of their windows done up with Halloween motifs. Witches on brooms are pasted to the glass. Craig knows he could be standing on any main street in the U.S.A.—the Halloween windows and the store names themselves would be identical.

Tonight he can feel America all around him, and he moves down Euclid Avenue past a dozen shoe stores: Allen's Shoes, Coles Shoes, Stetson Shoes. For a block or so Euclid Avenue is solid with shoe stores. In the windows are the heavy American shoes—perforated designs and slabs of leather for soles —available in large sizes for large American feet. Some European styles are displayed too—pointed toes and thin soles. These are not to Craig's taste, and he wonders if anyone ever buys them.

Though it is Saturday night there are few pedestrians. In the street under the lights Americans drive by in heavy American cars. Craig passes a group of Negroes on a corner, and a little farther on an unmarked police car, parked, with a cop behind the wheel and a riot gun locked upright in a stand.

He wanders on, looking into shop windows. He passes coffee shops, jewelry stores, a cafeteria. He comes to a row of movie houses. Marquees hang heavily over the broad sidewalk. Loew's State is showing a science fiction film. The RKO Palace has a costume epic. Craig looks at the photos and posters behind the glass. Should he go in? It is a way to forget tomorrow's game, and he needs that badly now.

Pennoyer stands in a dark bar, trying to make his mind a blank. In front of him is a shot glass of bourbon, his third, and change from a ten dollar bill, and a glass of ice water he has not touched. On the TV screen over the bar, a sports commentator is discussing tomorrow's game.

". . . The Big Red have shown themselves to be weak against the blitz, and the Browns figure to be around Pennoyer's neck all afternoon."

"Shit," mutters Pennoyer to himself. He empties the shot glass.

A voice down the bar says: "He's right, we gotta get to Pennoyer quickly."

Another voice says: "The book on him is that if you knock

91

him down the first three times he tries to pass, he'll be lousy the whole game."

"Pennoyer is over the hill," the first voice says.

Pennoyer, staring at his glass, concentrates on how much he likes to drink.

"What about Finney?" asks a third voice.

"He fumbles a lot. He can't hurt you like Craig."

"Craig is over the hill."

Everybody is over the hill, Pennoyer thinks, except barroom experts. He orders another drink. But the voices persist.

"If you ask me, the whole team is over the hill. Did you see them on TV against the Redskins?"

"They won, didn't they?"

"Yeah, but they played like a team that's over the hill."

"Craig doesn't hit in there like he used to."

"He's over the hill."

"Still, they're undefeated."

"They'll collapse any day. They got too many guys who are over the hill."

Pennoyer's head begins to get fuzzy. Tomorrow's game, which whirls about inside his skull, begins to slow down. He pours his shot into the ice water, and goes to the pinball machine. He begins to play. A dull rage comes over him as he realizes that he can't beat the machine. He asks the barman for more coins, and savagely keeps pouring them into the machine. He wants to forget tomorrow's game, but can't. He is fighting the game and the machine both.

Snatches of conversation still reach him.

". . . The fans sit there not understanding why the guy is open in the middle."

"The appeal of the game is, it's got a lot of mystery in it."

"Does the star player have animalistic type ability for which there's no explanation, or is it sheer brilliance?"

"The player may be a moron, but he has spurts of brilliance that come out in all of us. So you identify with him."

"Nobody can figure out how he does it."

"He doesn't make a great deal of money."

"Very few roll in money."

"Maybe he'll be found out, and won't be able to do the fabulous things he did last year."

"When a play works, they tell you why and how. Now, a catcher never tells you what he does with his fingers. But in pro football, every time they talk about it, it gets better."

"It's the mystique of announcing what they do, and then doing it anyway."

"Both teams are able to make success out of disaster."

"It's a basic confrontation. They come to a solution in two hours. That's the appeal."

"They're down on the field screaming numbers. They're winning the game and you don't know why."

Pennoyer thinks: On the field it's not philosophy. You get thrown on your ass by guys weighing a total of a thousand pounds and when you get up you can't remember what down it is. You try to find the scoreboard, but you can't focus your eyes on it. So you call the same play again and on your back this time you hear the noise which means the pass is completed and you're a hero. Or there is no noise, which means you're a bum.

What does anybody know about being alone compared with that?

What does anybody know about playing quarterback, except the four or five guys who do it well?

He rams another coin into the pinball machine and empties half his drink. Savagely he attacks the machine again.

He is a tall thin man with a leather face and gray hair. He has never been called the best quarterback in the game, but he keeps on playing year after year, while flashier men come and go. He rarely speaks. He believes life is something you go through alone. Although he likes being around his teammates, he believes the warmth he finds there is an illusion. The warmth he gets from bourbon whiskey is an illusion too, though it helps at times. He has a wife to whom he sometimes does not speak for days, though if she is not there he is restless and fidgety and does not know why.

Stoicism is his big card and he knows it now, but when he was a little boy it came naturally to him. Adults would fall all over themselves trying to make him smile or react. He learned to stare at them. He knew he had something. No one ever seemed to know what he might be feeling, because his face rarely gave clues. He has grown into a skilled phlegmatic football player. When hurt he never shows pain. He played one entire season with a separated shoulder, not telling anyone, for there was no other quarterback to replace him. No one ever guessed; how could they? When he is booed he appears not to notice. When cheered he does not smile. Cheers and boos come from the same place, and he has contempt for people who think they know but don't.

Looking at his lined, weathered face, listening to him in the huddle, it is impossible to tell whether the game is in the first quarter or the last, whether the Big Red is winning or losing. Pennoyer exerts his leadership by calling plays that work, and by hitting his receivers in the open. On days when the

93

plays don't work, and the passes miss their mark, then there is no leadership and the team falls to pieces. Pennoyer knows this and does not care. He hates defeat. If the team is going to lose, he doesn't care how bad the score is, and a little leadership is no better than none. No one else could do any better in his place and he is not going to holler and pretend to be what he is not.

His head is fuzzy now and his drink nearly empty. He thinks he has learned how to beat the machine. He has poured nearly five dollars into it, but there are five more where that came from if necessary. To Pennoyer, winning is everything. He rams another quarter into the machine so hard that the lever breaks off in his hand.

"Shit."

Whether winning or losing, he does not listen to information players bring back to the huddle. He has never met a receiver who didn't think he could beat his man, nor a lineman who didn't think he could clear a hole. Nevertheless, sometimes he hears the information and sometimes he uses it. On the field he trusts Craig's judgment most, for Craig has played this game almost as long as himself. He does not trust rookies at all, and never calls on them in tough spots, a trait the defense knows about all over the league, and which influences their thoughts and moves in key situations. If a lineman misses a block, causing Pennoyer to be clobbered by tacklers, he never reprimands the lineman. But he might climb slowly to his feet, then toss the ball over his shoulder with disgust. Pennoyer's disgust is eloquent. It is virtually the only emotion he shows.

Every summer the team brings three or four other quarterbacks to camp, trying to find one better than Pennoyer. Every summer the press writes glowing reports of one or more, the fans talk excitedly in barrooms; but Pennoyer looks the candidates over. He hasn't seen anybody yet and knows he never will. He knows he can play this game as long as he wants to. He knows how good he is, even if few other people do. He is the rare human being who does not need praise. At the end of each summer, the same reporters who gushed over some other candidate come to Pennoyer for interviews. They ask what it feels like to have won the job again. They work very hard to worm answers out of him that will make a story, and he works just as hard to prevent them from getting a story. The reporter begins to sweat. He works harder than ever. But Pennoyer's answers are so stolid and bland that in the end the reporter has no story.

"Did it worry you to see Conroy throw the ball that first day?"

"Any player who can help the team is okay with me."

"But you must have been worried."

"It's up to the coach to decide."

"Still, Conroy had a big reputation."

"Yes."

Pennoyer gives such answers deadpan, though Craig in the next locker, knowing the rules of this game as Pennoyer plays it, may be nearly in stitches.

Once or twice, to the rare reporter he respects, Pennoyer says what he feels.

"They say you can't throw the long ball, Jim."

"I can throw it. We just ain't got anybody who can run under it."

"Did Conroy worry you?"

"Every year I look over these phenoms. I ain't seen nobody yet."

Coach Dreuder, listening, adds thoughtfully: "Jim knows how good he is. He doesn't need anybody to tell him."

Pennoyer is a gambler. Perhaps he has no imagination. Perhaps he has only instinct which, in every field but sports, is considered a baser quality. But he knows when to go for the touchdown instead of the first down. Off the field he gambles too. Down home those early years he put his money in tobacco, and lost it, and then into cotton, and lost it. Now he takes his wife to Las Vegas every winter and shoots craps and sometimes wins. He stays as long as his money lasts and is a big man there. He has invested in nothing and saved nothing. When football ends he will start looking for something else. Whatever is to come after football, he knows it won't be as good.

The pinball machine has a broken lever; this is therefore the final game. Pennoyer feels very drunk, but tomorrow's game has at last ceased to whirl round his brain. He plays the machine carefully, cannily, and in the end beats it. All the lights start flashing.

"Hot damn," he shouts inside himself, and he gives an interior grin that would have lit up the room.

Outwardly he drains off the last of his melted ice and makes his way carefully, drunkenly, out of the bar. He comes out into the cool air. The fine for standing at a bar, he remembers, is $250. He straightens up with righteous dignity. A thirty-five-year-old man ought to be able to go into a bar if he feels like it. He makes himself walk without lurching. As he passes a cafeteria he realizes he has not eaten, so he goes in and drinks two bowls of soup and eats the Saltines that come with them. He decides he will go back to his room, watch Marshal Dillon shoot up the town on TV, and go through his playbook another time.

As he walks down Euclid Avenue in the cool night he feels excellent. His arm feels strong and confident, and without even trying he can feel the way it is to throw a touchdown pass, the sensation shooting from his brain into his shoulder and all the way down his arm and through his hand to his fingertips releasing the ball. To throw a football as hard as he can to an empty point in space so that the thrown ball and the running man reach that space simultaneously is an incredibly delicate thing to do, and to Pennoyer doing it is the greatest thrill life can offer. Each time a perfectly thrown pass of his smacks home, and the referee's arms go up, and the crowd noise comes up strong, Pennoyer feels like God. Nothing could add to his pleasure at such moments, nothing. Such moments are what he lives for.

At the Sheraton Plaza apartment hotel six hundred miles east, an amateur bridge tournament is in progress. It is organized by Flora Pennoyer for the players' wives, and is played on the Saturday nights that the team is on the road. The entry fee is ten dollars. This pays for coffee and cookies, and at the end for the prizes that Flora will buy. Flora always buys prizes for everyone, even the last-place pair.

This season sixteen wives are entered—four tables of bridge. Fifteen of the girls live in the hotel. The sixteenth is Carribel Craig, who has not lived in the hotel since Duke's early years with the team.

Tonight as always there are doors ajar all along the hall. Each table is in a different apartment, and the girls like to move back and forth when dummy to gossip and kibitz. More importantly, with all the doors open they can hear if one of their children cries out.

Usually all the games are on the one floor, but Jane Polski's son is sick, and so the fourth game is in her apartment downstairs. One of the players there is Anne Slade; Flora, two floors above, has agreed to listen for Anne's kids, Anne's door being left ajar for this purpose.

The conversation at all the tables is about clothes and hairdos and children's illnesses—women's things. The girls rarely talk football, partly because it is a dangerous subject, partly because few of them have ever been to a game with an adult male in their lives (their boyfriends and, later, husbands were always playing in the game) and they don't know that

96

much about it; football on the pro level is too technical, too complicated to be of much interest to them, apart from the winning or losing of games. They can't talk personalities, as this subject is taboo, and they have an explicit rule against any discussion of their husbands' salaries. Sometimes some of the younger girls bring money up anyway, at which point Flora, or Sara Morris, or one of the older wives will draw her aside and lecture her.

Incessantly, tonight as always, the girls gossip.

Sometimes it is harmless gossip: "Felicia's three days late."

Sometimes it is potentially dangerous: "Donald says the coaches are down on him."

Flora Pennoyer organizes the tournament partly as a responsibility, because the girls need something to do on the weekends they are alone, and she is the senior wife living in the hotel and team spirit among the wives is judged to help the team spirit of the team itself; and partly because she simply loves the gossip she picks up, even though Jim won't let her talk about it even in bed, and she knows better than to pass it on among the other, younger wives. When she tries to tell something juicy to Jim, he usually says: "I don't want to hear it."

Few of the girls are dedicated bridge players; for most the game is a social get-together. But Carribel, a fierce competitor, always plays to win. Tonight Carribel and Flora are paired against Sara Morris and Felicia Finney.

"Your bid, Felicia," says Carribel.

But Felicia says to Flora: "What did y'all do with your bonus money."

"It paid for our honeymoon," answers Flora. Though money is a dangerous and usually taboo subject, Flora doesn't mind remembering her honeymoon and Jim's small—by today's standards—bonus which paid for it.

"Jimmy's gonna buy a business with his."

"Times have changed," admits Flora. "Bonuses are bigger now."

Carribel, intensely loyal, leaps to the defense of her best friend Flora.

"At least Jim Pennoyer has proved he was worth his bonus," says Carribel sweetly. "Your bid, Felicia."

Felicia makes a show of looking over her cards. She is twenty-one years old, blond, with long fluttering eyelashes and a thicker southern accent even than Carribel's. She is very pretty and talkative, and she has perhaps been stung by Carribel's retort.

"Some *Life* photographers were up heah to take our pictures the other day," Felicia says. "Ah cain't imagine what for. Of course Jimmy's a wondahful football player. He really is. But why, you know, me?" Her eyelashes flutter.

Carribel flutters her own right back. "Those *Life* photographers really take an awful lot of a person's time," Carribel drawls. "Why, Duke and Ah hardly had time to do any courting."

Flora Pennoyer looks from one to the other.

Sara Morris, Felicia's partner, says: "Your bid, Felicia."

But Felicia gives Carribel a strange look. "You mean *Life* once took your photo, too?"

"For the, you know, the cover," says Carribel.

Felicia's eyelashes cease to flutter. "Ah bid two spades."

Carribel's hand is weak, but Felicia Finney seems to think herself the first girl in the world who ever married a college football star, and this makes Carribel throw caution to the winds. "Three diamonds," Carribel says sweetly.

"Three spades," responds Felicia doubtfully. But she looks at Carribel with new respect. "Tell what it was like, bein' on the cover of *Life* and all," she says.

"Kinda amusin'," drawls Carribel. "Seeing your face all over all those newsstands for a week. And for months after that coming across it, you know, unexpectedly at the beauty parlor, or at somebody's house that kept old magazines around."

Now Felicia looks humble and Carribel's eyelashes are the only ones fluttering.

"Four diamonds," adds Carribel sweetly.

"Double," says Sara Morris.

"Jimmy says Duke is a wondahful football player," says Felicia. "He really did." She has recovered. "Four spades." Her eyelashes flutter anew. "Ah just hope Jimmy is as good as that when he's as old as Duke is."

"I pass," says Flora Pennoyer. "Why don't I put the coffee on?"

When the games end, Felicia goes to her own apartment to bed, saying: "Ah'm three days late, you know. Ah better start taking care of myself."

But Anne Slade comes in, and some of the other girls, and they all sit drinking coffee and gossiping about the shows they have seen or plan to see, the clothes they have bought or plan to buy. Some of them envy Carribel aloud, because she lives in the city all year round and can see the shows, or buy the clothes any time she wants.

Carribel basks in this attention, and she loves being one of the girls—they are small-town girls as she is, and she believes she understands them and the disconnected lives they live for a few months each year here in the big city.

But deep down she is troubled too, though she scarcely realizes it. She is troubled by Felicia Finney who thinks (as Carribel once thought) that life is a constant succession of being on magazine covers and being married to her own personal football hero. But life isn't that way at all. After a while the magazines forget about you, and concentrate on some newer hero, and you aren't young and giddy anymore, and neither is life, and you don't know why. Nobody knows who Duke Craig's wife is anymore, or cares, or envies you, or thinks it's exciting that you caught Duke Craig, made him marry you. And Carribel finds herself wishing Felicia Finney could see what's ahead of her, because that would take the smugness out of her.

Tonight has brought Carribel's disappointment with her own life up close to the surface, so that even while she is outwardly happy and relaxed sitting sipping coffee with these other wives, her girl friends, nonetheless underneath she is upset, and she knows that tomorrow she will be blue all day.

She wishes that she and Duke still lived in the hotel with the other families. Those were the good days. The hotel did the cleaning and made the beds, and all a girl had to do was take care of her children (and Carribel only had one then) and do the cooking. The doors were open on the halls most of the day, with the girls popping in every now and then to borrow something. Nobody had a complete set of kitchenware or appliances, for instance, but among them they had one of everything, and each wife, next to her telephone, had a list telling which other wife had what. Carribel still remembers the list: Charlotte Plog had an electric mixer (the Plogs are back in Alabama now), and Flora had almost the first steam iron, and Rosemary Lynch (Jack is now an insurance salesman in Minnesota) had a waffle iron, and so forth. So you could always borrow what you needed. But the best was just to have so many other girls around all the time, and always have somebody to talk to, and Scrabble games and bridge and canasta and things going all the time.

Carribel hates living in a suburb here in the North, but doesn't realize it. She only vaguely realizes, underneath the laughter and gossip of this evening, that she is disillusioned by life. She wishes they could live in the hotel again. She wishes they could live in Texas again, too. She imagines she would feel at home and content there; it's warm, and you can get colored servants to wait on you. She wasn't made to be a suburban housewife. She was meant to be a southern belle with lots of parties and dances to go to, she decides. She was meant to live in Texas where being Duke Craig's wife would be important to people and if she, for instance, had another baby or something you know it would be a big story in all the papers.

In the movie Craig can no longer sit still. Restlessly, he walks uphill through the darkness of the theater and outside and starts back to the hotel, thinking: if the defense can hold them to two touchdowns, we have a chance. But in his mind that big Number 32 comes bashing around end all the time, and that left guard who pulls out to lead him is faster than he is, and the two of them coming around is like stopping a train.

Crossing Public Square this time there is a man waving a Bible and screaming: "Jesus tells us that fornicators and adulterers will taste hell's fires."

People stand grinning, watching the lunatic or missionary or whatever he is. A sign leaning against a lamppost reads: "Listen all members of the Hebrew faith unless ye be baptized, ye shall taste hell's fires."

Craig stops to watch, for it is better than worrying about the game. He has seen such men, such signs, listened to such harangues on Times Square, on Sunset Strip, and outside the St. Francis Hotel in San Francisco.

This is as much America as football, he thinks.

Upstairs Pennoyer lies on his bed staring at the television. Beside him lies his playbook, open.

Craig goes into the bathroom to take a shower. He hates to feel any dirt on him. He is compulsively clean, an automatic taker of showers. Most athletes are.

The two big men, reflecting on their beds, watch television wordlessly for an hour. Several times Craig glances over at the gray-haired quarterback, wondering what he is thinking. No one ever knows, on or off the field. Perhaps he is thinking deep thoughts. Perhaps he is thinking nothing.

Presently Pennoyer slides under the covers, turns his face to the wall, and goes to sleep.

When the program ends, Craig gets up to turn off the TV.

He lies in the dark, thinking about Margie. But even she cannot keep his mind off the game very long. And he begins to visualize Number 40 breaking up pass plays. He realizes there is nothing special about tonight. Every Saturday night in his life is the same, whether it is the Browns tomorrow, or the last-place team.

He thinks: By this time each week our apprehensions are so strong it is a wonder any of us can sleep at all.

CHAPTER | 8

Eight A.M. Pennoyer, wearing the T-shirt and shorts he has slept in, switches on the television, then lies in bed staring at it while Craig shaves. Craig likes to go into games clean-shaven. Most of the players shave after the game.

Combed and dressed, Craig stands at the window staring down at Cleveland.

Eight forty-five A.M. Pennoyer, dressed, says: "I'm going down." This is Pennoyer's way of saying: "Let's go down." He never comes closer to a direct invitation.

But Craig does not want to meet Boyle and get invited to the Mass. "I'll wait a bit longer."

Pennoyer shrugs as if indifferent, and goes out.

Nine A.M. Confident the Mass has begun, Craig goes down and buys the *Plain Dealer*. On the front page of the sports section is a picture of himself, the reflectors throwing blinding light on his face, rushing straight at the camera. His face wears a fierce expression and he is doing a parody of a straight arm. This photo was taken on the first day of training camp. Similar photos exist of every player on the team. Craig is embarrassed by the photo, because it looks faked, which it is. The story which accompanies it is full of misinformation; this does not surprise him. He is used to reading stories about himself; they never give him pleasure, because they are always so full of mistakes and stupidities.

Yet the fans think the sportswriters are experts.

Nine thirty A.M. Breakfast in the ballroom. The steaks are piled in the middle of the round tables. The orange juice is in big aluminum pitchers, and so cold the pitchers are beaded on the outside. The Catholic players arrive a few minutes late. Many of the players read the sports section of the *Plain Dealer* while eating; most have turned first to yesterday's college games. They want to see the results in whichever conference

101

they themselves came from. Only one or two older players glance at the political news.

Upstairs, Craig packs his shaving gear in his kit. This is the only luggage he has with him. Then he sits in the chair by the window reading the paper. Pennoyer has stripped off shoes and trousers. His shirt is open and his tie loose, and he reclines in shorts and socks on his bed staring at television.

Eleven twenty A.M. The buses wait in front of the hotel. The players stand in the sun waiting for the order to board them. They wear team blazers, business suits and from their fingers dangle their shaving kits. Coaches stand separate from the players, and wear hats.

Margie Berger comes out of the hotel.

Craig, surprised, looks at her. Standing with several older men, she smiles and nods at him, and then at certain other players. Her coat is in autumn colors, an orange and brown plaid. Her dress, Craig can see, matches the coat. She carries a crocodile handbag. Her pointed shoes are crocodile too. In the morning light she looks cool and new.

For a moment he intends to nod, then look away. He has been concentrating on the game, trying to nerve himself up for a superior performance. If he breaks this concentration he might never get it back.

He is afraid of being seen with her besides, for something might show in his smile or hers, she might hold onto his fingers a fraction too long. Somebody might notice, make a joke, start a rumor.

But he cannot help himself. He goes over to her.

He has eyes only for her. "What are you doing here?"

"We're making a commercial on the field before the game."

He shakes hands with her, wanting, needing to touch her. He convinces himself it will look more innocent to take her hand than to avoid doing so.

The meeting has brought color to her cheeks, and to his own.

They smile at each other.

"Well, nice to see you again," he says.

"Nice to see you."

He goes back to the group he was with.

"Good luck," she calls.

"Thank you."

After that, he refuses to look at her.

Ten paces away, Francis X. Boyle observes this and says to himself: What the hell is going on here?

Shocked, upset, Boyle realizes that something has hap-

102

pened between Craig and that woman. Or is about to happen. He decides she is trying to seduce Craig, who looks more than susceptible.

Boyle feels furious, and at the same time weak with fear. His stomach begins to churn and he blinks his eyes. He does not know what to do. Craig is a winner, but he is only human, and this woman is the type to flaunt her sex in a man's face.

He is furious with the woman, and with himself, too. He thinks: I knew she was dangerous the minute I saw her—all that makeup. I should have run her off at once.

But there was no way to run her off then.

I could have found one; I'm in charge here.

He feels sick to his stomach. He rams some gum in his mouth.

"Isn't that right, Frank?" says Father O'Malley.

He has not been listening. A woman like that could destroy any man, destroy Craig, and if Craig goes, there goes the season, and the team.

Boyle has always distrusted beautiful women. And for this one he feels fear. She is obviously on the make. She is the temptress. He must find a way to get rid of her, for how long can any man hold out if the temptress is constantly before him. A scandal could ruin the season, drag the name of his team down in the mud. All a woman has to be is beautiful, Boyle thinks, and she feels superior to the entire moral order. Flaunts sex all over the place. Morality goes out the window.

Perhaps the woman is honorable, though he does not believe this for a minute—all that makeup. Even so, she must go. There are thirty-five healthy young men on the team. He must protect all of them. The worst of it is, she has apparently singled out Craig. Is it too late? Should he warn Craig, or what?

It is eleven thirty. Coach Dreuder cries: "Let's go, everyone."

The players board and are counted. The coaches and reporters board. Dreuder sticks his head out the door and calls to the Pepsi-Cola group: "You people want to ride with us?"

A man answers: "We'll take a cab, Coach."

The door closes. Dreuder says to the driver: "Roll 'em."

The bus ride lasts five minutes. The bus comes around the massive stadium into the deep shade on the lake side. The players, staff, and reporters unload and enter the stadium through the back door. Most of the players hurry. They want to be first in line to be taped. Craig lingers outside.

The stadium is on the edge of Lake Erie. Craig finds a spot where he can look down at the piers where cargo ships are

103

moored. Some sailboats glide in the Sunday morning sun, and far out there is a liner. Craig is trying to reform his concentration. He tries to feel himself hitting into the line, to feel the arms and hands raking at his body and at the ball while he wrestles and struggles forward for extra yards. He visualizes moves he will make coming out of the backfield on passes. Number 40 is vulnerable inside, but not outside. Number 22 can be beat short, but not long. From a 6–1 defense they blitz nearly ninety percent of the time.

Turning, Craig gazes nervously up at the stadium, surely the biggest covered stadium in the world, and to him the most—ominous.

Ominous because every time we come here it is to play that rough team.

Ominous because it is so high, and therefore so dark and gloomy. The temperature is ten degrees colder on the field than outside.

Ominous because it holds 84,000 fans, all screaming for the Browns, and this rattles you. Then when you drive toward a touchdown of your own, making brilliant plays, those 84,000 people are mute, and that rattles you, too.

Craig goes over the frequency chart in his head. On first and ten they blitz nearly always from the 6–1 defense, and never from the 4–3. If they get you on the blitz making it second and long yardage, they will almost always blitz again, and if they get you twice you know they are coming a third time. It is a blitzing team this year, and they are very good at it, and that is why we put in all those fans and flare and screen passes all week. We can hurt them with those passes, and if we can get through the line on dive plays there is nobody to stop us but the safety man, so we will run a lot of dive plays.

Craig is very nervous now. Out on the lake, all is peace, and behind him is the great gloomy stadium and war. The Browns always wear white. White to Craig has always meant hospitals and pain. White makes the Browns look bigger than other teams, and more ruthless. They look as ruthless as hospital attendants. Heavy-shouldered, helmeted, sadistic hospital attendants. And you powerless against them.

Looking out at the sailboats, Craig imagines how this city must appear from the lake. The first sight of Cleveland, coming in by sea, is this stadium. In another culture, Craig supposes, they would have a cathedral on this spot. Well, football stadiums are America's cathedrals now. This is where Americans do their praying now, and are shriven, and purged of every emotion. Every Sunday afternoon this is where they watch avidly, safely, while two football teams beat each other up. Boxing used to perform this function, but pro football is better, for there are more bodies mauling each other at once, the participants are college boys, not mental defectives, and they don't get paid outrageous sums like important boxers, don't get paid much at all, considering the punishment they take. The pay is in no way out of scale with the national economy, no one is going to get a million dollars for throwing a few punches.

I think too much, Craig tells himself nervously.

He goes over the frequency charts again. In the Frisco defense they do this. In the goal-line defense they do that.

He walks inside, into the visiting team dressing room which is, as always, too small. It is so dingy that Craig's nervousness goes immediately into depression.

He hangs his blazer and trousers in a locker. After waiting his turn, he stands in shorts and T-shirt on a rubbing table with his right heel elevated by the cover of one of the cylindrical containers the rolls of surgical tape come in. This makes his right knee slightly flexed, and Dr. Flaherty, who only tapes knees, and only the knees of a few favorites like Craig and Pennoyer, pats the two-inch wide elastic tape into place in crosswise strips from mid-calf around the kneecap to midthigh, until the leg is encased in it with only the kneecap, surrounded, poking out in front. This tape is pink, and being elastic cannot be torn and so Craig, holding the scissors, cuts each strip where Doc Flaherty orders as the physician holds it stretched and half stuck in place. Then Dr. Flaherty pats it flat.

There are four tables going at once. The two trainers and the equipment man all tape ankles, and Dr. Flaherty tapes knees. Half-naked players wait to hop onto each table as soon as the previous player slides off.

Jimmy Finney, on one table, says: "I got an idea for a secret weapon. We paint Lincoln Hamilton red."

Players laugh.

Hamilton, on the next table, fixes Finney with an approximation of the evil eye. "The Mau Mau Club gonna take a vote on you, Finney."

"Oh God, not that," cries Finney in mock horror.

The Negro players often refer to themselves as the Mau Mau Club. Lincoln Hamilton pretends to be president of this club. It is a joke the players have.

"A vote," says Hamilton again. He has a deep bass voice.

The players are laughing.

"But I'm a nice kid," says Finney. Naked except for a jock and one taped ankle, he hops up onto the table. "Aren't I, fellows?" he pleads.

He pirouettes upon the table. "What am I bid for this beautiful body?" he asks. "Not a surgical mark on it."

"The Mau Mau Club will buy it," says Hamilton, showing very big, very white teeth. "Something to stick pins in."

Craig laughing, finds his depression is gone. He is part of this team, and together they can defeat anybody. He is eager for the game to begin.

"There you go, Duke," says Dr. Flaherty.

From mid-calf to mid-thigh, Craig is encased in several thicknesses of pink tape, a cumbersome feeling, but one he is well used to. Now he sits on another table, legs outstretched, toes pointed at the ceiling, while Pete tapes his ankles with rapid deft strokes, tearing each strip of tape with a single rip from calloused fingers. The trainer works less than two minutes on each shaven ankle, not looking up, not even knowing whose ankle he is taping until the end, and then tapping the sole of Craig's foot to signal that it is done, and Craig slips off the table to be replaced by someone else.

Back on a shaky bench in front of his locker, Craig strips naked except for the white spats, and the pink tape which puckers his right kneecap, and then puts on a jock, making himself comfortable in it. A gray T-shirt out of a bin goes over his head. Sitting, he pulls on sweat socks, wrapping tape around the tops as garters, then red outside socks over these up to his knees. He wraps tape around the top of the red socks too, above the bulge of his calf, tight, tearing the tape with his fingers, then tossing the roll to Joe Morris, who sits across from him in the same stage of dressing.

Craig then stands in jock, T-shirt, high red socks, and pink-taped knee, for the circulation in both legs feels a bit constricted. He flexes his knees and ankles to make the tape sit comfortably and get the blood moving again underneath.

After pulling his silver stretch pants into place, Craig pulls on his red jersey with the big No. 6 front and back, and takes the long tongues of the jersey which are designed to button under a man's crotch, but which few players ever button, and shoves these tongues down into the pants and draws the belt tight, and is now ready for the warm-up. He wears no pads. They go on last, just before the game.

Twelve fifty P.M. The players, ready for the warm-up, sit

106

on benches, the floor, radiators, the tops of the gear trunks. The trainers move about dispensing chewing gum, and patting lampblack under eyes against the sun. Craig accepts the lampblack out of habit, though he no longer believes it does any good. But it used to impress the girls back in high school. It is part of his football-hero image now.

The small room is crowded with overflowing lockers and huge men. Coach Dreuder barks: "We ready?"

No one answers.

"All right. Let's have a good warm-up."

The players spring up. Chairs and benches scrape. Cleats sound on the cement floor, and the players push through the narrow door and down a tunnel leading to the baseball dugout. As they come up onto the field they begin to run. It is forty minutes before game time. The stands are about a third full. About half the field is in sunlight. The sun is very bright.

Lincoln Hamilton and Joe Morris, the captains, lead calisthenics. Then the squad breaks down into groups. Backs and ends form two lines and Pennoyer and the substitute quarterback Rocco begin throwing passes over the middle, first to the man on the right, then to the left, lobbing the ball at the start, then firing it as their arms loosen up.

High above Craig, the great roofed stands form an almost complete oval. Waiting his turn, he thinks of Margie, who will watch this game. He is glad he doesn't know her location, for it might make him look for her amid all that mob, the way he used to do in high school when he played hoping to impress some girl whom he was afraid to ask out on a date, afraid almost to talk to at all. He used to look for her, trying to read her reaction to his whole personality, after every play.

Craig runs. Pennoyer's pass slaps into his hand.

One twenty-five P.M. The players sit again on benches, radiators, gear trunks. This time they are bulky in their pads. Some wear helmets, faces grim behind the cages. Some, helmets between their knees, suck oranges, or sip from paper cups filled at the cooler. Some, nervous, respond to last-minute urgencies, and there is a symphony of flushing toilets in the background. The trainers move about taping final fingers and wrists and socks that don't feel snug. The few voices are whispers. Nearly everyone yawns again and again.

Coach Dreuder says: "I don't need to tell you—"

A final toilet flushes. Mel Slade comes into the room, shoulders a yard wide, drawing the belt tight around his narrow waist.

The silence builds up.

"It's them or you," Dreuder says quietly.

He goes out and the coaches and trainers follow him. The door slams shut. The team is alone.

Outside, Dreuder listens to silence build up behind that door. Then there is a roar, many voices shouting: "Let's go, Big Red!" But the roar comes through the door as unintelligible noise.

"Let's Big Red, Big, Let's Red, Go, Let's Go."

The door is ripped open as if to rip it from its hinges. The team floods out through the narrow door, some of the players grim-faced, some contributing to more unintelligible noise.

"Whatdyasay Bigred drive 'em, Big Red, way to go."

There are people under the stands hurrying to their seats. They part, wide-eyed, to let the team through.

CHAPTER | 9

In a front row box in upper section three, where the open end of the oval curves in close to the goal line, Margie Berger listens to the thunderous roar as the kickoff teams spill onto the field.

The sun is on her lap. Her coat is open and she sits with one stockinged leg over the other. Around her everyone is yelling. The band is beating out some brassy march that can barely be heard. The receiving team in red, after huddling briefly, jogs into position, like a star shell bursting in slow motion. The deep receivers nervously bang their shoulder pads against the goalposts.

The noise does not let up, and Margie feels the adrenalin pouring through her own body. She is excited by the game about to begin, excited about the way her commercial went earlier. Most of all she is excited because she has seen him. And he stared like all the rest, only in a deeper, more intimate way.

This has convinced her that she looks lovely today. Her matching coat and dress in autumn colors are a success. Her crocodile bag and shoes were expensive, but worth it. She wears now a chrysanthemum which one of the agency men bought her, and she can imagine the way this sets off the colors in her cheeks. She has caused a stir everywhere today. Even during the commercial down on the field she caught cameramen staring at her a bit open-mouthed. That kind of thing can't be faked. The agency men around her have been very solicitous—it's almost amusing. She has been able to excite men for many years, but each time is a new time, and always a thrill. She knows what clothes and accessories set her off best. She knows how to wear beautiful clothes beautifully. This is not easy to do, and she is delighted with herself today.

And of all the men who have stared, the best was the way he stared, as if she were his wife, and he was especially proud of her today.

She supposes he has had many women—a football hero like that. She must be just one more in a long line. She tells herself it is silly to be in love with him. It can lead only to heartache and another terrible morning. She saw the way his color rose, and he seemed to catch his breath, and his fingers seemed to grope for her through her gloves.

Ahead of them is despair, if they go on.

When she was in college at Southern California, football was king. There was supposed to be an aura of sex around college football—all those nubile cheerleaders and screaming coeds, of which she was one. A star player was supposed to be able to bed any twenty girls he chose. But when she got to know some of the players, she found they were rather more interested in football than girls, would rather talk to their teammates than to her, and she soon drifted away. She found no sex in football then and sees none now. The uniforms are even anti-sex, for the shoulder pads come up to the ears, and the helmets swing around like turrets.

So what does she see in Craig?

Or is he only a conquest at a time when she needed a conquest badly.

A sensitive man where she did not expect one. Kindness. She has known only two types of men, those who, because she is so good-looking and so carefully dressed, are afraid of her; and those who overcompensate for this fear by pretending indifference to her—a pretended indifference which soon becomes real indifference when, either in irritation or despair, she breaks herself against it.

But Craig is kind.

Oh, he attracts her physically, too. The crinkly smile in his blue eyes, his few freckles which at times make him look boyish. His lithe way of moving. His big, rather heavily muscled body with its scarred knee and shaven legs.

But he is a married man, and for her there is only heartache ahead.

She loves the excitement with which he touches her. No one has touched her that way for a long time. That's what a woman is for, to excite a man. One man. Him.

110

As for the heartache to come, she will not think of that. She will take the moment.

Now around her the noise rises to a still higher pitch. Down on the field Number 76, who is an older man than the others as you can see by the stiff way he carries himself and by his belly under the white jersey, comes striding forward, the whole line advancing with him; he swings a swift heavy leg into the ball. It rises end over end, cartwheeling in the sunlight.

To Margie the whole ritual seems beautiful to watch: the big man striding through the ball with a strange kind of grace, and the lazy way the ball hangs up there tumbling so that she catches her breath and holds it as the ball drops down. Everybody is running now except the man waiting for the ball, all of them converging as if by prearrangement at one spot.

The two groups collide with an impact she can see, even though she can't hear it or feel it.

The personnel changes. Then Pennoyer barks signals she can't hear—a play chosen in the locker room twelve minutes ago to test how the Browns linebackers plan to defense the Big Red today. The play was slightly altered too, so that three men will hit Number 35, the Browns middle linebacker from three directions, possibly to scare him, certainly to make him wonder where all the blockers came from, and to make him worry about that particular play again. A physical and psychological probe on the first play of the game.

But Margie high up in the sun does not know this, nor hear the shock as the three men slam into Number 35, a delay between each, nor hear the grunts, nor the "oof!" that Number 35 makes as he goes down under the third blocker and the play tramples over him.

For her the game is silent. There is no noise at all, a pantomime, and she has eyes only for Craig. She sees him plunge into the heaving lines of men and spurt out the other side, running very low and then straightening to leap over Number 35 who nonetheless gets one hand up and hooks Craig's foot or leg, so that Craig begins to stumble, his momentum diminishing, out of control but lunging forward still. Then somebody smashes into him from the side and he goes down under bodies.

Margie has leaned forward in her seat, then stiffened seeing Craig with the ball, then half risen, her lips parted and her tongue between her teeth. Now as the play ends, having gained eight yards, she relaxes, turns to the agency man next to her and smiles.

He smiles back, and says hopefully: "Want a hot dog or something? A beer?"

Shaking her head, she leans forward to watch Jimmy Finney with the ball. She has lost sight of Craig, who has plunged into the line ahead of Finney to ram into some lineman who outweighs Craig by sixty pounds, who is coming just as hard the other way, and who, struck, does not budge. The noise Margie cannot hear is like a man running full speed into a tree.

She has watched football off and on all her life, and never enjoyed it as much as she is enjoying this, and as the game goes on and her enjoyment and tension increase she thinks: I guess I am enjoying it because of *him*.

I guess I am in love with *him*.

Where is this going to end?

To her the game is as intricate and at times as lovely as ballet—but ballet composed by two choreographers instead of one, each working against the other. She has never considered football as ballet before, but there is beauty in most of the patterns and in all the runs once a man gets any running room at all and the blockers form and the defense comes sprinting from all directions, big men but as fast and agile as small ones, and small enough from up here. The uniforms are perhaps lumbering looking, but only when stopped. In motion they have a logic and line and form all their own—the opposite of the ballerina's tutu, but just as much as a costume for scrolls and arabesques, the field just as much a stage, the thick-thighed players just as active as dancers. It's just that football accentuates the opposite of ballet: power instead of lightness, violence instead of grace.

And the punts are beautiful, slicing through the autumn air, one of them once rising so high that the lake comes into view behind it; most of all the passes are beautiful, because you can watch two geometric lines intersect—the curved parabola of the thrown ball, and the straight line being traced by the man sprinting to catch it.

She is enjoying the game so much, and wishes she could tell Craig. She wants to tell him also how she has seen the game almost as a ballet—what a beautiful game football can be seen that way. She wishes she could see Craig after the game to tell him all this and more, but the team will go directly to the airport and home. She won't see him.

Even if she did see him, would he grant her the comparison with ballet? Would he be impressed by what she has seen and felt and enjoyed? Would he try to understand? Or would he scoff, perhaps laugh at her, make some mocking remark?

She realizes she doesn't know what he'd do, she hardly knows him. Perhaps she has imagined everything, even his kindness, and the excitement when he touches her. Perhaps she bores him. Perhaps he will never call again.

She tries to reassure herself that she looks lovely today. But this does not mean that Craig cares for her. She is suddenly without confidence. What have her good looks ever brought her? Men following her in the street. Men trying to pick her up at parties. A husband who never seemed to need her.

She gazes down at the game.

But soon it draws her outside herself, as it is designed to do.

In the second quarter, behind 7–10, the Big Red is faced with fourth down, one yard to go on the Browns' forty-one-yard line.

What to do?

The safe play is a punt. Or a very long field goal. It seems madness to go for the one yard, yet this is what the Big Red seems determined to do. The two teams line up tight.

Margie catches her breath. Football has this at least over ballet: you never know what will happen next.

The two teams are intent on a plunge into the line for the one yard. It seems a crazy play for the Big Red. If they miss, they probably lose the game right here.

Margie leans tensely forward. She hopes against hope for the one-yard gain, the first down.

The ball is snapped, the lines converge. Finney dives past Pennoyer into the heaving, struggling mass—and doesn't make it.

But Pennoyer, she suddenly sees, still has the ball. Margie, who has lost sight of Craig, suddenly finds him again, as do the Browns and 84,000 other fans. He is alone in the flat, and the ball, lofted his way by Pennoyer, hangs on the air.

An incredible thing. The red jerseys are not going for the one yard at all. They are going for the touchdown. All or nothing.

The ball hangs there an eon of time. Is it on target? Will Craig catch it? The Browns, Margie senses rather than sees, have already recovered and flood toward Craig, no doubt wondering as she does how he got there alone. What has happened? What will happen? Tension compounded by mystery, surprise. Spectators screaming.

The ball settles in Craig's hands.

He sprints for the goal line forty-one yards away.

The Browns' safety men sprint to cut him off. They are

faster than he is, and appear to have the angle on him.

He crosses the thirty-yard line, the twenty-five, the ball under his arm, sprinting hard, the two pursuers closing in on him, 84,000 people screaming, all three men sprinting for the far corner of the goal line.

It lasts five seconds or more, time enough to calculate the three trajectories. Time enough to plot the relative speeds, to see the sides of the triangle form and judge where they will intersect. Time enough for Margie to raise one gloved hand to her mouth, her scream of encouragement cut off. They will catch him!

The first tackler hits him on the seven-yard line. Craig shoulders into him, lurching forward, fighting for balance. The second man hits him at the four, but he keeps his churning legs under him a yard longer, two yards—the three bodies tumble across the goal line. They sprawl, a tangle of arms and legs, sliding now across the turf. Craig springs up waving the ball.

Touchdown.

Margie is grinning and screaming. The nearest agency man has his arm around her, squeezing her.

But she is too elated to notice.

"What a play!" the man cries.

Margie's eyes are shining. "Isn't he marvelous?"

The agency man explains how the play must have worked. Craig hit into the line faking a run. The Browns' defensive backs must have decided there could be no pass, because no receiver showed, everyone was packed into the middle. Craig then slid off into the flat.

Margie watches Craig through the glasses. His helmet is off. He stands watching the extra point. There is sweat on his face, and grass stains all down one side of him. He is breathing hard. It is like seeing him in a private world she cannot enter; but he can come back from it, and she can have it then.

If he cares about her enough to come back to her.

The agency man hands her a container of beer, which she sips. It leaves foam on her upper lip, which she wipes off with her wrist.

At half time the Big Red leaves the field leading 14–10. In the locker room the players sit on benches and the floor, many of them breathing hard, most of them sucking on oranges. The assistant coaches move about showing Polaroid snapshots taken from the upper deck of the Browns' formations.

Beady Stein huddles with the backs and ends. The Browns aren't blitzing as much as expected. Stein tells Pennoyer to go

114

with deep passes to the sidelines, and with end sweeps to both sides.

"They seem awfully quick off the ball," Dreuder suggests. "Let's change our cadence. We'll go with an irregular cadence in the second half. That will give them something to think about."

Pennoyer nods.

Moving to the blackboard, Dreuder also rearranges the blocking on the sweeps to cope with the free safety man who is coming up much faster than anticipated.

Under the upper deck grandstand it smells of spilled beer and boiled hot dogs. The crowd buzzes bitterly about Craig's touchdown. Margie moves back out into the sun, where the band fills the center of the field. She watches the baton twirlers through the glasses. There is a girl with long naked legs, and Margie thinks: If you're a girl you spend your whole life trying to please men, and after you have pleased them they don't even want you particularly, even though that is when you want them most.

A boy begins to twirl, all hands and fingers manipulating the blurred baton. At the climax, he tosses two batons high overhead—and misses both coming down.

The crowd laughs. A low, rumbling, sustained laugh.

Through the glasses, Margie sees that the boy is about fifteen years old. His chin is trembling and he twirls on while trying to keep from crying.

Margie thinks: Poor kid.

She wishes she could tell Craig how her heart goes out to the boy, wishes she could tell Craig how much watching this game means to her.

But she won't talk to him again until he calls. If he calls. Oh please call, she thinks.

She watches the teams deploy for the start of the second half. This time the red jerseys kick to the white.

Craig rushes into the line. The gap between tackle and guard is the barest slit until he rams his shoulder into it, smashing it open enough to get through. He has scarcely heard the war in the line, the grunts and gasps, the noise of pads crashing together, nor does he feel the raking hands. All his weight and power are behind that shoulder until he bursts into the secondary, where he sees the nearest linebacker lunge for him. Craig veers so the linebacker gets only a piece, not enough to stop him, and lets the impact start him in a new direction, accelerating fast. As a new tackler appears, Craig retracts his limbs like

115

a turtle, while still barreling forward. Grasping, the man finds only the shell, nothing to hang on to as Craig's lowered shoulder plows into him. The man grunts and falls down. Planting his left leg, the good one, the only one he can cut on at all, Craig veers, eluding a cornerback who has studied the frequency charts, knows Craig can cut only one way, but in an open field forgets. Craig is running hard, but a defensive end, having recovered from a block, engulfs him from the side. Craig, as his knees buckle, gives it second effort, fighting forward another two yards, then crashes down.

The bodies unpile. This late in the game, Craig gets to his feet slowly, shakes himself, and searches for the yard marker. He has gained nine yards. He is breathing hard, not from having run nine yards, but from the exertion of smashing into all those people, and then the ceaseless struggle to stay on his feet.

In the huddle, Pennoyer mutters: "Two right green. L turn-in and make it deep. R down and in. The two back flies. On hut."

Pennoyer is going for the bomb. Another quarterback might have said so. But in the huddle Pennoyer never speaks anything but signals.

With the clap of hands, the Big Red breaks the huddle.

The Number two back, Mel Slade, goes wide right as a flanker. He will sprint straight down the field and is the primary receiver.

From his three point stance behind Pennoyer, Craig can see nothing except the backsides of his own men, and the anxious faces of the three standing linebackers across the line. His own face, from long habit, is absolutely blank, his eyes look nowhere, his weight leans in no direction that might tip the play.

"Hut!"

Pennoyer, ball already grasped to pass, eyes already searching downfield, ducks back past Craig.

The left end, Donald Fox, runs a deep turn-in—too deep for the linebacker to cover. The safety man on that side must come up to cover him, and the cornerback will come over, and on the opposite side there can now be only single coverage.

There the end runs a down-and-in pattern taking the safety man downfield.

Craig is set to pass-block. In front of him a white uniform stained with grass and dirt rolls off a block, looms over him, so close Craig can see his beard, see the fearful gap-toothed grimace behind his lineman's cage, hear his heavy breathing. He seems twice the size of Craig, and coming both in slow motion and at tremendous speed, and he lunges for Pennoyer as if Craig does not exist.

Craig, planted, rams his shoulder into the soft place below the shoulder pads; he hears the man grunt. His own exertion to stay on his feet is tremendous, but the man is too heavy, too strong, coming too fast. Craig feels himself going down, and then he hears the soft *woosh* as Pennoyer, behind him, looses the ball.

On the turf, with the salt taste of sweat in his mouth, and more sweat dripping into his eyes, Craig listens for the roar of the crowd, hears it reach a peak of tension and fear, then subside with relief. He knows the pass has missed.

It is now third and one, a vital play, for they need urgently to get a drive going, get another score, or at least keep the ball away from Cleveland.

Now is no time for trickery. A straight power play for the one yard is the only choice. Pennoyer watches his teammates jog back to the huddle. He looks at Craig, his most dependable back, but Craig looks gray, and the Browns will expect Craig anyway. Slade has just sprinted forty yards straight downfield for a pass that was slightly overthrown.

"Give me the ball," says Finney, tight-lipped.

Finney weighs 225, and is the biggest man in the backfield. But he is a rookie, and Pennoyer never calls on rookies in tight spots. Nonetheless, the other two backs are winded, and smaller than Finney besides. And Finney wants the ball.

Against his better judgment, Pennoyer calls Finney's number.

At the snap the two lines surge up. The noise is tremendous. Finney smashes in where there is no hole at all, then rolls off, looking for daylight. Hands and arms grapple with him. He wrestles forward, fighting for the desperately needed yard.

A white uniform curled into a fetal position hurls itself at the side of Finney's still planted leg.

There is a pop and a scream. The ball squirts loose. Men dive for it.

When they get up Finney lies on the turf alone, moaning. The players of both teams stand several paces away, staring at him.

Craig, knowing at once what has happened to Finney, thinks: It hurts so much you can't even writhe or squirm. You are rigid with pain. Craig shuts his eyes, as if to block off the low sustained moan coming from Finney. As always, it sounds like it is coming from a wounded animal, not a man.

Both teams back off ten yards from where Finney lies. No one looks at him. Then both teams remember that the ball has changed hands; the Browns have recovered the fumble.

117

The old personnel straggles off the field, as the new personnel runs on.

Pete, the trainer, has reached Finney's side, where he attempts to remove the injured player's helmet. Finney's mouth is tightly shut; he has stopped moaning. The helmet won't come off easily; when Pete yanks at it, Finney screams. Dr. Flaherty, a lumbering little man with a black bag, reaches Finney and kneels beside him, fingering Finney's knee. Each time he touches it, Finney's teeth bare, and he gasps. The two fresh teams stand twenty yards apart; no one looks at the group formed by Finney, Pete, Dr. Flaherty, and the other trainer, Paul. Most stare at the ground or off into the stands.

Craig watches from the sideline. His helmet is off. He rubs his sweaty face. All the old memories come flooding back.

Am I through?

Though you have never had a knee injury before, you know immediately what has happened to you. It hurts so much it isn't even localized; every nerve in your body screams with pain. The pain is absolutely exquisite. So is the fear.

Am I through?

Will I ever play again?

Is my life over?

Craig swallows hard. For a football player there is a loneliness that no one who has not been in that position can even conceive of.

The two husky trainers have Finney by the shoulders. Two substitutes have run on to grasp Finney's legs. When they lift him, Finney screams. The substitutes look back, alarmed, and adjust their grips on his legs. Dr. Flaherty waddles ahead. As they near the bench, Craig sees Finney's face. The sweat is running down Finney's nose and his teeth are clenched tight. Nonetheless, when they set him down, he gives another muffled scream.

What am I bid for this beautiful body? Not a surgical mark on it.

Craig looks away. His eyes fill with sweat, or is it tears?

On the field the Big Red defense gives ground grudgingly, but concentration is lost. Inexorably the Browns grind their way down to and over the goal line. With less than five minutes remaining in the game, the Browns lead 20–14.

Finney's replacement is Donald Fox, a second stringer every year he has been in the league. He has a second-stringer's mentality, and eyes that say: In a tight spot, you better give the ball to someone else, I might screw up. Not: Give me the ball, I can make it for us. Fox isn't comfortable under pressure. He is embarrassed. Pennoyer knows this.

Fox is big and fast with many skills, and Pennoyer knows how to use them, but they disappear inside the twenty-yard line, and Slade isn't too brave inside the twenty either. This is one more detail Pennoyer, who already has too much to remember, has to keep in mind. His only clutch back is Craig, who has already carried twenty times, and whose bones must feel like jelly by now. But there is a communion between Pennoyer and Craig. They understand each other, and what needs to be done. The two of them together are a team within a team. Now, as the remaining minutes dribble away, they put strength, and most of all faith, back into this team.

Pennoyer sends out five receivers. The fifth and last is Craig, who delays until the other four have taken their men deep, then filters into the empty short zone and takes Pennoyer's pass. He gains eighteen yards before the pursuit runs him down.

"Way to go, Big Red, way to go."

Craig is hollering and clapping as he runs back to the huddle.

Now Fox carries three times to another first down. Then Slade catches the Browns in a blitz, and, on a draw play gains twelve yards. The team begins to believe.

Pennoyer sends his backs hammering at the line, but the Browns get tough. He passes again, but the ball is batted down. On third and eight Slade catches one for a first down on the ten.

The official signals two minutes left in the game. Pennoyer trots to the sidelines for instructions from Coach Dreuder. Time is not a factor. Two minutes is ample to make ten yards and the winning touchdown.

Pennoyer sends Craig into the line. Shrugging and wrestling, he gets to the three-yard line. On the next play, Slade fumbles the handoff and loses three yards. It is third down and six. Pennoyer calls time out. He confers with Dreuder. They decide on a crossing pattern, Slade on one side and the split end on the other crossing in the end zone, with Pennoyer throwing probably to Slade. The clock shows a minute, forty-six seconds to play.

The play unfolds. Slade is open as Pennoyer fires the ball, but Number 40 makes a sensational play and bats the ball down.

It is fourth down, six yards to go.

Last chance.

The noise is tumultuous. Pennoyer barks signals, but the noise is so great his flankers can't hear him. He raises his hands for quiet. The official waves a time out. Pennoyer calls his team back into the huddle. His voice there is as monotonous

119

as always. He calls the same play. There is no emotion in his face or voice, yet the game will be won or lost on this one play.

He has called a swing pass to Craig. As the lines collide with a crash, Craig loops into the right flat. But Number 40 has read the play and is there. So is the linebacker, who embraces Craig a moment after Craig grabs the ball. But Craig brings his free arm up under the tackle in what is virtually an uppercut, and the tackle is broken. The linebacker sprawls on the turf and Craig has only Number 40 to beat. He whirls, darts toward the center of the goalposts, then suddenly veers back for the corner. Number 40 hits him, but Craig does not intend to be stopped and Number 40 has left his feet too early. Craig drags him into the end zone for the touchdown.

On the bench, his teammates mob Craig. Even Pennoyer grins and hugs him.

They lead, 21–20, with a minute and thirty-five seconds to play.

The men on the bench watch anxiously as Jones kicks off—a scary play at best. Here a good runback could ruin them.

Jones has tried to kick it away from Number 32, but that is where the ball drops anyway, and the man makes a brilliant runback of sixty-two yards. With a minute and twenty-two seconds left, the Brown are close enough for a long field goal, and have all their time-outs left besides.

Number 32 hits the line. Bulling and fighting, he gains six yards and the Browns immediately call time-out to stop the clock.

On second down, Number 48 sweeps left end for five yards. The Browns call another time-out. The ball is on the Big Red's twenty-seven-yard line, and there is one minute to play. On the Big Red bench, players are pleading and exhorting their teammates.

"Be big out there."

"Get *TOUGH*." The last word is a beseeching kind of shout.

Two passes fail. A third gains twelve yards before the receiver steps out of bounds. The Browns are on the nineteen-yard line, easy field-goal range now, with thirty-six seconds to play.

Number 32 hits the line, but is stopped. The Browns call their final time-out to stop the clock.

Number 76 trots onto the field to try for the winning field goal from point-blank range.

At the sideline, Dreuder has his arm around Lincoln Hamilton, president of the Mau Mau Club, and the Big Red's offensive captain. He sends the big lineman into the game.

CHAPTER | 10

Coach Dreuder stands gnawing his fingernails as the teams line up for the field-goal attempt. Behind him some players are reconciled to the defeat and sit with heads down, not wanting to watch. Others pace up and down, agonized expressions on their faces, exhorting their teammates on the field.

The crowd noise swells, the ball is snapped. The lines converge and rise up. Hamilton bulls into the center of the line, then smashes through, and as the ball starts to soar throws himself across its line of flight.

The ball strikes the side of his helmet and caroms off sideways. The crowd roar subsides into the sighs and muttering of 84,000 people.

Springing up, Hamilton shakes himself off, and, helmet in hand, his knotty skull illuminated by grinning teeth, jogs back to the bench, where he is hugged and pummeled by his teammates.

Throughout the vast stadium, Browns' fans disgustedly shred their tickets.

In the Big Red dressing room, Hamilton is still being embraced by his teammates.

Photographers snap pictures of Craig and Hamilton, both of them half naked, with their arms around each other. Pennoyer is brought on. He is photographed pouring orange soda over his head.

Presently the dirty ankle tape forms a mound in the center of the floor, the last photographer leaves, and Craig goes through to take his shower.

As he crosses through the trainer's room, he sees that Dr. Flaherty has prepared a hypodermic syringe for Jimmy Finney's knee. A few drops pop from the needle as Doc holds it to the light.

In an instant, Craig sees the old scene, hears the old voices.

121

"I don't like the look of your knee, Duke. I don't like it at all."

"It *is* a bit swollen."

"We're going to have to aspirate it."

Craig, who didn't know the meaning of this word, was afraid to ask.

Dr. Purcell, the university doctor, was an irascible little man with a raspy voice. First he shot the knee with Novocain, further scaring young Craig, though it did not hurt.

Then Dr. Purcell prepared a syringe the size of a small football pump. Craig, watching this, licked his lips. Dr. Purcell had to push hard to get the big needle into the knee cavity. It made a tearing noise. He worked it around in there, while Craig wiped sweat off his forehead.

Dr. Purcell attempted to withdraw fluid, but nothing happened. The glass pump did not fill up.

Angrily, Dr. Purcell yanked the needle out, ripped it off the glass pump, and threw it in the floor.

"Nurse, goddamit—"

This time when the needle went in, Craig could hear something grating.

"Doc, I think you're touching bone in there."

"Shut up."

Craig was sweating freely now. Again Dr. Purcell attempted to withdraw fluid. Again the syringe did not fill up. Dr. Purcell, furious, began pushing and wiggling the syringe.

"Doc, are you sure you're not touching bone?"

Dr. Purcell, cursing, was wiggling the syringe. Craig imagined the needle scraping the bone inside his knee.

"Doc, I think you're touching bone."

"Bullshit."

The glass football pump began to fill up with water blood. Dr. Purcell gave a sigh of pleasure: "Ah, there we go—"

Craig, who was nineteen at the time and had been hoping against hope all week that the worst was over, fainted.

"That's it, Jimmy, baby," soothes Dr. Flaherty, "Little Novocain to kill the pain so we can get you home."

As he draws the needle out of the inner side of Finney's knee, Craig can hear the same old soft tearing noise.

"That'll hold you till we get you into the hospital, Jimmy, baby. You don't want to go into a hospital here in Cleveland, do you, Jimmy, baby?"

Dr. Flaherty rubs the skin with an antiseptic. "Don't worry about a thing, Jimmy, baby."

*What am I bid for this beautiful body? Not a surgical mark
on it.*

Craig goes into the shower. He stands under water as hot as
he can stand it, his eyes closed, the water washing down what
feel like seams of age in his face.

Pete helps Finney dress. Finney's knee is bulky under Ace
bandages. Pete fetches baggy sweat pants to wear in place of
trousers. Pete then gets a pair of adjustable crutches out of a
gear trunk, measures them by eye to Finney's height, and
screws them together.

"Think you can get on the bus with these, Jimmy?"

Finney nods. He seems afraid that if he tries to speak he
might weep.

The trainer knows this. But there is nothing he can do. He
pats the boy on the back.

"I'll get you an ice bag, Jimmy."

In the coaches' room, Dr. Flaherty is on the phone to the
hospital.

"Let me speak to Malvin. Hello, Malvin? Yeah. That's right,
yeah. Pretty bad. Yeah. We'll need an ambulance at the airport. That's right. And reserve an operating room for me tomorrow morning. Yeah. Yeah."

Dr. Flaherty's hand goes over the receiver. He says to the
United Airlines representative who travels with the team and
who now stands at his elbow: "What time do we land?"

"Tell them our office will notify them directly, as soon as
the plane is in the air."

Also present are Coach Dreuder, who is knotting his tie at
the mirror; the two airline pilots, who have changed into their
uniforms, and F. X. Boyle.

Boyle thinks: A promising halfback is lost for the season;
the operation will cost three hundred dollars, and the hospital
expenses will be another four hundred dollars. Workman's
compensation pays most of it, and other insurance pays the
rest. We won the game, that's the main thing. We are on top.
We can replace Finney. Fox is a good back.

Boyle feels sorry for Finney. However, getting hurt is mostly
a player's own fault. Finney hasn't learned to button up as he
gets hit. Perhaps now he will learn.

Boyle remembers trying to sign Finney in Georgia last
winter. Finney kept hesitating, raising problems, raising his salary demands. Boyle, who wanted Finney badly, was afraid they
would never get him to sign. At last Finney gave Boyle a play-

123

ful sock in the arm, saying: "Don't worry, stud, I'll sign with you."

Boyle hates to be touched by anyone.

Now Boyle mutters: "Well, one good thing—maybe when he comes back, he won't be such a fresh kid." Boyle gives a short laugh to show he is joking.

"If he comes back," says Dreuder.

On the plane, nobody wants to sit next to Finney. He lowers himself into a front-row seat next to the porthole. The place next to him stays empty.

Behind Finney there is much loud laughter and calling across seats. The stewardesses pass out the first round of beer as soon as the plane lifts off. Players stand in the aisle in stocking feet, ties loose and shirts open. Some are still sweating. In conversation, they go over every play, congratulating and praising each other, gloating over the victory.

Finney sits alone in the front of the plane, staring out the porthole.

At last Craig goes forward and sits beside him.

"I've got some books home on the human knee, Jimmy. Perhaps you'd like to see them."

But Finney does not turn from the window.

Craig tries a new tack. "Did you know that guys with long torsos and short legs never get knee injuries?"

No answer.

"Very rarely," Craig says.

Craig adds: "If you're one of these guys who can't touch his toes, a really stiff kind of guy, then you'll probably never get a knee injury either."

No answer.

"Lots of times I've wished I was such a guy." Craig gives a laugh. "Of course that would make you a lineman, and you'd get your brains scrambled instead."

Craig hopes for a smile, but when Finney turns from the window, his eyes are damp, and he looks close to tears.

"I know a lot about knees," Craig offers. "I've been treated by about half the knee specialists in the country."

When Finney does not answer, Craig says: "Do you want me to go away?"

"No," Finney says in a husky voice.

Craig says brightly: "The knee is a little like two baseballs sitting one on top of the other, with a ring of, like, felt in between so the top one won't roll off. The felt is the cartilage. Actually it's in two pieces, two semicircles, one on the inner

124

side of the knee called the medial meniscus, and one on the outer side called the lateral meniscus."

Craig, like most players who have had knee injuries, knows the anatomy of the knee like a surgeon.

"Well, there are also four important ligaments tying the two baseballs, the knee, together: one down the inner side of the knee, and one down the outer side, both about two inches long; and two short tough ones inside the knee joint itself, inside the ring of cartilage. They're called the cruciate ligaments, because they cross."

If those are gone, sonny boy, you might as well forget it.

How would you like to have someone tell you that, Craig thinks. Amid the pain and the terror, a doctor says that to you.

Craig says: "The usual football injury is to the inner side ligament, which becomes stretched or torn completely, and to the cartilage there which can be torn. The ligament, if it's torn, can be sewn together with catgut or silk, and it will heal. If it's only stretched it will heal by itself. The cartilage never heals and has to be cut out. You can live without it," he tell Finney.

You have to learn to, Craig thinks. Because the damaged, well, feel of it is always there. There is noise in it, fluid in it, and frequently pain in it. When you are tired you will limp, and then your pride in your body will make you push back on that heel so the limp won't show—and that hurts. You must exercise every day or lose flexibility of the knee joint, and you realize that when you are older and don't have time for the exercises or they hurt too much, then you may start, like many of the old players, to limp permanently.

"It will keep you out of the Army," Craig says cheerfully. "It did me." You won't play golf again, or tennis, or dance or ski either, he thinks.

The fear of re-injury never leaves you, and that is a formidable psychological barrier in itself. Wrapped in so much tape you'll never have quite as much speed again, and by the end of each season your leg will be as raw from the tape as a bad sunburn all the time. You will dread putting the tape on there before each game, knowing that once the game is over, you must somehow get it off.

In the films you will notice that you are not making the sharp cut you used to make, and they are nailing you where formerly you went for good yardage. You must work out substitutes: shoulder fakes instead of hip fakes, for instance. You can only cut one way, because you only have one strong leg to push off on.

"So your knee winds up with a couple of scars," says Craig

125

cheerfully. "You didn't want to go into that box on the ground in a hundred percent condition, did you?"

Finney watches Craig intently.

"It's an easy operation, only a little over twenty-five minutes, usually. Then you're in a cast about two weeks, then you start walking on crutches." Craig thinks: And then the exercises start, the pain will be beautiful, and if you can't do the exercises because you can't stand the pain, then we will never hear of you again.

"Listen," Craig says earnestly, "it's not the end of the world. You can come back from this, that's the main thing."

Finney, his leg bulky under the sweat pants, licks dry lips.

Behind Craig, his teammates celebrate the victory. He longs to join them, to listen to the talk and jokes, to relive the good plays, to swill the two cans of beer per man which are enough to get a dehydrated player quite drunk. But he must give this up; he can't leave Finney alone now.

"When I got hit and went down," Craig says, "I couldn't believe it could have happened to me. I knew right away what it was."

After a moment, Finney says: "So did I."

"The pain was so bad I thought I would black out."

"It was the worst pain I've ever had."

"I know a doctor who says a knee injury doesn't rank too high in the scale of human pain."

"He never had a knee injury."

"I was running down under a punt. It was the second punt of the game. I made the mistake of looking up for the ball, and somebody hit me that I didn't even see. My cleats caught in the grass and he came rolling across my knee." After a moment, Craig adds soberly: "Mine popped just as loud as yours."

Finney says: "It sure does make a frightening noise. I think it's the most horrible thing I ever heard."

Craig does not want to live through it again, but it all comes back so vividly that he blinks his eyes.

Running. Looking up for the punt. Heavy breathing that he did not hear in time. The shock of impact, followed by the ligament snapping with a report like a gunshot. Then the flood of pain.

"The coach came running over to where I lay. You know what he said?"

"What?"

"He turned to the bench and shouted, 'Get me another half-back.'"

Finney smiles.

Craig heard that, without being aware of what it was. The

126

stadium was jammed and noisy, but he could not see it or hear it. He floated blind and deaf on clouds of pain and fear. Am I through? Will I lose my scholarship?

"Get him off here, quick," the coach ordered, for he wanted to save the time out, if possible. Four substitutes hustled Craig off the field.

He sat in almost intolerable pain at the end of the bench. When the game ended, two players lifted him under the arms, but the pain was so great he could not support himself, and two others lifted his knees. He must have moaned or screamed for he remembers that the boy's face turned in surprise, and he then sought a grip which did not involve the injured knee. But there was no such grip; Craig's lower leg dangled and swung all the way to the locker room.

His knee was too swollen to get his pants off. After a while they stopped trying and carried him out to someone's car. At the hospital, the pants were cut off him. A doctor twisted the knee this way and that, and he screamed.

He heard them talking about an operation. He wanted his parents to be there. He was aware inside his pain and fear that his parents would have no influence on the decision to be made; they were three hundred miles away. The coach would decide.

The surgeon explained how the operation would be done. One simple incision, one cartilage removed.

"Just one cartilage, Doctor?" Craig felt towering relief. If it was only one cartilage, he felt sure he would play again.

The next day the surgeon drew diagrams, trying to soothe Craig, who was then nineteen years old. For the first time Craig heard certain words: ". . . simple excision of the medial meniscus . . ."

But he must have awakened on the operating table, because as he came out of the ether he was aware they had cut out both. Tears streamed down his face.

"You sonuva bitch, you cut both of them out."

"You're going to be fine, son."

"You promised you'd only cut one out. You promised."

"You're going to be fine, son."

"Why didn't you kill me, too."

The pain after the operation seemed worse than before. He remembers a lady who, visiting the patient in the next bed, came over to console him. But his pain was so intense that when she bent down over his bed, he couldn't see her.

No position was comfortable. There was no way he could lay his cast to make the pain less, and at night he could not sleep. Night after night he lay alone with his rage, frustration, exhaustion, pain, worry. But I was supposed to be All-American this year, he thought once, and started to cry. When he had wept enough he at last fell into a doze—only to be jolted awake later by another burst of pain.

Craig, remembering, thinks: Pain is hard to remember, usually. But the pain of a knee injury to a football player lasts so long and recurs so often that he never forgets it.

"Jimmy, you come back, or you don't come back, depending on how much suffering you're willing to go through after they take the cast off."

By the time Craig's cast was removed the muscles of his thigh had atrophied slightly, especially the ones on top, so that he was unable to straighten his leg against the strong underneath tendons. The joint was full of fluid. He would sit for hours in the whirlpool bath, which was very boring, and he would sit for more hours under infrared heat, which was both boring and painful. The trainer would give him lengthy, hard-thumbed massages every day, trying to work the fluid out of the knee, massaging away from the swollen knee joint, trying to force the fluid upward into the thigh, downward into the calf.

"This is gonna hurt, kid."

Craig nodded. The trainer's thumbs dug into Craig's knee, which was swollen hard. Despite himself, Craig winced.

"I gotta push hard, kid."

Craig bit down on his lip. "I know it."

"It don't do no good otherwise."

He was willing to pay any price if he could play football again. He vowed that the world had not heard the last of Duke Craig. He lifted weights with his bad leg while lying on his back, the weights attached to an iron boot which was strapped to his foot. He climbed up and down the stadium steps, all the way to the topmost row, ZZ, a thousand times, perhaps more, sometimes pausing at the top to gaze wistfully down on his former teammates as they practiced for Saturday's game with S.M.U. or the Aggies or Baylor.

"Hello up there."

It was the team clown, his hands cupped to his mouth. Some other boys waved up at him.

After a moment, Craig called: "Hello down there." He knew some jovial response was called for, and this was the most jovial he could think of.

He missed being part of the team as much as he missed playing. The boys scrimmaging down on the field were still his teammates of course, but not really, for each Saturday

128

they won or lost without him. The desire to be one of them was an ache inside him.

There were periods of stupendous gladness when he thought he noticed full flexibility returning to his knee; he could almost feel himself running on it again, visualize himself scoring touchdowns. And there were relapses, when he had done too much and the knee filled up and in his despair he thought hopelessly: What's the use, I'll never be able to play football again.

Craig tells Finney: "I only missed one season, and I've had eleven others since, Jimmy. It's up to you. How much do you want to come back? The guys who don't come back are the ones not willing to suffer."

An oversimplification. What about the knees that are too chewed up inside? What about the players who can't bring themselves to trust this "new" knee, or are unlucky and get a second shot in the same place? What about the surgeons who do a poor job? The surgeons never admit it, but that is why some players don't come back.

Those who do come back are not the same, Craig thinks. If you ignore the knee, you won't last long, and if you worry about it too much, you won't last long either. You must change your game to protect the knee, and usually alter your stride slightly, too. One leg or the other is sore all the time, the weak leg because it is weak, or the strong one because you have been putting too much strain on it trying to protect the other. Your body gets as used to pain as a woman's, but that doesn't mean you enjoy it.

The injured knee is always there, and every blow on it will make you miss several games. Each time you feel the sudden scalding pain which by now no longer surprises you, you will think hopelessly: Here we go again. The iron boot, the massages, the endless climbs of grandstand steps, the whirlpools and heat; the weeks of not being part of the team anymore, for they have closed ranks, and go into each game without you.

In training camp each summer, you are always lame for the first month. Perhaps, like Craig, you cannot bear being treated with pity—the constant: How's the leg, Duke? And so you begin to pretend that "the" leg is really fine, you're just trying to sneak out of practices. You acquire a reputation for malingering, but anything is preferable to seeming fragile.

He does not mention this to Finney.

"The only problem afterward is that your knee may lock on you sometimes, Jimmy. I remember once against the Redskins, it locked when I was down in the three-point stance and Pennoyer had already started the cadence. Pennoyer is hollering, hut-one, hut-two, hut-three, and my knee is locked. The snap signal is four, and I'm kicking my leg out behind me trying to free my locked knee before Pennoyer can count to four."

Finney laughs—his first genuine laugh.

Craig, pleased that he has helped Finney this much at least, says: "I wonder what *that* looked like from the grandstand."

It wasn't funny at the time. It sent him making the rounds of the orthopedic surgeons, hoping one of them had some secret cure for Duke Craig's knee.

He does not mention this to Finney either.

Behind them, the beer has started to take effect. The players, some of them exhausted and all of them dehydrated, are becoming boisterous. The stewardesses move down the aisle serving filet mignon dinners.

Craig may have helped, but Finney does not touch his meal. Presently the stewardess, who is about as young as Finney, pretty, with a mouthful of big white teeth, leans over him saying: "A big strong boy like you has gotta eat. Why, you'll die if you don't eat."

Finney tries to smile for her, but his smile falls apart. She removes the tray, perplexed, wondering if her makeup is not on straight, or something.

Now the plane starts its landing approach, and the seat-belt lights come on.

As Finney turns from the window, Craig sees that his teeth are clenched tight and his brow beaded with sweat. The Novocain is wearing off.

"I'll get Doc," Craig says.

Finney grabs his arm. "I'll be—all right."

The runway rises up under the landing lights. All the players suck in a chestful of air, holding it. As the plane touches down, all the players expel that air.

"The only way to travel," they sing out with one voice. This is ritual for every landing. They laugh and applaud themselves.

Finney's hands, gripping the armrests, are white.

"I'll get Doc."

Craig stands. "Doc!"

The stairs bump against the plane. The players crowd toward the doors.

Doc Flaherty leans over Finney. "What's the matter, Jimmy?" To the trainer, who is leaning low to peer out the porthole, the physician says: "Do you see the ambulance, Pete?"

"It's there, Doc."

"Let's get him off."

Outside on the tarmac Craig stands in the cool dark with Pennoyer, whom the victory has made talkative.

"Pro football is above suspicion," the quarterback muses. "We score the winning touchdown with a minute and a half to go. They come all the way down the field and with twenty seconds left try a certain field goal and we block it. No other sport could get away with that."

"It doesn't sound too believable, does it?"

"If it was a boxing match, they'd hold up the purses. If it was a basketball game they'd subpoena everybody."

As the two trainers and Jimmy Finney's legs come through the door of the plane, Finney screams. Floodlights have come on, and in their glare, the players, watching, can see that Finney is weeping.

Craig says to Pennoyer: "Is your knee injury the worst pain you ever had?"

After a moment, Pennoyer responds: "When I was about eight, sliding down a tin roof with the other kids, I caught my balls on a roofing nail. *That's* the worst pain I ever had."

Craig begins to laugh.

Finney, weeping, is laid out on a stretcher.

A player's voice out of the gloom says: "Jimmy's one tough guy. It must really hurt."

Some distance off, Boyle watches with Coach Dreuder.

"We never had one who cried before."

Dreuder nods.

"This is no game for babies," says Boyle.

"He's probably more scared than anything else," suggests the coach.

"I don't care *why* he's crying."

"I wouldn't have thought it of a brash kid like that."

"If Finney comes back from this injury, I'll be surprised. He isn't tough enough for this game. If you ask me, you can cross him off your list right now."

The stretcher is lifted into the ambulance, and the door slams shut. The floodlights go off. The players, in ones and twos, drift away from the plane, not quite willing to separate yet after their great victory this afternoon. But in the street they must split up and head home, the few to their houses and apartments, the many to their hotels.

CHAPTER | 11

Craig decides he must not see Margie again. With a new game each Sunday, he has too much else to worry about. Each morning there are new plays and formations to memorize on the field, sprinting through them in sweatsuits for ninety minutes, working for precision and timing, committing them to the subconscious. After each practice there are lectures to listen to, blackboard diagrams and frequency charts to study. Then come the films. Each day there are defenses to take off the films and analyze, defensive personnel to study, watching the same play or the same sequence over and over again until it begins to come clear not only how each opponent reacts, but even how he thinks.

The Eagles have moved a big, fast rookie in at cornerback. Sitting in the dark with his teammates, Craig watches him intercept a pass against the Giants last Sunday.

Beady Stein, the offense coach, reverses the projector. On the screen the cornerback is now running backward away from the ball. All the players unpile and run backward into position. The switch is flipped again, and here comes the cornerback up to intercept the ball.

"He comes up awfully fast on turn-ins," says a voice from the dark.

They watch him intercept the same pass four times.

"Seems like you could beat him on a zig-in," another voice adds. The zig-in looks like a turn-in, but becomes something else.

"Coming up that fast he could never recover."

Stein has already decided to put in patterns built around a zig-in route. He wants the players to decide on the zig-in themselves. That way, they will run it in the game with more confidence.

The next play by the Giants is an attempted end sweep. They watch the cornerback spoil it.

"Look at him come up on sweeps."

"What about an option pass?"

At four o'clock, the coaches let them go. The conscientious players, half a dozen on offense, another half dozen on defense, stay to study films on their own.

Each group takes a projector and cans of film into side rooms. Craig, Pennoyer, and others watch the Eagles against themselves earlier this season. The film has been edited, and the Eagles are shown only on defense. Mel Slade runs the projector. He stops and reruns certain plays as much as ten times. Craig's head reels with football, but this is the way he wants it —not to have time to think.

But to his surprise, leaving the stadium at night, he finds the desire to be with Margie as strong as ever.

There is a phone booth under the stands. He has a dime in his pocket, which he fingers, eyeing the phone booth.

"You coming, Duke?"

"I'm going to make a call first."

He enters the booth, drops his dime in.

They wait for him a few paces away. He has not counted on this.

"Craig's phoning his agent."

"He's out of cash and wants the truck sent around to the bank."

He can hear them through the glass. Though he has dialed several digits of the number, he hangs up, recovers his dime, and trails his teammates out onto the street. It is dark, and cold, and his face feels clean in the night air.

He must concentrate strictly on football.

He owes it to his teammates, and to his family. He is a public figure, and he owes it to his reputation as well. This other thing—this image of a naked girl—is madness.

"If they throw a six-one at us, the twenty-eight and forty-nine sweeps should work consistently," says Mel Slade.

Someone lights a cigarette. The smoke rises into the streetlight. Craig feels hungry. He is aware of his body, healthy and alert.

"They've won two games in a row and that jerk on the *Daily News* thinks they're unbeatable."

"I gotta speak to the goddam Knights of Columbus tonight."

"That Number 56 is gonna be awful hard to root out of there."

Craig feels the November cold in his newly combed hair. He has sweated the same amount of sweat as these men, worn the same tape, washed off the same mud, celebrated the same

133

victories, wept over the same defeats. Life is a football in your fingers. Life is Sundays. All the rest is time in between.

He stands laughing and gossiping under a streetlight with his teammates.

A good moment, and better than this other thing that haunts him.

Reluctantly, the group breaks up. "Well—"

"Good night, boys."

" 'Night."

Driving home he convinces himself that his body, and his mind as well, is for football only.

This is how it has always been. From the age of fourteen he has kept his mind strictly on football. This is what made him an All-American—and kept him one. A life of self-denial. You don't become the present Duke Craig any other way. All he ever wanted to be was such a great football player that fans would remember him as long as the game is played. He didn't choose to become Sir Galahad too; that was merely an accidental side effect.

The traffic is heavy, and he drives his big Buick slowly, brooding.

Are not most of the others the same as himself?

Every team has its Donald Fox, who has his own apartment in the first big city he has ever been, and who brags about populating it with stewardesses. But who ever sees the stewardesses? Is Donald all talk?

Craig doesn't know.

Once he saw Donald, drunk, wrestling with a girl on a couch at a party. Donald was trying to get his trousers off, and the girl was trying to stop him. Every once in a while Donald would try to undress himself again, amid shrieks from the girl and howls of laughter from everybody else.

What did this indicate?

Craig doesn't know.

He considers professional athletes basically unsophisticated men, and he feels sure that few have ever learned their way into boudoirs. When would they have had the time, and enough purpose, to excel at this, too? They grow up under strict training rules dominated not only by parents and the clergy, but by coaches, too. From childhood on, football demands time, energy, concentration. Their coaches scream clean living at them night and day. When and how would they learn to manage a seduction—don't think that doesn't take learning, too. Of course a few probably stumble onto it early. They have always had girls. But most have not.

Craig wishes he could talk seriously about the subject with

his teammates. But it is hopeless. Sex is the one object every-body lies about or jokes about. You couldn't get an answer you could believe from anyone.

He himself would never give a straight answer either. What could he say: I was married by almost the first girl I ever went with, and when I was nearly thirty-one, for reasons I don't understand, I suddenly found myself in bed with another woman.

And I would like to be there again. But that is out of the question. The right and good thing is never to see her again, because if I see her I will want to go to bed with her, and may do so, and that is wrong and, for me, unthinkable. My duty is to the team, and to my wife. I have contracts with both of them, and an implicit contract with those (particularly the kids) who admire me. Think of the scandal. Sex, a worthless thing as everybody knows, captivates Duke Craig. Duke Craig, adulterer.

Flushed with guilt and shame, Craig vows he will not see or attempt to phone Margie again.

But what about Margie?

As he steers his Buick into his own street, the lamplights are dim amid the bare branches. He imagines Margie waiting by the phone for the call that will never come. Perhaps he owes her an explanation at least, and should call her tomorrow.

But he is not strong enough both to call her and to prevent himself from going to see her.

In truth he owes her nothing, and need not call.

Inside his daughter pulls him down for a kiss, and while he is bent over his son leaps on his back and he nearly collapses. This makes him smile: the great Duke Craig knocked down in the open field by a tackler weighing sixty-eight pounds.

His son already looks like him, and promises to have his own halfback's build: somewhat low in the hips for balance, power-ful thighs, thin calves, and small feet.

He carries Bobby into the kitchen on his back. There Car-ribel is preparing dinner for the kids: canned spaghetti. She can rarely be bothered to cook for the kids, serving them canned and frozen meals every night, and all winter they are out of school with colds or worse.

Carribel kisses him on the cheek: "Nice of you to come home for a change."

This is a dig at his many speeches at night, so he says: "I've often thought that fresh vegetables and meat might help their attendance record and put some color in their cheeks."

"Are you criticizing me again?"

"It's just that—"

135

"Ah don't have any maid, you know. It's all Ah can do to keep this house running as well as it does. Ah don't have time to cook for the kids every night."

He decides to drop the issue of the kids' diet. Better to have peace than an argument he can't win.

"Well, you certainly have *color* in *your* cheeks," Craig says. "You certainly look nice tonight."

Her anger disappears. She beams and pats a curl into place. "Do you think so?"

She is hungry for affection and praise, but he does not see this. Instead he is irritated that she has succumbed so readily to his compliment.

He is skilled at manipulating her in the interest of peace. In earlier years he used to work out elaborate routines. When she was in a temper or nagging him to do something he hated, such as paint a room—he would bring forth a routine. "Say, a man I know was looking over the players' wives in Section Twelve last Sunday. He said the prettiest girl was the one in Row B, Seat Three. Who could that be?"

Carribel's anger would cool as curiosity got the better of her. At last she would go to find her ticket stub.

"Why it's me!"

"Imagine that."

"Why isn't that sweet."

But now it seems to Craig that with Carribel, a single bald compliment is as effective.

"Make me a drink, will you?" she asks.

He makes her a martini. From the way she watches him, he realizes that tonight's compliment was not as effective as he hoped.

"You put too much vermouth in it." She hands the glass back.

"Sorry."

"Throw this out, will you, and make me one right."

He protests. "There are two shots of good gin in there."

"Ah'll do it myself."

"No, I'll do it."

At the liquor cabinet he adds gin to the martini. His back to her, he makes the ice clink.

"Here." She sips it.

"All right now?"

"Fine."

She didn't even notice, he thinks. He looks around at his living room, at the inexpensive modern furniture they bought ten years ago. Margie's apartment is far more attractive and comfortable.

136

Presently Carribel tells him of buying a chicken in the super-market, and then getting home and deciding that the chicken didn't smell quite right. Driving back to the supermarket, she demanded another chicken. The manager assured her the first chicken was fine. It wasn't till she started to storm out of the place that they at last agreed to change her chicken.

"That's the last time Ah go to that place."

"We're having chicken for dinner, then."

"When Ah got home, that one smelled bad too, so Ah threw it out."

Craig keeps his face blank, for Carribel, watching him, is attuned to the slightest criticism of herself.

"Ah've got some TV dinners in the icebox."

"Oh."

Craig wonders how much the jettisoned chicken cost. They have not managed to save money in ten years in pro ball.

"Well, TV dinners are really good," he says, "but you know what I was hoping for tonight? Scrambled eggs and bacon."

"Ah've been working hard all day, and Ah was hoping for once to serve you something simple."

For once? Craig has been out speaking four of the last five nights.

"Why don't I do the cooking?" Craig offers. "How will that be?"

She shrugs and looks away. He studies what he can see of her face, thinking: She must be as disappointed in this marriage as I am.

In the kitchen he mindlessly beats the eggs, he fries the bacon. He rather enjoys this, for he does not want to think out what to do about this marriage now, nor remember how he got into it in the first place.

Craig at eighteen was a sophomore at Texas University, and a second-string halfback on the varsity team. He had always been the star of his team before; colleges fought to sign him up. Now he was hardly playing, and he was confused and desperately unhappy. What did he have to do to convince the coaches he was a star? What did he have to do to convince the girls he was a star? Craig wanted only the best girls, the pretti-est and most knowing, the ones everybody else wanted, and these either went with the juniors and seniors on the team, or else made him feel, when they were with them, that they were not impressed.

Among those girls was Carribel, who came from his town. He had been attracted by her at home and had dated her. But although she was pretty, she was not his type, or something. He could not explain it, but no sparks flew and he sensed there ought to be sparks.

But now he tried for Carribel, because it was clear she was popular, she seemed available, and he knew her already. He had to have someone, for there were dances and parties after every game, and if you didn't have a girl you didn't go. Couldn't go. Couldn't be part of the team, cutting up and laughing and getting drunk on 3.2 beer, or pretending to get drunk. College was supposed to be a heckuva good time, something to remember all your life, and although it was never this for Craig, because he was too busy looking around trying to work out what life actually *was*, since it obviously wasn't a heckuva good time either here or anywhere, still he kept hoping that if he could get to play more, and score some touchdowns, and keep trying to be part of the laughing and cutting up, perhaps college and life itself actually might start being a heckuva good time after all.

So he tried to date Carribel for the Fall Fling, an important dance in the gym (the baskets folded up high and the girders festooned with streamers and hanging Japanese lanterns). But he had waited too long, and someone else dated her before him. So he slunk in alone and watched.

But since he couldn't have Carribel, he began to want her. She still didn't excite him much, except that necking in parked cars and in the living room of the Kappa Sigma frat house excited him well enough.

There were parties Saturday nights in the frat house, dancing to records and a buffet supper, and then later the lights would go out one by one until the room was dark, only the light from the controls of the phonograph still gleaming and the 78 rpm records dropping. It was a big room with many sofas and soft chairs, and the couples paired off in the dark, and you heard some giggling, and some rustling and much silence.

And Carribel's voice in a loud whisper: "You naughty boy, don't."

Craig, who had done nothing, was afraid others might hear: "Ssshhh!"

"You are fresh. Nice fresh, but fresh."

It made him wonder if he was not being fresh enough. It gave him ideas, but not for here, where at any moment some jokester might leap up and switch on all the lights.

He sought to get her to an empty room then and afterward, but never with success, and alone with her in a parked car was not much better.

After each session he wandered about wondering if he was in love with her. He felt consumed by needs which were not

138

entirely new to him, but new enough. And although the turgidness always faded after a day or so, and was forgotten completely during preparation for each game, nonetheless, it was always rekindled the following Saturday night, if he could get a date with her, which was never a sure thing.

"Ah promised Jim Henderson."

"Oh."

"Ah cain't break a date. It wouldn't be fair."

He wondered if Jim Henderson, who was president of the senior council, and starting left end as well, a very important man on campus and two years older than himself, dared anything with Carribel which he himself did not dare. And if Henderson was successful.

Sometimes she would put off his request for a date saying: "Ah'll have to see."

"See what?"

She would mention Jim, or perhaps Barney or Ralph: "He said something about something. Ah may have to go out with him."

Craig knew she was not emotionally committed to him, and this, given his lack of time and mood to find another girl, made him committed to her.

He called back an hour before the proposed date.

"Are you free?"

"As a matter of fact, Ah am."

"Why didn't you call me?"

"Girls don't call boys, silly."

That night they reclined in the dark, listening to the music, and to the rustling and giggling in the shadows.

"I wonder what's going on over there," he whispered, hoping her answer would give some hint of what she expected of him —what she would permit.

"Oh, things."

"Things?"

"You know, silly."

During an hour or more of torrid kissing, he several times stroked her sweater.

"Let's go somewhere else."

"No. Ah like it here."

That night, Craig's roommate entered their room with a bra dangling from his arm. He claimed to have removed it from a girl, with her permission, in the dark downstairs. He did not say which girl.

Craig didn't know whether to believe him or not.

Toward the end of the season Craig got to play more and more, and made a number of dazzling touchdown runs. It became clear he was the star of the future. Coach Buzzy Claypool gave interviews about him. Sports Publicity Director Harley Hanley arranged for photos to be taken of him, and feature stories about him appeared.

Carribel seemed to become easier to date as his star rose.

He always felt eager during the date, and turgid the next day, and then did not think of her again until just before he was to pick her up the following Saturday night, at which time he wished he was dating someone else. He really didn't feel at ease with her, and he wasn't sure he even liked her.

What he really like was being a couple among other couples, his contemporaries, and moving about from parties to dances to jukebox joints in several cars, eight or ten couples, all of them paired off as exclusively as if they were married. He couldn't be part of this without a girl, without Carribel or someone else, and he didn't know anyone else. And in any case, he enjoyed the kissing later.

That summer he worked on a road construction gang to build his muscles, which took him up to north Texas, so that he rarely saw Carribel. Also he was back on the campus a month before she was, a month before school started, practicing twice a day for the opening game of the season against Baylor on September 15. When the other students did convene, he had one date with Carribel, and then came his knee injury. There were of course no dates while he was hospitalized, or in a cast and on crutches, although once he sticked his way over to her outside a campus building.

"I thought we could go to the movies tonight."

"Ah'm sorry, Ah have a date."

"Tomorrow then."

"Ah have to study for an English Lit test."

"What about Sunday?"

"Barney's taking me to a party."

"Oh."

"Ah'm sorry."

He thought she looked genuinely sorry, so he said: "The following Saturday then?"

"O.K. Ah'll sure be looking forward to it."

When he could walk again he pursued her, but she was elusive. Barney, a defensive back, was having an excellent season, and they were seen everywhere together.

There were of course other girls on the campus, but Craig did not see many he liked. He was a shy boy. But more than this he was used to being a star in a certain area—the football field—meaning that in this one place he always knew exactly what was expected of him, always knew exactly the perfect move to make, always had exquisite reactions to anything untoward. Outside of that area—with a girl, and all girls seemed deliberately to keep him off balance—he was just another fumbling nineteen-year-old. He hated the awkwardness he felt with girls. It always made him want to retreat back into the world where he was a star—football—and where his experience assured him of never making an ass of himself.

None of the other girls he dated set off any sparks either. He did not know why he was so sure there should be sparks. Perhaps it was instinct, or an idea he had got from the movies. He found that when he was with a girl who didn't excite him at all he could be lighthearted and charming, and the girl would laugh and her eyes would begin to sparkle, and she would start touching his sleeve all the time. With one or two of these girls he took liberties. This was all too easy, and it rather disgusted him.

He also found that if he really liked a girl, he would quickly become awkward with her, and she would sense this and stop giving him signals altogether, so that he would become even more awkward. He always imagined such girls going back to their dormitories and sorority house and remarking: "Duke Craig is really a stiff, isn't he?" And because of this, he never asked them out again.

There was also a third type of girl on campus who, because of a kind of reverse snobbery, refused to date any student with an athletic scholarship. They called the athletes "jocks," which is not a pleasant word to know some girl has called you. A guy was never sure that a certain girl might not be this type, and waiting to be approached only so she could give him a haughty brush-off. She might not only refuse, but then go around bragging about having refused. A football player like Craig had a lot of pride, perhaps too much. He had to be careful. He could not risk this.

When spring training began in April, Craig was terrified that his knee would betray him, break down completely. But he never spoke of this, or of the dull constant pain, keeping it all bottled up inside him, and he learned to keep his face blank most of the time. On the field he ran with recklessness. He had only this one season to prove what a great football player he was—and his knee could fail him at any time. Coach Buzzy Claypool and Sports Publicity Director Harley Hanley watched him with awe. He was better than he had ever been, they decided, and the machinery was set in motion to make Craig into an All-American next season. This was to the interest of both men. If the team had a losing season, Coach Claypool could nonetheless claim to have "groomed" or "produced"

Craig, and the alumni would not be so quick to scream for his scalp. As for Hanley, his job was solely and simply to make the teams and athletes of Texas University famous throughout the country. The easiest way to do this was to manufacture an All-American halfback out of a boy like Duke Craig. Hanley knew exactly how to manufacture All-Americans, given a player of Craig's talent to work with.

First he prepared a film of all of Craig's touchdown runs as a sophomore, and his several as a junior before he was injured. Hanley then added sequences of Craig catching passes, throwing passes, and blocking for the passer and for other backs. The idea was to present him as a complete football player. Hanley prepared a commentary for the film which was recorded by Coach Claypool speaking in a partly pious, partly awed voice.

Nowadays such films are fairly common, but back then they were not; Hanley was years ahead of other college publicity men. He knew just how to distribute his film, too. That summer copies went to all major magazines preparing preview All-American teams—*Life, Look,* the *Saturday Evening Post, Collier's,* a few others—and also to the Chicago *Tribune,* the New York *Daily News,* and certain other major northern newspapers. Copies also went to all the NFL pro teams.

For Hanley knew that most selectors of the All-American teams are sportswriters who, though pretending to be experts, are extremely uninformed. He had often seen ballots signed by the most prestigious sportswriters in the business; players would be selected who did not attend the college named, or did not play the position selected for, or, once, a player who had been dead for two years. Some selectors, being conscientious, would ask advice from contacts on pro teams (who now would have seen the film on Craig); some would demand to see the film themselves. All who had seen the film would vote for Craig on the basis of the film, if only because they hadn't seen any other films, and Craig must really be great to have a film made on him. The film was a big plus, the major trump in Hanley's campaign. But he also sent excellent still photos around on Craig, and many publicity releases studded with anecdotes and details. In the releases he stretched some things. For instance, he called Craig 195 pounds, although he was a lanky 175-pounder at the time. Hanley also quoted past football heroes, sometimes with their permission, sometimes without, to the effect that Craig was the finest back to play in Texas since Sammy Baugh.

Hanley personally clocked Craig in a football uniform in a

hundred-yard dash, Craig sprinting the length of the empty field. "What did I do?"

"Christ," said Hanley, flicking the watch back to zero. "Nine point seven."

"You're kidding."

Just being a good halfback was not enough. The publicity was what counted.

"You ought to go out for track, Duke. I knew you were fast, but Christ—"

Craig laughed, not even realizing that Hanley was as good at publicity as Craig was at carrying the ball. Craig knew Hanley was faking a bit for publicity purposes, but he was enough in love with his own wonderful body and its performance to enjoy thinking of himself as a 9.7 sprinter for an hour or two. He was fast enough, in any case. Not many were going to catch him in an open field, and he had moves to shake off those. Provided his knee held up—

Sometimes he would look down on the two long scars and almost want to bawl. He had a recurring nightmare in which his lower leg was amputated and he tried to play football on one leg and the stump.

But he said nothing.

When he went under the heat lamp, into the whirlpool, he had a way of making jokes to the effect that he preferred the treatments to practice. The treatments weren't necessary, he pretended, he was really only malingering. He acquired a reputation for this which was to carry into the pros: Duke Craig, the book said, was a hard man to make practice.

From the outside he became again the powerful confident youth who had once carried his high school team into the state championships and who now would carry Texas to a Bowl game. From the outside he seemed the one boy so favored by fortune that life for him was an unending succession of triumphs which he didn't even have to pay for. From these college triumphs he would go on to bigger, better ones: pro football, big money, people falling all over themselves for such a hero; he would be invited to the best places; he would get a spectacular job when his playing days were over. Craig at twenty had what other men seek all their lives: adulation, fame—success.

No one knew about the fear he lived with. It all could end in an instant of searing pain up the inside of his leg into his skull. He was like a man with one eye living in terror of the blindness most men don't even think about seriously; or like learning to live, at twenty, in constant fear of death. For football was everything to him, and without it he would not want to live. The admiration and affection he got from his team-mates (and gave back) was the best he had ever known of love. And he was, in addition, a genius at football (in that he did it splendidly, almost precociously). And at nothing else.

As the season started, as he performed gorgeous acts on the field and victory followed victory, he found that it became easy to date Carribel again. This was nice. But in truth his thoughts —and his heart—were always on the football field.

In October teams of reporters and photographers representing northern magazines descended on the campus. They followed him everywhere and began asking who his girl was, as photos were urgently wanted of the two of them together.

"I don't really have a steady girl."

One photographer went to Harley Hanley, who realized that to complete Craig's hero image, a girl friend was vital. "Sure he's got a girl."

Hanley sought out Craig. "What about that girl I've seen you with?"

"She's not my girl," said Craig stubbornly.

Hanley went to Carribel. Later that day, coming down the steps of the chemistry hall, she called out to Craig: "Wait up, honey."

She trotted up to him, took his arm, and looked lovingly into his eyes as a dozen cameras clicked.

"Could I have your name, miss?"

She gave it to them.

"Would you spell that first name, please?"

"Are you Duke's fiancée, miss?"

"Well, we're not formally engaged, are we, Duke, honey?"

Craig, confused, said nothing.

"Have you known each other long?"

"Simply ages and ages. We went to high school together."

"Childhood sweethearts, eh?"

"Y'all might say that."

They copied down her replies.

"Duke is takin' l'il ol' me to the Fall Fling tonight, aren't you, honey?"

"Well," said Craig, confused, "I'd be happy to."

At the dance, flashbulbs popped until Craig's eyeballs felt seared.

The *Life* photographer wanted pictures of Craig in uniform and Carribel in Craig's letter sweater as a possible color cover. Craig was vain enough not to want to share the cover with Carribel or anyone else, but did not know how to get out of it.

The cover appeared less than a month later, probably a record in speed for *Life*. Craig and Carribel were billed as America's sweethearts.

Such publicity accomplished what Craig had failed to accomplish in previous years. Other boys considered Carribel taken by Craig, and never asked her out again. She was always available for dates now; they were often invited places jointly, almost as a married couple, and this pleased Craig. Also he began to feel a duty toward her. If she expected to accompany him to every dance and party, how could he invite another girl? That would be to leave Carribel sitting home waiting for him; since he knew loneliness so vividly himself, how could he condemn her to it? Besides, she was certainly a pretty girl.

Having borrowed his letter sweater for the *Life* cover, she never returned it, and when she borrowed his fraternity pin for another photo he did not expect to get that back either. He didn't mind. She wore it on her left breast all season. She was lapping up all the attention, loving it, and he didn't begrudge her that either. How could he when he was loving it all himself? She made him feel very much the man—man enough even to confer the status of Duke Craig's girl on her.

People now assumed they were engaged and would marry when Craig got his bonus money from the pros. Craig would like to have contradicted this, but how do you contradict something that is never spoken of out loud?

In any case, he became very close to her, and once tried to tell her what his junior year had been like—his despair then, and his fear now, because it could all end at any moment.

"Don't think about it."

"I try not to."

"No you don't, you think about it all the time. Ah can tell."

"Well—" said Craig.

"You just tell me such things because you want sympathy."

But he believed he was telling her because of the need to tell someone, anyone. It tortured him too much to go on keeping it to himself, but now she had cut him off with most of it untold.

"And then there's the pain, of course."

"Pain? When?"

"Most of the time. A kind of dull ache. After a game is the worst. On Sundays I guess I eat half a bottle of aspirin."

"A man cain't run with the ball like you do if he's in pain."

"Well—"

He never saw her change her opinion, then or ever.

"Everyone thinks you're the big hero, but you're really more of a hypochondriac, aren't you?"

"Maybe so," said Craig glumly. Was he ever going to meet a girl he could share things with—worries as well as triumphs? Carribel was great to share triumphs with; at parties she never got tired, never wanted to go home. But she wasn't much to share yearnings or worries or defeats with.

"You're really sort of a baby. But a nice baby. My baby."

He was pleased with her for softening her rebuke. He thought he liked her a lot at that moment, for he had been able to open his soul to her a little, even if she hadn't been too receptive.

During the torrid kissing sessions in dark places, she let him go a little further than in the past, but when he pleaded for more she said: "Not until we're married." Everyone took it for granted that they would marry. And of course she herself accepted it, or seemed too. From the outside perhaps it looked like an ideal union, but to Craig it seemed less than this. There ought to be at least as much exhilaration to love as to scoring touchdowns, he reasoned. There ought to be at least as much love and affection between a guy and his girl as between guys on a team. He began to feel he was being steamrollered into marriage, and there was not much he could do about it. There was no one to talk to. His father was dead. His brother and sister were too young. Harley Hanley lacked discretion; anything you talked over with him would be all over the country in an hour. Coach Claypool, Craig knew, would give a pious answer to any question; Coach Claypool, like most college coaches, was a cynic.

Nor was there anyone else on the team he could talk to on this level.

Like all else that year he kept it bottled up inside himself. Others began to ask when the marriage would be.

"Ah ain't the marryin' kind," joked Craig.

"Ah cain't marry her on account she ain't secretly mah girl, she's secretly mah sister," joked Craig.

"They's ladies all over west Texas tryin' to marry me," joked Craig.

The jokes got back to Carribel, who was furious.

"Ah reckon it's time we set a definite date."

"Well—"

"Well what?"

"It's just that—"

"Have you been trifling with my affection all these months?"

146

She began to sob. "Have you just been fixing to make me out a fool all over this country?"

Craig, distinctly uncomfortable, said: "It's just that I guess I never have been too convinced that—well—that you really loved me." He said lamely: "Do you?"

"Ah don't know what more Ah can do to prove it."

They were parked in the dark at the edge of the lake. There were other cars there, none too close. They would not be disturbed.

She began kissing him. He tasted the tears on her cheeks and to his surprise found them real. Perhaps this was the best that love had to offer anyone. Perhaps all the rest was only in the movies. She allowed his hand to search under her skirt.

"Ah do love you, Duke. Ah'll do anything to prove it, even that."

His hand withdrew with her panties.

"Just one time before we're married. It cain't do any harm, can it, Duke?"

"No," he said, kissing her.

And so the American folk hero consummated the American dream on the wide front seat of the American bedroom.

On the way back to the campus, she said: "Now when are we gonna marry?"

He accepted the idea as inevitable.

He prepares dinner for himself and his wife: crisp bacon, scrambled eggs, slices of Wonder Bread soaked in bacon fat and fried, and broiled tomatoes that come out split and juicy. Arranged on two TV trays, it looks colorful and appetizing—the yellows, browns, and reds are the colors of autumn (the colors of football) more or less. In the living room he sets one tray in front of Carribel, who sits staring at a so-called adult Western on TV, and the other in front of his favorite chair in which he can sit with his back to the TV.

"Get me a cup of coffee, will you?" Carribel asks.

"Okay. Is there any beer in the house?"

"I forgot to buy some."

"Oh." He realizes he really wanted that beer. "Is there any wine?"

"You're the only one who buys that."

She leans forward, intently watching something happen on the screen.

He serves Carribel's coffee, which she sips without taking her eyes from the program. Sitting with his back to the screen, he begins to eat his dinner.

147

He was invited to play in the Senior Bowl in Alabama, the East-West Game in California, the Hula Bowl in Honolulu. He couldn't play in all the games, for some conflicted, but any of the *places* was a good spot for a honeymoon, Carribel pointed out, and all expenses would be paid, and he would get several hundred dollars for the game as well.

Looking back, he cannot blame Carribel. He was proud to be getting married—the only twenty-year-old on the campus mature enough, and financially solvent enough to start a family. Everyone was in favor, his family and hers, Sports Publicity Director Harley Hanley who got several good stories into the papers, Coach Buzzy Claypool who made fatherly statements to the press—everyone. The Dean congratulated him one day on a campus path. All this turned Craig's head. When Carribel, his almost wife, clung to him in public, he felt a grown man compared with his teammates who were still boys. In public Carribel was as adoring as any youth could wish his fiancée to be.

F. X. Boyle selected Craig on the first round of the draft, then came down to Austin to sign him. An Austin oilman offered to represent Craig without fee. Boyle's first offer was $10,000 for the first season, more money than Craig thought there was in the world. The sum was already typed onto the contract, for Boyle had expected to deal with the player directly.

"Take it," Craig told the oilman.

"He'll go higher."

Boyle went up to $12,500.

"Take it."

"I sense that's still a little soft."

Boyle was beginning to lose his temper.

"What else can Craig do to earn so much?" Boyle snorted.

The oilman said: "I'd pay him more than that in my business. He doesn't have to play football."

Boyle was furious.

Craig was scared. Alone with the oilman, he said: "I don't want to be an oilman, I want to play football."

"Yes, but he doesn't know that."

"He drafted me. I have to play for him or no one."

"You could play in the Canadian League."

"That's a bush league. I want to play with the best."

"He'll go higher."

"He's got me. I've got to take whatever he'll pay."

"No you don't. Trust me a little longer."

The oilman pried a $16,000 offer out of Boyle. "Okay. Now, what about a bonus?"

Boyle's face got red. "I'm paying him more than any rookie I ever hired, and you have the nerve—"

"Yes."

"It's out of the question."

"Craig is the best college football player in the country."

"I can't afford him. Let him play in Canada."

"I don't want to play in Canada," Craig blurted out. He turned beseeching eyes on the oilman.

"I want a ten thousand dollar bonus for him."

"No."

"They need it to buy a house."

Boyle may have hated the oilman. But he loved Craig's attitude, his frightened silence, his eagerness. Perhaps Boyle wanted to show up Texas and Texans on the subject of money. He offered $6,000, an excellent bonus in those days, and the oilman took it.

Boyle stayed for the wedding, which drew a crowd of 2,000 people. Harley Hanley had a special roped-off section of the church reserved for newsmen. The wedding was front-page news throughout Texas, and some other places in the country as well. On the church steps, Carribel tossed her bouquet to the crowd calling: "Well, Ah got him."

The spectators laughed, Craig felt proud, and Harley Hanley sent the remark out on the wires to amuse America.

At the reception the minister drew Craig aside.

"The love you feel for each other today is only the beginning."

Craig, who was wearing his first tuxedo, nodded. In those days he believed nearly everything told him by older men, for they were reputed to know.

But what was this notion that he ought to be more excited than he was, or more exhilarated, or more—something? What was the vague insistent whisper inside his most secret thoughts that he had just made a terrible mistake?

Carribel, dancing with F. X. Boyle, signaled the music to stop.

"Ah want you all to meet the man who made this wedding possible," she announced, and threw her arms around Boyle and kissed him on the cheek, while the assembled guests laughed and applauded.

And Boyle has had a soft spot for Carribel ever since, Craig thinks.

He carries the trays into the kitchen and begins cleaning up. If he leaves the kitchen spotless, perhaps it will make Carribel feel *friendly* later. She does not often feel friendly

149

in that way. He tries not to compare Carribel with what he knows of Margie, for he has never lived with Margie, and all marriages are no doubt like his own, after the first few weeks. Once you start living together, there is no more romance.

He tries to make himself believe this.

One Saturday afternoon when Craig gets home from practice, his daughter Suzy is ill. Craig phones their pediatrician, who prescribes something over the phone.

But when Craig looks in on Suzy before going to bed, her breathing is stertorous. Alarmed, he phones the pediatrician again, who suggests that Craig drive the child over to his office.

"But she's feverish and can't breathe. Can't you come here?"

The doctor says firmly: "It's very late."

There is a silence.

"I'm pretty sure it's the croup," the doctor says. "Bundle her up in a blanket and stand outside the front door with her. Usually the cold air clears the bronchial passages and they can breathe again."

Craig does this, hoping it will work, for it is plainly useless to call that doctor again. After a while the child sleeps. He returns her to her bed.

Carribel is sitting up in bed with a magazine.

"Are you going to sit up with her?" Carribel asks.

"I've got a game tomorrow."

"The doctor's not worried."

"I'll stay awake an hour or so longer."

He thumbs through *Sports Illustrated*. After midnight the stertorous breathing starts again. Bundling Suzy, Craig stands outside the front door a while. It is cold out, and he is weary.

When he comes back to bed, he wakes Carribel.

"I've got to get some sleep. I've got a game tomorrow."

"I've got work to do tomorrow, too."

He can't sleep, but Carribel does. The doors stand open on the hall, and after a while Suzy is rasping loudly. His coat on over his pajamas, and Suzy inside his coat, Craig stands outside in the night.

Again he lies in the dark, groggy with sleep but worried about his daughter. Half in a dream, he hears the child call out. He nudges Carribel, who mutters: "You go, you're awake."

Suzy has vomited in her bed. He mops up, moves the child to the guest room, and for an hour or so sleeps.

He dreams that his daughter is drowning.

"Carribel," he shouts.

150

His wife rolls over.

"I've got to get some sleep, Carribel."

"All right, Ah'll go."

Carribel is shaking him awake.

"She's coughing. I've been the last two times. It's your turn again."

A little later the child is sleeping peacefully. Craig looks out the window at the dawn. His mind feels fuzzy and his body aches. It is eight hours until kickoff. Exhausted, he thinks: That woman is ruining my life. Suddenly he shrieks this thought, or perhaps only imagines he does: That woman is ruining my life.

On the first play from scrimmage Craig races out of the backfield on a deep circle pattern and Pennoyer puts the ball out there on the end of his fingers—and he drops it.

He was wide open, and in the huddle he can feel his teammates worry. A perfect play wasted. Pennoyer mumbles the same signals. Craig thinks: Hit them again before they work out how to stop it.

With the clap of hands, the huddle breaks.

This time the linebacker, whom Craig never spots in time, cuts him down with a block from the side. Pennoyer has no one to throw to and is smothered for a loss.

Nothing feels right to Craig. When Pennoyer sends him plunging into the line he seems to hit the hole too early or too late. He goes down from tackles he should have broken. He becomes more and more discouraged. Around him, the offense sags.

At half time he drops his pants, Dr. Flaherty aims a hypodermic beside the buttocks strap of his jock, and shoots him full of vitamin B-12.

The shot sometimes helps, but this time doesn't seem to.

With Jimmy Finney out, the defense keys on Craig, smashing him down. Most Sundays he plays with such enthusiasm that he never feels the bruises until afterward. Today his flesh logs each blow as it lands.

His play gets ever more ragged. He worries about getting seriously injured; half the people who hit him he hasn't even seen coming. He worries about committing the unforgivable sin: anticipating tacklers and flinching before they even hit him.

Coach Dreuder sends in an extra end, and the team goes into a double-wing offense.

Craig, on the bench, stares at his cleats thinking: That woman is ruining my life.

But they win the game on a desperate field goal; the chewing-out Craig will get when films are shown Tuesday will be relatively mild. Nor is he as sore as he feared.

By the time he gets home he has resolved to patch things up with Carribel; he can't go on resenting her this way. He tries to make himself feel love for her. He remembers how she looked when they slid her into the room after giving birth to Bobby: pale and wet, groggy with drugs, and under the blanket her stomach so slack. How he had loved her at that moment. He also remembers how childishly happy she was the day they bought this house, whirling round and round the empty rooms laughing. He remembers how angrily she as always defended him at parties, if anyone ever suggested he was not perfect. He remembers how earnest she is about collecting for charities, and other such community jobs.

In bed in the dark he draws her close.

"I'm sorry about last night."

"She's your daughter too, you know."

Magnanimous, he decides to ignore this. He strokes her face, her breasts. His hand seeks her thighs.

"Just what do you have in mind?" she says coldly.

The question freezes him.

Then his hand resumes. "I want to make love to you."

"You insulted me, last night."

He is not sure whether he shrieked his rage last night or dreamed he did.

Perhaps he shouted at her. "Did I?"

"You think all you have to do is apologize, and Ah'll accept you with open arms."

His hand, stilled, lies on her hip.

"Well, Ah don't happen to feel like it, if you want to know the truth."

When she rolls to her side of the bed, Craig lies furious, staring up into the darkness.

He makes his decision, or believes he does.

He bites off each word: "After the season, I'm leaving you."

Silence.

"You can keep this house. Keep everything. I'm getting out."

More silence. Then a noisy sigh. "All right, what's the matter?"

"Nothing," he shouts. "I just want a divorce." The word is out for the first time. He takes a deep breath.

"Because Ah don't happen to feel like making love."

"Because we're ruining each other's lives."

152

"That's what you said last night."

"Do you think I didn't mean it or something?"

"All right," she says resignedly. "If you want to that badly, come on."

At first he doesn't comprehend what she means. She arranges herself in the dark.

He gives a hollow laugh: "Oh, no."

"Come on." She tugs on him.

"You think agreeing to make love fixes everything."

"You're the one who wanted to," she says. "Come on then."

Her nightgown is hoisted up, and her legs spread in a V. He can feel his nerves twanging. His muscles are tense, and he is aware of all his bruises. He needs a woman to bathe his wounds and hold him in her arms. Margie—instead there is only Carribel.

"I meant it," he says hollowly.

She tugs his pajamas. "Come on."

Why not?

Perhaps afterward he would sleep. Otherwise, barely able to keep from screaming, he is liable to lie awake until morning.

Why not?

What does it signify? Sex works both ways. Inside or outside of marriage it can mean everything, or nothing.

He feels the top sheet on his bare rump. On top of his wife's body he thinks: To relax—and afterward to sleep.

He rocks back and forth waiting for momentary exaltation, waiting for—release, sleep—everything.

"You don't have to be careful," Carribel says, matter-of-factly. "This is the safe time of the month."

In Craig's marriage, this passes as a sexy remark, and tips him over the edge. He can't remember in the moment left to him if it is the safe time or not, but the effort to remember and decide spoils the moment totally. He seeks to withdraw in a hurry, but Carribel grips him tight.

He gives in to it, tries to enjoy it; it's too late to worry now.

"What did you do that for?"

She giggles in the dark. "Don't you want another baby?"

"No."

"At least you won't divorce me until it's born."

"Yes I will," he says wearily.

"You won't divorce me at all. Ah know you too well for that."

"Let's get some sleep."

153

CHAPTER | 12

He decides to telephone Margie. He invites her to have lunch with him. Perhaps, knowing her better, she will haunt him less. Some confusion will go away. He'll be able to see his marriage clearly. He knows a restaurant which, at lunch, is crowded with businessmen discussing million dollar deals over three martinis each: he will meet her there. He reasons that such a public place is above suspicion. It will seem he is meeting her as a representative of the Pepsi-Cola Company, not a woman at all.

Seated at a table, he waits for her. Despite himself, his eyes are glued to the door she will enter. Suddenly she is there, peering about for him.

Though aware of the beating of his heart, he is trying for a noncommittal smile as he rises to shake hands with her. To his dismay there seems no special meaning to her smile either, no special squeeze to her fingers. But she is so lovely that his own smile fades, and he wets his lips.

"How are things going?"

"Fine. And with you?"

"Fine."

She sips a manhattan, Craig a beer.

"I'm doing Mel Slade's son this week. He's only six. I'm a little worried."

"Yes."

They eat lunch slowly, and the conversation never moves off this level. Behind those lovely blue eyes is she anxious, bored?

"How did you happen to become Miss Pepsi-Cola?"

"It was somebody I knew."

He nods.

"I'm being test-marketed. If the idea catches on here, next year they may go national with it."

154

He nods again.

"There would be quite a lot of money if they do that."

Over coffee, with time running out, he says urgently: "Could I—could I see you from time to time? I mean—"

This is awful. He does not know exactly what he wants from this girl, but whatever it is, from her point of view, he has nothing to offer. What does she get out of it?

"I think—" she begins in a low voice. Her hand toys with the stem of a glass. He yearns to touch that hand, establish some contact. But in this public place that is impossible.

Avoiding his eyes, speaking to the glass, she says: "To go on seeing each other would be too great a strain on you, the risk, considering the way you feel—"

Her eyes come up to his. They gaze at each other so long and anxiously that Craig wonders about patrons observing them. How much can be interpreted from a look?

But it is too late to worry about that.

"Will you have dinner with me tomorrow night?" He names a time, and the restaurant near her apartment.

He watches the expression flickering across her face.

"And then?"

"Just—dinner."

After a moment she says in a low voice: "All right."

In the street they shake hands, then walk off in opposite directions.

He begins to meet her for lunch or dinner in dim restaurants. Craig convinces himself that most people who might recognize him would take her for his wife. Anyway, a restaurant is not that compromising a place.

One night, when they come out onto the bright street, she says: "I've been invited to a party that I really must go to."

Craig hesitates. "Do you want me to drive you there?"

"You could come on up, too."

Craig shakes his head. "No."

"It's mostly writers and artists." With a smile she adds: "I doubt much of your fame has preceded you there."

"Well—"

"We only have to stay a minute."

He has been longing to show her off to someone for days. To stand up before the world, and shout: "Look what I've got!"

Perhaps no one there will know him. Even if he is recognized, surely just appearing there with Margie would not be enough actually to start a scandal, would it?

"All right," Craig says.

A maid takes their coats. They go into a living room jammed with people. There is loud music and the blur of many voices. It is very crowded. After a moment their hosts come forward, the man's arm around the woman.

Margie presents Craig: "I'd like you to meet—"

Craig, offering his hand, interrupts: "I'm Wallace Craig."

Margie gives him a look.

"Glad to know you, Wally," the man says. "What line of work are you in, Wally?"

"I'm, er, in the entertainment industry."

"Do you play something?"

"What's that?"

Margie, amused, says: "You mean, like, a musical instrument or something?"

"Yeah. He has the look of a musician, doesn't he, Nancy?"

Craig, looking around, says: "It isn't an instrument you'd be likely to have on hand."

"Ask him what instrument he plays, George," says Nancy.

George, smiling, socks Craig on the arm. "Don't worry, we're not going to ask you to perform for us."

"I bet he plays the oboe," says Nancy.

"No, the tuba," jokes George. They are both a little drunk.

A waiter passes with a tray of drinks. His tray lightens by four.

Nancy sweeps more people into the group. "You know Margie, and this is Wally Cray. He's a musician."

"What do you play, Mr. Cray?"

Margie's eyes smile at Craig over the top of her glass.

Nancy giggles. "I think he plays the tuba."

Craig decides to relax and enjoy this. "Actually I play the bass drum."

"Not really."

"As an artist I'm considered probably unique in the classical bass drum field."

"I've never met a bass drum artist before."

"The degree of vibrato and obligato—smash, we call it— I can coax out of my bass drum, is considered without peer."

Craig looks around at grinning faces. The performer in him responds.

"I was the man who invented the technique for playing a bass drum pianissimo. You blow on it, you see. Before me, no one had ever done anything but sock it."

They begin to laugh.

"What else do you play, Wally."

"The cymbals, of course. The subtlety of my cymbal playing is considered without peer."

156

"What did you say your name was?"

Somebody whispers, "Wally Cray."

"Your face looks familiar, Wally."

"You may have seen it in connection with the Nobel Prize."

"Nobel Prize?"

"I gave a cymbal recital at the Nobel Prize dinner last year. Several of the critics were kind enough to call it without peer."

They are laughing.

"The King of Norway—" says Craig.

Somebody says: "Sweden, you mean."

"He may have been, I was a little drunk. In any case, this king said to me: Cray, he said, the degree of smash you get into your bass drum performance is without peer. That's when I knew he was a student of the bass drum art—when he used our word for it, *smash.*"

"What kind of man was the king?"

"Well, he was a little drunk, of course. He wanted to know how I could play the cymbals with such subtlety. King, I said, the secret of subtle cymbal playing is to use *only one cymbal.*"

Craig sees Margie laughing with the others.

"That's what I told him," Craig says seriously. "We cymbalists know that the key to our art is to remain inconspicuous, and to do this, you have to use *only one cymbal.* King, I said, there is no other way."

Craig looks around at the faces.

"The minute you take that second cymbal out of the closet, inconspicuousness is finished. Because you won't be able to resist." Craig does a pantomime of a man trying to resist smashing the cymbals together. The temptation becomes too strong, he bangs the imaginary cymbals together, and a beatific expression comes over his face as he listens to the noise.

"Playing the cymbals teaches you a lot about human nature," Craig says, nodding vigorously. "Given two cymbals, no man is strong enough not to."

"But with only one cymbal how do you—"

"Precisely."

A woman whispers to Margie: "Is he really a musician?"

"Wally Cray?" she says. "I somehow doubt it."

"What an attractive man."

Margie beams. She frees Craig from the group. "This way, Mr. Cray—"

Later, outside in the street, she takes his arm: "That was fun in there."

"I enjoyed it."

"You're quite a performer."

He laughs. "Don't be so surprised. That's what football

157

is, showing off before crowds. And I've done that since I was about fourteen."

"People don't scare you at all, do they?"

"Not in groups."

"But as individuals—"

"Yes."

"Do I scare you?"

After a moment he says: "Yes."

"Why?"

But he knows she knows why.

"Is it because you don't know what to do with me?"

He looks at her.

"I know what I wish you'd do with me. I wish you'd take me home."

Craig says: "I wish I'd met you ten years ago."

She replies softly: "I wish you had, too."

Craig looks for a passing taxi to flag down.

"Are you going to send me home in a cab again?"

He nods.

The night is chilly. The upturned fur of her coat seems to nestle her face.

"Do you ever see your husband?" Craig asks suddenly.

"We have dinner together every Friday night."

"In a restaurant?"

"I cook for him at home."

Quick jealous pangs knife through Craig. And after dinner, what do you do, he wonders.

They gaze at each other. Margie's face is grave. She does not offer the denial Craig hopes for, and he does not dare ask for it.

Instead she says quietly: "He is my husband, you know."

A cab pulls up. Its door opens gratingly.

Taking Craig's face between her gloved hands, Margie kisses his lips. Craig watches her cab move off, then glances up and down the street to see who might have observed the kiss. But the sidewalks are empty in both directions. He finds his car and drives home.

On Saturday after practice, Craig picks up Margie. He wears a dark turtleneck sweater, a suede sports coat, and a black cashmere topcoat. He is freshly combed and shaved.

She wants to see a house which a friend is having constructed in a suburb to the north. They drive there in Craig's Buick. The lawn is mud, and they approach the ultramodern house over duckboards. To their surprise they find the architect looking through the rooms.

158

He stands with them, obviously hoping for praise.

Ill at ease, Craig remarks: "These glass walls sure give a feeling of space."

"I hoped you'd say that."

"You make the trees and grounds seem part of the house."

"Exactly."

"What about the cost of heating?"

"It won't be excessive."

Craig doubts this, but nods. After shaking hands again, the architect departs.

Margie looks at Craig. "You don't like it, do you?"

"It's very attractive, I suppose."

Craig's own house is a standard split-level, built of the same materials and from virtually the same plans as every other house on his street.

"But is this practical?" he asks. "What about noise?"

They stand in the master bedroom from which steps drop directly into the living room. The wall between bedroom and living room is only a partition. It stops several feet below the high beamed ceiling, which is common to both rooms.

"There will be no privacy in either room," says Craig.

"Why didn't you ask the architect about noise?"

"I was afraid he'd have no answer. I didn't want to embarrass him."

Margie laughs. "Architects always have answers."

"Noise is serious. You don't know what it's like to live with screaming kids."

He sees her drop her eyes. "You're right, I don't."

Afraid he has hurt her, he goes on quickly: "Let's say you're trying to sleep in here, but the kids are having a party in the living room. The noise would drive you crazy."

He smiles and adds: "Let's say people are trying to play chess in the living room, while you are making love in here."

"The noise would drive you crazy."

"Right."

He watches her laugh. It is nice to be able to speak to her, conversationally, about making love.

"You're very conservative, aren't you?"

"It probably comes from football. Fancy stuff never works. It makes much more sense to go with something solid and tested."

"And the same with houses?"

"Absolutely," says Craig with a smile. "Football, houses, playing the cymbals one-handed—it's all identical."

Arm in arm they go out over the duckboards. At the car,

159

Craig says: "You never talk about children. It's as if you don't care one way or the other."

"Don't care?" she bursts out.

"Well, you don't seem to miss not having any."

She says in a low voice: "I've been to every doctor in this state trying to find out why I can't have children. I'm a human guinea pig."

He doesn't know what to say.

"Of course I care," she adds.

After a moment she says: "Why do you think I try to be around them all the time? Your son, all the others I've had on the show—I can't keep my hands off them."

He knows that after college she attended dramatic school, and later had small parts in movies. With the Hollywood studios collapsing, she came East to try for parts in television, but got married instead. Later she worked for the advertising agency which handles Pepsi-Cola.

"Don't think I wouldn't like to have children." There is a wistful look in her eyes. "I would. I just—can't have them."

He holds her close.

Opening her handbag, she produces tickets to a concert. "You need to be introduced to some culture," she says cheerfully.

He hands one ticket back. "I'll meet you there."

"Come and pick me up."

He shakes his head.

"Don't trust me, eh?" she says with a smile.

"It's myself I don't trust."

In truth he does enjoy the concert, the first he has ever attended. The music seems to soar, and him with it, so that his spirit floats free under the dark vault. Though his senses are attuned to the music, his thoughts solve the Steelers' defenses of next Sunday, he gloats over touchdown runs made three days ago, three weeks ago, three years ago. The music induces a kind of double vision, he sees everything clearly: his own excellence, the soundness of the team, the beauty of the girl beside him. The rest, which the music also discloses, he will not think about until after the season.

"Now tell me that was lovely, and you enjoyed it," Margie says when it ends.

"It was lovely, and I did enjoy it. I had no idea it could be so—so exalting. Or something," he adds, embarrassed.

"You don't have to be embarrassed with me."

"You won't squeal on me to the team, will you?"

There is amusement and more—love—in her eyes.

He drives to a dim cocktail lounge near her apartment. She orders cognac. "And you should have one too."

"Why not?" he agrees.

But as they sip it, a man drapes an arm around Craig's shoulders.

"Duke Craig, I just want to tell you I think you're the greatest ballplayer in the entire league."

"Well," Craig says. "Well, well. Thank you very much."

"You're just great."

"Thank you."

"There's just no back in the league as great as you."

"Thank you."

"Is this Mrs. Craig?"

Craig watches Margie. After a moment her head nods assent.

"Honey, your husband is the greatest."

"Thank you."

"Would you sign this for me, Duke?" The man presents a ball-point pen and a damp bar coaster. "Otherwise my kid won't believe I've talked to you."

Craig signs.

"Now you, Mrs. Craig."

Margie shakes her head.

"Come on," the man insists.

"No, please."

"I'd really like it. My wife would like it, too."

Again Margie declines.

The man looks at Craig, who says firmly: "You know how women are." Seeing the mystical expression on the man's face, Craig adds: "But I'd gladly sign it again, if that would help out."

The man laughs, shakes hands with Margie who gives him a weak smile, and then again with Craig whom he socks in the arm, saying: "Just remember what I said, you're the greatest."

They watch him go back to the bar. He looks over and waves.

Craig sips his cognac, watching Margie, who only stares into her glass. Presently, he says gently: "Come on, I'll take you home."

Outside her door he turns off the engine.

Margie says in a low voice: "Please come upstairs with me."

"That would only confuse things worse."

"Not tonight."

They are silent.

"The trouble is, I wish I was Mrs. Craig."

161

His willpower is not equal to this. In the elevator he holds her. He can feel her trembling under her coat.

"I was afraid I'd never feel you there again."

"Do I feel good?"

But her eyes are fluttering, and she says nothing more for a time.

"Will you have dinner with me Friday?"

"I have a—previous engagement."

He remembers this is the night she cooks for her husband. Sobered, he asks: "Is there anyone else in your life besides me?"

"Apart from my husband, no."

He nods.

"And in your life?" she asks.

"Just my wife."

She nods in her turn.

He thinks this a curious kind of fealty to pledge to each other.

Presently she says: "I do see a great many people."

"Here?"

"Sometimes."

"How do you keep them off?" he asks, believing that all must try to seduce a girl like this. Do some succeed?

"I put a tray on their laps, and a jigsaw puzzle on the tray, and we work on it together."

"And they can't make a move without upsetting the puzzle."

"That's right."

He smiles. "Very ingenious."

"Men seem to think that with a woman who's separated from her husband they have a very good chance. They're not too different from you in that respect."

He laughs.

"When you have no husband, you really attract them. I have to be very firm, or I'd be in bed with everybody."

He begins to kiss her. "You better—get your puzzle—quickly."

"I—will."

"Too—late."

CHAPTER 13

Outside the San Francisco airport a sixty-passenger bus waits for the players. The players stand in groups, grumbling, unwilling to wedge thick thighs and wide shoulders back into cramped seats so soon. All day, sealed in, they have ridden high across their vast country. Far below the states slid magically backward while they fidgeted and squirmed and got tired of card games and ran out of things to talk about. Now in this new place it is not yet night, though their stomachs tell them it ought to be. They are stiff, resentful, hungry.

This is Tuesday. The team flies to nearby games Saturday morning, but trips to the West Coast are made nearly a week in advance. The players' finely tuned, oversize bodies must be allowed to adapt to the jet lag and the three-hour difference. At the Napa Mission Inn, sixty miles north of San Francisco, a training camp will be established for this purpose; the team will practice there Wednesday, Thursday, and Friday. Saturday morning the team will come into San Francisco by bus and workout at Kezar Stadium. Saturday night, and Sunday night after the game, the team will be quartered at the Fairmount Hotel.

Now Coach Dreuder barks orders and the players, grumbling, board the bus. They grumble about being stuck in an empty resort sixty miles from the city; they grumble about being forced back into the monastic life of summer training camp. They grumble about this long, and to them unnecessary, bus ride to close out the boring all-day plane trip.

"Couldn't they find any place farther out than Napa?"

"Los Angeles would do. It's only about four hundred miles away."

"If they want to lock us up for a week before the game, they should have hired Alcatraz. It's not being used, I understand, and it's a lot closer."

The humor is heavy-handed. There may be delicacy to the way a long pass lies out on top of the air, but this is almost the only delicacy connected with the game and the men who play it.

In the front seats the coaches and Boyle pretend not to hear the bitter remarks.

At last the bus pulls up in front of the Inn. Inside, dinner waits on the tables. Boyle has telephoned from the airport so it should be. The players go directly from the bus into the dining room, where they devour shrimp cocktail, stacks of steaks, limp toast, apple pie. There are pitchers of iced tea and hot coffee on the tables.

Coach Dreuder raps on a glass: "Curfew is eleven P.M.," he calls out. "There will be a bed check. Practice is ten A.M."

Players give an exaggerated groan.

"When you finish eating, go out and get your suitcases off the truck."

The trainers and the equipment man enter. They have had to unload the trunks and the individual gear duffel bags off the truck. They are accompanied by the truck driver, who sits down to eat with them. Players are drifting out of the dining room, many of them picking their teeth. The uniformed bus driver, who has eaten fast to keep up with his new friends, goes out with a group of them; he is asking rapid questions about football. He has never had a team on his bus before, and this is a memorable day for him.

Meanwhile, Dr. Flaherty is in the kitchen castigating the chef for having served shrimp cocktail: "We told you no fish and especially no shellfish. Are you trying to make them all bloat up, or something?"

Dr. Flaherty leaves a menu for the rest of the week. "And remember, nothing fried."

After dinner players sit out on the front steps in the failing light. Eventually the bus and truck motor off. A few cars draw up, and some teammates are driven away amid ribald advice and warnings about the $250 fine for missing curfew.

Inside, a fire burns in the paneled sitting room. Craig sits in a leather chair in front of the fire reading the San Francisco papers. Linemen, Ox Polski and Mean Gene Gardner enter.

"What's that crap on the phonograph?" demands Gardner.

"I'm innocent," says Craig. "It was on when I sat down."

Gardner snatches the record off. "It's Puccini," he says, reading the label. "One of those Italian singers."

"The Italians got good voices, usually," says the gentle Polski. "Look at Perry Como."

"Look at Vic Damone."

"Look at Eddie Fisher."

"He's no Italian, you jerk."

Polski and Gardner, the team's defensive tackles, are inseparable. Polski, despite his size, is a gentle, mild soul. He wears steel-rimmed spectacles off the field, and contact lenses on it. He is the youngest and best of four brothers from a Pennsylvania coal mining town. His three brothers all played in the league, and all own restaurants in the Pittsburgh area now.

Gardner is from the Ozarks and never wore shoes till he went to high school. He went to college at Arkansas and was the most feared lineman in the Southwest. He is still feared. He likes to knock opponents' teeth out with his elbows.

Now Gardner shuffles through the records. "Put this on," he says to Polski.

A song comes on, a cowboy kind of voice.

> *When Ah'm eatin' ice cream*
> *Drinkin' beer*
> *In the sunshine of your love.*

It is the type of song Craig grew up with—the popular songs of the rural South and Southwest. But it no longer sounds right to his northern ear.

He goes outside through the group on the front steps. It is full dark now, but a warm night. Comfortable in just a sweater, he walks across the road and through the trees to the practice field. Across, in the moonlight, he can make out the high school to which the field belongs, and he is assailed by memories. The year he was a rookie this was the team's training camp all summer. This is where he learned what pro football was all about and, although he thought he knew the game by then, was amazed at the violence with which the pros played it. On this field every afternoon would end with a full-scale scrimmage full of busted plays and pile-ups (since nothing was polished yet) and usually with one or more players standing with blood running down his face, cut open by cleats. Or else the player would be lying on the ground all alone, all his teammates ignoring him, the scrimmage line being moved forward so that practice could go on while Dr. Flaherty found his bag and came hurrying out onto the field to attend the youth on the ground.

Craig fingers a scar from the bridge of his nose across under his right eyebrow, seven stitches earned on this field before he had been a pro three days, seven stitches sewn neatly into his flesh without any anesthetic in that high school locker room while he lay on a rubbing table.

"There you go, Duke, boy." Stitch.

"And another, Duke, boy." Stitch.

The curved upholsterers' needles, gleaming, pre-threaded with short lengths of thread, lying in a row on a towel.

"And another, Duke, boy." Stitch. Reaching for another needle.

"And you never felt it, did you, Duke, boy?" Stitch.

"And one for the road, Duke, boy." Stitch. Tying the knot tight.

Malverde, the publicity man, just out of college then, watching fascinated, horrified.

Craig, wanting to impress both Doc and Malverde, saying in a matter-of-fact voice: "That was quick. You really have things down to a science in the pros."

Craig remembering, smiles.

F. X. Boyle comes out of the dark trees and stands nearby.

"We had a lot of good training camps here," he says.

"It was a good place for a camp."

"It never rains in this valley in summer. That's one of the reasons we chose it."

They nod at each other in the dark, both of them remembering the baking heat of those days, the burned-out hills all around. But they remember it differently, for Boyle wore an open-necked white shirt to practice, and Craig wore full uniform and pads.

"A man sure was thirsty by the end of the afternoon," says Boyle.

"The last half hour of practice, thirst was all any of us thought of."

Boyle imagines they share these memories, but Craig knows differently. After practice, Craig and the other players would walk to the candy store down the road, guzzle soda pop, and talk worriedly about their chances of making the team. Boyle and the coaches would meet in Doc Flaherty's room where liquor and setups were kept locked in the closet; Malverde would fetch ice and glasses and mix drinks for them. This was known as the Five-Thirty Club, and the conversation would get hilariously funny at the expense of certain players.

"He isn't *an* end, he's *the* end. Gives away every play pointing with the whites of his eyes."

"That one must have big feet or something. He always looks like he's running in the mud."

Craig thinks: We knew about the Five-Thirty Club, and had a pretty good idea what was said there, and almost the very jokes with which the coaches and Boyle poisoned their minds against certain of us. There were a few players who used to walk past the window, looking up at it fearfully, every afternoon.

"I remember your first year with us," Boyle says. "That was a good summer."

"Yes," agrees Craig. They believe this, though it was a miserable summer for both of them.

For Boyle, there was no television income from exhibition games that year, and little enough television income at all. The Big Red had only seven thousand season-ticket holders, and a bad record in the six exhibition games could kill the ticket sale at home for the rest of the season. Boyle, like most of his colleagues, was conducting a fringe business operation then, all but four or five of the clubs losing money most years. His team was weak, and several bad seasons in a row could put him under for good—and then he got the idea to take his team west for their exhibition games. Training was cheaper on the West Coast, and if they played their exhibitions there on Saturday nights, these games would end too late for results to get into the Sunday morning papers back home: they could be lost to the strong West Coast teams (the Rams and Forty-Niners were the class of the league then) with impunity, and the large West Coast crowds would pay Boyle's training camp expenses. The Big Red then could go back east with the home fans still buying tickets, not knowing how bad their team actually was.

This idea possibly saved the team. That summer and the next, Boyle bought and scrounged and traded for players who built the team up, and hired George Dreuder as coach, and got Pennoyer from the Cardinals and Craig from the college draft.

Looking back, Boyle thinks of Craig's first summer as a happy time, but the owner was desperate and worried all through it. Once he even gave a tryout to an ex-convict who claimed to have been the star of the San Quentin team. "You better keep *every*thing locked while that guy's around," was one of Boyle's comments which delighted the Five-Thirty Club. Boyle brought in more than eighty players that summer. There was a busload coming and a busload going nearly every day, but by summer's end there was a middling-strong thirty-five-man squad which eventually finished third.

"Do you remember King Farouk, Duke?"

"Sure."

"Right over there behind those bushes is where the King used to upchuck his breakfast in the middle of practice every morning."

167

The King was a portly lineman from a Negro divinity college, a mild soul and forty pounds overweight.

"What was his real name?"

Boyle's fantastic memory is equal even to this. "Evans. Lloyd Evans."

After a few days Boyle sent the King home, relieved to have got rid of him before he suffered a gastric rupture of some kind. He might have lasted longer, and perhaps even rounded into shape eventually, had not Boyle hung the name King Farouk on him, making him an object of laughter and ridicule to all.

The principal thing Craig remembers from that first summer was thirst. There was a two-hour workout each morning in shorts and T-shirts, the players sprinting through drills and plays under the sweltering sun. In the afternoon came full pads and contact, starting with sixty or more men (however many were in camp) blasting singly or in pairs into the sleds, the players' shoulders smacking against the padded posts with a ring and echo, the sled lurching forward a few yards while the coach who was standing on it screamed at them, and the players' cleats dug into the burned-out turf and bits of dirt and grass spit out behind.

Then came one-on-one blocking drills. Sometimes when it was Craig's turn he drew a man his own size, sometimes a 260-pounder. The collision rang out over the field. When the coaches had put every player through this several times, it was the turn of the backs to try to plunge through two tacklers, a coach tossing the ball to whoever's turn it was, blowing a tweet on his whistle, then leaning forward to watch the ball carrier sprint toward two linemen who waited blank-faced behind their cages, literally with open arms. There was a variation of this: two blockers facing the two tacklers, giving the ball carrier some protection as he tried to plunge through into the clear; but the result was usually a pile-up anyway. After these drills came an hour of the full-scale warfare of scrimmage. And although putting his shoulder into someone was one of the pleasures which had first drawn Craig to football, and he enjoyed it, still he got awfully sore after a few days; parts of his body stayed tender all summer.

The bashing was fearful, but the mental anguish was worse. Everything was being graded on the coaches' clipboards, and filmed by Boyle himself (to save money) from a wooden tower, and players who didn't measure up would be sent out of there on buses and trains with no pay at all for the sweat and pain of the days or weeks they had lasted.

Some of the veterans and all of the rookies, Craig included, worried constantly about being cut from the team; there was no way to tell who would go and who would stick. The coaches might keep a bad guard because they needed guards, and cut a good end to make room for him. Certain star players had no-cut contracts, and if you were trying to beat out such a player you were doomed from the start; they couldn't cut him so they would have to cut you. The dormitory was rife with rumors about who had no-cut contracts. Or a player could sweat and struggle for eight weeks to nail down a job as, say, reserve quarterback, only to have Boyle bring in a Pennoyer on a last-minute trade—sending the presumed reserve quarterback home on the next bus. Craig knew very well how good he himself was, but what guarantee was there that the coaches would see this? They might form a prejudice against him. They might find they could trade him or sell him for a player they needed more, and all the work and sweat would have to be done over somewhere else. He was a piece of merchandise now, and his contract could be voided at any moment for any reason. Days of mental torture; his contract no protection at all. Pay checks did not even start until the first league game in late September. If he got cut, he would not get paid a cent.

"I love training camp," Boyle says, an intimate kind of admission for him. For Boyle, each training camp is to watch a new team bloom like flowers—a new season—a rebirth of youth and hope.

"Yes," Craig says. In a way he loves it too, for it brings excitement back into his life after six dull months. But he also sees the brutal, ruthless quality of it, the way it inexorably tightens, tautens the team, at first flinging players off casually, the King Farouks; then paring a few almost surgically, then grinding the others off in the final days. The last almost make it, are desperate to stay, will never be flung off or pared off, and now must be ground off to expose the final facets of the jewel.

"Remember Billy Botts?" asks Craig.

"Yes."

Billy Botts got cut; nonetheless, Boyle remembers him fondly. "He didn't have the right emotional makeup for this game."

They listen to the birds in the dark trees. A car passes on the road behind them. They look out over the field in the moonlight.

Billy Botts was newly married. His wife, living with her parents back in Oklahoma, was already pregnant; he used to phone her every night. They had a house picked out and would make a down payment as soon as Billy collected his first checks in late September.

Billy was so anxious to make the team that he ran himself into near exhaustion every day. He was the most enthusiastic rookie they ever had, but also the most highly strung. The more other rookies were cut, the harder Billy ran. Finally he collapsed on the practice field. Heat prostration. He swallowed his tongue. He went into shock. It was virtually a heart attack, and Dr. Flaherty barely saved his life. Two weeks later Billy was out of the hospital. The coaches told him not to worry, take it easy, but he must have felt he had two weeks to make up now—he ran harder than ever. After he collapsed the second time, they cut him. They were afraid he would die otherwise.

"Billy could have been a good football player," says Craig.

"I hated to let him go," agrees Boyle.

Craig at twenty-one loved the brutality and ruthlessness of football, loved to shoulder into tacklers and knock them down, so once he knew he had made the team, he loved training camp, too, because he was as tough as it was. But in later years he saw more and more that no man can stay tough enough long, himself included, cannot go on enjoying the pain he causes, and even less the pain he absorbs, cannot go on ignoring the suffering of the men and boys the team would shed, adding their crushed egos to its own, unifying the survivors with glue melted down from the carcasses of the destroyed. The survivors have come through the selection process. They are the strong. The thirty boys and men cut each summer are vital not only for the bodies and sweat they contribute to scrimmages, but also because, once cut and sent home, they represent all outsiders, all non-team members, the non-elite that the now elite can exclude from itself. No team can exist without excluding all but its own, and this precious ability is forged each summer in training camp. The team is the team, and the publicity man does not belong, nor the trainers, nor visiting former players, even former teammates. The owner does not belong, nor reporters traveling with the team, nor Doc Flaherty, nor the coaches. Even some of the team's own players do not belong. Jonesy, the left-footed kicker who only kicks, does not belong; injured players who are not playing do not belong. Any player suddenly discovered to have odd-ball interests does not belong and will be closed out at once as definitely as if he were an epileptic. The others would feel they could not understand him, and therefore could not rely on him in a crisis. This could happen in midseason because the team was losing, and if it did happen would accelerate the losing. But mostly it happened in training camp.

"Remember Foster Newton?" Craig asks.

"You mean Fig Newton," says Boyle caustically.

Foster Newton was a rookie end from Princeton. In mid-training camp a short story appeared in the *Saturday Evening Post* called "The Ball Carrier." It was by Foster Newton.

In the locker room a veteran end from Georgia named Dusty Plog read "The Ball Carrier" aloud in stentorian tones and a cornpone version of a Princeton accent. Two dozen other players crowded around to listen.

"Wayne Savage took the ball and faded to pass," intoned Plog.

Newton, standing by the door with a canvas bag of balls over his shoulder, said in an anguished voice: "Come on, fellas, let's get out on the field."

"Hold on," said Plog. "You men ain't heard what this Wayne Savage done next."

Craig watched Newton, who stood by the door scraping the cement with his cleats, not knowing whether to go or to stay.

"Stiff arming the safety man, Savage broke into the clear."

"Way to go, Savage," somebody cried.

Plog read on until Savage crossed the goal line. "Three cheers for Wayne Savage, guys," Plog demanded.

The cheers rang out. Some of the players were laughing and wiping tears from their eyes. Foster Newton stared at the cement floor.

On the field after that, first Plog, then several others as well, mocked Newton's every move.

"And Foster Newton makes a savage catch."

"And it's a savage block by Foster Newton."

"When you put that helmet on, Newton, let's put it on savagely."

"Foster Newton listens savagely to instructions from the coach."

The coaches did nothing to stop this, and Boyle in the Five-Thirty Club began to refer to Newton as Fig. The tag of course stuck.

On the field after that: "And Fig Newton does savage push-ups."

"Fig Newton savagely fumbles the ball."

A few nights later, Newton rapped on Boyle's door. "I think I better go home."

"We're sorry to lose you," Boyle lied. "Here's a voucher for your plane ticket."

Craig remembers that he saw the cruelty but did nothing.

But what was there to do? He might have offered friendship, for Newton all but cried out for help. But Newton was doomed and no rookie, Craig included, wanted to go near for fear of being sucked down with him.

Craig picks up a blade of grass and sucks on it. "At least he was man enough to leave."

"What do you suppose he wrote that idiotic story for?" asks Boyle.

"He wanted to be a writer."

"I hope he turned out a better writer than he was a football player."

The team, Craig reflects, is a communistic society. Everyone contributes his maximum, and the team is what counts, not any individual member. That is why it can be so harsh toward its own members. Pro football is a cruel and ruthless way of life. Although all the players have been to college, and some intellectually are very bright, nonetheless the mental level of the team as a whole—its attitudes—is on the level of schoolboys. The humor is schoolboy humor, and the cruelty is schoolboy cruelty. The players have the schoolboy's lack of interest in any form of sophistication—except the sophisticated brand of football they play. Conversation invariably is shop talk—very very technical. Craig has found that he cannot speak to his teammates of that part of life that troubles him, because this is serious stuff and they always react to serious stuff by mocking it. Craig no more wants to be mocked than the next man, but he might have risked mockery. What he cannot risk is the chance that his teammates will find out who he really is, will decide he does not fit in, and will slowly, inexorably close him out.

King Farouk did not fit in, nor Billy Botts, nor Fig Newton nor hundreds of others, and they disappeared. Every player now playing will not fit in eventually, succumbing to an unwillingness to stick his head in the hole anymore, or perhaps only the inability to do so, which is a kinder way to say it. The kindest way to say it is supposed to be "old age"—as if any reference to that can be kind. Every player will succumb unwillingly. They will wait all winter for contracts which do not come; a few will then insist on a final chance, and at the end of the summer weeks will be cut like any rookie—except that Boyle, who respects the pride of old, formerly great players, will announce to the press that they have "retired." But who ever retires, especially an athlete only, say, thirty-five who is sure he has one year left, just one more chance to dig the old shoulder into somebody, and to hear the noise of the lines coming together, and of the distant crowd, and to taste the dirt and sweat in his mouth, and to feel the love of teammate for teammate in the heat of the game.

Craig knows it will happen to him. An athlete faces old age twice, the first time when he reaches thirty. And so in a sense he faces death twice, too, faces debilitated powers, unwantedness, thoughts of mortality—which is perhaps more than any man ought to be asked to bear twice.

Somewhere an owl hoots. The moonlight paints the field with a sheen of illusion.

"Shall we walk back to the Inn together?" suggests Boyle.

"Why not."

All of the players will not fit in sooner or later, and then will be shed ruthlessly. Such ruthlessness in the face of years of love and devotion is hard to understand if the game is really only a game. Of course it is not a game; it is two other things, a ruthless quest for perfection on the one hand, and an entertainment spectacle on the other. Every aging perfectionist ceases in time to close in any further on the ideal of perfection; every aging comedian loses the knack of making the mob laugh. Boyle understands this, Craig knows. Boyle always has new actors ready to come onstage.

The game goes on, and the nation is full of ex-players who never again will fit in anywhere; ex-players who go out into the world with false hopes along with their false front teeth and their wrecked knees and no reputation that can be sold anywhere. And they must begin again at thirty-five or so, on nothing. Craig does not mean to blame the game, for it is not the game's fault. Many players go out into the world as beer salesmen and insurance agents, and a few as lawyers and doctors and dentists, and a lot seem happy to become coaches. So why worry about the weak, who are doomed anyway?

In the hall, the owner and player bid each other good night. Boyle imagines they have shared some intense communion in the night. Craig knows they have not.

He goes up to his room thinking: The trouble with me is that I have begun to see myself in everyone, even in the King Farouks and Fig Newtons and Billy Bottses, and I have learned to think too much and suffer too much, and life is easier if you see it as most of these rookies see it—as the simple matter of bashing the guy in front of you over and over again. I used to see it that way myself, but I don't anymore, and maybe I have been hit in the head too much.

When he is almost asleep his door opens, and a flashlight beam shines in on his face. The beam crosses to Pennoyer's bed, then is withdrawn, and the door closes.

Craig hears the muffled voices in the hall.

"Anybody missing?"

"Ox Polski and Gardner."

"That'll cost 'em two hundred and fifty bucks each."

"Polski had some pillows rolled up under his blanket. I knew it couldn't be him—it was too small."

"He should have stuck an armchair under there."

"The other intellectual didn't even bother to pull the bed-spread down."

"If Mean Gene's that stupid, we ought to fine him more."

"They said he was mean. They never said he was smart."

The voices drift down the hall.

In the other bed, Pennoyer mutters: "A thirty-five-year-old man ought to be able to get some sleep without having flash-lights shined in his face in the middle of the night."

Polski and Gardner, shoes in hand, are caught trying to sneak back to their room at midnight. They explain that they were appearing without fee at the California State Orphanage at Sonoma. They bitterly resent being fined.

"Why didn't you ask permission?" Coach Dreuder demands.

"Suppose you said no?" asks Mean Gene Gardner.

"Then it's no."

"But we promised," says Polski. "The kids were counting on us."

"The fine sticks. Now get to bed." Coach Dreuder, in his pajamas, goes back to his own room. He will have to find a way to remit the fines—but not until the team leaves this place. Otherwise, he tells himself, half the team will stay out all night every night.

In the morning it is warm and sunny, but on the field the players are edgy and the practice is flat. Boyle, who has taken part in the calisthenics wearing a sweatsuit, kneels at the side-line watching the practice, and he knows it is flat and after-ward says as much to Dreuder.

"I hope they sharpen up by Sunday."

"Right now they're not thinking about the game at all."

They watch the players trooping across the street toward their showers.

"Well," says Dreuder, "I've been in this game twenty-five years, and I've never learned how to tell if a team is 'up' for a game."

This is true, but not the same thing. What is certain is that if the players don't run new and unfamiliar plays sharply and eagerly in practice this week there is no chance they will do so in the game Sunday.

In the locker room beside the Inn's empty swimming pool, there is more grumbling.

"What do they make us stay at this dump for."

"There aren't even enough showers, for God's sake."

Lunch is Campbell's vegetable soup, green salad, slices of ham, roast beef and cheese, and Jell-O for dessert. The beverage is iced tea. The big, healthy young men, almost all of them wearing crew cuts, sit in the dining room with their muscles bulging. They wear sports shirts and sweaters, or sweaters over T-shirts. An outsider might think they all look alike; and since most of them are complaining about something, they all sound alike.

The afternoon meetings end at three thirty, whereupon bored players strike out for San Francisco. Some don't get back on time, and there are more fines.

The next day's practice starts as badly as the first. The team is leaden.

"Talk it up," Dreuder shouts. "Let's get a little life in this thing."

"Talk it up, you guys, talk it up," Polski's voice cries. A few other players take up the chant, but it soon dies out. The squad is broken down into groups. The linemen drill at one end of the field, the backs and ends catch passes thrown over the middle by Pennoyer and by Sal Rocco, the second string quarterback.

Ball after ball is fired. Too many are dropped. Finally Pennoyer, in disgust, throws one as far as he can. The receiver is Craig, who sprints after a ball thrown sixty yards in the air.

"Look out," Mel Slade screams.

The thrown ball has drifted out of bounds, where a young woman with a baby carriage watches practice. Craig, looking back over his shoulder for the ball, doesn't see them.

"Look out—" The whole team screams.

Craig spies the baby carriage, glances back for the ball which he catches in one hand, and then hurdles the baby carriage—he sails over it without breaking stride. He falls on the other side, but rolls over and springs to his feet without having dropped the ball.

"Way to go, Duke!"

It is such a fantastic feat that the team breaks into spontaneous applause and whistling.

"How to go, Duke."

Dreuder says to Boyle: "Christ, what an athlete!"

"I thought sure we were going to kill a baby or a halfback or both."

The team comes alive. A line of chatter springs up, the

175

receivers have stopped dropping balls—they begin counting consecutive balls caught without a miss. It gets up to twenty-seven when a pass from Pennoyer skitters off Donald Fox's fingertips. Their teammates razz and boo both of them.

Dreuder blows his whistle and the herd of linemen lumbers in from the far end of the field.

"Moo," go the backs and ends, imitating cattle. "Moo, moo."

In the shower room after practice no one grumbles. Ox Polski talks about his infant son who died last winter of leukemia. "In one way it's a blessing, because I know he's happy in heaven, and if he lived I'd be worrying that he might turn out bad, and maybe end up in the electric chair." Polski says to Gardner, "For all you know, Gene, your boy could turn out bad and end up in the electric chair."

"If he keeps on the way he's going," says Gardner, whose son is five years old, "he can't miss."

Boyle and the coaches are undressing in the lifeguard's room. Dinsmore, the end coach, who has stayed behind to watch Jones practice field goals, enters. "Jonesy was hitting 'em pretty good," he says with a pleased smile.

That afternoon in the meeting they watch the Forty-Niners against the Bears the previous weekend. The offense studies new blocking on the 28 and 49 sweeps, and the defense is given keys designed to stop the Forty-Niners' screen pass before it gets started.

Friday's practice is as good. Dreuder announces that all fines will be rescinded if they beat San Francisco. Everybody cheers.

That night, Craig sits out on the front steps with some of his teammates. The game is on all of their minds, but no one talks of it.

"I don't like to actually hurt people," Polski says.

"I like to hurt them," says Gardner. He lights a cigarette.

"I just like to make a clean tackle," adds Polski. "It gives me great satisfaction to make a clean tackle."

"I like to hurt them," says Gardner. "I like to hit them so hard they don't get up."

"But why?"

"Why do you think they call him Mean Gene?" asks Slade with a grin.

"I like to knock people around, I guess. Before I was married, I never cared for girls much—you have to treat girls gentle, and it sort of went against my grain."

Slade says, "We all like to hit, I guess. Otherwise we'd be baseball players or some other type of non-contact athlete."

They sit smoking.

"You can hear the birds," says Polski.

"I sat here many a night when I was a rookie," says Lincoln Hamilton.

"Me, too," says Craig.

"My first year we trained in Oregon," says Polski.

"That was a good camp," says Slade.

Hamilton puffs on a cigar: "You 'member that cat one year wore tight pants and Italian suede shoes and done drove up in a sports car?"

"A defensive back from U.C.L.A."

"I don't recollect his name. They run him off too fast."

"You didn't see many sports cars in those days," says Craig.

"I guess the coaches didn't hold with them suede shoes none, neither."

"But Gene," says Polski earnestly, "I just don't understand liking hurting people."

Craig watches the coals glow as cigarettes are inhaled. He listens to the conversation of his teammates. He feels their warmth all around him. It is comforting not to have to face the world alone.

CHAPTER | 14

There is a place up near Kezar Stadium with a vista over-looking the Golden Gate Bridge, and after practice Saturday morning Craig makes his way up there and stands gazing at the bridge for a long time. He remembers his surprise the first year to find it red, not golden at all. He remembers one year driving out to see it in a taxi, only to find it so shrouded in fog that only the base of the near stanchion was visible. None-theless it thrilled him then as it does every season, and when he got back to the hotel he made the mistake of talking about it, and someone, Dusty Plog he thinks, said: "You a bridge fancier, Duke?"

The warning light went on in Craig's brain.

"What do you fancy most, Duke?"

It was all very light. "The only bridge I like is the kind you play for money," Craig said, shutting it off at once, ordering himself to be more careful in the future.

Now he watches a freighter, very tiny so far away, heading under the Golden Gate and out to sea. He stoops for a blade of grass and sucks it for a time, while romantic longings col-lide inside him.

For dinner he goes to the Blue Fox with Gardner, Joe Morris, and Mel Slade. The restaurant proves too elegant for the other three, and it adjoins the city morgue besides.

"This steak tastes like they cut it off one of those stiffs next door."

"In a place like this, it was probably a vintage stiff, though."

"Get a whiff of that cheese?"

"It smells like the inside of a Globetrotters' sneaker."

Afterward, four very big men in topcoats, they walk along a street of honky-tonks.

Doormen try to hustle them inside: "Fifty beautiful girls, fifty."

But the game is on their minds and they are too restless to sit down anywhere.

They hop aboard a cable car which rumbles and grinds partway up Nob Hill toward the hotel. But the cable car is too noisy and too slow and they have ridden cable cars too many other seasons.

Jumping off, they walk uphill through Chinatown.

"Step inside, mister. Beautiful Chinese girls."

At the hotel they wait at the newsstands for the early editions of the Sunday morning papers. Slade leafs through some girlie magazines. Pennoyer comes up and stands picking his teeth.

Soon a dozen players wait for the papers to arrive. They want to see what the papers say about tomorrow's game.

"Where'd you go to eat?" Gardner asks Polski.

"DiMaggio's."

"Any good?"

"Not bad."

A man hurries in under a bundle of papers—when it drops with a thump beside the newsstand, all the players crowd forward with their money.

Craig, waiting at the elevator, reads the front page headlines.

"Hello there."

To his astonishment it is Margie. For a moment his face is suffused with delight. But he cuts this off abruptly.

"How do you do?"

"Good to see you again."

"Good to see you."

Margie nods to the other players. Then the elevator doors open and they all board, Margie trailed by a bellboy carrying her suitcase.

In her hand is a slip of paper. It bears her room number and its price. As she pretends to study the figures, Craig sees that her room is 1422.

The elevator stops at the fourteenth floor.

"This way, miss," says the bellboy.

"Good night, gentlemen," she says. "Good luck tomorrow."

As the elevator continues on up, Craig is having a nervous reaction. His hands sweat. He wonders if it shows on his face.

Craig and Pennoyer enter their room. Craig deposits his paper. "I'm going downstairs and buy some aspirin."

Pennoyer watches him narrowly.

"I've got a headache."

Pennoyer says stolidly: "Curfew is eleven."

"I've got to get something for this headache."

179

Pennoyer pulls the sports section out of his paper. Craig has paused at the door.

"If there's a bed check, tell them I went to get some aspirin."

From behind his paper, Pennoyer grunts.

The elevator drops to the fourteenth floor. Craig walks along a dim corridor. Suddenly a door opens—and Craig finds himself face to face with F. X. Boyle.

"Good evening, my boy," says the owner expansively.

"I didn't realize you were on this floor," says Craig.

"How do you feel, my boy?"

"Great. Just great."

"I thought I'd go down and get a paper."

"Yes, they're in now."

"Well, curfew is at eleven," the owner jokes. "I'd better hurry."

"Same here. I've got to see one of the boys first." This is a mistake, and Craig knows it at once.

"Oh? I didn't know we had anybody on this floor besides myself."

"Oh, yes," says Craig, moving off.

Boyle descends to buy his paper. Something strikes him as false, and he isn't sure what to do.

Crossing to the desk, he asks for his team's rooming list, but the night clerk doesn't recognize him, and refuses.

"I suggest you hand it over before you find yourself in bad trouble," Boyle snaps. This is the first he realizes how upset he is.

"My instructions—"

"Do you know who I am?"

"No, sir."

It might be sorted out calmly, but Boyle is not in a calm mood. Suspicion gnaws at him. Refusing to identify himself, he orders the clerk to phone the manager.

"But he's retired for the night, sir."

"What is your name?"

Intimidated by Boyle's wrath, the clerk phones the manager, and Boyle has the satisfaction of listening to this sleepy fellow's apologies. For a moment this soothes Boyle.

The chastened clerk produces the rooming list, which Boyle studies.

"I'm terribly sorry, sir."

Boyle ignores him.

"It's just that I had no way of knowing who you were."

The clerk, moistening his lips, says: "It was for your own

protection, you wouldn't want us to furnish the list to just—just anybody."

Suspicion has become certainty; there are no players on the fourteenth floor.

"Will you kindly shut up."

Another certainty is screeching in Boyle's ears. Crossing to the house phones, he asks the operator: "Do you have a Mrs. Berger registered here?"

"That's room 1422. Shall I connect you, sir?"

But Boyle hangs up. For a moment he rubs his eyes. Craig has never been in trouble before. Perhaps it should be over-looked—

But it is not one player. The integrity of his team is at stake.

Boyle's stomach begins to burn, and for a moment he feels dizzy. He has never made a compromise with what is right, and he does not intend to start now. He phones Coach Dreuder.

Beady Stein answers. "We're watching a movie on TV."

"I'll be right up." He shoves gum in his mouth.

In the elevator Boyle feels sick with dread, or perhaps it is grief. Thirty-five players depend on his judgment. How could Craig betray him this way? If Craig has no honor left, who has?

Stein, in pajamas, opens the door. There are liquor bottles and a cardboard ice bucket on a sideboard—left over from the Five-Thirty Club this afternoon. Boyle downs a glass of ice water. It seems to cool his stomach.

"Curfew is eleven," he says.

"They're pretty reliable the night before the game," answers Dreuder.

"Are you going to make a bed check?"

"They'll all be in tonight."

"I'd make a bed check."

"Oh, Christ," says Stein.

"I have the feeling you'll find one bed empty."

Coach Dreuder looks at him: "Who did you see?"

But Boyle still hopes a bed check will prove him wrong. "Maybe you'd better just make the bed check."

Stein looks at Dreuder, who nods. Stein begins to put his clothes on. After dressing, the assistant coach crosses to his suitcase and gets out his chrome-plated, three-battery flash-light.

"Wait till midnight," Dreuder cautions. "The night before a game is not the night you want to nick somebody."

Stein phones down to the desk for a passkey, and a clerk to accompany him on a tour of the team's rooms.

At midnight the bed check starts. Some of the rooms are still bright when Stein opens the door. "Get that TV off and get to bed," Stein growls.

Boyle trails Stein and the clerk down the hall.

"Get that TV off and get to sleep."

The flashlight beam probes other rooms already dark.

Passing the elevator, Boyle says: "I'll be in my suite. Call me when you finish." His stomach burns so much he must go back to his room for his pills. In any case, he doesn't want to be there when they find Craig's bed empty.

The elevator drops to the fourteenth floor. In the dim corridor Boyle stands outside room 1422. He imagines he hears Craig's voice in there, and other sounds he wishes did not exist.

She sits Buddha-fashion on the bed, laughing.

"You looked so surprised to see me."

"I *was* surprised," Craig concedes.

"All the color drained out of your face."

She has her hands clasped in front of her nose as if in prayer, but behind them she is smiling.

"In a blasphemous kind of way, you look like you're praying," Craig says.

"Blasphemous?"

"With those things sticking out over your arms." He pokes gently with his forefinger.

Her eyes close; she concentrates on what he is doing. But she is still smiling.

"I had no idea you were coming out here," he says.

"I didn't know myself until yesterday. And then it turned out we were getting in so late I was afraid I wouldn't even see you."

He pushes her back so her hair is on the pillow. "If you open your eyes now, you'll see me."

Below her window, the city drops toward the bay. They look down on dark rooftops, and the lighted ravines that are streets. The bay is dark and vast except for points of lights that are ships, and the scintillating bridge slicing across it like a scimitar.

Wrapped in a blanket, they sit on the bed which they have pulled close to the window.

"I'll bet all the team rooms face the courtyard," says Margie.

She is proud of the view she can offer him.

"Always. Football players spend hours looking into courtyards hoping we might see something."

"Do you ever?"

"Never. Ten seasons of wasted hours."

His right arm is around her under the blanket; his other hand is on her stomach. She holds both her hands over his.

"I love San Francisco," says Craig. "When I was a rookie we were having a wretched season, couldn't move the ball, couldn't score. Then we came here and scored five touchdowns. I got three myself. And after that we were all right."

She is amused by this idea. "Is the number of touchdowns the way you tell if you like a city?"

"I don't know. But I hate Chicago because of the Bears. And I've never felt comfortable in Cleveland."

"I like San Francisco, too," Margie says.

"But it's the hills, the bridges, the views, that you like."

"More than that. I like it because when I was in college we used to come up here to play California and Stanford. They're across the bay." When she points, the blanket slips from her shoulder and a breast escapes.

He watches her draw the blanket around herself again. "Were you a cheerleader?" he asks.

He is trying to imagine her ten years younger, a girl in a thick sweater and brief skirt and long cold legs leaping about in front of a screaming grandstand—the essence of young American girlhood.

"No. I was just a girl in college, and piling into rickety old cars and driving to games was the thing to do." She describes a game in Berkeley across the bay, and after it a Fiji party in the Phi Gamma Delta fraternity house. The girls wore cellophane hula skirts and the boys wore swimsuits (the motif being imitation south sea island) and they ate pineapple on the floor until someone set a girl's cellophane skirt on fire. Afterward Margie slept in the Berkeley chapter of her sorority— Kappa Gamma Gamma—and Sunday they all drove home.

Talking of her college days she seems wistful. "College is a silly time," she says. She laughs and tells him of hoping for dates with boys who usually never asked her, and trying to avoid boys she didn't like but knew were going to ask her—

"The worst was hoping against hope to be the Rose Bowl Queen."

"Were you Rose Bowl Queen?"

"Judy Hemple got it. All I got was to be one of the princesses."

Her tone is bitter: "You've seen the Rose Bowl pageant?"

"On television."

"There were six princesses my year. We all had our own floats and they paraded us around the field at half time. Only

183

the queen's float was twice as grand as ours. When all the floats came together in a cluster, there was Judy on her throne, lording it over us, smirking."

He laughs at her. "Still rankles, doesn't it?"

"I felt so humiliated. I was much prettier than she was. I hated her."

"Poor Margie."

"It sounds so silly now, and it was so important then. My only chance to be Rose Bowl Queen." She gives a wry laugh.

That she is confident of her beauty, and impressed by it, and prizes it, surprised Craig at first. Why make so much of what is only an accident of birth? But now he sees that her beauty and his football skill are essentially similar: accidents of birth, which, however, formed their personalities, made a certain kind of life possible, separated them forever from other people—and which in effect exposed them like two flowers to brief and short-lived glory. Nor was the gift at birth sufficient. Each of them had to learn to use it, perfect it, protect it, he via years of training and self-denial, she by learning about clothes and hairdos and jewelry and makeup, learning how best to accentuate her beauty, by learning also how to walk and talk and laugh and listen.

Craig has one hand on her hip, the other on her flat stomach, and he turns her slightly to kiss her. They gaze down on the city and the rim of lights across the dark bay.

"Football players don't converse about sex much," says Craig presently. "Did you know that?"

"I'm not surprised."

"What does that mean?"

"I knew quite a few of them in college."

"Did they tend to maul you less than other boys?"

She laughs. "Much less. It almost gave me an inferiority complex."

"Almost," Craig says, amused.

"We used to wait for them after the games, then all go off to parties and things. Always big groups. Always very platonic. I always felt they were more interested in being with each other than in being with girls. Most of them got really quite shy when alone with you."

"And?"

She laughs. "Well, I had a lot of pleasant evenings, but nothing very exciting."

"I'm glad to hear that," says Craig seriously. "Because I always wondered whether Texas was different, or I was odd, or something."

"They always seemed terribly wary of making the wrong move with a girl."

"The religious influence is still very strong in football. That might have something to do with it."

"Football is a game of terrible rectitude," says Margie.

But Craig is serious. "In training camp every summer, the rookies have to put on a show for the veterans. They sing their college songs, or perform skits mocking the coaches. Sometimes they tell mildly dirty jokes. But one summer we had a rookie get up and start telling about this masturbation contest he won. You could see the veterans start to squirm. They didn't think it a bit funny. Soon they started hollering: get him off there."

Craig is silent, remembering.

"Boyle made a terrific stink. He chewed out the veterans' committee which organized the show, and within two years he had traded both those guys. The rookie, of course, they cut."

Presently Craig says: "It seems to me about half the big football colleges in Texas are run by churches. The Methodists run S.M.U., the Baptists run Baylor and Hardin-Simmons. T.C.U. is the Disciples of Christ, and so on. That means a divinity school on the campus, preachers around all the time, and all students must take an hour of religion a week."

Margie says: "Elsewhere in the country the Catholic colleges have all those wonderful teams."

Craig asks: "Are you Catholic?"

"I was once."

"What does that mean?"

But she drops her eyes. "I don't know."

"Religion isn't going to church. It's a pervasive thing. It pervades football. Religion is in slogans like 'sound mind in sound body' and 'straight and narrow.' The coach of the Dallas Cowboys leads the Lord's Prayer in the locker room before games. Did you know that?"

"No," she says, surprised.

"We say the Lord's Prayer, too. I don't know who started it. It happened when Dreuder became coach. Five minutes before we take the field, he and the coaches go out of the locker room, leaving us players alone. For a moment no one says anything. Then somebody coughs, or drags a cleat across the floor. Then Joe Morris, the defensive captain, says something like: 'We gotta beat these guys, Big Red.' Then everybody starts to holler. Then it stops and we join hands and say the Lord's Prayer."

Moved, Margie says: "I think that's very nice."

"Sometimes it makes me choke up. I know it helps us play better. The team spirit, the love we have for one another, is very intense during that prayer. It's the most religious experience I've ever had."

Her eyes are misty, and she kisses his cheek. "You're very sweet."

They look down on the city and the bay.

"A lot of the lights have gone off down there now."

"It must be very late."

He can feel her body against his under the blanket.

Presently he says: "Sometimes I think that moment of prayer is the best part of all this."

She says: "Because it means that without each other, you're nothing."

"I always thought marriage meant that, too."

"It didn't for me," she says in a low voice.

"Nor for me either." Though he hadn't wanted to tell her this, his love for her at that moment is too strong to hold anything back.

They lie back, wrapped in the blanket, her face against his, the lengths of their bodies touching.

"What's your husband going to do."

"Oh, I expect he's going to divorce me."

Craig is silent.

With false brightness, Margie says: "I saw the girl he's interested in, the other day."

Surprised, Craig says: "But I thought you said there was no other girl."

"Well there is, it seems."

The false brightness is gone from her voice now. "A friend pointed her out to me in a restaurant. She's tall and thin. About twenty-one years old, I should think."

Her voice is husky. "My friend, the woman I was with, said: 'Margie. I don't think she looks a day younger than you do.' "

She is near tears and Craig holds her, thinking of the "friend." The bitch. Oh, the cattiness of women to each other.

"My husband likes them young, you see. He's forty-two himself, and it seems I make him feel old."

When he kisses her eyes they are damp, and he can feel her chest heaving against his as she fights to hold back sobs.

"Old age is creeping up on both of us," he says.

She begins to cry and he kisses her eyes, her chin, her throat, her breasts, trying to convince her in the only way he can think of that she is as lovely, as exciting as she has ever been, a flower newly bloomed, petals opening to receive her lover the sun.

186

"Do you feel old now?"

"No."

"I wish you were sixteen and I was your first man."

"At sixteen I didn't even let boys kiss me."

"Seventeen, then."

"I was about twenty-five. I was an awful prude."

Craig says: "I feel about sixteen. I could go on and on doing this to you and never stop and never get tired of doing this to you."

"We're both sixteen, and this is terribly illicit, but I'm glad we're doing it, it's so nice."

"You don't feel old anymore, do you?"

"Oh, oh, oh, don't talk, just do it, oh, oh, oh, oh I love you, Wallace Craig."

CHAPTER | 15

Sometimes they doze, awakening to find each other in the dark to writhe joyously or luxuriously, tiredly, perhaps falling asleep that way, on their sides, coupled. Or else they lie awake talking in low voices.

When they notice the ceiling start to lighten, they sit wrapped in the blanket and watch the dawn come up over San Francisco. It comes up slowly behind the mountains across the bay.

Now there is a slash of rose crayon atop the ridge of mountains, and then the sun explodes above it, and into their eyes. It glints off the corners of buildings near them but below them the rooftops of San Francisco are still dark the streetlights still glowing in the ravines of the streets Now the surface of the bay turns purple, then mauve. The peaks of the bridge turn red. The lights on the bridge wink out. The bay has turned to gold.

They rub noses, delighted with the dawn that is now over.

"That was nice."

"Let's take a shower."

"One shower or two?"

"One if you like But you musn't get my hair wet. I have to go on television later, and it is not a rainy day."

Soapy water runs down their bodies.

"I can't get over seeing you naked."

"I look just like other girls."

"It's not that. It's just that with clothes on you look so slim. But really you have a very emphatic figure."

She laughs, pleased.

Both are famished, there is a basket of fruit and nuts on a sideboard, and they eat all of this.

When she sits cross-legged on the bed again, he kisses her knees.

"Do that," she suggests.

"No."

"Why?"

"I just—couldn't," Craig says.

After a moment she says: "You don't hate me for suggesting it?"

"No, why should I?"

"I suppose it might seem disgusting to you."

Since it did seem disgusting, though already less so, he denies this.

But he is interested. "It's something that's been done to you before?"

She grins. "I didn't say that."

"But it has been, hasn't it?"

She nods.

"Your husband?"

"No."

"Before you were married or after?"

"Before."

He doesn't suppose she stayed virginal until her marriage. But he knows little about her sexually, and wants to know everything, particularly this.

"The strange thing," she says, "is that the man who did that to me—well, I never made love with him."

Craig finds this hard to believe. "Why not?"

"Because I didn't—love him."

"But you liked that."

"Oh yes. That was splendid."

"But how can you permit that, and not go to bed with the man?"

She laughs. "I suppose it sounds, well, curious."

Presently she explains: "I was a virgin at the time, and I used to date him. We were sitting in a drive-in movie necking and he wanted to make love to me—he had me half-undressed—but I wouldn't let him, and suddenly he started doing that."

"Then what?"

"I was very surprised and very excited and I didn't really care about the guy. I figured if he wanted to, let him."

"And it was pleasant?"

"Delightful."

He is amazed to be able to talk about this.

"Rather an intimate topic of conversation, wouldn't you say?"

They both laugh. She sits cross-legged on the bed. She has lovely shoulders. The line from her collarbone curving out to the point of her breasts is lovely too.

189

"Tired?"

"No, not at all. Are you?"

"I feel wonderful."

He pushes her back on the pillow.

"How do you feel now?"

"Even—better."

When he enters his own room he can hear Pennoyer in the bathroom, and he sits in an armchair reading the paper until the quarterback, shaving kit in hand, comes out.

"Well, well," Pennoyer mutters.

"Good morning."

"Get rid of that headache yet?"

Craig has to smile. "It's gone altogether."

"Swell."

Deadpan as always, Pennoyer packs his suitcase.

"I'll go in and shave," Craig says.

As Craig withdraws his shaving kit from his bag, Pennoyer says: "Stein ran a bed check."

"What did you tell him?"

"That you had a headache."

"Did he believe you?"

"Would you have?"

Craig shrugs and enters the bathroom. But he is no longer smiling.

When he comes out he considers trying to get some sleep. But he is not sleepy so he goes down and out through the lobby with Pennoyer, who wears dark glasses and looks as mysterious as a film star. Outside it is very bright and warm, though the month is November. They listen to a cable car grinding up California Street. Craig squints against the sun. San Francisco is always warmer than one expects, Craig thinks. He feels alert and hungry.

During the steak breakfast Craig is aware of the coaches eyeing him. But nothing is said. He goes back upstairs to his room, where he packs, then sits with the papers. Again he considers taking a nap, but doesn't feel tired. He is eager to play football.

To avoid a possible scene, he delays going down to the bus until the last moment. As he comes out of the hotel his teammates are boarding the buses. Some kids clamor for his autograph, which he gives. A man comes up and introduces himself and his wife. Craig smiles and shakes hands with them.

From the corner of his eye, he sees Dreuder watching him; the coach grinds out a cigarette.

190

As he waits to board the bus, Craig feels a hand on his arm.

It is F. X. Boyle.

"Morning, my boy."

"Great day for a game," offers Craig.

"How do you feel?"

"Great."

The owner's face darkens. "I wondered if there was, well, something you might like to talk over with me."

Craig frowns. "I can't think of anything."

The owner's lips compress in a thin line. "I thought there might be something."

They stare at each other, a confrontation Craig would have preferred to avoid.

"I can't imagine what you mean," he says. Unsmiling, he steps up into the bus.

There is an empty double seat, but if he takes it, Boyle might sit down beside him. Instead, he wedges himself onto what is left of the double seat occupied by Ox Polski.

But Boyle does not get on. Stein counts heads, and after conferring with Dreuder outside, gives the command to the bus driver.

"Okay, roll 'em."

Craig moves into the empty seat, and stares pensively out at passing San Francisco.

At Kezar Stadium, after he has been taped, Craig stands forcing thigh pads into his skintight silver pants.

"How's your headache?"

It is Dreuder, looking grim.

Craig feels that all of this is childish, but knows they do not think so.

"Great."

"That's good. That's very good. Because you're going to run kickoffs back today, and I may have to use you on other special teams as well. So I hope you're feeling perfect."

Dreuder stares at him, then turns away.

Craig is furious. Dreuder is sticking him on the suicide teams (like any rookie) to punish him. He has broken a rule and violated the code as well, and that makes him a child who must be punished. F. X. Boyle is mixed up in this, Craig knows. Boyle is horrified and aghast, and this is none of his business and would be funny except that you can depend on him to make it his business. His team and the sanctity of his players are sacred to him. Craig hopes that Boyle at least does not know that Margie is involved; if he does know, he will make trouble for her, too.

Angrily Craig jerks his belt tight. The hell with F. X. Boyle.

Outside, Craig fields punts in the sun. The stands are half full now. Dreuder calls Winfield Green aside. Green is the fastest player on the team.

"Green, I'm holding you off the kickoff return team." Ignoring the puzzled Green, Dreuder shoots Craig a hard look. This makes Green stare at Craig, who in turn stares at the turf.

"Ball!" Mel Slade screams.

"Mine," shouts Craig.

He locates the punt dropping nose first out of the sun, catches it, lopes forward four strides, then throws the ball to Pete, the trainer, who relays it to the center.

Later, inside the locker room, Pete moves among the players collecting bridgework. Wrapped in Kleenex, it goes into a drawer which will be locked in a gear trunk. Most of the linemen are gap-toothed now, and many of the backs. Some of the players who still have all their teeth suck on fighter's mouthpieces, softening and shaping them for the game.

"Any more valuables?" calls Pete.

A few last-minute wallets and watches are handed over. Pete locks them into the gear trunk, which is now a safe.

The players are tense, silent. The final minutes are always the same. The men feel hot and weak, they imagine they have forgotten important details or entire plays, and they ask frantic questions of the coaches.

"On the thirty-six from the spread," asks Stablinski, "do I drive him in or out?"

"Suppose we're in a zone on my side, but man to man on the other?" asks Winfield Green.

The coaches answer in soothing voices.

The suspense is overpowering. Everybody wants the game to begin.

Dreuder tells them where they stand, as if any don't know. "You lost last week. You're one game below Cleveland. You gotta keep the pressure on. You gotta win today. You can win. If you have any pride you *will* win." He is practically snarling at them.

"Win."

His voice gets stronger. "Win."

The third time, he shouts the word: "WIN!"

He strides out the door. His entourage follows.

The players are alone.

No one moves or speaks.

"Let's get 'em, Big Red," a voice shouts. Everybody hollers. Cleats bang on cement.

Outside the door, Dreuder looks at Stein and nods his head. The door is flung open and the players, some grim, some hollering, hurry out. As they come onto the field, a roar goes up.

The kickoff return team has huddled; it trots into position. Craig, who has not run a kickoff back in ten years, waits at the goal line.

Lincoln Hamilton, turning to look behind him, spies Craig. "What you doing there, Duke?"

But Craig's anger has passed. He feels both the old excitement of last night and the new excitement of this moment—eagerness to get his hands on the ball.

All his senses are alert. As the whistle blows and the ball rises into the air it seems to him he can hear the clean *thunk* of the kick sixty yards away. Now the ball gets bigger and bigger. He can see the laces clearly, then even the grain of the leather. He wets his lips, feeling the leather in his hands already.

"Mine," he shouts.

Joe Morris drifts over beside him.

"Mine," he shouts again. Four hands reach for the ball. He and Morris bump together, and Craig wrenches the ball away from him. Craig sees the scene with such clarity that even the expression on Morris' face sticks in his mind. As he starts upfield, he can see almost in slow motion every member of the Forty-Niner team as they converge in a melee to force the runback into the center of the field. They are supposed to guard their lanes, but there is always a laggard if the ball carrier can find him, and Craig's vision is so sharp that he spots this laggard at once and veers that way. As men start to get knocked down, all sorts of information registers on Craig's brain. Two men have overrun the play. Hamilton knocks his man over backward—another lane free—Craig hears the helmet strike the ground. He hears feet pounding, his own and others, feels his cleats biting the turf, and he sprints for the gap. Hands and arms lash at him—it is like plunging through bushes. He sees a face behind a cage, mouth open, toothless, and veers to miss the arms attached. He shoulders into somebody, and bounces off.

The onrushing line of Forty-Niner players swells and bursts like a tire blowing out, and Craig spurts into the clear. Even though this is the way the play is supposed to work, it almost never does, only one kick in two hundred is run back each season, and he himself hasn't run this play in ten years. Nonetheless he feels no surprise today. He sees all the patterns too sharply, is thinking too clearly. He hears all the noises as well, smells the torn-up turf, and a touchdown is what he expected

193

from the moment he caught the ball. He thinks: No one can stop me the way I feel today.

At the fifty-yard line he has only the kicker to beat, a small-ish man and normally a defensive back. Though they are closing fast, Craig reads his eyes, and sees him decide to protect the center of the field. Craig checks this against the frequency charts studied all last week. It checks. Craig shifts the ball as if to cut into the middle; his eyeballs work over that terrain; his shoulder seems to lunge that way. The kicker, who is running too, leans to protect the middle, realizes he has taken the fake, and dives for Craig, grapples with him.

But Craig, who does not intend to be stopped, goes under the tackle. The kicker has his arm and shoulder, but Craig flings him off, hears him smack the turf full length. Craig listens for the pursuit, hears the pounding rhythm broken as they have to leap over the prostrate kicker or run around him, and knows it is clear city now to the goal line. But Craig sprints all the way, the white stripes whipping past under his low-cuts; he has energy to burn. Curling back under the goalposts he thinks of Margie. A smile comes onto his face and he murmurs, that's a present for last night, and I hope you like it.

As he jogs up the sideline, his excess energy is converted into high spirits. He goes past Coach Dreuder with his nose in the air and a smirk on his face. Dreuder refuses to look at him.

But when the Forty-Niners make a field goal, Dreuder puts Winfield Green back on the kickoff return team.

Craig grins, thinking: That's one victory for my side.

Green runs the kick back to the 28-yard line. On first down Craig gains four yards on a dive play. Then he gets five on a draw. On third down with a yard to go, Pennoyer bobbles the snap, Mel Slade bumps him, almost missing the handoff—and is thrown back short of the first down.

So Craig crouches in the fullback spot to block for Jonesy's punt. Only one Forty-Niner rushes, Number 66. Craig, braced, catches him on his right shoulder, lifting him. He hears his shoulder pads creak and the man grunt, sounds that most Sundays he is not even aware of. But Number 66 is coming too fast—he goes over the top of Craig and into the punter, and all three men go down. Craig, squirming out from under, sees the penalty flag down, and Pennoyer and the Big Red offense coming back onfield. Craig is elated. He wants to run with the ball again.

On first down Craig, pass-blocking, slams into Number 52, stopping him. But the pass is incomplete. Craig shakes his pads back into place. When Pennoyer calls the same play again,

Craig stops Number 52 a second time. But the pass is intercepted. He hears the Forty-Niner players screaming "bingo, bingo." He sprints upfield ready to make the tackle, but Mel Slade gets there first. As the whistle blows, somebody smashes into Craig from the side and he goes down. His lips are caked with dirt and grass, which is not a taste he enjoys, but it reminds him of how alive he feels.

On the bench he spits out a dipperful of tepid water. His body is wet with sweat, and one of his wrists is scraped. He licks it absently.

The Forty-Niners get another field goal. The score is 7–6.

On the field again, Craig gains four yards on a draw. They hit him hard and he enjoys it. That's the way to play this game, he thinks. On second down he pass-blocks as Pennoyer throws twelve yards to Donald Fox.

On another draw, he hurdles the pile-up, running across red jerseys and silver legs. He can see even the seams of the pants and the grass stains. He gains eleven yards before they smash him down.

He runs a deep circle pattern, making it look sincere, clearing out a zone for Jake Simmons, the tight end, who gets another first down.

He runs two more hard, sharp decoy pass patterns, clearing out zones. But both passes are incomplete.

So it is third down and ten. The Forty-Niners have eight men rushing the expected pass. Craig takes the handoff from Pennoyer, slithers through the full blitz, sheds a tackler, veers to the sideline and runs forty-seven yards to his second touchdown of the day.

As he passes Dreuder this time, his smirk is broader still. The coach wears the red team blazer and a straw hat. He smokes nervously. The smirking Craig he ignores.

A warning light flashes in Craig's brain. Don't push this too far. But he ignores it.

"Heckuva game, Coach," he says exuberantly.

Dreuder does not reply.

The Forty-Niners go in for a touchdown, and the score is 14–13.

Craig skirts left end. He can see all the blocks set up in slow motion, hear each of them, and he bulls and shrugs his way forward for eight yards.

Pennoyer throws three passes in a row. Craig pass-blocks on the first two, then runs a decoy pattern deep. When Simmons grabs the ball behind him, Craig doubles back to throw himself into a possible tackler.

With first down on the fifty, Craig sweeps left end for eight, then picks his way for seven yards through fallen players on a draw play. On the next play he leads Slade into the hole, smashing a linebacker out of Slade's path.

It is second and seven. Craig knows Pennoyer will call a pass, and he wants to be the one to catch it. On the last three decoy patterns, the cornerback on that side has played him loose, taking away the deep stuff.

Waiting for the huddle to form, Craig tells Pennoyer: "He's playing three yards off me. On a square-in I can run away from him."

Pennoyer, though he pretends not even to have listened, calls this play.

But a linebacker lines up at Craig's head. At the snap, Craig gives the linebacker an outside move which doesn't take, and the linebacker flattens him.

Craig hits the ground rolling so the linebacker can't pin him, and in an instant is up and running again. But he has lost a second or more and must run the square-in pattern shallower than intended. He breaks his pattern off so sharply that the middle linebacker, who has picked him up, falls down, and Pennoyer hangs the ball out perfectly. Craig catches it on the dead run on the twenty-yard line, veers, and sprints for the corner. The safety man comes racing to cut him off, and slams him near the flag. The two of them slide across the flag in a heap. The official runs up with his arms raised, signaling a touchdown, Craig's third.

The safety man, irate, screams that Craig never crossed the line. He rips his helmet off for emphasis. He screams and curses and stamps.

"You tell him, Jack," laughs Craig.

Passing Dreuder at the bench, Craig again cannot resist. "This is the most marvelous game," he smirks.

Dreuder sucks on a blade of grass, staring out at the field.

The Forty-Niners score almost at once on a long pass. At half time the Big Red team leads by only 21–20.

In the locker room Dreuder is furious. He lashes the defensive team for making mistakes, and the offensive team for missing opportunities. "If you blow this game, you blow the season.

"You know what the score ought to be?" he shouts. "It ought to be twenty-eight to seven. At least twenty-eight to seven. Instead of that they're only one point behind."

He goes on in this vein. Craig wonders if Margie is enjoying the game. He is eager to get his hands on the ball again. He is confident that he can get at least one more touchdown before this is over. He remembers every detail of last night. In the first half he expected to score every time he took the ball. Each time he didn't he was surprised. He can smell Margie's perfume, taste her skin. He feels seven feet tall.

Stein moves to the blackboard and outlines a variation of the halfback option. The Forty-Niner secondary is coming up too fast on end runs, and the option should go. He wants the option tried the first time the Big Red gets the ball.

Pennoyer calls the play with the ball on their own seventeen-yard line. As Craig whirls for the handoff, his concentration is so acute that the parts of the play seem to fall into slots in his brain. Don't run into Pennoyer, don't snatch at the ball, and when he sticks it in your middle don't drop it. Don't cut the guards off and don't run into them—he sees them dart out of line, he ducks in behind, and from the other side of the line he knows this looks exactly like the Big Red's strong sidesweep. He races toward the sideline. The ball is tucked under his arm—this is still a run to the Forty-Niners—and he does not even feel for the laces. Above all he does not look for Slade downfield; Slade must have filtered through the line by now. He remembers not to belly the sweep too much. It has to look real, and obviously it does, for here comes the Forty-Niner secondary up to stop the run. He thinks: You boys are in for a surprise.

Straightening, he searches for Slade, finds him all alone forty yards downfield, and throws the ball carefully, confidently. He sees the safety men recover and sprint for Slade. But they are too late—the pass has perfect elevation, perfect lead. Slade makes a nervous, basket-catch of it, and runs forty more yards to the touchdown.

It is about as easy a touchdown as Craig has ever been involved in, and a stunned silence fills Kezar Stadium.

Slade runs back up the field, and he and Craig jog to the sideline together. Slade is grinning broadly.

"The perfect play."

"They never knew what hit them."

Coach Dreuder watches them. As they pass him he gives a brusque nod.

"That'll hold 'em," says Craig smugly.

Craig sits on the bench feeling alert and happy. He will meet Margie after the game. He can't wait to talk to her about all this. He remembers last night. He has had no sleep. Why isn't he tired? He not only is not tired, he can't wait to get back into the game again.

But the Big Red's eight-point lead lasts barely five plays, then is cut to one point again. The Forty-Niners seem to have shattered the Big Red defense, and Dreuder rails at the defensive players as they troop wearily off the field.

The score is 28–27, the mob is in an unroar, and the Forty-Niner defense gets tough.

Craig gains four yards through the middle. They hit him hard.

Craig takes a screen pass, but Number 52 reads it, and smashes into the middle of it screaming "Screen, screen" at the top of his lungs. Four men throw Craig for a big loss.

On third and eleven, Pennoyer passes. Craig, blocking, catches Number 52 on his shoulder, but the man is coming very hard, and the impact filters down through Craig's body all the way to his shoes.

But the pass is good for a first down. Next Craig carries on another draw, wrestling forward for five yards.

Craig leads Mel Slade into the line. About five tacklers hit Slade, and Craig goes down under all of them.

But it is first down again. Pennoyer completes three short passes in a row, Craig sprinting hard out of the backfield on decoy routes each time.

Craig runs a sweep to the left. The Forty-Niners break it up, trap him behind the line, but he wriggles through for a two-yard gain before men hit him from all sides and he goes down.

Slade gets a yard. Then Craig carries four straight times. He gets seven yards, seven, six, and nine. He has got the Big Red moving again. His body begins to feel hot from the pounding, and his mind is a little feverish, but he loves this; carrying the ball is his art form, and he knows that the picture his cleats and shoulders are painting today is epic—one of the best he has ever done. This is football. This is what he loves.

A penalty sets them back. Inexorably they smash forward again. Slade gains five yards, then three. Craig bulls into the middle for three. Pennoyer completes another pass. When not carrying the ball, Craig pass-blocks or runs a decoy route. On the nineteenth play of the series from seven yards out, Craig drives his shoulder into the line and through it, trampling bodies under his cleats, shrugging, bulling over for the touchdown, his fourth of the game.

The score is 35–27.

But this time when he leaves the field there is no smirk on his face. He feels the punishment now, and he can't catch his breath. He sits on the bench trying. His uniform is soaked with sweat, and stained with grass and mud. The bones of his shoulders feel scraped nearly raw by the pads. The tape on his leg has worked loose, tearing some skin off with it no doubt, for his flesh there feels raw also.

He hears the crowd roar. When he looks up, the Forty-Niners have scored again, and he goes back into the game. There are still four minutes to play, and their lead is cut to 35–34.

On an attempted draw play, Craig is ridden backward, and goes down on his back with men on top of him. His helmet smacks the ground.

In the huddle, Pennoyer watches him narrowly. "You all right?"

He closes his eyes, waiting for his head to clear. "Sure."

Pennoyer calls a pass. Craig, racing across the middle, reads zone. His vision seems to encompass the entire secondary, freezing every man in it while he searches for an opening in the zone—finds one. But as he runs into this gap, the secondary unfreezes. Men converge on him. The ball floats to him too slowly, a mallard. He grabs it, but a linebacker is on him. He attempts to stiff-arm the linebacker, who grabs his arm and slings him round and round and down.

Pennoyer calls another pass. Craig braces himself to pass-block, but the rush doesn't come. There is no one to hit. Blessed momentary relief. Craig feels as if he has just had a week's vacation.

He runs another draw play, their big gainer today. He gets sixteen yards, the last of them bounding from tackler to tackler, before the traffic churns him up; somebody lies across his helmet; his face is in the dirt.

He hits the hole ahead of Slade who gains four. He hurls himself into the linebacker ahead of Donald Fox, who gets four more. He races out of the backfield as a decoy as Slade plunges for six. Again Pennoyer fades to pass. Craig aims a block at Number 66, misses him completely, and the guy clobbers Pennoyer.

It is second and fifteen on the Forty-Niner 45-yard line. The blitz is on, but Craig wriggles through on the draw. Someone is on his back, slowing him enough for several others to recover and slam into him all at once.

But he has gained six yards. It is third and nine on the Forty-Niner thirty-nine. Craig stands up out of the huddle trying to catch his breath. Pennoyer looks at him, then calls a pass play. It is a play action pass, and if Craig is too tired to do much, it doesn't matter—his function is to blast into the line without the ball in order to hold the linebackers in. He does this, and the impact is as great as if he actually had the ball. Over his prostrate head the pass goes to Donald Fox, who is thrown out of bounds on the one-yard line.

They all troop downfield to the new scrimmage line. Craig is breathing hard.

"What the hell, Duke," says Pennoyer beside him. "You might as well get another TD."

Craig grins. The adrenalin courses through him, and he knows he can blast over for this touchdown too.

But a substitute comes onfield with orders from Dreuder. Slade is to carry on the thirty-six slant.

But Slade is thrown back.

On the next two downs, Dreuder sends in a substitute with orders for a certain play, and it is obvious he does not want Craig to get this touchdown.

Pennoyer kicks at the dirt after both plays are thrown back. "Childish," he mutters.

It is fourth and one yard still to go. Pennoyer throws a disgusted glance toward the bench. This time there is no substitute. He ducks into the huddle and calls Craig's number.

Craig lunges forward with the handoff, and as the seething line collapses, he dives over it into the end zone.

The mob is silent. Thousands move toward the exits.

Craig's old exuberance comes back. He wants to rub Coach Dreuder's face in it. As Jones comes onfield to kick the point, Craig says to Pennoyer: "Let me kick the sonuva bitch, Jim."

Pennoyer's leather face creases in a grin.

"Jonesy," Pennoyer orders, "hold the ball for the Duke."

"I don't know how to hold the ball."

"Try," says Pennoyer. He jogs to the sideline, where he stands watching.

Jones, mystified, gets down on one knee.

When the ball comes back, Jones bobbles it. He gets it down, tries to spin the laces away from the kicker as Pennoyer does. But as Craig strides forward, the ball is leaning sideways. Craig boots it anyway. It squirts over the line, bangs into the upright and then through for the point.

When the official's upraised arms signal this, Craig starts to laugh. By the time he reaches the bench he is virtually hysterical.

Dreuder stares at him, lips compressed.

Craig shakes his head, laughing. He is exhausted, and can't stop.

The hysteria lasts all the way to the locker room. He is laughing behind his sodden jersey as he tries to tug it off the pads and over his head. He is seated on a bench, and when the jersey comes loose, Dreuder is there standing over him.

"I can't fine you," the coach says curtly. "I promised I'd rescind the fines if we won, and I will."

This sobers Craig.

"But I won't forget this."

Craig doesn't know what to say or do, so he shrugs.

A moment later, from behind the lockers, he hears George Dreuder talking to reporters.

"Was that your game plan, Coach, to stick mostly to draws and short passes."

"No, that's the way the game developed. Pennoyer found he was getting adequate running out of Craig, and he stuck with it."

"Adequate? Craig was a one-man team."

"I didn't see it that way at all," says Dreuder coldly.

"It was all Craig the way I saw it."

"What about the offensive line?" demands Dreuder. "What about Slade and Fox. What about Pennoyer's play calling."

"I saw it as all Craig."

"Well, I saw it as a great team effort," snaps Dreuder.

Craig, slumped on his bench, gets the pads off his scraped shoulders. This is a great relief. He slides his pants down, unbelts his hip pads, and gets them off—another great relief. He looks forward to slicing the tape off his ankles and knee— the greatest relief of all.

The reporters loom over him. "To what do you attribute such a great day, Duke?"

The question tickles Craig's sense of humor, and he knows Dreuder will hear.

"I guess I got an especially good night's sleep. I felt great all day, really great." He almost tells them that all day he could see the ball so clearly that, even when it was spinning, he imagined he could read the printing. But he decides against this. The reporters wouldn't believe him, the players might mock him about it, and such a statement might make Dreuder really mad.

The reporters show him the statistics. He sees that he carried the ball twenty-two times for 167 yards, ran one kickoff back for 101 yards, caught three passes for 33 yards, threw one pass for 83 yards and a touchdown, and scored five other touchdowns and an extra point.

"That was quite a performance, Duke."

Craig smiles. He is so proud, he can't help it. But he thanks them politely for the praise, then answers their questions, though what he longs to do is get the tape off his legs. They crowd so closely around him that it is dark where he sits, and when they leave him finally it is as if the lights have come back on.

He gets his pants and socks off, and probes the slicer down

201

under the spats around his ankles, slicing the tape off cleanly there. There is a mound of dirty tape in the center of the floor; he adds his own to it. He calls out for scissors, and when a pair is tossed his way, he works the nose of them under the pink leg tape and cuts gingerly down the outside of his leg, then begins to peel it off. It hurts to pull on the tape, but it must come off. After much grimacing and waiting for the pain to abate, he gets it all off. His flesh is raw and there are many small cuts where the edge of strips have cut into the skin.

But it is off, and he is relieved. However, much gum remains stuck to the skin, so he sits naked on a rubbing table in the trainer's room and pats at it with ethyl alcohol for as long as he can stand it.

The pain is too great to rub all of it away. He goes through into the shower and lets hot water run down his tired body. When he comes out and stands on the scale, he sees he has lost eight pounds.

"That's nothing," says Ox Polski beside him. "I lost fifteen."

All this time there has been laughter and loud conversation, and at the cooler, water burbles constantly as glass after glass is downed. Craig stands among his teammates, dressing slowly, luxuriously, fond of all of them in this moment of victory.

He puts on a clean shirt and knots his silk tie and goes outside with his topcoat over his arm. Some kids there wait for autographs, which he gives, and wives and friends of the Forty-Niner players wait glumly.

As Craig separates himself from the kids, Stein leans out of the first of the team buses and calls: "This one is ready to roll. Anybody else coming?"

No one replies, and the bus motors off.

The sun is going down, and the air feels cool and clean. Craig hails a taxi and rides in it with the windows open across the Golden Gate Bridge to a French restaurant in Sausalito where he has arranged to meet Margie. He does not expect to meet football people in such a place, and he does not really care if he does. He wants to show Margie off to the whole world. He feels exuberant, confident, careless of any consequences.

She is not there yet. Extremely thirsty, he orders a Tom Collins which tastes so spectacular he drains it almost at a gulp.

Margie comes toward him, her eyes alight.

"My hero!"

"Did you enjoy the game?"

"You were spectacular."

"I almost always play well when I go to bed early the night before."

She laughs.

"Tell me the one you liked best?"

"The kickoff runback. I thought the kicker had you."

"I knew exactly when and where he'd make his move. It was like telepathy. I was surprised he even got a hand on me."

They sip drinks, replaying the game. "How did you like the seven-yard plunge? That was our sixty-seven." Craig laughs. There's a moment when you hit a line, when you feel it start to give. Every bit of power is packed behind that shoulder, and then the line sort of splits, and you're through, trampling everybody all the way to the touchdown. It gives a feeling of—of—it's fabulous."

It is all vivid in his mind. He is giddy with success. "What a fabulous day! Did you like the option pass?"

Margie's eyes meet his, grow misty; she blinks the mist away.

"What's the matter?" he asks.

"Nothing. I'm just very happy, that's all."

The restaurant is small and crowded, with lamps on each table. Craig has ordered the oldest and most expensive wine on the menu, a 1953 Chateau Margaux.

"Can you afford that?"

"Well, I can this year."

But it reminds him even in this moment of joy of the funny life he lives. The future is uncertain for everyone, but for a professional athlete most of all because he is building toward nothing. In a year or two, perhaps he won't be able to afford beer.

"But you can sell your name and fame afterward."

"Perhaps. Some players seem to manage that."

He tells her of the jobs he has had during the off-seasons. Presidents of beer companies, of a brokerage house, of two insurance companies have made him lavish promises, and he has gone to work for them.

"My first job usually would be to play golf with the boss and his cronies at his country club. The bosses always like to show you off. Then you sit around the office for a couple of weeks, all the while playing golf with the boss every Saturday. Then finally they send you out to sell something—usually something no one else can sell because it isn't any good.

"I'd give my name to the customers, and some would be impressed and want to talk football to me for two hours. But others would get very edgy. Sort of: 'You think you're better than me because you're a football star; well you gotta show me, brother.' "

"Really?"

"After a while I'd always give my name as Wallace Craig,

and if the customer didn't recognize me, I'd try to feel him out first before telling him who I was. Sometimes I wouldn't tell him at all. and probably not make the sale either, and the boss would hear about it and think: I hired Duke Craig, not just anybody, and if I'm not getting the benefit of Duke Craig, out he goes."

Margie looks at him.

"And out he went," says Craig with a smile. They both laugh. But presently their laughs fade.

"I guess it's not really too funny."

"Well, it has its funny aspects, I suppose."

Selling beer is not the life Craig is looking for, nor playing golf with bosses. It must be a career in something he could learn to be the best in the world at.

"Or the whole," he says, "I think a player's name is worth nothing on the market. The image of the football star is a myth. It's nothing but smoke, and when it blows away there's nothing there. You can see a thousand miles. For the first time you can see where you are. For all those years you haven't been able to see."

"What do the other players do?"

"Some get trainee jobs each winter. A lot of them don't even bother. They make speeches two or three times a week from January to July because it pays better than working."

"And when they finish playing?"

"They go back to the town they came from and take a small job."

She takes his hand.

"Very few football players have college degrees," Craig says. "Only five or six on our team." He drops his eyes, because this is a confession he feels he has to make. "I don't have one."

"But how—"

"You miss an awful lot of classes traveling with your college team. There are an awful lot of nights when you're too tired and beat-up to study. And then, well—nobody ever makes studying seem that important. It isn't that I failed courses. I just didn't take enough courses. The result is that now I find I've had almost no education at all."

They have ordered lobster bisque, followed by a rack of lamb. Craig is famished at first, but as the lamb is served he can feel his body cooling and stiffening, and the pain comes on. His knee begins to throb as it often does after a game, but tonight the rest of his body aches too. He loses interest in the food, but seeks to conceal this from Margie.

The waiter is at their table.

"Dessert, madame? Monsieur?"

For Craig no position is comfortable. It is all he can do to keep from squirming. He hopes Margie will refuse dessert so they can go.

"I'd like some sherbet," she says.

He watches her eat it.

The waiter returns. "Coffee, madame, monsieur?"

"Not for me," Craig says hurriedly.

"I'd like some," says Margie.

She sips it. He watches with a fixed smile on his face.

"Can we go someplace else now?" she asks.

Craig says: "I don't know any places in San Francisco."

"I know one."

"Would you mind terribly if we went back to the hotel?"

She is instantly concerned. "What's the matter?"

"It's just that—I'm in a certain amount of pain."

He has had bad Sunday evenings before. This is one of the worst.

In the cab he tries to make conversation, but he is counting the minutes to the hotel.

As the cab climbs Nob Hill, Margie asks: "Would you like me to get out here so we wouldn't be seen together?"

"That's not important."

She watches him, concerned. At the desk he asks for his key. He manages a smile, "I'll be all right." The elevator stops at her floor.

"If you can put up with me—" he says.

In the corridor she holds him, her face against his neck.

"Of course I can put up with you."

Her door closes behind them. "Can I take a bath?" he asks.

He lies in water as hot as he can stand it, his eyes closed, and after a time the pain diminishes. When he gets out of the tub he lies face down on a cool sheet and Margie pats his body with eau de cologne. His skin is scratched and bruised.

"Your body looks like you've been beaten with a club," she says. "I had no idea."

"It's often like this."

Her hands are cool. The eau de cologne is cool. She pats the big bruise on his right side, and the one on his left buttock. The eau de cologne cools the scrapes of his shoulders.

"Your forearms are black-and-blue too."

"They're sore after every game. I break tackles with them."

He explains. His free arm hangs full length against his side. When the tackler throws his arms around Craig, Craig brings this arm up in an uppercut to break the tackler's arm loose.

"So after every game my forearms ache. My shins and my knee and my thumbs, too. People on the ground are always

205

whiplashing their legs into your shins. And my knee hurts because there is no cartilage in it. I never have known why my thumbs always hurt, though. I guess they're sticking out and catch on things and I don't even realize it."

"Poor hands." She dabs eau de cologne on his skinned hands. She smooths a handful of it up his arm to his shoulder.

"That feels lovely."

She smooths eau de cologne up and down his back. "You won't feel like making love tonight."

"I'm so sore."

She smooths eau de cologne down his legs to his feet.

"Turn over and I'll do the other side." He does so. "Why—why you do feel like making love after all."

"But I'm so sore."

"Too sore to do it this way?"

"No, not if you do it that way."

"There. I'm not hurting you?"

"No."

"You're sure I'm not hurting you."

"No. Not at all. No."

"Just lie still and don't move. I wouldn't want to hurt you."

"You're not hurting me at all."

"You don't mind if I move, a little?"

"No."

"Tell me if its feels soothing."

"It feels oh—oh so soothing."

"As good as the eau de cologne?"

"Better. Much better. Much much much much, oh, much—better."

"I'm trying to be very careful and not hurt you."

All of the tension goes out of him, and for a moment there is no pain, just the exquisite torment of the moment, and the thought: How could any man leave a girl who would think to do this for him. And he says; "Oh, Margie, oh, oh, I want to marry you."

"All right," she says, "you can marry me if you want to."

When he awakens it is daylight, he feels much better, and he begins to kiss Margie. One eye opens, and there is a sleepy half-grin on her face. "Good morning," she says.

Her skin smells of soap. He feels her body quicken. "What are you doing now?" she asks.

"Just this."

Her hand is in his hair. "No, don't."

"I want to."

"No you don't."

"Yes."

"You said you didn't."

"I want to now."

"No," she says, biting her lip. "Don't."

But he does. He finds that it has to do with how much you love someone.

A little later, he says: "I meant it, about wanting to marry you."

"So did I."

There seems nothing more to say after that.

The team's United Airlines charter takes off from San Francisco Airport at eleven A.M. In the air the stewardesses move through the plane hanging up the players' blazers and suit jackets. The card games start at once. Shoulders and necks bulge under white shirts with loosened ties. The reporters on board settle beside an unfortunate player or coach, and start interviews. Kevin Tierney, Boyle's son-in-law, moves up and down the aisle distributing envelopes containing the players' game checks; each player's contract salary is broken down into weekly checks, one after each game, and these are handed out either in the locker room after a home game, or on the plane if it is a road game.

The stewardesses begin serving canned fruit juice.

"You want to play bridge, Duke?" asks Joe Morris.

There are bridge games going on each side of the forward compartment where the seats face each other, and also in the lounge. Gin rummy games are in progress up and down the plane.

Craig declines the bridge game.

Instead he stares out the porthole down onto his country, far below.

Oh, Margie, oh, oh, I want to marry you.

From up here it seems to him he can see every state he has ever played in—which means most of them. He knows a hundred stadiums from the inside, each of them different, and the crowds that fill them different too, for some are rabid and some only curious, and if you are sensitive you can tell which almost as soon as you take the field. He knows hundreds of TV stations and newspaper offices where men have interviewed him; once the interviewing was done between races at a greyhound track, and another time while wreckage was being cleared away at a stock car track. These are still the only times he has ever seen dog racing or car racing. He knows hotels and motels and restaurants and airports and train stations, but he knows the country itself too. He knows the tall fir trees edging the

207

horizon in Oregon, and the way the Columbia River boils down toward the sea not far from Multnomah Stadium in Portland.

He knows the state of Washington, which has deserts where you'd never expect them, in the southeast corner around Walla Walla That is rodeo country in there something else you'd never expect. He knows Spokane where the golf courses have tees and greens with precipitous valleys in between And there is a lake in Idaho where a bunch of them went water-skiing one time, and he alone was able to get upright on the skis. The motorboat wasn't strong enough to pull the heavier boys fast enough which had never occurred to the man who invited them out, and the party was a bust, and he apologized all the way back to the hotel.

Craig remembers posing for pictures with Pueblo Indians in Arizona and other Indians in Wisconsin Dells, Wisconsin— what tribe were they, he wonders. That was the place they lived in cabins and worked out on the first fairway of the country club and then went into Milwaukee and got murdered by Green Bay. That was also the place the governors of Wisconsin Michigan, and Minnesota met in a conference, and asked afterward to be photographed with Craig and Pennoyer, and Craig didn't know the names of any of them. Neither did Pennoyer.

There was another governor the next year in Oregon, a Democrat coming up for reelection in a Republican state. The Republican-controlled press in Portland would not give him any publicity at all, and one day he wandered out onto the field and asked to be photographed with Duke Craig. The city editors, he explained, were forbidden to run his picture, but there was a chance, if Craig would pose with him, that the sports editors hadn't been told and so would use the picture. While waiting for the photographer to set up, Craig asked what he did before becoming governor, and the governor said he was formerly a radio announcer. Which is what he probably has become again, Craig thinks, for he lost that election in a landslide. But that man represents the only interest Duke Craig has ever had in politics.

All right, you can marry me if you want to.

He looks down at the blue deserts of Utah. Presently the Rocky Mountains begin to pass, vast fields of snow pierced by spiky peaks. Then come the great plains that the wagon trains crossed not all that long ago, and that he crosses every year in a few hours to play football.

Everywhere down there people who follow the game know the name and reputation of Duke Craig. He knows what that reputation is, for he has read the articles about himself too. He is sincere, correct, irreproachable, and so for all of those people below he is an ideal, as well as an athlete, and this is a puritan country, and conduct which is permissible for them is not permissible for him.

It begins to get dark.

The stewardess's voices come on. "Will you fasten your seatbelts, please."

Craig wonders were Margie's plane is—nearby, no doubt, for her flight was to take off at the same time as this charter. He hopes he will see her again when they land, even if only from a distance, even if only a glance. The plane bumps down.

"The only way to travel."

To Craig's surprise, Carribel and Bobby are waiting for him at the baggage rack. A little distance away stands Margie, watching them, a stricken expression on her face. He wants to go to her, but cannot.

He lifts his suitcase off the moving belt. "Let's go home."

That night, having made his decision, Craig says to his wife: "After the season we've got to end this."

"What do you reckon Ah've done wrong this time?"

"It's just that we have nothing together."

"Ah believe you mean it."

"Yes."

"May Ah ask why?"

"This isn't the way marriage is supposed to be."

"What would you know about how a marriage is supposed to be?"

Craig says nothing.

"Is there another woman?"

He has decided to answer no to this.

"You wouldn't know how to get a woman, apart from some fool like me."

Craig says nothing.

"Ah thought there might be another woman. You haven't been bothering me these last few weeks. For you, not to bother me is unusual."

They stare at each other, then Carribel leaves the room. He does not know what reaction he expected. A fight? Hysteria? Instead there was nothing. She doesn't believe he is serious, or hasn't thought out what divorce would mean.

It will all have to be done again.

Later he lies in the dark, unable to sleep.

CHAPTER | 16

By Tuesday the game films have been graded, and Coach Dreuder must preside over the distribution of "incentive" money. On this team and most others, awards totaling several hundred dollars are given to players each week. Linemen who attain a certain blocking percentage, or pass rushing percentage, get ten dollars each. An interception or a fumble recovery is worth ten dollars. Dumping the other team's passer wins ten dollars, as does a key block of a run of twenty yards or over. A run of that length is worth ten dollers, and if it culminates in a touchdown it is worth twenty dollars. Now Dreuder finds that the big winners this week are Ox Polski with thirty dollars, and Duke Craig with sixty dollars. It galls Dreuder to hand six ten-dollar bills to Craig, but he does it.

By Thursday, which is Thanksgiving Day, Dreuder is in a foul mood, for he can feel that the team has gone flat again, and though he shouts and rails, each practice has been sloppier and more lethargic than the one before. Coaching football is an inexact science, and Dreuder is not sure how to counteract the team's deadness. But his instinct is to get tough, and so he drives the players through a Thanksgiving Day workout when, in other years, he has sometimes given them Thanksgiving Day off.

After practice he would like to show them last Sunday's game. The Forty-Niners, one of the weakest teams in the league, scored thirty-four points on them, and their own offense was pitiful except for a few runs by Craig. Nobody else did *anything,* and the films prove this, and Dreuder wants to show them these films, but decides he can't, because the players would simply sit back and watch themselves win the game. The films would only make them smug.

So he shows films of the Big Red getting trounced by Green Bay two years ago. Green Bay is their next opponent.

This film, he can tell from the muttered comments, bores them. No one takes it seriously: two seasons ago was another century.

So he sets up two television sets, one for the offense, one for the defense, and makes the players watch the Detroit-Cleveland Thanksgiving Day game which begins in Detroit at noon. He orders them to watch only the Cleveland team, for they meet Cleveland again this season, and they don't meet Detroit at all. Instead he hears them all watching the game like fans, and rooting for Detroit. During the commercials Dreuder sometimes snaps the light on, and diagrams a play they have just watched, and then asks for questions on the play. But there are rarely any questions.

Dreuder, in disgust, gives up. Perhaps they are all thinking about getting home to their families. Perhaps practice will go better tomorrow.

At five o'clock there is a Thanksgiving Day dinner and party thrown by F. X. Boyle in the ballroom of the apartment hotel that the majority of the players and their families live at.

Boyle stands with his hands in his side pockets, beaming paternally down on the children of his players. There are little girls in party dresses, a few babies in high chairs, and some small boys playing tackle football with a rolled-up newspaper in the middle of the ballroom floor.

"Stop the game, children, and come and eat."

"Come and eat, Billy."

They dine, three or four families to each big round table. Dreuder sits with his wife, and with the other coaches and their wives. His end coach, Dinsmore, has two small children, and Dreuder watches their mother spoon food into reluctant mouths. At his own table and others, the kids squawk and complain and some pitchers go over, and Dreuder thinks: I'm nervous enough, I didn't need this, too.

The men talk football across the tables and between the tables. Turkeys, provided free by the concessionaire at the stadium, are devoured. They are huge, tend to be tough and were previously frozen as well, and they have been overcooked so that the flesh is dry. With them is cranberry sauce, sweet potatoes, canned creamed onions, canned string beans, and a thick gravy. There are glasses of water beside every plate, ice cubes swimming in them, and there are big aluminum pitchers of milk on the tables also, and pots of steaming coffee. Some of the children demand and get Pepsi-Cola (provided free by the sponsor) to drink with their meals. There is no beer or wine, and Dreuder himself sips a watery manhattan—this being a festive occasion, each adult was granted one cocktail before dinner, and the choice was manhattan or old-fashioned. Most of the players drink milk or coffee, fork swift quantities of food into their mouths, and praise the food frequently.

"Gravy's delicious," says Ox Polski across the table to his pal, Mean Gene Gardner.

"Turkey's great," agrees Mean Gene.

For dessert there is ice cream and pumpkin pie, as much as anyone could eat.

Dreuder himself is too preoccupied even to taste what he is eating. Once he finds that he is chewing on a wad of his own cheek. The pain shoots all the way through him. He puts his fork down. When the ice cream comes, he inflates his cheek with an icy gob of it, letting it cool the wound.

The small boys resume playing football in the center of the floor. The adults smoke amid the noise. Some of the players chew on cigars. The cigars jut out of puffy young faces under crew-cut hair. Dreuder watches F. X. Boyle move from table to table, leaning over with his arm around some favorite player, accepting thanks for the lavish spread.

"It cost me five hundred, but it was worth it."

"We sure appreciate it, F. X."

"You boys mean a lot to me."

Dreuder tries to shut his mind to the crying babies, to the high-pitched small boys' voices shouting signals ten feet away. Tonight he must study films of the Packers against the Bears two weeks ago. The blocking needs to be rearranged on the 67. It is too late to change the game plan he has drilled the team on all week, but he wants to study that again, too. He wonders how soon he can leave without incurring Boyle's displeasure.

Craig sits with the Pennoyers, the Slades, and Joe and Sara Morris. The Morrises have a baby in a high chair. The Slades have two small children, and the Craigs have two. The childless Pennoyer has a silly grin on his face. He is delighted to be surrounded by kids, and had a try at spooning food into Suzy Craig earlier. Now he has turned his chair to watch the small boys play football with their rolled-up newspaper which is gradually coming to pieces. He begins to root aloud for whichever team has the ball.

Carribel says to her husband: "Bobby's gonna ruin his clothes."

Craig's son wears long pants and an Eton jacket, and his short tie carries a big Windsor knot which Craig tied for him at home. He is struggling forward with the ball, and one tackler has him by the sleeve and another by the tie, and they wrestle him to the floor.

"He's all right," says Craig.

"Ah can see you're not the one has to iron his clothes."

Craig can tell that Carribel is yearning for a fight, and he fears she means to begin her counterattack here, where he can't fight back.

"Are you gonna make him stop, or am Ah the one?"

"Yes, of course," says Craig hurriedly.

"Are you man enough for that? Are you a man at all?"

Craig flashes a grin all around. But his teammates and their wives have seen other spats between the Craigs, and pretend not to notice.

Craig thinks: Carribel's instinct always is to fight back, but she usually chooses the wrong issues to fight about, and always the wrong place. But he starts to call his son out of the game.

"Duke's got a girl friend," Carribel says suddenly.

Sara Morris leans forward, eyes fluttering: "Tell us about it, Carribel."

Apparently, Sara thinks Carribel is kidding. Craig, shocked, looks from one to the other. Is Carribel taking a shot in the dark, or what?

With a grin, Craig says quickly: "Women are crazy about me. Always have been."

"Her name is—"

"Shut up, Carribel."

"Duke doesn't want me to tell her name."

Craig can feel Pennoyer eye him.

He calls his son. "Mommy doesn't want you to play anymore."

"Aw, gee, Dad, we're—"

"Look at your tie," Carribel cries.

The tie now is long and thin. Craig begins to retie it.

Carribel remarks: "Duke thinks all you need to get a girl is a big knot in your tie."

The table has fallen silent. Craig works on Bobby's knot.

"Y'all should have seen the size of the knot Duke wore in college. He was so gauche. Y'all have no idea. He's still that gauche, if you want to know the truth."

Craig, wanting to get his son clear of the scene, gives the boy money. "Go buy some candy," he orders. He decides that the only way to silence Carribel is to disappear.

"Excuse me," he says, and leaves the table.

When the men's room door closes behind him, he finds he is quivering with rage.

Outside, Boyle says to Coach Dreuder: "Are you going to say something to him, or should I?"

Dreuder thinks: He's a grown man. Leave him alone. You

have no right to meddle. But all he says is: "I've got nothing to say to him."

Craig throws cold water on his face. After a while he stops quivering. He is washing his hands when the door swings back, and Boyle enters.

"Hello there, m'boy."

"It's a fine party, F. X."

"Glad to be able to do it for the team."

The owner watches him. Craig, carefully washing his hands, knows what is coming.

"I have the feeling something's troubling you, m'boy."

Craig soaps his hands. "Whatever gave you that idea?"

Boyle thinks out what he wants to say. "Well, missing the bed check, and all. And this little scene out there. Well, I've had the feeling things aren't going between you and Carribel the way—like in the past."

"Yes, well—" Craig, pretending to dry his hands, edges toward the door.

"She's a lovely girl, Carribel."

"Yes."

"I've always been fond of her. Remember at your wedding, when she stopped the music and introduced me to the guests and then gave me that big kiss?"

"Yes." The owner, apparently deliberately, is blocking the door.

"I've always looked at you two and thought, there goes the ideal couple in this league."

Craig dries his hands until the paper towel disintegrates.

"She's crazy about you, and you're crazy about her, I know."

Craig stares at the shredded towel.

"It would certainly be tragic if anything went wrong. I'd blame myself."

Craig takes a new towel.

"It's not too late to—to right the boat, so to speak. I'm sure it's not too late for that."

Craig goes on rubbing his hands.

"Two lovely children. People all over the country look up to you, Duke. You're one of the finest players we've ever had in this league, and one of the most admirable. You wouldn't want to spoil that, would you? Think of all the fine youngsters who look up to you. Not to mention your son, Bobby. A fine-looking boy."

Craig says nothing.

"So I wondered if there could be something you'd like to talk over with me."

214

"You see, there's nothing—"

The owner gives a chuckle, cutting Craig off. "I just wanted you to know I was available, any time of the day or night as they say." He claps Craig on the shoulder—unblocking the door.

"Everything's fine," says Craig. "And we sure do thank you for the party." The door slams behind him. Outside, he wipes his brow, and his hand comes away damp.

In the hotel lobby there are potted plants and bellhops standing. He steps into a phone booth.

"Happy Thanksgiving," he says, when Margie comes on the line.

"I'm going to have dinner with friends, later."

"I wish I could be with you."

"My husband's lawyer called this morning."

"So it's started."

"I said I won't make any trouble. I don't want anything from him."

He can tell how upset she is. "I wish I could be with you."

Back in the ballroom, avoiding Carribel's table, he stands talking with Joe Morris. Father O'Malley joins them.

"Say, Joe, can I see you a minute," calls a voice.

It is Boyle, summoning Morris, leaving Craig alone with the priest.

Craig thinks: Am I supposed to assume I am alone with him by accident?

"How are things going, Duke?"

"Couldn't be better."

"I just thought there might be something you wanted to talk over."

Craig annoyed, says: "Like what?"

But the priest laughs. "After all, I am the chaplain of this team, and if I don't pretend to do the job once in a while, they won't let me sit on the bench."

Craig is forced to smile.

But the priest gets down to business again. "Carribel sure is looking pretty today," he says. "If I hadn't been a priest, Carribel is the kind of girl I would like to have married."

Craig says nothing.

The priest watches him. "Anyway," the priest says presently, "if you ever want to talk anything over, I'm there. No one can force you to talk anything over, if you don't want to."

"I'm hired to play ball."

"That's right, Duke, and to be a credit to the team and the league. Something that might not be a credit to the team and the league—well, that's what we're trying to prevent. Right?"

"Right," says Craig. He turns away, recaptures his kids, and tells Carribel it's time to go home.

Leaving the table, Carribel says: "Duke hates for me to make a scene. You won't beat me when we get home, will you, Duke?" She is in good spirits now, Craig sees. Her counter-attack has started and was a success. She turns to the table again, and whispers, "Duke doesn't really have a girl friend, do you, Duke? He'd like to have a girl friend, but he wouldn't know how, would you, Duke?"

"That's me," says Craig, forcing a grin. "Happy Thanks-giving, everybody."

Saturday morning the team flies to Green Bay. When the team works out in Green Bay Stadium at noon the temperature is above freezing, and the strip down the center of the field, skinned of grass this late in the season, is a film of mud. There are reports that a blizzard is moving down from Canada.

After practice, outside the stadium, George Dreuder talks to his counterpart, the Green Bay coach.

"I'm sorry about the condition of the field. We had a high school game in there last night."

Dreuder observes that the field is okay.

"The crew will cover it with tarps and straw—in case we do get a blizzard tonight."

"Fine," says Dreuder. "It's the same field for both of us anyway."

They look at each other. Dreuder thinks: Football is a gigantic live chess game. Tomorrow, whatever the fans and TV viewers might think, it's not Green Bay versus the Big Red, it's this man against me. He moves his pieces, and I move mine, and the man with the sharper brain and the steadier nerves wins.

They have nothing to say to each other.

"Well, good luck."

"Good luck."

Buses wait to take the team back to the Holiday Inn in Appleton, Wisconsin, twenty-seven miles away. Dreuder has clocked it. On a dry road the trip takes twenty-eight minutes. If there is snow on the road tomorrow, how much time do I allow? Dreuder asks himself.

For twenty-eight minutes, Dreuder listens to the players gripe.

"Why do they stick us way out here for?"

"There's nothing to do."

They are edgy. Dreuder tells himself this is good.

It was Boyle's idea to quarter the team in Appleton. Green

Bay is a rabid football town, and on a Saturday night could be full of drunks, Boyle pointed out. Appleton would be quiet as a tomb, and there is a highway outside that runs straight to the stadium—half an hour by bus, no more.

Drunks in Green Bay could involve players in a disturbance; noise could keep the team awake. Dreuder approved the idea of Appleton.

Now he wonders if this was wise. The players could get so nervous sitting around Appleton for the rest of today that they would sleep badly, use up all the energy they will need tomorrow.

"It's like dealing with racehorses," Dreuder mutters.

Across the aisle, Pete the trainer says: "Did you say something, Coach?"

Dreuder realizes he has spoken aloud. "Only that I'm losing my mind," he says.

The trainer, reassured, smiles.

Dreuder thinks: It's like dealing with racehorses. You never know whether they're going to feel like running. They are as highly strung, as unreliable and often no smarter.

Dreuder was once an All-League end on the Bears. He knows the tension the players live under. It comes on Saturday night, gets very strong Sunday morning, and vanishes the instant a man smashes into some other guy on the field.

Whereas the coach's tension never leaves him from the first game to the last. During a game is the worst. For two and a half hours you pace up and down, chain-smoking, suffering, and there is almost nothing you can do.

Back at the hotel a late lunch is served. After lunch, Dreuder meets with his coaches and they go over plays and defenses in case of an icy field.

At two o'clock a college game starts on television. The players watch it, sprawled on beds in their rooms. Dreuder watches it in Boyle's suite, with most of his assistant coaches on hand. He has the reports from his college scouts, and watches specific players on both teams, grading those of them he can see on each play. The Big Red may get a shot at one or more of these boys in next winter's draft. Often he curses the TV cameraman. When a specific player runs out of the picture, Dreuder never knows if the boy makes his block or misses it.

Dreuder never sees college games in person. This is the closest he can come to getting a line on boys he might draft next year.

After the first game ends, there is another on another channel. Dreuder wants to watch all of it, but at five thirty Malverde comes in with the reporters and the liquor, and Boyle with

217

some former players who live in the area. Malverde gives all of these people liquor, and Boyle gives the old players tickets to tomorrow's game.

One of the former players is Ox Polski's oldest brother, who used to be known as "Babe," and who now weighs about three hundred pounds.

"Hey, Babe," says Dreuder, "what are you doing here?"

"I happened to be in Milwaukee, so I thought I'd come up for the game," answers Babe Polski.

"How's the restaurant?"

"Good."

"It's in Allentown, isn't it?"

"No, Pittsburgh."

Boyle comes over with Wayne Griffin. From 1938 to 1941, and again from 1945 to 1948, Griffin was the best running back in the league.

Shaking hands with Griffin, Dreuder says: "Good to see you," but what he is thinking is that the gray-haired Griffin is a much shorter, slighter man than he remembered. Griffin would be too small for today's game.

"What business you in now, Wayne?"

"I sell a little fishing tackle up around home."

"That's right, you come from around here, don't you."

"The fishing tackle business is pretty good up in the northern part of the state. You should come up some day. I'll take you out after some pike."

Griffin never liked coaching, or was never any good at it, Coach Dreuder thinks, so now he fishes all the time, and when the team comes to Green Bay he comes down to the game to remember old times. Tomorrow Boyle will take him around in the locker room and introduce him to the players who will be polite, a little distant, and preoccupied with the game; none of them will have the slightest notion who Wayne Griffin used to be. They'll know who Babe Polski used to be only because of Ox. This is a game without a past. Ancient history is last season, and further back than that, to the players, is unrecorded time.

Dreuder feels a little sorry for Wayne Griffin. He hopes Griffin has been in enough modern locker rooms not to expect the players to recognize his name, or be interested in talking to him.

The amenities past, Dreuder goes back to watching TV. From time to time he politely answers the questions of Wayne Griffin and Babe Polski and the others, while trying to watch and grade the TV game at the same time.

At dinner, Dreuder announces a meeting for seven thirty.

The players groan; normally they are free Saturday nights. But tonight the coaches must show them the new defenses and plays in case of ice or snow.

"So shut up," Dreuder snarls. "You're not going anyplace tonight anyway."

Realizing he sounds meaner and angrier than he intended, he sits down and tries to finish his dinner.

But he is not hungry and he has a raging toothache in an upper front tooth though the tooth is perfectly sound. The toothache comes from grinding his teeth in his sleep. Probably he needs root canal work, four or five visits, and he doesn't have time for that during the season. Besides, perhaps it will clear up when the season ends and he stops grinding his teeth in his sleep.

This time each year his body breaks down in a dozen small ways. Just now he has a toothache, sores in his mouth, an infected toenail and a permanent cold. He knows it is his body's way of telling him to ease off. But he can't ease off. Already there is not enough time in the day to do all that needs to be done. He works every night to eleven o'clock or later, studying films, designing new plays, rearranging old plays to take advantage of this or that weakness observed in the films. There are scouting reports to study, interviews to submit to, TV shows to appear on. There are vital conferences with his staff. There are also dozens of calls each week from old friends he hasn't seen in ten years but who want 50-yard-line seats for Sunday.

Leaving the dinner table, Coach Dreuder asks Doc for pain pills for his tooth.

"How's your cold?"

"Give me some cold pills too."

The team is a traveling pharmacy. There are citrocarbonate pills to ward off pulled muscles, salt tablets to ward off heat prostration, antihistamines to ward off colds, and enzyme pills to prevent swelling. There are pills to loosen the bowels, and pills to tighten them. There are dextrose pills for energy, and sleeping pills for insomnia. There are penicillin shots at the slightest provocation, and vitamin B-12 shots for anyone who asks. Most players swallow five or more pills a day. Some of this is hypochondria. Some of it is psychosomatic. And some of it is real. Dreuder thinks his own problems are part real, part psychosomatic. He goes up to Doc's room for the pills. The pain pills dilate his eyes and make him feel groggy, so he decides to let Beady Stein conduct the meeting. Stein, at the blackboard, draws what he calls "blizzard formations."

Nobody laughs.

219

"It's snowing," says a player who sits by the window.

They all rush to the windows to watch the snow fall.

"Sit down," cries Dreuder. "Haven't you ever seen snow before."

The meeting goes on. The windows frost over, and the players near them scrape the frost off from time to time to peer out.

When Stein ends the meeting, chairs are pushed back. The players bump each other going out through the door. Downstairs in the lobby stands Boyle's son-in-law, Kevin Tierney, shaking snow off his coat.

"Just get in?" asks Coach Dreuder.

"We were the last plane. They've just closed the airport."

"What if it's closed after the game?"

"I'm going to call United now."

At the elevators, Tierney hands over some letters. "These came into the office this morning, George."

Dreuder opens them in the elevator. There are four letters, all from people he doesn't know. Three are unsigned. All enclose a clipping from the Detroit *Free Press*.

Dear Coach: Your days are numbered if you blow this season.

Dear Coach: If you haven't seen this clipping—

Dear Coach: If what this clipping says is true, you—

Dreuder sits with his toothache in front of the TV. The clippings are in his lap. He does not need to read them. He knows the words by heart, for there are a dozen other copies in his suitcase, all sent by "friends" who forget to sign their names. According to this column, if Dreuder doesn't win this year he is out. F. X. Boyle is supposed to have said privately: "I know football as well as George does, and we really have the horses this year. If we don't win, I'll have to believe it is George's fault."

Boyle must have seen the clipping, too. Boyle has said nothing. Therefore, the clipping is true.

Dreuder, staring at the TV, tortures himself with this information the same way he keeps prodding his aching tooth with his tongue.

If he doesn't win, he is out, and he no longer believes in victory, for his team has cracked. He does not know how or why, but it has cracked. He would have to be blind not to see the signs: the loss to the Giants two weeks ago; the shoddy defensive performance against San Francisco last Sunday; the sloppy workouts for nearly three weeks now. Polski has ballooned up to 280—he ought to be down to 250 by this time of the season. Pennoyer's passing is not sharp. Donald Fox contributes nothing. Craig's mind is not on football at all.

This is the crucial time every season. Any coach can keep his team up there for nine games. That's not what they pay off for in sports. If you crack there, you're just another loser. The winner is the guy who pours it on now, and forces everybody else to crack. He's just as worn out as they are, but doesn't let them know it, and they crack and he wins.

Beady Stein laughs at something on the TV.

The loud laugh causes Dreuder to clench his jaws spasmodically, and as his front teeth bang together, the pain shoots up into his skull. He concentrates on the pain for a moment, enjoying it.

Moving to the window, he sees the snow still coming down hard.

Dreuder swallows another pain pill. Later he lies in the dark, hoping for sleep.

At three A.M. in his sleep he bites down on the side of his tongue, and snaps awake with his mouth tasting of blood. In his dream he has just solved the Packer goal-line defense again. He first solved it Tuesday afternoon, and gave it to the team Wednesday morning, and solving it again now means he has been working as hard in his sleep as he does awake. He lies exhausted, and the pain of his tooth comes on again, hard.

He gets up to take another pill, then stands at the window. Outside it is still snowing. The snow is so thick he can barely make out the streetlight down below in front of the hotel.

In the morning, snow still falls, and when Dreuder comes downstairs some of his players are outside in team blazers and loafers throwing snowballs at each other.

He rushes out into the snow screaming: "Are you morons trying to catch pneumonia?" Abashed, they troop back into the hotel with Dreuder berating them.

The steak breakfast begins at nine thirty. Dreuder decides they must leave for the stadium immediately afterward—there is no telling how long the trip will take.

The players, edgy and resentful, board the buses. Up front, Dreuder sits with Stein.

"They're nice and nervous."

"They're tense all right."

The two coaches are trying to reassure each other.

"I like them this way."

"Me too."

Dreuder begins to hope. This kind of tension has a good feel to it. Football is an emotional game. If they take the field still tense, and if the Packers should be a little flat, they could conceivably tear the Packers apart.

221

But the road is crowded with cars. For a while they move steadily through the falling snow. Then traffic slows to a crawl. Dreuder can still feel the tension all around him. He thinks: The isolation of Appleton, this snowfall, a bus with the windows frosted up—this could give us the edge we need.

The bus has stopped. There is no sound but the windshield wipers rasping across the glass.

Then some of the players begin to scrape at the frost on the windows. They try to peer out into the snowfall. But the heat and moisture of the football bodies quickly frost the windows over again.

The bus moves slowly forward; it stops.

"What time is it?"

"What's holding us up?"

There are a few feeble jokes. Advice is shouted to the bus driver. Some of the players attempt to sleep.

The bus moves forward, then stops. A cop bangs on the driver's window and shouts instructions inside. The bus skirts a stalled car, but a little farther on stops again.

Outside, the snow falls steadily.

One or two players pace up and down the aisle. Conversations start, but soon die out. Players begin to gripe.

"They couldn't have wanted to win much, sticking us out in Appleton in a blizzard."

An hour passes. The windshield wipers rasp across the glass. Players use keys and coins to scrape frost off their windows.

Dreuder and Stein stare straight ahead. The keen edge of tension is gone. They can feel this. Instead the players are bored and sullen.

The bus moves forward, stops, starts, stops again.

At last the driver says: "I can see the stadium."

Players crowd the aisle.

"We can walk it."

"Let's get off.'

"Yeah."

Dreuder shouts: "Everybody sit quiet and wait."

Time passes. The players grumble and squirm. They have forgotten the Packers. They are thinking only of getting off the bus.

The bus does not move. "Can you see anything, driver?" asks Dreuder.

"Seems to be some cars with locked bumpers."

"All right, men, bundle up and let's walk from here."

Outside the bus the players trudge through deep snow to the stadium.

By one o'clock the snow has stopped falling. The grounds crew labors to get the tarps back. Other crewmen rake the underneath straw off the field. The day is very cold, but when Dreuder tests the turf with his shoe it is soft and muddy in places. He knows that parts of it will freeze fast, and other parts slowly. By half time it should all be frozen.

The teams work out on the cleared part of the field, while the grounds crew drags the tarps off the rest of it.

Dreuder makes Craig, Slade, and Polski do sprinting and dodging movements. Craig wears normal cleats, Polski wears mud cleats, and Slade wears sneakers. Dreuder is trying to decide what footgear his team should wear.

"Normal cleats are fine," says Craig.

"I'm gonna wear these mud cleats," says Polski.

"Sneakers," says Slade.

Dreuder decides that in the first half the players can wear what they want. In the second half they will all wear sneakers.

Worrying about the cleats means Dreuder doesn't have to worry about the game itself. But his team is listless. Jones, kicking field goals from the thirty-five, barely reaches the goal line. When Dreuder snaps at him, Jones says plaintively: "The balls are frozen. They have no resiliency and won't travel. It's like kicking a block of wood."

Dreuder watches the stands filling up. The fans are bundled like Russians, but they are there, drinking from flasks and banging their hands together.

In the dressing room, jerseys come off, and players put their pads on over the blue thermal underwear. They are all worried about what footgear to wear, asking advice from each other. On a gear trunk, Pete is filling and lighting handwarmers. Paul is distributing the down-filled capes to each player.

"We're going to get murdered out there," Dreuder mutters to himself. The players talk listlessly about the weather. No one is anxious to go out into the cold again. No one is eager to play football.

Dreuder thinks: An entire squad has to be fired up for a team to play over its head. But it takes only a few men who don't care to drag a whole team down into a shoddy performance. And now Dreuder reads the mood of his team and knows the Packers will murder them.

To his dismay, he soon sees that he is right.

The players' hands are warm enough at first, and Pennoyer takes the team down the field to the 35-yard line, where Jones tries a field goal which is short. Pennoyer comes back to the bench and kicks at the turf, while Jones, behind him, complains in a loud voice that the ball is frozen and dead. The offensive team sits inside capes, hands around the handwarmers in the pockets. But these do not heat the backs of hands, which get steadily colder as the defensive team, onfield, is pushed backward by the Packers. The Packers score.

There are still a few players on the Big Red who play to win, and Pennoyer is the same as always. But these few can't do the job alone. The line isn't hitting, and the backs and ends, their hands stiff with cold, are having trouble catching the ball, or holding onto it. Pennoyer finds he can't grip the ball hard enough to have any faith in throwing it accurately, and so waits a second or two too long, hoping a receiver can get wide open. The line, playing apathetically anyway, can't hold the Packers out this long, and Pennoyer gets thrown for losses again and again.

On defense Polski is skating around on the mud cleats, the Packers move him in whichever direction they choose, and he comes to the bench with his bland, puffy face contorted and changes into sneakers. Back in the game, the Packers still move him.

There are fumbles on both sides. The ball pops out of Slade's hands, strikes the frozen turf, and rebounds waist-high so that Slade grabs it almost without breaking stride, and keeps running. But other fumbles the Packers recover.

By half time the field is frozen. In the locker room the players work on their hands, trying to massage the numbness away. Dreuder strides up and down, railing at them.

In the second half, the Packers get stronger still. The field is the same for both sides, and every player who gets smashed down parts with the skin of his elbows, knees, and other joints. The difference is that the Big Red, losing, feels this, and the Packers, winning, don't. The Big Red players ease up, for it hurts less that way; and what difference does it make since the Packers will trounce them regardless.

Pennoyer, disgusted, gives the ball repeatedly to Craig, who keeps hitting the line, finding no hole, and getting thrown down on his back while skating around looking for one. After a while Craig, too, is thinking about punishment rather than winning. He hesitates, waiting for the hole to open before making his move. He tries to dance outside, looking for daylight. The plays are not designed to work this way, and the Packers throw him down hard every time.

The score goes to 20–7, not a rout at all on the face of it. Frozen fans in the stadium, and other millions on TV, hope or fear the Big Red might still win. It is a rout only in the minds of both teams. The Big Red has given up.

Snow starts falling again. Soon the field is white everywhere except the area around the scrimmage line.

Pennoyer doggedly keeps trying to move the team. The snow is coming down. He fades to pass, the Packers blitz, and three tacklers wade toward him, arms spread for balance. Pennoyer slips and is already falling as they hit him. A 250-pound linebacker lands knees first in the small of Pennoyer's back.

Pennoyer lies there, and Coach Dreuder screams: "Rocco—"

The substitute quarterback, who has been on the press box phone all through the game and whose hands are frozen the same temperature as the instrument, runs onto the field.

He is trailed by Dr. Flaherty, whose face is half hidden in a muffler, and who waddles out to Pennoyer's side as fast as he can. Presently Pennoyer is carried off on a stretcher.

The game goes on. It is second down and eighteen. Rocco takes the ball, fades to pass, the pocket collapses, and when the Packers hit Rocco, he drops the ball.

The game ends.

In the locker room Coach Dreuder aims a vicious kick at a gear trunk. Too late he remembers his infected toe. The pain makes his eyes close.

The players, most of them stripped down to sweat-soaked, blue thermal underwear, sit morosely in front of their lockers. Most of them suck greedily on cigarettes.

Reporters have entered the locker room. Dreuder's rage is so apparent none dares approach him.

Youngblood of the *Tribune* moves among the players with his notebook out.

"Is that the worst weather conditions you ever played under?"

He jots down the answer and moves on.

"Is that the worst weather conditions you ever played under?"

Craig gives Youngblood a wan smile. "In old Forbes Field one time it rained so hard there were puddles two or three inches deep around the second base area. I caught a pass and went sliding in there face first with somebody sitting on my helmet. My face was under water and I thought I was going to be the first man ever to drown in a football game."

Youngblood jots this down. "Good note," he says. "Any other game you remember?"

"No."

Youngblood is going to get a fine article out of this. As he moves down the row of stalls, his voice carries back to Craig: "Is that the worst weather conditions you ever played under?"

A reporter approaches Dreuder. "How's Pennoyer?"

Dreuder snaps: "We don't know yet."

Dreuder orders the room cleared of reporters. While Pete is doing this, Dreuder thinks over the game plan he devised for this game. In his head he checks everything out, and sees that the Packers played exactly as he figured them. The plays he put in should have worked. The defenses he put in should have stopped the Packers cold.

His mind studies it over and over. It stays the same. The concept—his concept—was perfect. The breakdown was in the execution. He remembers key blocks, key tackles missed. He put each player in the perfect spot, and the player failed to execute. The defeat is their fault, not his.

However, the fans, the owner, blame him, not them. He is the one who suffers, not them. They will be back next year and he, if that columnist is right, won't be.

Boyle comes up to him.

"It's not your fault, George."

Dreuder tries to figure out what this means.

"They didn't even try, George."

Hope now mixes with Dreuder's rage. His job can be saved. If he can bring them back, win these last two games—

Pete says: "The room's cleared, Coach."

Dreuder, his voice hoarse, begins to berate his team.

"—sloppiest team effort of any team of mine ever.

"I won't stand for it.

"I got ends who can't catch, guards who can't find the men coming over them—

"Polski—" Dreuder shouts the word out. Polski does not look up, but his face turns red as Dreuder's tirade comes down on him.

"Jones. If you can't reach the posts from thirty-five yards out, Jones, we won't carry you—"

Jones says: "But the ball was frozen."

"Don't you talk back to me," screams Dreuder.

He starts on Craig. "You're supposed to be a leader of this team, but I don't think football is your game anymore, eh, Duke?" Dreuder's voice lowers; it becomes sarcastic, almost confidential. "Because, gentlemen, Duke Craig's got his mind on something else. Duke Craig's got his mind on—on *stuff*." Dreuder shouts this word.

He paces, his footfalls the only sound.

"That's all Craig cares about, *stuff*. If you think you can stay up all night and play on my team, Craig, you can't."

Craig realizes that today is his birthday. He sits with head down, taking it.

"I won't have any player on my team who has his mind

on—on *stuff*, Craig. You hear me, Craig?" Dreuder accuses Craig of letting the tackler through who injured Pennoyer, and although this is not true and the movies will prove it, Craig sits there, head down, taking it. His face burns. He is thirty-one years old today.

"So now let's all get our minds off *stuff* and everything else except football." Dreuder rants. "We will scrimmage Wednesday, and if I'm not satisfied we'll scrimmage Thursday, too, and maybe Friday and even Saturday, and if anybody has enough energy left Saturday night before a game to go out looking for—for *stuff*, I'll be surprised." At the door Dreuder says softly, "I'll be very surprised." The door slams behind him.

Someone kicks the side of a trunk, hard. Many voices rise.

No one looks at Craig, or mentions his name.

The locker room slowly empties.

Outside, Craig finds that it is night. It is cold, and he looks up into the winter stars. The sky is clear and bright. The night, muffled by deep snow, is soundless.

The two buses are bright islands of light.

Craig overhears Dreuder talking to Kevin Tierney.

"They've been able to get a Convair in," says Tierney. "But we won't be able to take everybody."

"Leave the goddam reporters."

"They'll squawk like mad."

"Let 'em."

At the airport, an ambulance with Pennoyer in it waits beside the plane. The players board the plane. Presently a cargo hatch up front is opened, and Pennoyer loaded through that. An icy blast of air blows through the plane. Card players are cleared out of the front compartment, and the stretcher laid across the tops of the seats.

The plane lifts off. The stewardesses begin to pass out beer, and soon conversation comes on. Dinner is served.

After dinner Craig goes forward to see Pennoyer, but the quarterback is doped up.

"Will you fasten your seat belts, please."

Craig straps himself in.

"The only way to travel."

An ambulance is waiting on the tarmac. Here there is no snow. Pennoyer, wrapped in blankets, is lifted out of the cargo door and slid into the ambulance. Doc and two other players climb in, too. The players are Mean Gene Gardner, who suffered a concussion in the second quarter, and Donald Fox, who has a possible broken hand. Doc takes no chances with head injuries and will keep Gardner under observation for forty-eight hours; Fox's hand must be X-rayed. In addition the defensive end Greg Wagner has a massive charley horse and is probably through for the season.

Craig phones Flora Pennoyer, who says she will leave for the hospital at once.

"Do you want me to meet you there?"

"You're awfully nice, Duke."

He is in pain himself, his right biceps swollen, and all he wants to do is get home. But he waits two hours at the hospital with Flora, and when the X-rays show that Jim has a broken transverse process of the spine and is out for season, he comforts her. This is a common football injury, he tells her; Jim will be fine in a month or so. He keeps on in this vein until he sees she believes him, then takes her back to her hotel, where she kisses him on the cheek, saying: "You always do the right thing, Duke. And I know—I know you always will."

So the gossip must be all over the team.

It is past midnight before Craig gets home. His right arm hurts and he goes to bed with an ice bag on it. When the pain keeps him awake he gets up and takes two sleeping pills. He lies there waiting to become unconscious.

CHAPTER 17

In the morning his business agent calls.

"I think I got a contract lined up with Wheaties. You know their All-American Boy series?"

There is also an article extolling virtue which the *Reader's Digest* wants him to put his name to; and Pepsi-Cola wants him to do some ads. "They'll film you giving some tips to youngsters, and then you and the kids take a break and drink some Pepsi on camera."

Craig asks the terms.

"Nothing's nailed down yet."

"Listen," says Craig. "It's more important to me to get the money quickly than to hold out for the best terms."

"Something wrong, Duke?"

"No," he says. "No, nothing's wrong."

His swollen arm throbs. He spends the day sending out his photo to kids. He takes aspirin. He keeps putting fresh ice into the ice bag. The rule is twenty-four hours of ice, after which the internal bleeding is presumed to have stopped, then the switch to heat to speed the resorption of the dried blood now trapped within the muscles. At dusk Craig gets into a hot tub, and lies there for nearly two hours. When he gets out he fixes his own dinner; Carribel is not speaking to him. After dinner he spends two more hours in the tub. The heat soothes the pain, and he thinks he can feel the swelling begin to diminish.

Wednesday morning at the stadium the players, grumbling, put their pads on for the punishment scrimmage.

"If he thinks he can scrimmage us today and get a good game out of us Sunday, he's crazy," a voice says loudly.

"Yeah."

"He's trying to ruin us."

Dreuder, in the coaches' room, hears this through the door. His team, though favored to win in the East, has lost two of its last three games. Once the disintegration starts in a football team (or presumably any other team) it follows predictable lines. The one team breaks down into several cliques. Players whisper together in corners. Dirty looks shoot across the room at teammates or coaches. Where there had been good humor, there is now only grumbling. On the field the players lose concentration, or desire, or whatever it is, and stop paying strict attention, and then they not only lose, they start getting hurt. Winning teams have almost no injuries, and losing teams have four or five hurt a game. Dreuder does not ask himself why this is so. Football is not an introspective game. He just knows it is so, for it always has been.

Pete the trainer knocks on the door. He hands Dreuder a list of players too damaged to play in the scrimmage. The last name on the list is Craig.

"Craig's playing."

"Coach, if he gets another shot on that arm, he won't play Sunday."

Dreuder rarely overrules Pete. "Get Craig out there. Tell him the prima donna shit is over as far as I'm concerned."

When Pete backs out of the room, Dreuder studies the list again.

For next Sunday Pennoyer is out, Greg Wagner is out, Donald Fox (whose hand is broken) is out, Finney is still out, Wilson Cambridge is still out, and House DiRico is probably out.

Once the disintegration of a team starts, Dreuder reflects, it is almost impossible to reverse. A coach has only two options. He can make jokes and give the team several days off from practice. Or he can chew the men out, stage midweek scrimmages, blister them with work, and with sarcasm and anger. This is the course Dreuder has chosen. The work, sarcasm, and anger have to be exaggerated in order to cut through the thick skin of the team down to the individuals they are designed to affect.

So Dreuder starts the scrimmage, and he screams at them after every play. He watches Craig hit the line four straight times, not favoring his arm or trying to protect it, and then pulls Craig out of the scrimmage, not wanting to risk any longer losing Craig for Sunday. In all the scrimmage lasts only ten minutes, before Dreuder loses his nerve and calls it off. He can't afford to get anyone else hurt now.

In the locker room he makes another speech, wishing he had the guts just to snarl at them, instead of pleading with them to become a team again and fight to win these last two games.

He tells them they could still tie with Cleveland, forcing a playoff, if they win these two games, and Cleveland loses two. Failing that, they can finish second and make the Playoff Bowl in Miami in January: "A little extra money, a little free sun with your families. But if you go into these last two games with your present attitude, you'll lose them both."

He tells them Rocco is an excellent quarterback and can do the job—something no one on the team believes.

Dreuder goes on talking too long, and sullenness sets in, and at last he becomes aware of this and snarls at them: "You guys got no pride. No pride at all." He storms out the door.

Afterward, Craig sits with his arm under the heat.

He has a speech to make that night, but arranges for Joe Morris to take it. He wants to lie in a hot tub, then get to bed early.

When he gets home and is in the tub, Carribel to his surprise enters the bathroom. She stands, hands on hips, looking down on him. Obviously she intends to make some sort of dramatic pronouncement. Although he feels at a disadvantage, being flat on his back under water, he is nonetheless relieved. He wants to get this thing out in the open.

"Are you still fixing to divorce me?" she asks with mock sweetness.

But she seems too sure of herself. Something is wrong.

He nods, watching her.

"Is there anything Ah can do to change your mind?"

"No."

"Yes there is."

He shakes his head. "No."

"You see, there's something you don't know, Ace."

He masks the twinges of worry he feels. "What did you come in here to tell me?"

"You think you're so much better than me," she cries angrily. "For years you've treated me like a child—a dull child. You think Ah don't know?"

Craig stirs in the water. "You didn't come in here to tell me that."

"You don't know what it is, being married to Duke Craig. Half the year he isn't home, and when he is home he is lying in a bathtub. He's got time for every kid and drunk who calls him up on the phone, but do you think he's got any time for his wife. Not ever."

Craig says, "What's on your mind?"

"Ah don't want to stay married to you either. Unfortunately, Ah have to."

"Say it," snaps Craig.

"Ah have a little surprise for you, honey."

In the tub, Craig feels his body tense up. His stomach muscles contract.

"You cain't move out after the season, honey. After next season, not this season. On account of you are going to be a father again. Ah think you ought to wait around at least till then, don't you, honey?"

Craig looks at her. He feels his face start to burn.

"Don't you think you ought to wait around until the great day comes, honey?"

Under the water, his body goes hot too. Then immediately cold.

"Ah mean, how would it look, an All-American boy like Duke Craig walking out on his loving wife that he has just got with child?"

Craig is so cold he is unable to catch his breath.

"Ah mean, everybody would say 'he cain't hate her *that* much, if he can manage to get her pregnant.'" She adds: "Ah mean, how would that *look?*"

Craig, frozen in ice, hears her clearly.

"By the time the great day comes, you'll be about ready to go to training camp, honey, and after that you'll be in another season—cain't get all emotionally upset in the middle of a season, can you? So, say, a year, or a year and a half more with me. Then you can go, if you still want to."

She looks down at him. "You can wait that long, cain't you, honey? Ah mean, you ain't in any hurry, are you, honey?"

The physical reaction has passed. Craig tries to calculate how long ago he last made love to his wife. "Why didn't you tell me this before?" he manages to say.

"Ah was saving it for a proper occasion, honey. A girl cain't give her hero such thrilling news just any time, can she? She has to wait for a proper occasion."

But when Craig surges up out of the tub, she backs hurriedly from the room.

In a daze he towels himself off, dresses, stumbles out. He stands in the cold December night. He does not know what to think or do, and at last he gets into his car and drives. He realizes he is headed toward the city only when he notices skyscrapers ablaze with light, coming closer. What did I come here for, he asks himself. But he knows.

He parks outside Margie's building. He has to tell her. He can see her lights burning high above. In his ears he still hears Carribel's voice, her words nailing him to his cross for another year or more of his life.

Margie's door opens. She is surprised to see him, then delighted. She kisses him. But when he paces the room she knows something is wrong.

"I can't marry you yet," he blurts out finally. "My wife is pregnant."

He sees the stricken look come over her face.

"I don't know how it happened," he says. "An accident—but my fault."

Her chin quivers.

"I can't marry you yet. It's my fault, my responsibility. Don't you see?"

Margie hides eyes full of tears.

"It's only a little longer we have to wait. We can still be married—a year—"

"What's the matter?"

She only shakes her head.

He grabs her shoulders: "Tell me."

"There's nothing to—to tell."

But there is, and he guesses what it is. "Are you pregnant too? Is that it?"

The tears stream down her cheeks. When she nods, he lets go of her. The room is spinning and he puts out a hand to steady it.

"I'm sorry," she sobs. "I didn't do it on purpose. I didn't believe—all those doctors—they told me it was impossible."

She takes both his hands. He tries to swallow, tries to catch his breath.

"Your husband?" he says.

"Oh no. Not my husband."

"It could have been," he says doggedly. "All those nights you had dinner with him."

"It was always just—dinner."

"But you said—"

"I was so jealous of you with your wife. I just wanted you to imagine—wanted you to be—jealous of me, too."

She is sobbing. He is close to sobbing himself.

"No one has touched me since—since the first night with you."

He holds her in his arms.

"All those years I used to think that if I could just get pregnant I'd be the happiest girl in the world."

His cheeks are wet. He doesn't know if they are her tears or his own.

"I can get rid of it," she says.

"No."

"I know a doctor—"

233

"Absolutely not."

"I don't mind."

"No, no, no."

"What are we going to do? Oh, Duke?"

"I'll think of something," he says, holding her.

But what?

CHAPTER | 18

This season there is a new team in the league, Dallas. Made up of castoffs from other teams, plus untried rookies, the team is struggling on the field—it has yet to win a game—and also at the box office. Crowds have been sparse.

So the Big Red, like previous opponents, has been asked to fly into Dallas early enough Friday morning to attend a luncheon sponsored by the Salesmanship Club in a downtown hotel. Practice is to follow at the Cotton Bowl. With reporters on hand both at the luncheon and at the practice, much publicity will be stimulated.

In addition, certain star players, particularly Texans (and of the Texans particularly Craig) have been asked to appear on television programs Friday and Saturday.

Outside the hotel a warm sun beats down on the wide streets common to the big Texas cities. Glare flashes off the windshields of the cars, and the glass and aluminum skyscrapers. It is noon, and hot.

Inside, the players file past tables where girls write out name tags, then pin these tags to lapels. Salesmenship Club members and their guests file past other tables and are pinned with similar name tags. In the ballroom itself there is a long dais filled with local dignitaries, plus the officials of both teams. In front of this is a lower dais for all seventy of the players. A hundred or more other tables, each seating ten or twelve, fill the ballroom. There is much loud talk, grinning, and back-slapping. Every man wears a name tag, and is addressed always by his first name.

There are big glass pitchers of ice water on all the tables, but Dallas has been in the grip of a drought since summer, and the water in these pitchers comes from the Red River. This water, salty and full of chemicals, is almost undrinkable, and Beady Stein moves along in front of the players, warning them not to drink it—they might all get diarrhea.

After the main course, the toastmaster introduces every player in the room. The two head coaches then make speeches filled with platitudes. Dreuder, in his turn, says: "Dallas has a real fine football team, and I know they'll give us a lot of trouble Sunday." Everyone applauds.

To his surprise, Craig, the returning Texan, described by the toastmaster as a "legendary name in the Southwest," is asked to speak.

He stands at the microphone pretending to be embarrassed.

"They didn't tell me I'd have to speak. Shucks—"

The ballroom laughs.

"I'm as embarrassed as that time in high school in west Texas. I was about fifteen years old, wearing a helmet two or three sizes too big for me, and I hit the line and an opponent tackled me around the helmet. It was such a big helmet I don't see how the other kid got his arms around it, but he did. He kept twisting it and twisting it, and about half the mothers in the stands started screaming. They thought they were watching a child get his head screwed completely off."

Everybody is laughing.

"Of course only the helmet was turning. But when the kid let go of me, my helmet was on sideways, with my nose wedged into the earhole. It was stuck, and I couldn't get it off. I couldn't talk either. My voice sounded like a I was talking in a deep cave, and no one could understand what I was saying."

Craig describes how the perplexed referee signaled time-out. The referee had a try at "unscrewing" the helmet, then Craig's coach tried, then finally they led Craig to the sidelines like a blind man. The grandstand was in hysterics,

Craig observes: "A little rough on the ego when you're fifteen years old, wouldn't you say?"

Craig, smiling, waits for the laughter to slacken.

"You know what I was thinking inside that helmet? Well, I had just read *The Man in the Iron Mask*. I thought: The same thing's going to happen to me. I imagined I'd have to wear that helmet around until my beard started to grow, and then eventually my beard would choke me to death."

Craig then tells of another embarrassing game in which a tackler grabbed him by the belt, the belt snapped, and there was Craig sprinting toward the goal line with his pants falling down. He was holding them up with his free hand, but a tackler lunged at him, and he had to stiff-arm the boy, and as he did so, his pants lapsed.

Standing before the mike, Craig does a pantomime of his hand darting from his trousers, to the tackler, back to his trousers, back to the tackler.

236

He listens to the laughter. He does not tell them that he made the touchdown anyway—this would spoil the joke. Nor does he tell them that he was the best high school football player in the state that year. Every Texan in the audience knows this already.

When the laughter ends, Craig says he is delighted to be back in Texas, to be—home. He sits down to tumultuous applause.

Regaining the microphone, the toastmaster tells how proud Texas is of Duke Craig and the record he has made in pro ball in the North, and how he is a credit to his team, the league, the game itself, to Texas, and to the nation. The ballroom grows more and more quiet. The toastmaster, feeling this, goes on in the same vein. His voice becomes husky—Texas gets very emotional about football players, particularly Texans—and it is clear the toastmaster means what he is saying. Several times he is interrupted by applause.

Craig stares at the tablecloth, fearing this speech will end in a standing ovation for himself. Texas needs heroes and made him one when he was still the fifteen-year-old kid in the oversize helmet, and Texas wants to think of him as a king-sized hero now.

The eulogy takes an unexpected form.

"—And Duke and Carribel Craig are and always have been the very model of the best of the youth of this great country and the great state of Texas."

As always, applause follows the mention of Texas.

"—And I only wish Carribel Craig could be here now to see what Texas thinks of her and her husband."

The toastmaster demands: "Why didn't you bring Carribel down with you, Duke? How is Carribel? Stand up and tell us how she is."

Craig stands up at his table, so embarrassed he even slips into the old Texas accent: "She's right fine." What will his teammates think of this? He doesn't know what to say, and so blurts out what is on his mind: "Carribel couldn't come down here on account of—being as she's expecting and all—"

Immediately he wishes he could cut his tongue off. The applause starts. By ones and twos men begin to stand. Soon the entire room stands applauding Duke Craig. Craig, his ears burning, draws on the tablecloth with a knife. He thinks: Why did I say that? I wish I hadn't said that.

Outside the buses wait. The players shoulder on board and ride through the glare of streets to the Cotton Bowl for practice. There are new skyscrapers in aluminum and glass, and

237

older blocks of low buildings, and great wide streets filled with big cars, and signs everywhere to let them know they are in Texas and nowhere else: The Texas National Bank; Lone Star Gas; The Texas and Southwestern Cattle Raisers' Association.

The buses enter the state fair grounds and stop close to the walls of the Cotton Bowl.

Seeing it again brings many memories back to Craig, though he tries to close them off. He dons his sweatshirt and cleats and comes out onto the field, and looks around at the vast empty bowl which he used to play in every year. He toes the thick spongy Bermuda grass, broadleafed, dry, and a little dusty, the grass of all the Southwest stadiums, needing almost no water and a fine cushion to get tackled on, the best.

That night Craig appears on four Dallas television programs. On two, films of his college games are shown. One shows the finals of the high school state championships in the Cotton Bowl, when Craig was sixteen. He provides the commentary for all these films, and is not surprised at how vividly he remembers every play, although the men interviewing him seem to find his memory remarkable.

"But that high school game was fifteen years ago."

"Yes, but it was the biggest thing that had ever happened in my life."

"A high school game?"

Craig thinks: But it was for the Texas state championship, we could have been state champions, and we lost by one point and in the locker room every boy was weeping.

"We thought it was pretty important, though."

Saturday morning, after a brief workout in the Cotton Bowl, Craig catches a cab to the airport and gets onto a plane for west Texas. He is going home.

From the air he looks down on the brown land that bred and nurtured him, and in every town below he sees a high school football field, and he thinks: It must be the same down there as it always was. In Texas, football is the only sport anyone really cares about and every small boy dreams of being an All-American some day.

In Texas the coaching starts in the eighth grade. By the time he was fourteen, Craig was expert at giving newspaper interviews, and talking on the radio (there was no television in Texas then) and at sixteen he was known the length and breadth of the state. Texas junior high and high school teams are organized into leagues, and the season begins under the broiling midsummer sun with two workouts a day, as with

238

the pros, and then when school starts there is a game every Friday night under the lights, as the season builds toward the championship game between the two best high school teams in Texas.

Craig's town, like all the towns, was organized around the high school football team. Booster clubs raised money to hire the best young coaches, paying them perhaps $10,000 a season, with free housing and an expense account as well, and usually two assistant coaches. After a good season there would be a bonus; the coach Craig's senior year in high school was given a new Cadillac. The coach the year before lost two games, which was judged two too many and the booster clubs had him fired.

The shops along Main Street all closed early on Friday afternoons to allow merchants and customers to get home to an early dinner and then get back to the game on time. The pressure felt by the young players on the field, Craig reflects, was the same pressure a pro feels. They had been smartly drilled for wooks, they had studied game films day after day, they wore sharp new uniforms, and the roar that went up when they took the field let them know exactly what their fans and their town expected of them.

Craig played because he loved to put his shoulder into another boy and feel him go down, loved to run with the ball, loved to throw a ball into outstretched arms for a score, loved to compete, loved to win—and also loved all the adulation and applause that went with it, loved to walk down Main Street where all the grown-ups knew his name.

"Hello there, Duke. Say, I got a new shipment of ties in today. Why don't you come inside and pick one out."

"Feelin' thirsty, Duke? You just come inside and sit at the fountain and I'll fix you an ice cream soda."

He knew he was good. He knew he was important.

He loved football so much he played in many sandlot games in his school clothes with his pals—sometimes even on Friday afternoons when there was a game that night. He was fiercely competitive and had to win even these sandlot games. Although he was always polite to his elders, he never gave an inch to boys his own age, and so there were many fights. When he walked home afterward he liked the feeling of the dust stuck to him under his clothes.

He stands beside the river under the trees. The new stadium is a minature Cotton Bowl that holds 17,000, half the population of the town. It has replaced the wooden bleachers of Craig's time, and he looks up at it, admiring the lines, thinking:

239

I built that stadium. As much as any single person, I built it.

My stadium. A nice thought to have, he thinks, though it doesn't change anything in my life now.

He remembers standing back there and winging the ball to someone on play after play. If they rushed him too hard he would take off and run. During the time-outs, the sweat dripping down inside his jersey, he would hold the dipper in his hand, looking up into the lights through a million bugs, sloshing the water around in his mouth, then spitting it out.

He considered himself a tough kid. No one ever made him show pain, and on defense he loved to smash into people. In practice the coach would run them until they began to drop from exhaustion, but Craig never dropped and never complained.

"You gotta be in shape," the coach screamed.

"This is not a friendly game," the coach screamed.

Craig believed this.

The coach said no smoking or drinking. Some of the boys sneaked cigarettes. Craig never did. The coach preached the importance of clean living, and Craig believed him.

"You gotta pay the price of greatness," the coach screamed.

Craig was willing to pay it.

Of course his world widened later, though his love for football remained the same. In college he attended all his classes except those which conflicted with practices or game trips, and sometimes at night he studied until he fell asleep over his books. But in high school his world was bounded by those floodlights with the bugs swimming in them, which rimmed the football field.

"He can't play with that arm." They had a team doctor even then, and a trainer to tape ankles as well.

"Give him a shot, Doc."

"Not *that* arm."

"I gotta play, Doc. You gotta give me a shot. You gotta."

"You better have him out there, Doc. There's a lot riding on that game."

Craig, looking up through the trees at the stadium, smiles and thinks: I always sided with the coach then, against the doctors, against my parents, against my own best interests. Coaches formed me more than any parents ever formed me. They taught simple virtues: absolute dependence on myself, stoicism in the face of pain, facing up to the responsibilities of life. They taught no smoking or drinking, they taught respect for girls, and going to church, and loyalty to your teammates.

And playing when shot full of Novocain as well.

I don't know whether they really believed what they taught, but they made me believe it. Me and most of the others, as near as I can tell.

The house Craig grew up in sits halfway down a tree-lined, dusty street, and for a while he stands looking at it. To this house all during his last year in high school came the college recruiters. He would come home from school and find one of them sitting at the dining room table with his father, elbows and coffee cups on the oilcloth. Some of the recruiters pressured Craig. Most concentrated on his mother and father, and the pressure came from the parents later.

"Baylor's a denominational school, son. You'd get a good religious education at Baylor."

"They're Baptists at Baylor."

"A Baptist education is better than no religion at all, son."

Baylor sent three different men, a week apart. All emphasized religion. Oklahoma sent a wealthy oilman who landed at the town airstrip in his own plane and took Mr. and Mrs. Craig up for a ride in it. Later he flew Craig up to Norman, Oklahoma. He promised that if Duke went to Oklahoma, Duke would have a good job in the oil business as soon as he graduated.

Most of the colleges sent assistant coaches. Arkansas sent the same coach over and over again. Rice sent three different coaches.

"You gotta decide, son. Your mother and I—"

His parents favored whoever had put the most pressure on the most recently.

"At Oklahoma you'd get into the oil business on the ground floor."

"I wish you'd go to one of the church schools. That minister Southern Methodist sent down was so nice. I'd feel much better if I knew you were there with that man looking after you."

The president of the Texas A. & M. alumni association said that if Duke would sign with them, the booster club there would see to it that he had a new car to drive around in.

"Oh no," said Craig, shocked, "I couldn't accept that."

Finally Coach Claypool came up personally from Austin. He ate dinner with them, a new oilcloth tablecloth being laid on for the occasion.

"Why Mrs. Craig, I declare you do fix the fanciest spread I have set down to this year."

Mrs. Craig giggled and said he was only flattering her.

Looking back, Craig can see that Coach Claypool was too slick for all of them. He made Mrs. Craig feel the queen of

Texas cooking. He congratulated Mr. Craig for having sired the greatest high school football player Texas and the world had ever seen. He told Duke that he was building all his plans around Duke alone for the next four years.

Craig signed the letter of intent. Texas University promised him room, board, tuition, and books for four years, and he promised to play football during the same four years. Craig was relieved to have decided, to get out from under the frightful pressure of his parents, and of the recruiters breathing on him every time he turned around.

Three days after he graduated from high school, men from Texas came to get him. He was installed in a boarding house outside of Austin, so as to be hidden from other colleges who might decide to rerecruit him during the summer. He had a job loading packing cases a few hours each day, along with other high school stars waiting to play football for Texas U. He was very homesick. In August freshman practice began in 105-degree heat in a training camp set up on the edge of the desert. Coach Claypool had decided to build this freshman team into the toughest group of boys the state had ever known, and he did.

The house Craig grew up in is occupied by others now. Though he stands looking at it a while longer, he does not go in. Later he goes to the cemetery and looks down on the graves of his parents. He has a brother who is an Air Force officer in Germany, and a sister who teaches school in Houston and who might get over to the game tomorrow, or might not. That is all that remains of the Craig family, and of course of the high school football star of so many seasons ago there remains only—himself.

Craig has not been in this town in ten years, but he does not want to meet anyone from the old days. He goes back to the stadium beside the river and sits on a bench under the trees watching the water go by. He remembers it all, the past and the present, and wonders where he will get the courage to face the future. The only way out that he can see is to pay Margie to go quietly away somewhere, while he stays quietly with his wife and pretends things are fine. That is the advice anyone in football would give him. It is the practical thing, the only thing that can save him. Football is a strict game with a strict code, and he remembers the Italian movie director famous for his sexual prowess, whose name came up, and Beady Stein saying: "They better lock that guy up before he impregnates the world." This was followed by a roar of laughter, with Stein laughing louder than anyone.

Craig can hear the same voice saying: "They better lock

Duke Craig up before he impregnates the world." Followed by the same laughter.

He watches the water go by, brown and slow, and thinks of the new bowl stadium behind him. During his three years in high school, crowds doubled—they lost only three games in this town in three years.

How could his life have come from there to here? He blinks several times.

He cannot do anything like that to Margie.

But what about himself?

No matter what happens to himself, he cannot do anything like that to Margie.

After a time he catches a taxi out to the airport and then the evening plane back to Dallas. He has remembered much, but solved nothing.

CHAPTER | 19

George Dreuder watches his team warm up on the field. In the passing drill the balls are missing, or being dropped. The players shagging punts bobble them. Some distance away, the linemen being drilled by the line coach come sluggishly off the ball.

Dreuder's counterpart, the young Dallas coach, walks toward him. They shake hands.

"Good crowd," Dreuder says, for something to say.

They look around, admiring the half-filled stadium. This is easier than making small talk.

"What will the crowd be?"

"About forty thousand," the Dallas coach says. "Our best this year. It's a tribute to Craig. He's the one they want to see."

The two coaches discuss the problem: Texas fans are still loyal to high school and college football. They are not interested in their new pro team.

"You'll win them over in time."

"I hope so. We have to win some games first of course. And maybe pick up a player as popular in Texas as Craig was."

Dreuder asks: "Why was he that popular? Texas has produced plenty of other great players."

The Dallas coach gives his opinion. On the field, from high school on, Craig made exciting runs to win games in the final seconds. Off the field his life was full of suspense, too. Oklahoma University practically kidnapped him, and even announced he had signed to go there; but like a good Texan Craig went to Texas. Then came his knee injury. Could he come back? He not only came back, but was better than ever. Added to this was the fantastic publicity during his last year in college, his storybook romance and marriage, his big contract and bonus with the pros.

244

"He was the football hero everybody most admired," the Dallas coach says. "And he was a clean living boy too. Went to church. Always said and did the right thing."

After a moment, the Dallas coach adds cautiously: "I hear he's changed."

Dreuder walks back to his own side of the field. Nearby the band waits at the sideline to parade. The sun, reflected off the brass instruments, is blinding. Dreuder looks over the grandstands. Jewelry flashes, there are many fur stoles and capes. Texas is oil-rich and land-rich and it shows in the football crowd. Many of the businessmen wear cowboy hats, though there are few cowboys left in Texas now.

Dreuder watches his team drill. They are uninspired.

He orders them off the field.

Behind him, as he moves toward the locker room, the band blares a strident march, and a line of leggy girls struts onto the field. They wear brief costumes, with flashing bangles, and cowboy hats hang from their necks. They are all twirlers. The public address introduces them as the Apache Belles. The band is marching too, boys and girls in red uniforms. Ahead of them is a drum so big it takes two men to carry it. A third marches alongside, beating it.

"The band with the biggest boom in Dixie," cries the voice from the public address.

The booming drum, drowning out the music, fills the stadium with noise and excitement.

Inside the locker room at the blackboard, Dreuder diagrams the first play to run after the kickoff return. He has chosen a screen pass, hoping to spread the defense, pick up big yardage, and give his own team both information and an emotional lift. It is a good sound play to start with against this new, inexperienced team.

Dreuder has decided against haranguing his players. Perhaps they will make this first play work, and from it take enthusiasm for the game itself, and then begin to play sharply. He has seen this happen to other teams which were down, as his own team is down. It does not happen often, but it is possible, especially against a new and inept team like Dallas. Besides, even a bad performance by his own team should be enough to defeat Dallas.

He is hopeful as he trails his team out onto the field.

But his hope lasts just one play.

Joe Morris catches the kickoff on the 1-yard line, drops it across the turf while trying to pick it up again, and finally falls on it on the 8-yard line.

At the sideline, Dreuder curses. He stubs at the grass with

245

his short-cleated coaches' shoes, forgetting to order Rocco not to run the screen pass, to call some other play.

As Dreuder watches the teams line up for the first play, he convinces himself that Rocco will of course change the play on his own.

But Rocco, who did not play a minute this season until Pennoyer was injured, has no intention of disobeying instructions. He suspects the screen pass will fail this close to his own goal line, but he calls it anyway, fading back into the end zone with men chasing him. As he tries to loft the ball to Craig over the fingers of the Dallas rushers, one of them tips it, and it sails straight up into the air.

Softly thrown, the ball hangs there above the heads of two Dallas linemen, and when it drops finally, one of them wrestles it away from the other and hugs it to his breast. Since he is standing in the end zone, this is a touchdown for Dallas.

When Rocco comes to the bench, Dreuder berates him. The 40,000 fans cannot hear Dreuder's curses, but they can see Rocco's gestures as he seeks to explain. They see Dreuder give a snort of disgust and walk away from him. They see Rocco stride toward the opposite end of the bench, where he slams his helmet to the ground and meekly sits down.

The game deteriorates. Dallas is inept, the Big Red listless, and so the teams appear evenly matched.

Dallas finds a weak spot in the Big Red defense: the rookie tackle Otis Denson, who replaces the injured Greg Wagner at defensive end. Denson weighs 265 pounds and has a big college reputation; every summer he drives a jackhammer digging up streets, and in his free time he lifts weights. He thinks strength is the answer to all, but opposite him is a thirty-year-old veteran, a castoff from the Rams. This man weighs forty pounds less than Denson, but he has moves, and Denson does not. The veteran never attacks from the angle Denson expects, and when Denson tries to manhandle him, there is frequently nothing to manhandle but air. Denson knows nothing of guile, nothing of the feints and fakes of the big pro linemen. Most plays end with Denson and the veteran handfighting each other, standing upright, while the ball carrier scoots by them for big gains.

This weak spot not only serves to keep the Dallas offense alive, it also further discourages an already discouraged Big Red defensive line. The others struggle and claw at Dallas for two plays, only to watch the third go past Otis Denson for a first down.

The Dallas passing attack is poor. One Dallas pass is deflected twice before being intercepted far downfield by Winfield Green, fastest man on the Big Red team. He runs it back sixty yards, but when tackled he fumbles the ball into the surprised arms of the Dallas quarterback, who runs the ball back to midfield, is tackled, and fumbles there in his turn.

The crowd roars with laughter, or perhaps appreciation. On the sideline, Coach Dreuder kicks the turf and burns.

Soon the Big Red is backed up to its own 1-yard line. Jones goes in to punt, but the pass from center is low (nobody is sharp today) and as Jones grapples with it, he steps over the end line for a safety, and two more points for Dallas. Later Jones costs his team a penalty on a kickoff—neither he nor Pete can find the kicking tee, and they spend several minutes rooting around under the bench looking for it, while the referee steps off five yards for delay of game.

All this sloppiness is contagious. Dallas, on a later kickoff, is penalized twice for offside, and kicks the third time from their 30-yard line. Craig is in on kickoffs now, for Morris has been shaken up, and he catches the ball on the 15-yard line and races upfield with it, not thinking exclusively of the game, thinking also of how much more confused life is than football—football is absolutely clear-cut. Spying an opening, he tells himself that the football field is the only place in the world where all his instincts are perfect—and thinking this he reacts a shade too late and the opening is closed when he gets there. The tackler, wrestling him down, also wrestles the ball away from him. Craig springs on the man's back and in a rage flings him to the turf as hard as he can. The player gets up, eyes Craig speculatively, and trots off the field.

There is a penalty against Craig, and soon after that a series of penalties against both teams. Tempers get short, the officials get exceedingly strict, and the players start fouling each other as much to spite the officials as to settle private grudges: if those bastards want to call penalties, let's give them penalties to call. Mean Gene Gardner gets thrown out of the game for fighting.

Jones is sent in to kick a field goal which will cinch victory for the Big Red. This will be his eleventh field goal of the season if he makes it, and according to his contract he gets a $500 bonus for each one over ten. He is thinking of this money as the teams line up. The pass from center is wide, and Rocco (subbing for Pennoyer here too) puts it down badly. Jones aims a wild kick at the ball, seeing the $500 vanishing, and it is batted down by a Dallas lineman. As it bounces around the ground, Jones runs over and kicks it again; this time it rises and sails cleanly and illegally over the posts. As the officials confer to decide what the penalty for such a kick might be, the Dallas team is laughing. The entire crowd is laughing. Jones hangs his head and trots embarrassed from the field.

With a few seconds left in the game, Jones comes on to punt. The ball is on the Dallas forty-five, and the strategy is to kick the ball straight up in the air, so that Dallas will have to field it and run with it close to their own goal line. Since Dallas has no time-outs left, and thus no means of stopping the clock, this punt could well be the last play of the game.

But Jones is the leading punter in the league and according to his contract will receive a $1,000 bonus if he wins the punting championship. He comes onfield wanting to boom one, both to redeem himself with the crowd and to safeguard his punting championship. He reasons that Dallas will never score anyway; all a booming punt can possibly give them is a single extra play.

So he booms it. It sails over the end zone, seventy yards on the fly. The clock is stopped, and Dallas takes over on the 20-yard line.

Dallas is two points behind, and there are twenty-two seconds to play, time for two, possibly even three plays.

Coolly, the Dallas quarterback throws a down-and-out pass to the sideline for an eighteen-yard gain. Joe Morris, the Big Red defensive captain, sees the same play coming again. It figures: this is Dallas' strongest play, and it will give them, if successful, both enough yardage to make a long field-goal possible, and enough time (because it will stop the clock) to kick one.

Morris is thinking of his own contract. He gets $200 for each interception, and $500 if he can run an interception back for a touchdown.

Many of the contracts are written with bonuses. Pennoyer gets bonuses for each game won over eight games, and for the eastern and league championships, a possible $6,000 extra. But Morris doesn't know what bonus arrangements other players have. He knows for certain only his own contract; he is thinking only of his own bonuses.

He is certain that he has read the quarterback's mind right, and as Number 81 races down at him he reads this man's mind, too, and knows exactly where the pass will be thrown to. Number 81 is tall and skinny and very young, and easy for a talented defensive back like Morris to handle, and Morris is counting on the sure $200, and possibly $500 if he can find any blocking as he runs the ball back. He times the flight of the ball, and leaps in front of Number 81 to make the interception, only to have the ball go through his hands. He hears it sock home in Number 81's gut. Then he is chasing futilely

248

after Number 81. He chases him all the way over the goal line.

With seven seconds to play, Dallas has scored the winning touchdown.

Morris, sweaty, dirt-stained, tired, troops into the locker room with the others. They move head down, silent.

Defeat.

In the center of the room rises the mound of dirty tape. Clods of earth and grass fall under each chair. Socks, jocks, and T-shirts, all of them soaked with sweat, make limp piles on the floor.

Let Pete clean up. He cost them five yards by losing Jones's kicking tee that time. Five yards might have made all the difference.

This is nonsense, but comforting. It is a relief to blame it on somebody.

Voices begin to rise.

"That Denson is beautiful. He's gonna make all-league statue this year."

"The only time Mean Gene hit his man all day was when he punched him."

"Jones is not kicking well this year."

"In my neighborhood we say he can't kick."

"Do you think Morris was trying for an interception?"

"I didn't notice you making any big plays, you sonuvabitch."

"Who you calling a sonuvabitch, you sonuvabitch?"

There is a scuffle. Naked men drag other naked men apart. Dreuder screams for order, he berates them all. "I don't want to hear another word in here. The next guy who speaks gets fined fifty dollars. All of you just shut up."

The father silencing children.

In the bus, Craig sits beside Mel Slade.

"I think my ribs are busted," says Slade.

"We could have beaten them easy," Craig says. "It's just that everybody was thinking about himself instead of the team."

Slade makes no answer. It hurts him to breathe. He attempts to breathe as little as possible.

The plane rises into a pink haze. Stewardesses, trying to be cheerful, pass out beer. They get no response and don't know why.

No one can explain to himself how such a sloppy game was possible.

Craig gazes down on the country. Below now must be Louisiana, which produces oil and football players, and then Arkansas, which produces cotton and football players. That winding silver ribbon must be the Mississippi; a bit east of the river is Nashville, where he first met Margie.

249

As darkness gathers below, Craig gazes down on Kentucky, which produces horses and football players. The plane plunges into night. Below now must be Pennsylvania, which produces coal and steel and also hundreds upon hundreds of Catholic football players with Polish names.

He finds, when the stewardess comes for his tray, that he has eaten no dinner.

Ahead wait two pregnant women, and whatever he does will be wrong, and he will have to decide something soon, and he does not see any way out.

The plane bumps down.

"The only way to travel."

He draws his tie tight against his throat and reaches into the overhead rack for his team blazer and then his overcoat. Outside the night is cold—twenty or thirty degrees colder than Texas.

In Texas three hours ago he was home, and now he is home here, and no man can have two homes, and the answer must be that he, Duke Craig, no longer has any.

CHAPTER | 20

When he gets home Carribel, in her bathrobe, is sipping tea in the kitchen.

"You want a beer?" she asks cordially.

He is surprised. "No."

"Ah thought you might want a beer."

"We had some on the plane."

He can see the edge of her nightgown under her bathrobe, and she has her hair in rollers.

"You want a cup of tea, then?"

"Did any mail come?"

"It's there in the fruit bowl."

He sifts through bills she never opens, junk mail she never thinks to throw away, envelopes addressed in pencil that must be from small boys.

"How many times did you carry the ball?"

"Nineteen, I think."

"Are you sore?" she asks solicitously.

"Not bad." Is she trying to build up to a fight, or what?

"It must be the Texas air."

"You know how the Cotton Bowl is," he says. "The grass is thick and soft."

"Ah miss Texas."

"A lot of people were asking for you."

"Who?" she asks, pleased.

"My sister. Some of the sportswriters. Old Professor Legrand."

"Where'd you see him?"

"He turned up in the locker room before the game."

After a moment she says: "You lost."

"We were dreadful."

"Ah watched part of it on TV."

This annoys him. How can she watch only part of it, when football is everything in their lives?

"Ah saw it when you fumbled."

"You might try watching the whole thing some Sunday."

"Ah never have enjoyed football much."

"You liked it in college."

"That was different. You were the big hero and everything." In college she shared Duke Craig's glory; up here she has become just another suburban housewife. The glamorous life she expected to last forever didn't.

"Football is a stupid game."

"Well, it keeps a lot of nice young men out of gas stations."

"That's where most of them will end up."

"Maybe."

"—You included."

He yanks his tie off. "I'm going to bed."

But he is not quick enough. "Who is she?" Carribel demands.

"Who is who?"

"The other woman."

After a time, he says: "I told you there is no other woman."

"And you would never lie, would you. You and George Washington, or was it Jesus Christ. Who is she?"

Craig thinks automatically: So she knows.

But to protect Margie as much as possible, he goes on with the lie: "No one."

As he climbs the stairs, she pursues. "Tell me how much you are looking forward to your new son or daughter."

"I thought you didn't want to have any more babies."

"It was an accident, honey."

"Sure."

"It was. Accidents do happen, honey, don't you know."

When he turns, there is a hard bright look in her eyes.

"Tell me how happy you are about it, honey."

"When is it due?"

"You mean you want to know how soon you can escape from your wife?"

"When is it due?"

"Have you got a speech ready for the sportswriters when the baby's born? About how happy you are?"

He goes into his office, drops the letters there, and peels off his shirt. Carribel stands in the doorway.

"Do you remember what you told them after Bobby was born?"

"Would you like to leave me alone, please?"

With mock sadness, Carribel says: "You don't remember. And it was so precious. You said—"

"Never mind."

"Ah do believe it's coming back to you, honey."

"I remember."

"Your words are engraved on my heart. You said—"

"Stop it."

"Ah can still heah your poetic words—"

"Stop it."

"You said: 'He weighs about as much as a football, and sits in the cup of your hand like a football does, and holding him is like scoring my first touchdown for the Big Red, only better.'"

Craig, seeing these words in print, was mortified, and now he is mortified anew.

"Ain't Ah got a poetic husband though? He utters words that are right up there with Lincoln."

"Is there anything else you want to say?"

"Just that Ah do hope that when your new son is born, honey, you can think up some more such beautiful lines. Because you mustn't let on you ain't happy, just trapped."

She slams the door on him. He rubs his eyes. Then he snaps the light out, and stands at the window staring down into the garden.

Monday Craig tries to calculate how much money he has. He calls the bank to ask how much equity is in the house, and his insurance agent to ask how much his policies are worth, and his broker about the value of his few stocks. He adds up the figures in his bank books. He tries to remember exactly how much the club still owes him on past seasons, but can't, and doesn't dare phone to ask.

Money, a concrete in a sea of variables. Except that here money is a variable too. How long will it have to last, how can he get more, what will he have to pay for?

He begins to pay the bills that have accumulated. He signs and sends out photos to kids. He can hear Carribel moving about the house, and when she begins banging things he knows she is bored, or upset, or whatever she gets, and wants to fight.

He stands at the window. The grass is pale, and the rock garden overgrown with dead gorse. But it blooms every spring the way a football team blooms every autumn. In summer it will be ablaze with flowers. Great old elms rim the lawn, thick boughs to go with thick trunks, oversize among trees as football players are oversize among men.

If he could talk it over with someone, that might help. But to whom could he say: I have got two women pregnant, and don't know what to do next.

With a wry laugh, Craig imagines the response.

You mean you don't know what to do for an encore?

Don't laugh, it's not funny.

No, it's not funny.

It wasn't my fault. I didn't do it on purpose.

Whose fault is it then?

You've got me there.

You're an extremely careless young man.

Not careless. My wife did it on purpose, and the other girl imagined she couldn't have children and took no precautions, and so it just—happened.

I don't see how I can help you if you are unwilling even to concede your carelessness.

I concede it. Help me.

I'm terribly sorry, young man. You should have come to me before. There is nothing I can do for you now.

You refuse—

There's nothing I can do.

Craig turning from the window, thinks: I can certainly see the humor in all this.

On the wall above a leather sofa is a blowup of himself at eighteen crashing through the line against Baylor, head-on toward the camera. An old picture. He wears a leather helmet with no face guard. The hard helmets came in the next year, and face guards much later. Both his feet are off the ground, and his legs are bare: a photo (it seems to Craig) full of youth and strength and joy.

He was brand-new then, the way a racehorse is brand-new. Although he thought he was admired as something special, the one and only me, he can see now that he was admired more the way a racehorse is admired, or a pinup girl: as an example of the perfection of the species, and as proof of its yearly renewal. Useless, except to look at, and perhaps watch run. Isn't he, she, it, gorgeous? And isn't it great that next year there will be a new one just as gorgeous.

He has contributed pleasure to the lives of hundreds of thousands of fans. He has given them not his time, but his body, the most intimate thing he had to give.

What have they contributed to his life? He stares at the numbers on the pad on his desk: this much money. But it isn't very much money, considering, and he feels as he imagines certain prostitutes must feel at times: perhaps he has sold himself too cheaply.

He thinks of Margie home alone, with *him* swelling inside her. Loving him, trusting him to find a way.

But there is no way.

Outside his door is his wife, for whom he is responsible before the law and human opinion. Duty and honor demand a certain course now. He may have made only a mistake, but now he must pay for it.

To go with Margie would be to lose his children, to lose this house and its lawns and trees paid for with sweat and pain and his skill at performing rare acts under pressure, to lose his untarnished reputation, to lose football. It would also be to lose admiration and approval that he is not sure he can live without.

To stay would preserve some of that, perhaps all of it. But the cost would be to abandon this girl he loves, this female animal with her modesty and desire, her timidity, her passion, her trust—to abandon her to the storms. To see her reaching out to him, and then turn away.

They better lock that guy up before he impregnates the world.

He rubs his eyes.

They better lock that guy up before he impregnates the world.

At noon he goes down and fixes himself a sandwich. His face is haggard from too little sleep. Carribel appears in the kitchen.

"Do you still feel trapped, honey?"

Craig remains silent.

"Poor honey."

He begins eating his sandwich.

"Don't you wish you'd been more careful, honey?"

He chews steadily.

"If it's a boy, Ah'm fixing to name him Wallace Craig, junior."

He says carefully: "I thought we decided against that when Bobby was born."

Carribel, in mock surprise, says: "Why, Ah do believe you are finally taking an interest in your baby."

"I figure it's due about July first."

"Time enough," Carribel drawls, "for you to come to your senses."

He devours that sandwich and begins making another.

"She'll never appreciate what Ah'm saving her from."

"Who are you saving from what?"

"That actress. You know the one Ah mean."

255

He swallows half the new sandwich and is hungrier than ever. He starts on the other half.

"Ah'm saving her from being married to you. She has no idea how grateful she ought to be."

Craig swallows steadily.

"Does she know that you love that stupid game more than you could ever love any woman? That and your own image. Does she know how proper you are? That you can't sort out all the demands on your time, and so you say yes to everybody. Which leaves very little time for your wife and children —in fact no time for your wife at all. Does she know that? Does she know how much more intelligent you think you are than your poor wife? Does she know you don't have any love left over for your wife, because you gave it all to yourself?"

Craig wolfs down a third sandwich and a glass of beer.

"If she only knew what it is like being married to such a hero as you."

Craig swallows a banana.

"Wait till your children learn about you. See what kind of hero you are to them."

Craig starts on a fourth sandwich.

"Picks up some slut in heat and thinks it's love."

In the hall, Craig puts his coat on. He is still hungry.

"How are you going to explain to her that you got your wife pregnant? Have you thought that out yet?" Carribel begins to laugh. "Tell her it was an accident. Tell her you did it from across the room by accident."

Craig goes out. The door slamming cuts off Carribel's laughter. His stomach churns. He looks up through a lacework of branches at the pale light of winter. Gradually his hunger goes away.

At the hospital, Craig is admitted to Pennoyer's room. The quarterback's leathery face is pale, and there is sweat on his forehead.

"Hurt much?"

"It ain't too bad. It depends what you understand by pain. It ain't anything I can't stand."

They nod at each other.

Pennoyer says: "Cheer me up, Duke. Tell me something funny. Like how to lose to Dallas. That must have handed you all some laughs."

Small talk ensues. Craig finds that they are ill at ease with each other. If you never expose yourself to teammates, they never expose themselves to you, he thinks. Do he and Pennoyer know each other at all? The only one Craig has ever been able to talk to is Margie, and how can he give up that?

"Life is full of surprises."

"You can't win."

"But there are different levels of losing."

The conversation can go no further on this exalted plane.

"Shit," says Pennoyer.

They can't talk about Pennoyer's suffering, nor Craig's. For all those years their intimacy has been based on touchdowns, and they don't know how to shift that intimacy now. Their affection for each other is not enough.

"He's going to scrimmage us for an hour Wednesday."

"Madman."

"It's a good week to be in the hospital."

"Shit."

An edge of plaster peeps from the front of Pennoyer's gown. The silence is broken by Pennoyer offering candy from a box.

"Some kid sent it to me."

"That's very nice."

"Yes, it's nice."

What needs to be said, neither can find words to start.

"Most people are afraid of life."

"Most people try to get through life without being noticed."

"When the going gets tough they fill themselves with whiskey or drugs."

"They'd rather become a stone or a tree."

"Shit."

It becomes time for Craig to go.

"Tell them to win for the Gipper," says Pennoyer stolidly.

As Craig waves from the door, Pennoyer suddenly says: "Don't worry, Duke, you'll always do the right thing."

Craig thinks: I would if I knew what it was.

Tuesday morning at practice, Joe Morris and Lincoln Hamilton lead calisthenics. Near Craig, F. X. Boyle, wearing a sweatsuit with Pennoyer's name stenciled on it, does them, too. Boyle takes part in the calisthenics three times a week, always in a sweatsuit bearing the name of some back or end. The owner identifies with the stars of his team, and Craig has seen him toss linemen's sweatsuits back into the bin, claiming they would be too baggy.

After calisthenics, Boyle stands with the coaches in a jacket lebeled: Big Red Staff.

The players run. They run through windsprints, then passing drills, then plays. Craig takes a turn passing the ball. If anything happens to Rocco, the team will go into a single wing offense with Craig at tailback.

The team is quiet, and Craig senses determination. There is a feeling that they can win; they will win. They can beat Cleveland Sunday and close out the season on a victory.

Coach Dreuder runs them. The whistle tweets.

"Okay, run it again."

Sweat drips down their faces. On the sideline, watching, stand Mel Slade with strapped ribs, Donald Fox with a cast on his hand, and Jimmy Finney with sweat dripping down his face. Finney, out of the cast now, spends most of every practice session climbing up and down the grandstand steps.

The squad is depleted, but the determination is there.

When they come into the locker room there is some chatter. Everybody can feel the new spirit. No one knows where it has come from, but it is there.

This is the last game. Victory will clinch second place, and a trip to Florida for the Playoff Bowl game against the second place team in the West. That means another payday, and a week in the sun with all expenses paid. Victory will salvage the season. Victory will give an illusion of strength to launch next season on come July. Victory will make the Christmas holidays cheerful instead of gloomy. Victory will mean a better contract when Boyle comes around in a few months.

Most of all, to win is why they exist.

To lose is to be humiliated. Nothing is fun after a defeat. A week of depression sets in. Only the next victory can wipe out defeat for any pro athlete; to lose this last game would be to chew all winter on the bad taste of defeat.

They strip down. In the showers they joke. Practice is over for the day.

F. X. Boyle leads the coaches and reporters upstairs to the weekly press luncheon in the stadium club restaurant. About thirty men are present, including the Browns' publicity man, who will give a speech about the condition of his team. A bar has been set up. The reporters get half drunk. Boyle watches them, pleased; this makes for "friendlier" stories.

Malverde leads a Negro reporter to Boyle, introducing him as W. Rollo Poindexter, who is doing a cover story on Lincoln Hamilton for *Ebony* magazine.

"Link is the first person of his race ever to play for me," says Boyle.

The reporter asks Boyle's opinion of the race question. Annoyed, Boyle thinks: This is sports, not the race question; what are you trying to do, make trouble on my team.

But he thinks of a witty remark instead. Grinning, Boyle

says: "The race question all boils down to this: There are only two kinds of people in this world, those who are Irish, and those who wish they were Irish."

Though Boyle expects a big laugh, he does not get it. Puzzled, he adds: "Link Hamilton will be playing for me as long as he wants to, and after that he'll join my coaching staff. There'll be a place for him on this team as long as he wants it."

Boyle has no interest in Negroes or civil rights, but he admires great football players, white or black. Hamilton as a coach will keep future Negro players in line, which is important, and being a Negro, he won't have to be paid much.

When coffee has been served, Boyle calls the meeting to order. He has memorized a joke, and also memorized several amusing comments on last Sunday's defeat by Dallas. But the laughter is only polite. Though his jokes are always carefully thought out in advance, he has never been able to convulse audiences, and doesn't know why. He doesn't understand what tricks other speakers use to do so.

Meanwhile, downstairs in the locker room a tailor named Ben Schwartz is taking measurements for summer suits. There are still several players to measure. Ben Schwartz is present in the locker room every Tuesday, and sells a great many suits to players who, because of their bizarre builds, can never buy ready-made suits that fit. Schwartz scrawls *football player* across every order blank as he signs it: otherwise his tailors will refuse to cut the suit to the proportions indicated, believing that Schwartz must have measured wrong.

Today Schwartz sells seven suits, one of his best Tuesdays ever. He too can sense that the team feels good, and believes it is going to win.

Dreuder feels it. He cancels the scheduled Wednesday scrimmage.

Craig feels it. He runs hard every day, and so do the others. He watches the films, studying defensive personnel he knows by heart. He memorizes the new frequency charts—they have changed slightly since the first Cleveland game so many weeks ago. When the meetings end and the locker room empties out, Craig stays on to rerun films again and again for himself and others—sometimes for himself alone. He gets bleary-eyed from them, then rewinds them and shows them again.

From the moment that the football starts each day, until the moment the guard passes him outside the stadium at night, the disaster about to engulf him can be held off.

"Nice night, Mr. Craig."

That guard is the only one he knows who calls him Mr. Craig.

"So it is, Joe."

"Maybe we'll have nice weather for the game Sunday."

"Good night, Joe."

"Good night, Mr. Craig."

When he goes to see Margie, he is ill at ease with her, also.

"You look nice like that, with your hair damp and combed."

"I just left the stadium."

"I suppose I've seen you that way before."

"I guess so."

There is only one thing either wants to talk about, but neither dares broach the subject, and so they make small talk.

"Is everything all right?"

"Yes. Is it with you?"

"Everything's fine."

"I'm not sick or anything."

"That's good."

"Duke—"

"Yes?"

"No, nothing."

He tells her he can't stay long; he must speak at the Catholic high schools all-city football team dinner.

"It's just as well. I'm rather tired tonight anyway."

After a while he gets up to go.

"Good night."

"Good night."

In the doorway they embrace each other. Each wants to hear the other say I love you, but neither wants to speak the magic words first.

He can feel her heart beating, and her cheek is warm against his. Under her hair his hand cups the base of her neck.

"The doctor says I'm very healthy. Since this is my first baby, he said perhaps Mr. Berger would like to come in and have a talk with him."

She laughs. Craig laughs too.

"At least I'm Mrs. Somebody. That's better than most girls in my position."

He holds her close.

"I shouldn't have said that. I'm sorry."

"You say whatever you want."

"I wish—" She breaks off. All she wants is to be reassured of his love.

For a time neither speaks. Then Craig says; "I've got to go."

She bites her lip. "Have a good speech."

When he looks back, she is still standing in the doorway.

She smiles and waves. He is aware that the magic words have been spoken by nobody. Why didn't she say them? Why didn't he? The words are—only words, but they might help. The world is a poor place without them. Brooding, he takes a taxi to the hotel where the banquet is to take place.

At the hotel he steps into a phone booth.

Margie's voice comes on the line. "Hello?"

"I love you."

"Oh, Duke," she says, and starts to cry.

After he hangs up, he waits in the booth a moment for his own eyes to dry. Then he strides into the ballroom to face his public.

From the dais he looks down on the best high school football players in the city: a sea of big eyes and smooth faces. To either side of Craig on the dais are high school coaches and some priests, one of them Father O'Malley. The toastmaster is Bruce Bingham, who calls the Big Red games on TV. The guest of honor is the cardinal. Thumbing idly through the program, Craig sees to his surprise that he is to receive an award himself: the Catholic High Schools Good Sportsmanship Award.

When the cardinal arrives and says grace, the dinner begins. It follows predictable lines: bland jokes by Bruce Bingham and the cardinal, the award of plaques to the eleven best high school players. Then the cardinal picks up an extra plaque, and begins to eulogize Duke Craig as the type of clean-living, courageous athlete all of these boys should emulate.

It is corny enough, and Craig has received similar awards before; in a ten-year career they are inevitable. But tonight he looks down into those big round eyes, and it is as if he can hear the cardinal's voice saying: "Better that a millstone be tied around your neck, and you be cast into the sea, than that you scandalize one of these little ones."

Standing at the microphone, Craig is handed the plaque. The cardinal whispers in his ear—Craig expects something about prayer, but instead the cardinal pretends to be a betting man: "I like the Big Red by two touchdowns Sunday."

Craig flashes the smile that is expected of him, then stands with downcast eyes trying to collect his thoughts. The young faces look up at him, some smiling, all adoring.

Now is no time for jokes about the helmet that got screwed on sideways, or the game in which his pants nearly fell down. He has an inspirational type talk, and now he seeks to alter it for these boys in terms of what he himself has learned of life in the last few weeks.

He tries to tell them about caring. "To care is the most important thing in the world. If you care enough, anything is possible. If you care enough, then nothing can stand in your way for long." He sees he is losing them, so he explains that caring is the quality that enables a fullback to bowl over tacklers on the way to the goal line. It is the quality that enables a man to get ahead in business, or a mother to love a boy who plays football in his school clothes and comes home with buttons missing and grass-stained pants.

They chuckle.

He gets serious again, trying to explain it. When he feels he is losing them once more, he describes Jonesy, the previous Sunday, kicking the bounding football out of somebody's hands and over the posts. "That's what we call caring too much."

He has described it so well they are all laughing.

"Jonesy wasn't laughing."

They are convulsed.

When they quiet down, Craig says seriously: "But caring too much is the least of the errors men fall into."

They watch him.

"Caring is love. You can't be good at anything unless you love it. Do you know what separates the good teams from the bad teams in our league? The players on the good teams have respect and admiration—and love—for one another. The players on the bad teams get on each other's nerves."

He is over their heads now, but beginning to see some of it clearly for the first time.

Coming back to them, he tells of Pennoyer, a player who cares, a player the others will follow, a player for whom you will execute plays you don't think will work, simply because he thinks they'll work. Because he cares enough, you will try it—and often enough it does work, too.

When he finishes, and the cardinal has pronounced the benediction, boys crowd around to shake his hand and ask technical questions about football.

Father O'Malley's meaty hand comes over the top of the group to grasp Craig's.

"Great speech, Duke."

The priest draws Craig aside. Under the Roman collar the priest wears a dickey of pleated black silk. His nails are manicured, and he smells of aftershave lotion.

"You ought to be the team chaplain, not me," Father O'Malley jokes.

Craig's own nails are short. One is black, and another has been ripped sideways down across the quick.

"Anyway, Duke, I'm very pleased that you've made up your mind to put aside—I mean that you've decided to resume being the same Duke Craig you've always been."

The group of high school boys waits respectfully a few paces off.

Father O'Malley cuffs his shoulder. "F. X. is going to be very pleased, too."

"Yes, well—"

"Well, I just wanted you to know that you're doing the right thing, and you won't regret it."

Father O'Malley's grin turns away. The high school football players crowd forward to surround Duke Craig anew.

CHAPTER 21

When he gets home, Carribel grabs up the plaque.

"Sportsmanship Award. Sport of adultery. That's your sport, right, honey?"

He reaches for the plaque.

"But Ah want to hang it over my bed. To remind me of you."

"If you want to fight, let's fight in the morning."

"Are you too tired, honey?" she mocks.

She follows him up the stairs.

"Sportsmanshipping must be such a grind, honey."

He is trying to ignore her and strip off his shirt at the same time, and one of the buttons pops and strikes the wall.

"Now you'll have to sew that back on, poor honey. Or maybe the adulteress will do it if you ask her. But don't think Ah will. Ah'm only the wife."

"You'll wake the children."

"Ah'm only doing this for them." She begins to cry. He watches her work the tears up. "Their daddy doesn't care about them. Ah'm only trying to keep my happy home together for their sakes."

She never attacks from the same angle twice. "You amaze me," he says brokenly. "You truly amaze me."

Saturday morning he takes his time dressing after practice. But the Browns come in to fill the locker room across the hall—he can hear them milling around in there. Later he hears the rumble of their cleats in the corridor.

The guard, Joe, enters to clear Craig out of the room. The Browns' coach, a small, ice-cold man who has won many championships, wants no spies in the stadium during the hour his team has the field.

"I'm sorry, Mr. Craig."

"No, it's nothing, Joe."

"It's just for the hour they're out there."

"I know."

"He's a bastard, that man."

"I can see his point, though."

"I hope you boys wipe them out tomorrow."

"We'll try, Joe."

"Have a good day, Mr. Craig."

He goes home hoping for quiet, for he wants to concentrate on tomorrow's game.

In the kitchen he gets cheese and beer out of the icebox, and bread out of the drawer.

"You mean the adulteress doesn't fix your lunch for you?"

He fixes his sandwich.

"What kind of adulteress can she be not to fix your lunch."

"The children—"

"They don't know the meaning of such words as that, though they soon will, Ah'm sure. Their daddy will teach them, won't you, Daddy?"

Later he goes out to toss a football around with his son. Soon the lawn is crowded with small boys. From the kitchen door, Carribel orders the game off the lawn.

Some of the boys back away in several directions. Others stare at Craig.

Craig strides toward the kitchen door.

"That's what the lawn is for."

They glare at each other. At last Carribel drops her eyes and turns away.

Craig has won a small victory, and is pleased. "It's okay boys. Mrs. Craig has changed her mind."

It is a sunny afternoon, not very cold, and he is warm enough in a red sweater. The turf is firm underfoot, and the leather feels good in his hands. When he throws it, the football seems to ride on the late afternoon light. He enjoys the delight with which some boys catch it and run for touchdowns, and the disappointment with which others drop it, and look, for a moment, ready to cry.

"My fault," he always calls quickly. "Bad pass." In the huddle he whispers, "Same play again," to give the boy who dropped the ball another chance.

The streetlights on the corner come on. Soon there are dark shadows of trees across the playing field. The December night closes hurriedly in, and the game ends.

"Thanks for the game, Mr. Craig," say the more timid boys. "It sure was nice of you, Mr. Craig."

The braver boys call him Duke: "I hope you beat the Browns tomorrow, Duke."

Voices, high-pitched and excited, drift back to him out of the darkness.

"You got a great old man, you know that?"

"He's damn great."

"My old man can't play football like that. My old man is pretty useless, in fact."

The interval on the lawn has helped, and Craig's nerves feel soothed as he reenters his house. He opens a beer and sits sipping it and reading the papers in his office.

Presently Bobby and Suzy, who have been watching television in the living room, complain that they are hungry.

"Mommy's locked herself in her room."

He feeds them and himself, then knocks on Carribel's door.

"Do you want anything to eat?"

"Go to hell."

A little later he puts Suzy to bed, handling the small smooth body, the tiny pajamas. He squeezes her bottom affectionately.

"Do the big jump, Daddy."

With Craig's help, the child jumps nearly to the ceiling.

"Now flip me."

He flips her in the air so that she lands on her bed. Bobby, slightly jealous, watches from the doorway. "My turn next."

"You're too big."

But the boy is troubled. "Why is Mommy mad at us, Dad?"

"I don't think she's mad at you, just at me."

"Why, Dad?"

"That's a long story."

"Tell us a story, Daddy," cries Suzy.

"Did you hear the one about Snow White and Little Red Riding Hood's grandmother and the Three Bears?"

He has a way of telling several fairy tales at once, improvising, mixing characters together so that the familiar tales end up no one knows where. Usually he can make the children laugh.

"—then along came the sleeping prince, who happened to be awake that day—"

"He's not in this story, Daddy."

"All right, big mouth," says Bobby, "you tell it."

"The sleeping prince is in it," Craig assures Suzy. "I just put him in."

Craig, furiously inventing as he goes along, loses himself in the story, and in the big solemn eyes of his children. For each surprise he is rewarded by a whoop of laughter.

266

The story ends with Snow White eating the Three Bears for breakfast, for they turn out to be not real bears, but chocolate cake. "But Poppa Bear was too tough. Momma Bear was too soft—she went down like peanut butter. But Baby Bear was just right."

The children are laughing, and so is Craig.

"And then Snow White found that she had gorged herself so much that she fell right asleep, and that's what you two are going to do right now."

He tucks Suzy into her bed, kisses her, and closes the door. Bobby wants to take a shower, so Craig goes down and cleans up the kitchen. When he comes up, Bobby is in bed waiting to get tucked in and kissed, and then Craig goes out, closing the door.

Carribel stands in silhouette in the door to their room. The light is behind her, and it is like looking into a storm.

"You might at least have been discreet."

"About what?" he asks.

"About your sexual exploits."

There is a hard bright look in her eyes. "Ah do believe more people are talking about those exploits than your other kind."

"Why don't you go to bed," he says presently.

"You're such a child, honey."

"Fine. Now go to bed."

"Does the adulteress know what a child you are?"

He studies her.

"At least you admit she exists," says Carribel.

"I'm going to bed."

"Not until Ah finish what Ah have to say to you."

"Talk all you want, but don't expect me to listen."

When Carribel begins to laugh, Craig adds: "And don't try to work yourself into hysteria either."

"It's just very funny, honey."

"Look, I've got a game tomorrow. That's all I want to think about tonight. I need some peace, and a good night's sleep. What do you say?"

She wears a pink dressing gown belted at the waist. Her eyes are red, presumably from crying.

"At a time like this, all he can think about is football." She gives a broken laugh. "Ah always knew you were king of the jocks. Ah always knew you had never grown up. Ah just didn't realize you were such a child you could believe a cheap screw was so important."

His jaw clenches, and she sees this.

"You don't realize how silly you look, honey, sniffing after

267

that bitch in heat like a dog. Ah mean, you're supposed to be an adult. You've made such a fool of yourself."

He turns to pass her in the hall.

"Sniffing after her like that. Tell me, what does it smell like?"

He slaps her.

There is a moment's silence. Then he says: "I'm sorry."

"You stupid jock," she screams, half crying, half laughing.

He sees there will be no peace for him in this house tonight, and resolves to go to a hotel. Striding past her into their room, he gets an overnight bag out of his closet.

"Where do you think you're going?"

To jar her, he says: "I'm leaving."

"After next July perhaps, not before."

"I've got to get some sleep tonight," he pleads. "Can't you understand that?"

He is putting things in the bag.

"If you go out that door, you're not coming back."

"Have it your way."

Carribel begins to giggle. "I'll take you for every cent. You'll never see those children again."

"We'll see about that."

"Your precious team will drop you like a snake." She sees this strike home. "—A poisonous snake."

He goes past the bed into their bathroom and comes back with his toilet kit.

"Ah'll charge adultery. Ah'll smear you across every paper in the country."

He zips the bag shut.

She is giggling hard. "Ah only married you because Ah felt so sorry for you. You were such a baby. You wanted it so bad. You haven't changed." She begins giggling again.

He tries to concentrate on tomorrow's game so as to blot out her voice. But the game drifts out of sight, his mind can't find it. Perhaps, once he is safe in a hotel room—

"You've made me the laughing stock of this entire country. Ah'll fix you, though. Ah'll do away with myself. It'll be worth it to get even with you."

She is giggling wildly as he pushes past her. Behind him, she slams the door violently shut. When he turns, a crack has appeared in the plaster beside the door frame.

This sobers him. As he stands on the landing with his overnight case, the door is wrenched open again. Carribel, hair disheveled, a wild look in her eyes, giggles at him.

"You are going to have a terrible crime on your conscience. You won't be able to weasel out of this one."

268

The door slams again. The lock turns.

What does that mean, Craig asks himself.

Does she really expect me to think she's going to kill herself in there?

Carribel's not the suicide type, Craig tells himself shakily.

Who is the type then? People commit suicide all the time. What type do it?

He doesn't know.

But not Carribel.

Why not Carribel? If driven far enough, anyone would.

Has he driven Carribel this far? Would she kill herself just to destroy him? Does she hate him that much?

What weapons does she have in there?

Razor blades. My sleeping pills. She could always drown herself in the bathtub, I suppose.

He goes downstairs and slumps in an armchair in the living room.

He is no longer anxious to leave the house.

Presently he goes around checking that all the doors are locked. In the kitchen he sees that the burners are off, and the faucets shut. The house is quiet. In the dining room he turns the thermostat down to sixty degrees for the night. Then he sits in his living room again.

On the mantel is a row of his cups and trophies. They gleam dully, proof that he has been named most valuable player so many times. They are nice, but of no value in the future. They make him think of the ancient Aegean tribes who elected a man their king, allowed him a brief reign, and then killed him. It was a great setup for the tribe. It wasn't so hot for the king, though.

His overnight case in the hall. He carries it upstairs to the spare room. He will sleep there. No need to go to a hotel now. He convinces himself Carribel is probably sleeping soundly. She won't bother him till morning.

He gets Suzy out of bed, carries her into the children's bathroom, drops her flap, and places her on the seat. He listens to her do what she is supposed to do; it is a reflex, she is still asleep. He holds her so she won't fall in. Back in her own room, he tucks her into bed.

Bobby sprawls half across the pillow, sleeping dreamlessly. Craig draws the covers up over an exposed shoulder. A convulsion has occurred in the lives of his two sleeping children, though they don't know it yet. Looking down on his son, Craig hears again Bobby's thin high-pitched voice on the telephone last September.

My dad's home. Come on over and play.
My dad's home, get the gang.
My dad's home. We're going to have a game.

Craig ruffles the hair of his sleeping nine-year-old, then closes the door softly. Standing in the hall, he decides he will get his shaving kit out of his bag, take it into the children's bathroom and brush his teeth. Perhaps he will take a shower, too. His stomach muscles are contracted. The muscles of his shoulders and back too. A hot shower might relax him, help him to sleep. He must be at his best in the game tomorrow.

He stands in the hall looking across at the locked door of what was his bedroom—his and Carribel's.

A vague fear nags at him. At last he crosses and tries the door.

"Carribel," he calls.

There is no response, though his watch shows it is only ten thirty. She can't be asleep. She must be as tense as he is—sleep won't come easy tonight.

He stands indecisively in the hallway. She is probably all right, but determined not to answer.

"Carribel?"

No answer.

He rattles the doorknob.

But there is still no answer, which is not like her. When upset, she has never been able to keep silent. The violence inside her always comes out in shouts or sobs or curses.

You are going to have a terrible crime on your conscience.
Is her violence possibly self-destructive?

"Carribel, answer me."

He bangs on the door.

"Carribel, do you hear me?"

He waits.

"Answer me, Carribel."

He puts his ear to the door, but hears nothing.

"I'm going to break the door down, Carribel."

He rattles the doorknob.

"Carribel, you have to answer me!"

You are going to have a terrible crime on your conscience.

He is alarmed, and also angry. She has discovered a new method of tormenting him: silence.

"Carribel," he says in a level voice, "at the count of three I'm going to break the door in."

Absurdly, he hears himself counting, the way fathers threaten children.

"One."

Silence.

270

"Two."

With his ear to the door, he can hear no stir or sound within.

"Three," he cries.

But instead, he only bangs on the door with his fists.

"Carribel, open the door!"

Infuriated, he slams into the door with his shoulder, hitting it hard enough to provoke a reaction from Carribel, but not hard enough to damage either it or himself.

But there is no reaction inside.

The action, once commenced, seems to have a life and logic of its own. Backing off, Craig smacks into the door with the back of his right shoulder and arm, the way a halfback (himself) hits a line. However, this is no line of burly football players, but a heavy wood door, and as he bounces off it, Craig feels a searing pain from his shoulder almost to his hip. But he is expert at ignoring pain, and so ignores this pain. Backing off, he slams into the door again, and this time the frame splinters, and the door is flung back. It strikes against a bureau, toppling off a lamp, which shatters on the floor. Craig himself hurtles into the room out of control, and almost falls.

Carribel lies sprawled across the bed in a filmy rose nightgown. She lies on her back, legs slightly parted, one arm outstretched and the other across her breast. There is a slipper on one foot. The other slipper is on the floor beside the bed. Her mouth is open and she is pale as death, though breathing.

Carribel is the first thing Craig sees. The second is the message scrawled on the wall above the headboard in crimson lipstick.

ADULTERER
TAKE CARE OF MY CHILDREN

Craig thinks of his sleeping pills at once, and the empty bottle on the bedside table is the third thing he sees.

Their bedroom is big, measuring about twenty feet by twenty, and it has a connecting dressing room and bathroom, features which led them to pay forty thousand dollars for this house, more than they could afford at the time. The bedroom contains the queen-sized bed on which Carribel lies in a transparent nightgown, two bedside tables, and a kind of coffee table at the end of the bed with magazines on it. There are two bureaus and two armchairs in the room, and on the walls, which are painted pale blue, are several Utrillo prints and one large, unframed mirror. The wall-to-wall carpeting is pale blue also, as is the counterpane on the bed across which in a pale rose slash lies Duke Craig's wife.

Craig has lifted Carribel by the shoulders into a slumped sitting position, and he shakes her violently.

"Wake up."

He shakes her.

"Wake up."

But she slips from his grasp and falls back onto the pale blue counterpane.

Cupping her behind the neck, he lifts her enough to begin slapping her face with his free hand. Her mouth hangs slack, and saliva drools down over her chin. Though he slaps her again and again, she makes no sound.

He springs to his feet, clenching and unclenching his fists. He reads again the lipsticked message on the wall above the headboard. Picking up the sleeping pill bottle, he reads the label, but the information this gives is scant: One or Two Capsules Upon Retiring.

He calculates how many pills might have been in the bottle. He remembers taking two after the first Giants' game, and two more after the Green Bay game. Any more? He can't remember. Often after a game he has lain in bed in pain deliberating whether or not to get up and take pills. The deliberations would go on until he either did so or fell asleep, a confused state of mind in itself, and difficult to remember now.

But the bottle might have contained twenty-four pills at the start, perhaps even less, and he knows he took at least four of them. That seems to mean that Carribel has swallowed a maximum of twenty pills. How many are fatal? Unfortunately, he has no idea.

He gazes about the room. Carribel's clothing is lumped on one of the armchairs, and her dressing gown droops in folds from the other. The light in the room comes from both bedside lamps, which are lit. There are windows across two walls of the room, but the drapes are closed.

He imagines this room filled with the police emergency squad, while flashbulbs pop. He stares at Carribel's "suicide" note on the wall, and imagines photos of that in tomorrow's papers. At whatever cost, a scandal must be prevented. He cautions himself to think all this out carefully. If he panics now, he is lost.

How many pills are fatal? Once he heard Doc Flaherty say it depends on the size and weight and health of a patient; it would take far more pills to knock out Ox Polski, than Ox Polski's son, Doc said. It depends on whether the patient has built up a tolerance for the pills, on whether the patient has been drinking as well, on whether there is food in the patient's stomach or not.

Carribel has never taken sleeping pills before, as far as Craig knows; she has had no liquor today, but no food either.

Still twenty pills maximum. To Craig, this seems like enough to kill anyone, especially a young woman—this sprawled young woman in the transparent rose nightgown.

The lipstick scrawled on the wall still reads:

ADULTERER
TAKE CARE OF MY CHILDREN

I didn't realize she was that desperate, he thinks. Maybe she wasn't, he thinks; maybe she just hates me. Maybe she took six pills to simulate a coma, and flushed the rest of them down the toilet to scare me.

He tries to laugh.

If so, she has succeeded.

Getting his arm under her shoulders, he tries to walk her up and down the room. He knows the patient should be kept awake and moving. If he can get her awake and keep her awake, there will be no need to call in any emergency squads. The story will never reach the papers.

But as he walks her, she keeps collapsing. She's taken a lot of them, he thinks. He goes on walking her. She may have taken all of them, he thinks.

How long ago? How much time is left?

He puts her back on the bed, then decides to get her dressing gown on her over the transparent rose nightgown. He is concerned, if someone does come into this room, about her modesty. After he has worked her arms into the dressing gown, she falls back, and he buttons it all the way down.

But this is only stalling. He sees he must call their family doctor. If he can worm some information out of him, perhaps it won't be necessary for the doctor to come to the house at all.

A nurse's voice comes on the line: "Medical Group."

Craig feels greatly relieved. In a moment their family doctor will come riding to the rescue like the Lone Ranger and all the other heroes of American legend.

"Dr. Bascom, please," says Craig confidently. "It's an emergency." Dr. Bascom has a mellifluous voice and a posh practice, and Craig believes he knows the man well enough to count on his discretion.

But it is Saturday night. "I'm sorry, sir," says the nurse, "but Dr. Bascom is off duty. Shall I put you through to Dr. Rosenthal?"

"No. Dr. Bascom is our doctor."

"I'm sorry, sir, but he's not on call tonight. Dr. Rosenthal will be glad to help you."

But Craig doesn't know any Dr. Rosenthal. "No. It has to be Dr. Bascom. Can you give me his home number, please?"

"Who's calling, please?"

Craig gives his name. There is a pause during which he imagines the girl looking up Dr. Bascom's home number.

"Oh yes, I have you here on the card file."

"Fine. Now if you'll let me have Dr. Bascom's home number—"

"I'm terribly sorry, sir, but we don't give out the doctors' home numbers."

"You don't understand." Craig decides to add guardedly: "Someone is dying."

"Dr. Rosenthal—"

"Dr. Rosenthal is not our doctor. Dr. Bascom is our doctor."

"But sir, Dr. Rosenthal is the duty physician tonight."

"Will you please give the number?"

"I'm sorry, sir. Our policy—"

Craig finds it hard to comprehend all this. "But someone is dying—"

"I can't really believe that, sir. Otherwise you'd be happy to take Dr Rosenthal."

"Listen. Please—"

"Dr. Rosenthal is the one on call tonight."

"I've got to have Dr. Bascom."

"I can have him call you tomorrow, Sunday. Would that be all right?"

Craig gives a broken laugh. "The patient may be dead by tomorrow."

"Dr. Rosenthal—"

Craig hangs up. Thumbing rapidly through the phone book, he finds Dr. Bascom's name, but the only number listed is the one he has just called.

For a moment Craig convinces himself that Carribel has taken only a few pills, that there is no mortal danger, and that he can handle this crisis by himself.

But suppose she should die?

Chilled by this idea, he resolves to call Doc Flaherty. Being a physician, perhaps Doc Flaherty will in this case be discreet, even though Craig knows he tends to blab everything all around the team. Doc Flaherty gave him the sleeping pills and should feel some responsibility. But Doc might feel responsibility principally to the team, and might tell the owner or the coaches that Duke Craig last night spent several hours under considerable strain, and ought not to be relied on in to-day's game.

Craig decides he will have to take a chance on this.

So he phones Doc Flaherty, whom he locates at a party after three phone calls. As he waits for Doc to reach the phone, he hears in his head Doc's raspy voice saying: "Those movie stars that do it, they're all hoping somebody will find them first. You take the pills, you got several hours. Usually they have a cleaning woman coming in before that, or a boyfriend. But the car breaks down, and nobody gets there in time. That's not suicide, that's an accident."

At this moment, Craig is convinced Carribel has swallowed the whole bottle, counting on him to save her. If so, there can't be much time left.

Craig listens to the noise of the party in the background. Then Doc Flaherty comes on the phone. But his voice is fuzzy and jocular.

"Duke. How's ol' Duke? Why aren't you in bed by now, ol' Duke?"

"It's Carribel, Doc. She's—she's ill."

"We're just having a little fun here, Duke. Is it something that could wait till morning?"

"She's taken some pills."

"How's her breathing, Duke?"

"She's still breathing."

"Amplitude and frequency, Duke. That's the thing to look for."

Craig hears ice tinkling, and the noise of the party, and then Doc Flaherty laughing, with his hand half covering the receiver.

"Doc, how many is—" Unable to bring himself to say fatal, Craig says, "—dangerous."

"A lot, Duke. If they take that many, it usually makes a gelatinous mess in their throats. Gotta do a tracheotomy so they can breathe. They never think to take 'em one at a time. They try to take 'em all at once, and then they choke to death. Nothing like that here, Duke, right?"

"Is twenty enough?"

"Could be. Could be." But the physician's voice is still unconcerned, and now Craig hears him laugh, and call something across the room.

"Doc, could you possibly come over here now?"

"Hell, Duke, I'm an orthopedic man. Don't you have a family doctor?"

"I can't find him."

"There must be somebody. I'm an orthopedic man."

275

"Doc—"

"We're just having a little fun here, Duke. If you're really concerned, call the police. They know what to do. But I don't think you have anything to worry about, eh, Duke? Why don't you just take a couple of aspirins and—you gotta get some sleep for the game tomorrow, Duke."

"But Doc—"

"See you in the morning, ol' Duke." Click.

Craig stares at Carribel. Lifting her head, he tries slapping her again. But this is hopeless. It appears to him that her breathing is slowing down.

He dials Dr. Bascom's number and asks the girl to send Dr. Rosenthal at once.

"I'll have him call you as soon as he calls in."

"When will that be?"

"Well, he just hung up. He said he'd call in again at one o'clock."

"I can't wait."

"Look, I can't reach him right now. Do you want him or not?"

This is a crisis Craig has never faced before, and though he bids himself be calm, his hand is trembling as he calls two other doctors.

But it is still Saturday night, and both numbers funnel in to Dr. Rosenthal.

"Dr. Grissom is not on call tonight. Please call Dr. Rosenthal at this number."

"Dr. Rosenthal is handling Dr. Preston's calls tonight."

Craig's options have diminished to two. He can do nothing, letting Carribel die. Or he can call the police emergency squad, and the photographers and reporters who accompany them. There is a lump in his throat he can't get down. He rubs his face with sweaty hands.

Call the police.

No, let her die.

To let her die means that he is free. No lengthy, expensive, lurid divorce. Free of a detested wife. Free to marry Margie.

To call the police means flashbulbs exploding and headlines tomorrow:

> DUKE CRAIG'S WIFE
> IN SUICIDE ATTEMPT
> OVER OTHER WOMAN

Followed by the scandal that will scar all of them.

Carribel lies pale and slack-jawed, forehead beaded with sweat, and in his confusion Craig remembers that she looked

276

this way when they brought her down after Bobby was born; when her eyes opened, and she pressed his hand to her hot face mumbling "Hello, honey," he was suddenly sick with love for her.

Call the police, and hurry.

No, let her die.

Rage clouds his eyes. He thinks: You're trying to destroy me.

He is aware that if he does nothing, she might not die at all. But that is not his choice. His choice is to will her death, or to call the police.

Never mind the scandal. Call the police, and hurry. There's not much time.

Don't call them and be free.

He looks down on Carribel's limp form, thinking: You're trying to destroy me. His eyes fill with tears of rage, of exhaustion, of defeat. Grabbing up the phone, he calls the police.

There is still time, before they come, to try to scrub the lipstick off the wall, or even to move Carribel to another room. The idea either does not occur to him, or he is too exhausted and too guilty to act on it.

Instead he sits on the bed holding his wife's hand, muttering: "Don't worry, I'll save you," over and over again, until at last he hears the sirens wailing in the street.

The Associated Press has a man stationed at every hospital in the city, and so the news goes out on the AP teleprinter network within five minutes of the time Carribel Craig is wheeled into the emergency room. The city newspapers, and the wire services as well, have radio cars in the streets chasing down police calls, and these cars are ordered to the hospital at once.

The reporters and photographers find Craig pacing the corridor.

"Had she been despondent long?"

"Trouble over another woman I understand, eh, Duke?"

"You planning to play tomorrow, Duke?"

"Tomorrow hell," a reporter says, checking his watch. "It's today."

"How about it, Duke?"

But Craig has decided not to answer any questions.

The swinging doors at the end of the corridor part, and TV crews arrive and set up their gear.

The reporters plead with Craig for some response.

"Listen, Duke, we're just working stiffs, how about giving us a break?"

"Your children are alone in the house I guess, eh, Duke?"

277

This wounds Craig's pride as a father, so he says: "I had a neighbor come in."

"What about the lipstick on the wall?"

Craig gives a wry laugh. They ask you questions they already know the answers to.

Flashbulbs explode in his face. Blinding lights come on, and TV cameramen come up for close-ups. He strides to the other end of the hall. When he moistens dry lips with his tongue, another ten flashbulbs pop, and he knows they were waiting for just such an expression.

"Who's the other woman, Duke?"

They probably already know, he thinks. I'm sorry, Margie, he thinks.

"You planning to divorce and remarry?"

"I heard that all four walls were covered with lipstick. Shall I put that down as the truth?"

But he refuses to answer.

"Listen, Duke, we all got deadlines to meet. You gotta help us."

His shoes squeak on the linoleum under foot.

After a time a doctor comes out of the emergency room. With the press surrounding him, he says: "I think I can promise she will pull through."

The TV lights come on again, and an assistant herds the young doctor in front of the cameras where he is urged to repeat this statement.

The reporter says: "Craig announced in Dallas last week that she was pregnant, Doc. Will she lose the baby?"

The doctor gives a start of surprise. "In cases of this kind —" he hedges.

"The shock is usually enough to bring on a miscarriage, eh, Doc?"

"Well, there seems to be some bleeding—"

The newspaper reporters, listening to this off-camera, are copying it all down.

When the TV lights go out, the reporters crowd in to ask the young doctor his name, and for other details of the treatment, and about the presumed miscarriage.

"Where are there some phones, Doc?"

The doctor and Craig watch the reporters rush to phone in their stories. The TV crews fold up their gear and disappear. Only a few photographers linger, eyeing Craig from a distance. They are waiting for the patient to be wheeled out—a possible shot of the husband gazing guiltily down on his wife.

The young doctor says to Craig: "We did a gastric lavage—pumped her stomach. Not much in it, actually. I don't think

278

she was ever in any danger of dying. She probably only took a few pills, and got rid of the rest. That often happens."

Craig gives a wry laugh.

The young doctor says earnestly: "But we had to take all the emergency measures just to be sure, injections, stimulants and so forth, and that seems to have brought on some bleeding—"

Craig nods.

"—I'm terribly sorry to have to tell you that."

By the time they wheel Carribel out of the emergency room, all the photographers are gone—it's too late now to make even the final editions. She is wheeled into an elevator, which rises. Out of the elevator, she is wheeled down a long corridor and into a room.

"She won't wake up for an hour or so," says the young doctor to Craig. "Why don't you and I have a coffee, Duke? I've always been a great fan of yours."

Later Craig stands at the window watching the dawn come up over the city. There is a park across from the hospital, and the low sun turns the topmost branches into a network of silver and gold.

From time to time Craig turns to look at Carribel.

The young doctor enters, and does something for her.

"Duke, I think she's coming out of it now."

Craig moves to her side.

"I can't leave you alone for long. She's still very weak. This has been rather a shock to her system."

Craig nods. Behind him, he hears the door close as the doctor goes out. Carribel's hair is damp with sweat.

Her eyes, opening, rove the room unfocused. After a time they find him, and with an effort focus in.

"Who's looking after my children?"

"Ralph Lane came over." This is the neighbor.

Her voice is throaty and dreamy: "You must have had to wake him up."

"The sirens woke him up."

She looks away.

"You gave us quite a scare."

"You deserved it," she suggests.

She begins to laugh and cry. "You deserved it. Oh, you deserved it."

Craig finds the doctor outside the door. "Doctor—"

The doctor rushes in and leans over Carribel, who is laughing and crying.

"I think you better go, Duke."

He goes down the long linoleum corridor and down the

279

stairs and outside. It is daylight now. Feeling weary, he sits down on a bench in the park. People move singly through the park: an old man with a prayer book, a grandmother in black leaning on a cane; it must be time for the early Mass.

A little later the sun is higher and warmer. Crossing the park now are children in Sunday finery, most of them carrying prayer books also. The next Mass must be the children's Mass, Craig thinks. A little girl comes skipping along past Craig's bench, followed by three small boys who are laughing and pummeling each other. Coming the other way is a man reading a paper. Craig sees his name on the front page in big letters. Below that are some photos: his and Carribel's wedding picture dug out of the archives, and beside it the shot of Margie holding the ball for him that time in Nashville.

He looks away.

As the sun rises he opens his coat and lets it warm his chest. His collar feels stuck to his neck, though he moves his neck this way and that trying to free it.

At length he leaves the park and begins to walk toward the stadium. It is a fine day. Cabs pass him, but he does not flag one down; he has plenty of time. When he passes a diner, he realizes that he should eat, so he goes in and orders bacon and eggs and coffee. But when the food comes he can't eat it.

You've got a game to play today, he tells himself. You need your strength. You've got to eat it.

Slowly he forces himself to do so. Then he drinks two more cups of coffee. There is a mirror facing him behind the counter; he tries not to look at himself.

A man comes in and takes the next stool. His newspaper lies on the counter while he studies the menu. It is the same tabloid Craig saw being read in the park, and he wonders how the paper found out Margie's name. Any one of the players could have revealed it, he reasons. Perhaps the reporters traveling with the team already knew it.

Outside again, Craig walks through dark narrow streets down toward the river, coming out into the sun there and walking along under the bare trees. A tug is dragging a barge against the current, and a little farther on a speedboat starts up. Then there is a bend in the river, and the stadium comes into view ahead. He can see the flags flying all around the rim of the stadium.

CHAPTER | 22

His shoulder throbs. As he comes into the locker room he sees that he is a little late, for most of the stalls along both sides of the long, low ceilinged room are occupied. Some of the men have their silver stretch pants on already, and socks as well, meaning that they have already been taped. Others, although still wearing their own underwear, stand with the clean white tape already encasing their ankles.

After glancing at the clock over the door to see how late he is, Craig moves toward his own stall, halfway along on the left; he is trying to remember how he would have performed this act on any other Sunday. He is back in the realm of the poker face and the bluff here, and however he feels inside, he is determined that none of it will show.

The room is hot and damp as always, and in most of the stalls the Sunday papers are visible—that is normal too. The difference is that today many of the papers are being studiously read and then, as the room becomes conscious of Craig's presence, they are being stuffed guiltily under stools.

Coach Dreuder comes out of the trainers' room. "Who's next to be taped?" he cries. "There's no one even on line in there. This is not a reading room, for crissake."

There is a general movement toward the trainers' room.

Craig, facing into his stall, has removed his shoes and trousers.

"Did you get any sleep?" demands Dreuder's voice behind. Craig turns to face the coach. He shakes his head. "No."

"Do you want to play?"

"Yes."

Craig watches him.

"I wish I didn't have to use you."

Craig remains silent.

"But I got nobody else."

281

Craig nods. The season started with five running backs, and three, Finney, Fox, and Slade, are injured now.

"Is Carribel all right?"

"I think so."

Craig, who has been holding his trousers upside down, drapes them over a hanger which he hooks to the grill separating his stall from his neighbor.

Dreuder says: "Christ, what a mess."

Craig remains silent.

"I gotta use you. I got nobody else."

"I want to play."

When Dreuder leaves, Craig, naked, pulls on the clean jock, and gingerly works his sore shoulder into the clean gray T-shirt.

He hears Dreuder berating the publicity man, Malverde.

"Where are the programs, for crissake?" There are supposed to be fifty programs for the players in the locker room two hours before every game.

"I guess they didn't come in yet."

"Well, don't just stand there, go get them."

As Malverde goes in search of the programs, Craig goes through into the other room to be taped. There are three rubbing tables in use. Presently Craig stands up on a table, his knee flexed. Pete starts to tape his knee.

"Your thigh looks pretty raw, Duke. Maybe you should shave it again first."

"It's okay."

Pete pulls on each length of elastic tape to get it tight, then pats it flat.

There is a cubbyhole off this room which serves as Doc Flaherty's office, and Craig watches a steady line of players go in there, lean over the table, and get needles plunged into their rumps. Most of these shots are vitamin B-12, but some are penicillin. Craig does not believe in drugs, especially penicillin for incipient colds, but most players do, and Doc appears to. Or perhaps Doc shoots in water, Craig thinks. Most men around pro football think of the players as high-strung children, and treat them accordingly.

Craig, hopping down off the table with his knee and both ankles taped, considers asking Doc to look at his shoulder.

But he does not want to face Doc Flaherty.

Outside in the main room, Dreuder says to the two clubhouse boys: "I don't want any sportswriters in here at all."

Normally the press is allowed to roam the locker room

until an hour before game time, when they would be shooed out.

"And when we go out on the field to warm-up, I want all these Sunday papers to disappear."

"Okay, Coach."

"I don't want to see a single paper."

"Okay, Coach."

"I got a game to play today."

Craig, wearing gray T-shirt and jock and pink tape on his right leg, and white spats on his ankles, returns to his stall. His hip and shoulder pads hang from hooks in the back of the stall, and his bright red helmet is on the shelf above. His red jersey droops from the grillwork on one side of the stall, and his silver stretch pants hang from the other.

He sits to pull his socks on, and tapes them tight, and tears the tape across with his thumb, and a man stands over him, blotting out the light. When he looks up, it is F. X. Boyle.

There is an anguished look on Boyle's face, and an anguished throb to his voice. "Is it true?" Boyle asks.

Craig says: "It's true."

"That poor girl."

Craig lays the washboard thigh pads across his upper legs, and tapes them on.

Boyle's voice is husky. "How could you?"

"I don't know."

"You don't know—"

"It just—happened."

The owner's jaws work. "You'll regret this. You'll be sorry about this as long as you live."

Standing, Craig steps into his silver pants and begins to work them up his legs over the thigh pads.

The owner, his jaws still working, abruptly moves off. Craig sees him lift a game program off the stack on one of the trunks, then flip through it without seeing any of the pages.

Craig thinks: I never asked to be his hero.

That's not true; you wanted to be the hero of everybody.

I just wanted to be the greatest football player who ever lived.

But being a hero was good too, wasn't it.

Yes.

Dreuder's voice calls: "Five minutes, boys."

Craig tucks his bright red jersey, its big silver No. 6 fore and aft, into his silver trousers.

Dreuder comes over again: "You look awful."

"I'm all right."

283

"Drink this." The coach hands Craig a cardboard container of coffee. Craig drinks it.

"What's the only thing on your mind right now, Duke?"

"The game," responds Craig automatically.

"Good."

"I want to play." He puts his warm-up jacket on.

"I wouldn't use you, but I got nobody else."

It is time for the pre-game warm-up. Dreuder at the door calls: "Let's go, boys."

The locker room floor is carpeted, so that the rattle of cleats begins on the cement ramp outside the door. The players move down the tunnel and up into the baseball dugout and outside and begin to jog down the field toward the sun. Craig hears the muffled cheer of the crowd before he himself comes up into the light, up the wooden steps and then onto the hard turf and through under the goalposts, fanning out to start calisthenics at the far end near the bleachers in the sun.

There are photographers everywhere, and Craig can feel their long lenses on him. But the special cops keep them off the field itself. He does not mind the cameras, which are there every Sunday anyway. He just does not want to answer questions, for his concentration is coming on fine now. He can feel the tape and stretch pants encasing his legs, the old snug feeling he is used to. He is aware of the stubble on his unshaven face, and even his shoulder throbs less than before. He is trying to empty his mind of everything except the game, and when he runs the Browns' defensive personnel through his mind like a card file, all the information is there where it should be.

A punt rises lazily into the air. "Mine," he cries, circling under it.

He catches it lightly in his fingertips—so lightly there is scarcely a note of contact between the hands and the ball—jogs forward, then lofts the ball back toward the punter.

Soon his body feels oiled like a machine. The sweat is coming out nicely all over, and the sleepless night and fatigue go deep back inside him, and his shoulder stops hurting—and he feels ready to play. His concentration is not perfect. Every few minutes it is interrupted by a vision of Carribel's damp, pale face. Or, watching the crowd enter the stands, he imagines the whispers coursing down the aisles; any fan who arrived without knowing, would soon know. Some would feel disgust, and some pity, and he wants to put the old admiration back in its place. He can do this, if he can play a big game, score some touchdowns, and lead the Big Red to victory as he has done so often over the years. He means to show 60,000 men and women what it is like to see your life collapse, and put out anyway, and do the job you are paid to do, and do it better than anyone else in this league or the world. He means to force this crowd to give him back the admiration he has earned over the years.

After twenty minutes the red jerseys jog in toward the dugout again, passing, at the dark end of the field, the Cleveland squad in white jerseys and white pants. The two squads of players ignore each other.

At the locker room door under the stands there is a scuffle. Guards wrestle with TV crewmen, and with Bruce Bingham, who calls the Big Red games on TV. The scuffle goes on even as the players file past. The guards wrestle their adversaries aside, and the players, wide-eyed, file through into the locker room.

Snatches of angry voices reach them through the door.

"We've gotta do a commercial in there."

"You know the rules, Mr. Bingham."

"It's an emergency."

"There's no press allowed now, Mr. Bingham."

They hear curses, scuffing shoes, what sounds like blows, and they stare at each other. They are all listening hard, and no one speaks.

They hear Dreuder's voice outside the door. "What the hell is this?"

The scuffling stops, and the voices go low, though still agitated.

"All we need is five minutes for a new commercial, George. It's an emergency."

"I got a game to play, for crissake."

"Do you know how much money is involved?"

"Here's Boyle."

Inside, the players have stripped their jerseys off and now lace shoulder pads on, then yank each other's jerseys down into place.

Craig, his jersey taut over his pads, sits on his stool sensing exactly what is happening outside the door. They must have shelved Margie's commercial and now they want to film a substitute.

The door bursts open, and the TV crew enters, dragging cables. Blinding lights go on, and Bruce Bingham, mike in hand, faces the door he has just entered. This puts almost the entire locker room in the background. Bingham speaks a Pepsi-Cola commercial, then the lights go out. But they come on again almost immediately, and Bingham speaks the same commercial again.

285

This time the lights stay out, and the cables retreat through the door. However, some of the crewmen linger in the room, wanting to gawk at the team during these final tense minutes before the kickoff.

"Get them out of here, Bruce," orders Dreuder.

"You saved our lives, George."

An assistant producer says: "Thanks, Coach. Our regular commercial got shelved at the last minute. Otherwise we never would have forced our way in here."

"Okay, okay," says Dreuder. "Come on, Bruce, get them out of here."

"I didn't like it any better than you did, George," says the announcer's mellifluous voice. "It only leaves me about ten minutes to get up to that TV booth through this crowd."

"Okay, okay."

"I hope I make it."

The announcer feels himself part of the team, and wants the players to see him in this guise: about to enter combat also; part of the common effort to defeat the Browns.

But at last Bruce Bingham and his crew are out of the locker room. The players begin to worry about the game again. The nervous parade to the bathroom begins, and suddenly everything needs retaping. Players call out to Pete or Paul, who rush over and retape fingers or wrists or socks. Ox Polski scissors a cardboard tape tube lengthwise down the sides. This makes two curved cardboard shells eight inches long, and he peels his socks down and tapes these shells over his shins, then pulls his socks up again and tapes the socks tight under his knees.

"We've won the toss," says Drueder at the blackboard. The offensive team crowds around while he diagrams the first play they will run: a delay pass from Rocco to Craig over the middle.

An official sticks his head in the door. "Five minutes, Coach."

Rocco stands at one end of the room throwing a practice ball to Pete. The repeated sharp report of the ball smacking into the trainer's hands gets on everybody's nerves.

"Cut that out."

Everybody is tense now. More players rush to the bathroom to empty bladders and bowels that are already empty. Rocco drops his practice ball into a bin of T-shirts, walks into the bathroom, and vomits up what is left of his breakfast.

"Do we want to go to the Miami game in January?" asks Dreuder softly.

There is a short explosive yes.

"There's only one way."

A player roars: "Beat the Browns."

Then everybody is yelling, releasing tension, promising to drive the Cleveland team into the ground.

"Rocco, what's the first play?" demands Dreuder.

Rocco gives the number of the delay pass to Craig.

"Craig, where do you take the ball to?"

"All the way in for the score," says Craig. But he is thinking: That was Margie's commercial they shelved. Boyle never would have let them in here, unless he was responsible for shelving it.

He tries to see himself grabbing Rocco's pass. First the delay, to let the other receivers clear out the middle, then himself filtering in there and grabbing the ball and sprinting for the goal line, with two of his own men out in front of him, neither of them ferocious blockers, but at least screens he can cut off of, and a runner such as Duke Craig could possibly go all the way on such a play, or at least get a big gain—twenty yards minimum.

But instead Craig imagines Rocco missing him with the ball. Rocco is so tight he will never be able to hit a moving target on that first pass, although once the first play is over, he may be all right. And even if the ball is thrown true, Craig sees himself missing it, for he is suddenly inexpressibly weary, and sees no joy in playing this game, and wonders if the joy he remembers ever truly existed.

So he sees the first play ruined, and first plays are crucial, for they can establish momentum one way or the other. Football is emotion. You have to be so high you don't feel the pain, don't begrudge the terrific expenditure of energy, the sprinting, bashing, wrestling, tugging, dragging of each play. Momentum means having the emotion on your side, rather than theirs.

The door closes behind the coaches. The team is alone. There is no sound, then many tense sounds: a chair scrapes; a throat is cleared; a cleat rubs the rug.

Then Joe Morris shouts: "Let's go Big Red."

All the voices shout an answer.

The players bunch into a tight circle. In the center, hands clasp each other. Players who can't reach the hands, clasp the shoulder pads in front of them. The prayer begins. Thirty-five voices chant "Our Father, who art in heaven . . ."

When the prayer ends, Joe Morris shouts again: "Let's go Big Red."

Everybody roars an answer.

Grim-faced, they plunge out the door, most wearing their

helmets, a few with helmets dangling from fists by the face bar. Going down the ramp there are a few customers standing, and in the dugout where the players wait to be introduced other customers lean out and over the edge and try to talk to their favorites. But the players look at nobody, and no one speaks.

Joe Morris runs the kickoff back to the 28-yard line. When the huddle forms, Rocco wipes his sweaty palms and calls the delay pass to Craig.

But Craig gets knocked flat at the line of scrimmage. Springing up, he dashes into the middle, but Number 35 is on him, and the pass goes over their heads anyway.

Momentum to the Browns.

Craig thinks: You can cross that play off. They have read a key somewhere, for they recovered so fast as to be on top of him even before he filtered through the line.

Adjustments have to be made, and Craig, worrying, knows that Rocco is not the man to make them in the huddle in the few seconds available there. Peering over the defense, Rocco brushes dirt off his seat, then ducks into the huddle and calls Craig on a simple dive play. Probably he couldn't think of anything else. The other two backs are Duane Nevers and Winfield Green. Green is normally a defensive back, and although very fast, does not hit the line with the power a running back should have.

Craig, plunging for four yards, is aware he will be the heavy-duty back for as long as he lasts. But his shoulder aches, and he knows he can't hit the line many more times like that.

"We got four," says Rocco, pleased, in the huddle. Then he calls the same delay pass which failed on first down.

It is third and six as Craig lines up for this play. It'll never work, he thinks. But perhaps he can make it work, though it takes faith to do the impossible, and he is playing without that today. Instead, he is aware of tens of thousands of people looking down on him. This may be his last game, and he wants to make them remember what a great football player he was. Remember all the thrills I gave you. Remember the moment of glory I was in your lives. Remember the joy I used to feel playing, and communicated to you. Remember—me.

Crouched behind the right tackle, he tries to work out why this play failed two downs ago. The left end must have been the one who knocked him down; how will he get past that man this time? Since Number 35 was on top of the play, he didn't respond to Winfield Green swinging left out of the backfield; why?

It is very complicated, Craig has only seconds to work it out, and he listens for all his years of football, of loving this game, to send him some messages. But none comes, and he must try to work it out like a chess problem—and there isn't enough time for that.

Forcing himself to try, he decides that if he runs the pass pattern slanting across the middle instead of circling into the middle, then Number 35 won't be able to recover in time. But if Craig is not in the middle of the secondary exactly where the blackboard diagram says he should be, will Rocco be able to find him?

And how does Craig get past the end who flattened him last time?

Rocco is already barking signals, and the lines converge before Craig has found a solution. He hears the grunts of the impact and struggle, and as the left end looms up, a much bigger man than Craig, inspiration comes. Craig stands straight up and claps his hands as loud as he can.

He has a momentary vision of the defensive end's mouth dropping open behind his cage—surprise surprise what the hell is this they didn't tell us—and then Craig sprints past him, starts on a deep circle route, but breaks it off and slants across the middle.

He looks back and here comes the ball, looming swiftly larger, and it seems to him he can hear the laces whistling. The ball gets tremendous in size, and then Craig grabs it, just as Number 35, recovering amazingly fast, rams him full speed in the back.

But it is a first down.

"Way to go, way to go," hollers Craig, running back to where the huddle is forming.

They spring out of the huddle into position. Craig throws a block on Number 61, and Winfield Green circles right end for seven yards. Craig hits into the middle on the next play, but there is no hole. Though he struggles and wrestles, there are too many of them and they ride him backward still on his feet until the whistle blows. As he relaxes, Number 35 with a final effort, flings him to the ground.

Penalty.

The official strides off fifteen yards against the Browns.

This makes it first down past midfield, and Craig begins to hope they can move the ball all the way to a touchdown. But Duane Nevers is promptly thrown for a two-yard loss. Then comes a pass to Jake Simmons which is underthrown and nearly intercepted.

"Let's move that ball," Craig mutters as the huddle forms. "Let's move that ball."

But he sees they are deflated. He is deflated himself and fears that the team will now slowly dissolve. They have no confidence in Rocco as leader. His passing is not quite accurate enough. He doesn't read the defenses fast enough, and the Browns are jumping around back there to foul him up further. The players look to Craig as leader, but halfback is not the position a man can lead a team from, and besides, Craig is very tired, he has not been to bed.

Jones punts.

At the sideline, Craig confronts Coach Dreuder. "On the delay, who are they keying on?"

Dreuder, biting his fingernails, watches the game: "We don't know."

"They're on top of me as soon as I get past the line."

Calling over Beady Stein, Craig sketches an altered version of the play in the dirt. Rocco and the other backs and ends lean over the diagram.

"Suppose we run it like this?" asks Craig.

Steir nods assent.

Craig takes a dipper full of water, rinses his mouth, and spits it out. He stands watching the game.

As the first quarter ends, the Browns push across a touch-down.

"Let's get that back, Big Red," Craig cries as they run onto the field again.

But one drive after another stalls. The Browns score a second touchdown, and lead 14–0.

In the locker room at half time, the idea of a big play fills Craig's mind. A big play could put some hope back into the Big Red. But the Browns have been giving them the usual fierce beating in the line, and now in the locker room the players slump in their stalls or move wearily back and forth, their sweat-streaked dirty faces without expression. Craig sees they are not thinking of victory anymore, nor of the possible week in Miami and the extra game and paycheck there. They will take their final paycheck this afternoon. They are thinking about paying their hotel bills tonight and collecting their kids and their suitcases tomorrow morning and driving home to Macon, Georgia, or Wahoo, Nebraska, or wherever they come from.

The alternative is to stick one's body in front of blitzing linebackers, to hit into holes that don't exist, to get rammed in the back the instant you catch a pass.

The team seems to prefer to make the next hour a formality only.

Craig alone is still desperate to win, though his shoulder aches, and his body feels dry, empty, drained of sweat.

"Let's go, Big Red," he cries as the interval ends and the teams take the field again. "Let's go, Big Red."

It is a feeble enough cry, but something of his need communicates itself to his teammates. In the third quarter the blocking is better, and the Big Red moves steadily down the field. Craig carries steadily for short gains: four yards, three, five. Once he gets eleven yards, weaving through the secondary almost from sideline to sideline, sprinting, stopping, starting, juking a lineman so that the man lunges, misses, and falls down. It is an elegant run, but gains only eleven yards, and those eleven with the goal line still distant. Craig looks up into the grandstands hoping the crowd will realize what a rare skill they have witnessed. But the run gained only eleven yards, and it earns now only mild applause.

But he and Nevers hammer at the Browns' line, and a pass to Simmons picks up a first down, and finally Winfield Green skirts left end for the touchdown.

This picks the team up. Perhaps victory is not only possible, but will not cost too much. The score is now 14–7.

"We can win, Big Red," Craig keeps chanting. He stalks in front of the bench slapping his helmet against his palm. "We can win, we can win, we can win."

But the minutes plod on, and the tenor of the game does not change.

The Browns drive to another touchdown, which is scored by Number 32 over Joe Morris. Number 32 shoulders into Morris, and then stomps over him into the end zone, and Morris does not get up. Pete and Doc Flaherty run out, and presently help off the field a man who has forgotten what day it is, and what town he is in.

That means Winfield Green must play both offense and defense now, and somebody must field the punts and kickoffs Morris fielded, either Craig or Nevers. Coach Dreuder chooses Craig.

As the kickoff return team huddles briefly, Craig thinks: Just give me a chance, a single block or perhaps two. To Craig a kickoff return, with two teams rushing headlong at each other, is a play on which any kind of freak thing can happen: somebody can fall down, someone else can leave a lane unguarded. A kickoff return, in a game they are losing 21–7, is a time of hope. With a little help—

But he can't plead aloud for his help. All he can do is try

to meet as many eyes as possible around the rim of the huddle, silently begging. Some of the eyes regard him oddly, uncomprehendingly, and some look away. They do not believe in virtuoso performances by Craig or anyone else, for they are pros, and thus realists, and they realize this game is lost. Tomorrow they go home. They do not want to meet some opponent head-on at speed on this kickoff return and perhaps get seriously hurt.

The ball floats end over end, dropping down directly under the goalposts where Craig catches it. As he starts upfield he hopes for the old feeling of joy to invade his mind and body and tell him where to run and how.

But there is nothing, just weariness and the beginning of despair. Twenty yards ahead he cannot distinguish any patterns at all, nor guess at any possible opening. A wall of white looms up, and he is slammed down hard.

He arises groggy, shrugs his shoulder pads back into place, and waits for his head to clear.

The Big Red starts downfield, and the going is easier now, for the Browns consider the game won, and substitutes man their defensive line. Craig and Nevers punch out short gains, and another delay pass to Craig is good for seventeen yards. Winfield Green skirts right end for eight yards, and Nevers takes a pitchout the other way for seven more. Craig hits the middle three times in a row for four yards, six, three.

It is effective, bedrock football, but it is using up too much time. The Big Red team needs not one touchdown but two just to tie the game. Craig is on the edge of exhaustion, and plays he might have broken for big yardage earlier go for short gains now—when tacklers grab him he is too weak to fight to stay on his feet. His mind has become a little vague, and he mutters a prayer for one last big run: Please God one more to make them remember who I was.

At the 20-yard line the Browns throw their first team back into the game, and when Craig hits the line he is stopped for no gain. In the huddle Rocco again calls the delay pass, which, as altered by Craig, has been a consistent gainer all afternoon.

Again Craig eludes the onrushing defensive end; again he fakes to hold Number 35 in place; again he breaks the circle pattern off and slants across the middle. Again the ball and Number's 35's shoulder reach him simultaneously. Again the shock of impact travels all the way through his body. Again he holds onto the ball.

It is just an ordinary play, but perfectly executed by a man playing on memory alone and on the last of his physical reserves. Craig looks around at the shell of stands now so dark

292

in the late afternoon light that he can no longer see the bright faces and brighter colors. He thinks: I wanted to give you a bigger play than that, but that's the best I've been able to do today, and you didn't find it good enough, and now you'll go away from here remembering me in letters four inches high on the front pages today, instead of in letters almost as high on the sports pages for more than ten years.

The ball is on the 1-yard line, and on the next play Rocco goes over on a quarterback sneak.

So the score is 21–14 and there are less than two minutes left as the Browns receive the kickoff. They run two plays into the line and are stopped and as they line up on third down, Craig, watching tensely from the bench, thinks: If we can stop them now we will get the ball with time enough, possibly, to tie up this game.

But the third down play unfolds, and Number 32 bulls for twelve yards and the first down.

Craig's uniform is heavy with sweat, and his face is gray though he does not know this. He watches Ox Polski call time-out after each Brown play to stop the clock. He tells himself that if they can force a punt, there will still be time for one play or two. With one more chance to carry the ball, perhaps Craig can break one all the way. He pleads silently for this chance.

At last the Big Red defense holds. The Browns go into punt formation. Downfield, Craig waits for the ball.

It comes fast, a line drive of a punt, and Craig has to dash back and catch it over his shoulder. But it is the kind of punt that can be returned a long way, for there was never enough loft for tacklers to get down under it, and as Craig angles upfield he can see the row of red jerseys beginning to form an alley for him along the sideline in front of the Big Red bench. Craig cuts past one tackler, eludes a second, and then he has reached the sideline and is sprinting upfield inside the alley of red jerseys. Passing the bench he has a glimpse of Dreuder's face with a cigar in it, and Boyle's with his mouth open. Craig's exhaustion fades out of mind now, for it is overlaid with elation, and with the surprise he always feels when he breaks a play open perfectly, the way it is designed to break open but almost never does. With nothing to do but sprint straight up the field inside the red alley of blockers, he listens for the crowd and hears it, and thinks: I can't give you victory, but in another forty yards I can give you a tie. Will you love me then? Will you forgive me then? Will you remember me then? Running with the football is the only big gift I've ever been able to give anybody in my life, and I've given it to you all these years and you never even knew it was a gift from me to you. I wish you could know, but if you can't I wish you would take this last run of my life and remember it, and remember me.

With forty yards to go the alley of blockers funnels out into the open field and he is on his own, with only two men still to beat, Number 35 who circles warily in, and the kicker who is still some yards off. He knows he has to beat them at top speed, for the pursuit is very close. He can hear the hoofbeats, and he can hear the close heavy breathing. He is getting tired now, for he has sprinted more than forty yards already, and his uniform is heavy with sweat, and his legs are loggy from the beating he has absorbed for the past two and a half hours, and from no sleep.

Number 35 is trying to crowd Craig out of bounds, instinctively protecting the wide part of the field, and Craig knows this man almost always goes for an inside fake, and so Craig gives him one. The man lunges for where Craig seemed to be, but isn't, and one hand rakes down Craig's side without catching anything, and then Craig is past him with only the kicker to beat.

But his legs have become very heavy, and he can't breathe, and when a wave of blackness comes over him, there is an instant during which he can't see. He fights this off, but it comes again in a few strides, and though he does not know it, he begins to stagger as he runs. The kicker looms up. Recovering under this new urgency, Craig gives him a move, and cuts past him toward the center of the field, and then he begins staggering again, and this time he realizes vaguely what is happening to him, and tears come to his eyes and he begins to cry, for he knows he will never make it to the goal line and it will all be wasted. For this is sports in America, where only victory counts, only the touchdown counts—the almost great run is worth nothing.

The goal line is only twenty yards away now, but he is stumbling and the blackness blinds him and he fights to breathe, and when he fails at this, he fights to stay awake. Pleading with his body for one last jolt of adrenalin, he gulps at the air and nothing happens. He tries to keep on running though he can't see. He can only hear the pounding cleats behind him, and the heavy breathing getting louder and louder and louder, and then someone is on his back and he goes down hard with men on top of him, and the run is over.

The referee peels the bodies off him, and places the ball down on the 17-yard line. He has run sixty-four yards. Helped to his feet, he knows he is weeping and tries to stop but can't. He stands there with the tears streaming down his face while the teams form two huddles. He does not know which huddle to go to, so he wanders in on the Browns because the white huddle is closer and he is so awfully tired.

He is not aware of what happens next. Number 35, who is the Browns' captain, leads him by the arm to the referee, and the packed grandstands release all that accumulated tension in a long sustained roll of laughter.

Though the Big Red have no time-outs left, the referee stops the game and signals to the Big Red bench for someone to come out and get Craig. The stands still shake with laughter as he is led off the field, and then the referee's arm swings around to start up the clock again. Rocco brings the Big Red offense up to the line and throws one pass which is completed, but short of the touchdown, and then the gun sounds ending the game.

The final score is Browns 21, Big Red 14.

In the locker room Craig begins to retch, and though nothing comes up, he can't stop. He can't see either, and can't stop retching long enough to cry for help. It isn't till he crashes backwards out of the toilet stall that Ox Polski runs over and starts screaming for Doc Flaherty.

Doc Flaherty wraps him in blankets on a rubbing table and gives him a shot of something.

F. X. Boyle comes in saying: "Well, where's the team stud?"

He finds Craig on the table and stands looking down at him.

Just before he goes under, Craig says: "I did my best."

"No you didn't," says the owner. "You left your best in a bedroom somewhere."

CHAPTER | 23

The next morning F. X. Boyle goes to seven o'clock Mass as he does every day of his life, and kneels as always in a third row pew in the almost empty church with the gilt-edged leaves of his missal open before him. But today he finds he cannot follow the Mass in the missal. Numbly he watches the priest turn.

"Dominus vobiscum."

"Et cum spiritu tuo."

The Latin prayers on the altar drone in his brain. He knows what most of them mean, and he seeks among them for guidance, for he believes that Holy Mother Church in her infinite wisdom has an answer for everything, and he wants to make sure that he has chosen the correct answer in this case.

Later he moves to the altar rail, where he takes the host on his tongue, the body and blood of Our Lord, and with his eyes closed tries to see into heaven. He offers this communion up for the repose of the soul of his dead wife, as he always does, and also for certain dead football players whom he greatly admired when alive. He tries to keep his mind on holy thoughts, but an image keeps recurring of the first great quarterback he ever had, Fred Gillespie, of the way Fred used to throw the ball, and of the way he looked later dying of cancer. Fred died with the sacraments, and with Father O'Malley in attendance, and so is probably a saint now, possibly tossing a football back and forth in the presence of God, if that's the way heaven is, for even God would enjoy watching the way Fred Gillespie could throw.

Taking a chance, Boyle directs a special prayer for guidance to Fred Gillespie, if he is there, as he should be, a man like that. What should I do?

But no new answers come back to him, and he decides this is because the answers have already been given out many times.

The sixth commandment is: Thou shalt not commit adultery; and the ninth is: Thou shalt not covet thy neighbor's wife. It is all there and binding on everybody, not a Catholic commandment like attending Mass on Sunday, but God himself revealing his natural law to the Jews, and through them to all men for all time.

Kneeling, his face in his hands and his thanksgiving after communion only half said, Boyle remembers Fred Gillespie wearing jersey No. 42, and then he remembers Fred pale and dying in bed and hears his own broken voice saying: "Fred, no one will ever wear that number again."

With his face in his hands, Boyle can almost feel the tears of that day, and he remembers vividly calling a press conference and announcing that Gillespie's jersey has been retired for all time. Later Boyle retired jersey No. 19 also, a running back who played many seasons, the last of them wearing a spinal brace because there was no one that season to replace him. That was courage. That could choke a man up—a man like F. X. Boyle--just thinking about it.

No one has ever worn No. 42 or 19 since, and Boyle always thought that No. 6, Craig's number, would be retired too one day, because the man who wore it made the big play in the clutch time after time, and was so charming besides, and a model to American youth, and all in all the best football player Boyle ever had.

But that is all changed now, and Boyle as soon as possible will get jersey No. 6 on the back of some other player, so as to wipe out memories of the current Number 6, which keep recurring, though Boyle blinks his eyes and mumbles Hail Marys half aloud in the dim, nearly empty church, trying to make those memories disappear. But though he prays ever harder, Boyle keeps seeing Number 6 leap to make the one-handed catch that beat the Bears that time, and the magical run that beat the Giants in the rain, and the snaky punt return against the Eagles in old Shibe Park.

The most electrifying player Boyle ever had.

But all that is over now.

God is a God of love, who in heaven can make allowances for his errant children if he chooses to, though even God himself can't condone sin, and couldn't even be tolerant, Boyle believes, in a case like this. Thievery or drunkenness (the great sin of the Irish) Boyle can understand and forgive. Lust he cannot understand, and so cannot begin to forgive it. Perhaps God can, provided the sinner repents; but Boyle himself cannot.

Man is weak, but there can be no excuse for being weak in

that way, the most reprehensible of sins. Why hadn't the man fallen for whiskey, Boyle asks himself. A weakness and a sin, sure, but not disgusting. With his head in his hands trying to pray, Boyle imagines "them" performing disgusting acts behind hotel room doors—acts that might be useful and even good within marriage, but a perversion outside of marriage. The woman, clearly, is a slut and seduced the man, sordid enough in itself, though perhaps understandable. But the man, instead of reacting as you would expect, instead of rejecting and perhaps denouncing the woman and the temptation, chose instead to wallow in it—chose this perversion. He has chosen also, in effect, to drive his Christian wife to near suicide; has chosen to disregard his own children, the helpless children of that Christian union. Has chosen to disregard public opinion, too.

Amid such sordidness there can be no extenuating circumstances. Boyle tells himself he is not a prude, not an intolerant man. He is a man of the world and not easily shocked. But he is a just man, and thus condemned now to take whatever course is just, whatever the cost to him personally.

Holy Mother Church is very clear: man must not persevere in sin. If Boyle does nothing now, or merely announces his displeasure without any stern sanctions, this would be to encourage perseverance in sin. Therefore Boyle must make a stern judgment and act on it, or he will appear to condone both sin and sinner, scandalizing millions of fans who will imagine him capable of overlooking such—such debauchery, merely to keep a star player for next season.

Finishing his thanksgiving after communion, Boyle looks up from his hands. The candles glint on the chalice which the priest has tilted over his head and is drinking from. By the time the priest has turned and extended the jeweled gold chalice to the altar boys to take more water and wine, Boyle has made his decision. Though he dreads what must be done, he sees that before God he has no choice.

As the priest turns to bless the kneeling faithful, Boyle repeats in English the Latin words being intoned on the altar: in the name of the Father, and of the Son, and of the Holy Ghost, amen.

Later, from his office, Boyle speaks at length with the commissioner by telephone.

Already being hounded by reporters, the commissioner wants to dispose of the Craig scandal as quickly and quietly as possible. But he fears opposition from Boyle, who stands to lose a valuable player. Now, to his relief, he hears Boyle say that the best thing, from the league's point of view, is for Boyle to give Craig his unconditional release, and for Craig to drop quietly out of football.

"We're entering an era of unprecedented prosperity," the commissioner agrees. "We got to hush this thing up. Television—"

"We can't afford to be smeared by a moral turpitude scandal now," states Boyle.

They decide that if Craig refuses to retire, the commissioner will suspend him indefinitely under terms of the player contract for "conduct detrimental to the best interests of the game."

"But I think he'll retire," the commissioner says. "He doesn't want the bad publicity any more than we do."

Boyle says cautiously: "Suppose in a couple of seasons he tries to get the suspension lifted and make a comeback?"

"We'll see."

"I don't want that man playing ever again."

"Well, we'll see."

"I'd be entitled to at least two Number one draft choices for him," Boyle insists.

The commissioner at last concedes this and will so notify the other clubs; after all, Boyle has just given up a prominent player, sacrificing his own interests for the good of the league.

Boyle hangs up satisfied that Craig is finished in football. Two or more years from now no club is going to give up two first draft choices to sign a halfback (even a Duke Craig) who has not played in all that time and who, by then, will be in his mid-thirties besides.

But with the call completed, Boyle feels drained. As he rests his face in his hands, he tells himself he has been no harsher than the case demands.

Though the season ended yesterday afternoon, the locker room attendants are putting in a busy morning at the stadium. The laundry must go out: the mud- and grass-stained red jerseys in one sack, the equally stained silver pants in another, the sweat-soaked jocks, socks, and T-shirts in a third. Most of the used tape and clots of dirt were swept out last night, but now each individual stall must be cleaned, and the football shoes in them which were worn yesterday and which are the personal property of each player, must be cleaned and painted with shoe black, and worn or broken cleats must be replaced. The locker room attendants are paid $5 a week by each player for servicing the shoes, and today must hurry, for most of the players will drop by soon to collect their shoes. As each stall is cleaned out, the shoes go into a paper sack with the player's name scrawled on it with Magic Marker, ready to go home with the player for the winter. Some players have six or more pairs, worth more than twenty dollars a pair, and these could get lost in the stadium over the winter. Besides, the player could get traded over the winter, or not be invited back next season at all. In any case, the players will begin workouts at home in May, in order to be in shape when training camp convenes in July, and so will need their shoes then.

All morning players drift in to collect their shoes, and some have other belongings too: a raincoat, or a favorite baseball cap, or shaving gear. Some of the players, while they are there, sit for a while under the heat lamp or in the whirlpool bath. Yesterday's bruises hurt just as much today, though the season is over, as on any other Mondays, and most of these bruised players face a long, cramped drive to whichever distant state is home, beginning as soon as they leave the stadium.

The locker room attendants have orders to phone Boyle as soon as Craig appears, and they do so, and Boyle enters the locker room just as Craig is about to leave.

"Can I have a talk with you?"

After hesitating a moment, Craig says: "All right."

They enter the coach's office, and Boyle closes the door.

Boyle gestures toward a chair. "Sit down."

But Craig remains standing.

"How's Carribel?"

Craig says she will be able to leave the hospital in a day or two.

"Who's taking care of the kids?"

"I've had a woman come in."

Boyle nods. After a moment, he says: "Bobby's a great kid."

Craig remains silent.

"He looks just like his father," Boyle says.

Craig perceives that Boyle's voice is husky. Presently the owner asks: "How could you do a thing like this to that little boy?"

Craig says nothing.

"Forget Carribel for a moment," Boyle says. "How could you do this to that little boy who adores you so?"

Craig only shakes his head.

Boyle feels all the old emotion in Craig's presence: admiration for this gifted athlete who has done a hundred times all the brilliant things Boyle always wished he could have done himself. Boyle finds he has to fight down admiration for Craig

300

the football player, which is still there despite everything. He also finds he has to give Craig one last chance to—to come to his senses.

"What are your—your plans, Duke?"

"There's only one solution now."

Boyle asks: "Divorce?" When Craig nods, Boyle says: "But that little boy—"

Craig watches Boyle.

Boyle says: "You're determined, whatever the cost in broken lives?"

This is none of Boyle's business, and Craig doesn't know what to say, so he stares at the floor.

Boyle suggests hurriedly: "Perhaps you'd like to have a long talk with Father O'Malley. He knows your problems—"

"I'm not Catholic."

"Well, maybe a psychiatrist then?"

When Craig does not answer, Boyle says in an anguished voice: "But I just don't understand."

Craig, seeing Boyle's suffering, would like to help him understand, though he supposes this is impossible. Nonetheless, he chooses to say as lightly as he can: "Perhaps I'm in love."

"You're not going to pull that on me," says Boyle disgustedly.

Boyle's mood hardens as he remembers his own love for poor dead Rose. During all of their marriage they slept in the same room every night, except when he was on the road with the team, and when he would go over to her bed in the dark it was like two souls melding before God. That was Christian marriage, Boyle thinks. That's what love is, not this sordid coupling behind hotel room doors.

"The only love you were exposed to was poor Carribel. You've thrown that away. You don't even realize how much that poor girl loved you—must have loved you to do what she did."

Craig moves to the door and grasps the knob: "Yes—well—"

"Don't you walk out on me, I'm not finished talking to you yet."

Craig stays.

"Are you going to marry that—" After a moment, Boyle forces himself to say: "—that woman?"

Craig decides to say: "I think so, yes."

"Is there no hope you will come to your senses?"

Craig remains silent.

"Then there's nothing I can do for you, is there?"

301

"I suppose not."

"You've called the reputation of this team and this league into question. The very integrity of the game is at stake—"

But Boyle is suffering again. He cannot bring himself to do what must be done.

"I wrote you a letter," he says. But his voice quavers as he withdraws the letter. "Then I found I couldn't just send it to you. I had to try to talk some sense into you first."

Craig, holding the unopened letter, says: "I can see your point of view. I just wish you would try to see mine."

"There's no way."

"People go through their whole lives miserable—"

"What you did is indefensible."

"You have no idea of what went on inside my marriage—or outside it either."

"I don't have to know. I see adultery, near suicide, divorce, fatherless children. What could alter that? Holy Mother Church says—"

"I'm not Catholic."

Boyle says in a milder voice: "But the Church is so right on all these matters. It has all that experience, all that wisdom. It teaches that adultery and divorce are wrong not only on a divine level, but also on a human one. Oh, this woman looks very good to you now. But what will it be like after you have gotten used to her, and tired of her? You'll have ruined all these lives and you'll be no better off."

Craig says nothing.

"It's always that way," Boyle says, nodding.

After a moment, he says: "So tell me you'll think it over." He is practically pleading now. "We'll hold everything in abeyance while you think it over."

"No."

"You don't have any gratitude either, do you?" cries Boyle, angry and distraught at once. "I try to help you and you spit on it. That letter is your release."

Craig says in a low voice: "Perhaps I can catch on with some other club next year."

"The commissioner is ready to announce your indefinite suspension for conduct detrimental to the game."

Craig nods.

"The league has to protect itself," Boyle says. "If you refuse to come to your senses, then the only solution is for the league to cut you off."

Boyle steps to the door, but as he opens it, he turns back to Craig and his voice is anguished again. "I just don't understand how I could have been so wrong about you. You were never an All-American. You couldn't have been, and do what you've done."

Craig stares at the floor.

"You played the role, Duke. But in your heart you were never an All-American."

The door slams.

A little later Craig goes out into the locker room. The door is open and two men are dragging out a laundry sack marked *jerseys*.

Sam comes up and hands over a paper bag containing Craig's six pairs of low-cuts.

"I cleaned yesterday's, and changed the toe cleats, Duke. They're good as new and ready for next year."

"Thanks, Sam."

Craig gives the locker room attendant a smile and an extra $5. "Buy the boys a beer on me, Sam."

Craig takes a last look around the empty locker room: the grillwork of the stalls, the trunks lining the center of the room, the doorways to the smaller rooms opening off it. He sniffs the faint smell of sweat and liniment, and when he listens for it, he can hear the voices of his teammates coming in the door after a victory. Coming in sweaty, dirty, happy—what pleasure in life could match that moment?

Outside, he goes down the ramp and up through the dugout onto the field and looks around at the shell of grandstands, and when he listens for the cheers he can hear them, too. He thinks: It may be years before they find a halfback as good as I was. But this is no consolation. Maybe it is not even true.

He sees an open gate in the centerfield wall, with the street beyond, and he walks out of the stadium with his brown parcel under his arm. When he is a short distance from the stadium, he looks back at the mass of it rising up out of the parking lots. It seems to him that the flags still blow high up around the rim, and that the cars are arriving, and hordes of people pass him carrying blankets and flasks, the girls with chrysanthemums in their lapels, all of them talking excitedly, and his own name on their lips:

"The one I like to watch is Duke Craig."

"What number is the Duke?"

He is giving up his children, which is hard enough, and he is giving up the way a perfectly thrown football feels smacking into his hands when there is nobody between him and the goal line; and his throat and chest feel choked, and he doesn't know how much he can bear to give up at one time.

303

When he is a few blocks farther away he looks back one last time at the stadium. His eyes mist over and he sees the stadium blurred through tears, because he knows he will never play football again. He thinks: Why am I carrying on like this, it was only a game.